Return to Longbourn

The Next Chapter *in the Continuing Story of* Jane Austen's *Pride & Prejudice*

Shannon Winslow

For My Sister

Ruth

...who, by her unfailing support, humor, and enthusiasm, has added immeasurably to my life and to my writing career.

Soli Deo Gloria

Preface

It is no secret that I adore the work of Jane Austen. Her subtle stories of love triumphant and her witty, elegant prose suit my taste exactly. They have influenced my own writing more than anything else.

With Jane Austen's stories so deeply entrenched in my mind, I often find myself thinking of and alluding to various passages from her books as I write. Instead of fighting the temptation to borrow some of her expertly turned phrases, I went with it. After all, I couldn't hope to improve upon the master.

So, if you are a Jane Austen aficionado, you will no doubt recognize a quoted line here and there (a listing of which you will find in the appendix). I had a wonderful time tucking these little jewels in between the pages. My hope is that you will find just as much fun discovering them as you read. I trust you will accept this as I intend it – as a tribute to Jane and to her fans. Enjoy!

Respectfully,
Shannon Winslow

Let other pens dwell on guilt and misery. I quit such odious subjects as soon as I can, impatient to restore every body, not greatly in fault themselves, to tolerable comfort, and to have done with all the rest. – Jane Austen (*Mansfield Park*)

Mary had blossomed in the interval since her siblings left Longbourn... Thus, well seasoned by time, practice, and renewed dedication, she made great strides toward the standard of the truly accomplished young woman she had always aspired to be...

...Kitty, meanwhile, continued to divide her time chiefly between Heatheridge and Pemberley according to which house was hosting the more interesting social events. She fretted over being already almost twenty with no prospects for marriage immediately apparent...

– The Darcys of Pemberley

Prologue

The letter from London was a true Godsend. He knew it the instant it arrived, and just as quickly determined what he must do. Now the fertile Shenandoah Valley of Virginia – which until so recently had encompassed all aspects of his life and every hope for the future – lay half an ocean behind him, the distance widening with each passing day.

As the creaking timbers of the deck dipped and rolled beneath his feet, Mr. Tristan Collins kept one gloved hand ready on the rail. He had long since overcome his initial discomfort with being at sea, to the point where his legs had learnt to compensate for the perpetual movement without any conscious effort.

"Mr. Collins, sir," said the cabin boy, coming up behind him. "Capt'n says won't you take supper with him?"

The distinguished young gentleman with sandy hair turned into the icy wind to answer the lad. "Thank you, Patrick," he said with a wan smile. "Tell the captain I shall be along directly."

Pulling his great coat more tightly about his person, he turned his gaze aft once more, to where the sun had recently sunk below the western horizon. He had no idea what he expected to see. There was nothing there other than a fading glimmer of daylight and three thousand miles of cold, roiling brine – an impenetrable barrier, seemingly. But would only half an ocean be enough to keep the ghosts he left behind in America at bay... or to keep his own thoughts from forever flying back, like pigeons returning to their roost?

No, he would not feel truly secure until he once more set foot on the reassuring ground of his native country. In England, he would start again.

1

Ingathering

It is a truth universally acknowledged that every mortal being must at some point face the certainty of death and the day of reckoning. Despite his every effort to avoid it, this reality at last bore in upon Mr. Bennet, a gentleman who had long resided near Meryton in Hertfordshire. He had managed to live in tolerable comfort for nearly seven-and-sixty years, his contentment at least partially owing to the fact that he was rarely incommoded by bouts of serious intro-spection. Yet, in his final hours, he did at last pause to reflect upon the questionable quality of his earthly pilgrimage.

The traits of idleness and self-indulgence suggested themselves straightaway. Whereas these are not generally touted as virtues, Mr. Bennet reasoned that it would be outright hypocrisy to condemn in himself that which he freely forgave in so many others of his ac-quaintance.

With his conscience clear on that head, his two remaining sources of potential regret as he prepared to meet his maker were these. First, he had married unwisely and in haste. Yet he hardly thought it likely he would be chastised for that above, having already paid more than thirty years' penance for the folly below. Likewise, he knew the consequences of his second regret – failing to produce a male heir – would soon be meted out on the terrestrial rather than the celestial plane.

Finally, the dying man considered that perhaps he should have taken his domestic responsibilities more seriously – disciplined his five daughters with some diligence when they were young and made better provision for his widow. This belated remorse, however, proved as transitory as it was ineffectual. Thus, being serenely satis-fied with his deportment in this life and, therefore, confident of a favorable reception in the next, Mr. Bennet breathed his last.

~~ * ~~

"What is to become of me?" wailed Mrs. Bennet for what could be no less than the hundredth time.

Two days had elapsed since her husband's sudden demise, and Mrs. Bennet was really in a most pitiable state. She had taken to her bed upon the event with pains and paroxysms of every sort, according to her own exhaustive narrative on the subject. Mary and Kitty, being the only two of her offspring immediately to hand, had done what they could to quiet their mother's gloomy effusions. Yet it seemed the more they reassured her of future comfort and security, the more Mrs. Bennet persisted in prophesying her own wretchedness.

"I daresay I shall be left to starve in the hedgerows!" she continued. "Indeed, I most certainly shall. Your father's heir – whosoever he may prove to be – is sure to turn me out of this house before Mr. Bennet is quite cold in his grave. And if my family is not kind to me, I do not know what I shall do. Oh, why could we not have had a son? Then I should not be at the mercy of this horrid entail." Her sorrow lapsed into consternation at the thought of that longstanding grievance. "It is unaccountable that anybody should see fit to will his estate away from his own female descendants for the sake of some distant relation. I shall never understand it should I live to be ninety. And now your father has gone off and left me to suffer for his ancestor's madness on my own. How could he do such a thing? Then again, he never did have any compassion for my poor nerves!" Sobs again overtook her.

Kitty sat mutely by, her limited supply of consolation already spent to no avail.

Mary, with greater resources but perhaps less patience, took temporary refuge downstairs. She thus received the first intelligence of an approaching carriage. Hearing the unmistakable sound of gravel grating on the sweep, she hurried out to see which of the expected parties had arrived.

Immediately upon the apothecary's pronouncement that Mr. Bennet's illness was of a grave nature, an express had been sent to each of his other three daughters, all of whom lived at a considerable distance from Longbourn. The two eldest, Jane and Elizabeth, were both married (some seven years past) and resided not far from each other in the north of England. Lydia, the youngest, had been married, widowed, and then married again. She would be traveling from Plymouth where she was settled with her new husband's family.

Mary waited on the porch, clasping and unclasping her hands in an attempt to compose herself for what was to come. She knew it fell to her to convey the news of their father's fate to the occupants of the elegant equipage now approaching. From its size and grandeur, it belonged to one of her well-to-do sisters from the north rather than the more modestly situated Lydia. For this, Mary was profoundly grateful. Lydia's wild nature rendered her entirely unfit to soothe Mrs. Bennet's fears. Either one of the others would be of more practical use, both to their mother and to herself.

As the carriage slowed to a stop before her, Mary distinguished Elizabeth's anxious face at the window, looking for some sign of encouragement. Mary could give her none. Instead, she slowly shook her head, allowing her somber countenance and conspicuous garb of mourning to answer Elizabeth's unspoken question. Papa was dead, yet to be spared the necessity of speaking the words aloud was some little relief.

Elizabeth disappeared again into the depths of the carriage – and presumably into her husband's arms – not to emerge for several minutes. Mary did nothing to hurry her. She preferred that the office of bearing with Elizabeth's initial spasms of sorrow should fall to her brother-in-law, Mr. Darcy, instead of to herself.

The tide of grief had already threatened to overpower Mary more than once. Yet she dared not give in to it. Outward expression of emotion was both foreign and frightening to her, so long had she practiced the art of stoicism. That philosophy had served her well in the past, enabling her to endure the disappointment of every one of her sisters being favored, complimented, courted, and three married ahead of her. Now, however, its strictures allowed her neither vent for her own sorrows nor protection from the false presumption of others that she had none.

By contrast, *no one* thought it possible Mrs. Bennet would demonstrate herself mistress of her feelings now, considering how little facility she had shown for it in the past with far less provocation. Kitty could not or would not exert herself either. Because of their weakness, Mary felt doubly obligated to play the unassailable tower of strength, at least in their presence. She was certain her relations could not even conceive of her crumbling, having never witnessed any symptom of it before. As a point of personal pride, she intended to keep it that way. So, when Elizabeth finally alighted from the carriage with the help of Mr. Darcy, Mary embraced her but shed no tears with her.

"We are too late, then," surmised Elizabeth when at length she pulled away. "Papa is already gone?"

Mary nodded. "Sadly, yes. Two days past. It was very sudden."

At once, Mr. Darcy stepped forward to place an arm firmly about Elizabeth's shoulders. She leant back against him and, after a pause to collect herself, she asked, "And Mama? How does she do?"

"Exactly as you might expect," said Mary with a significant look. "Kitty is with her now, and Lady Lucas and our aunt Phillips have attended her every day since the crisis began. Still…"

"Yes, yes, I see. So Jane and Lydia are not yet come?"

"No, although they are every moment expected."

"Then the weight of this has fallen primarily upon you, dear Mary. I am sorry for that. You look pale. How much you must have gone through!"

"Come, Lizzy, steady yourself," urged Mary, seeing her sister on the verge of breaking down again. "Mama will be eager for your company."

"Yes, of course," said Elizabeth, drying her eyes. "Let me to her then, although I know not what comfort I may be."

~~ * ~~

By the end of the day, the family was fully gathered to Long-bourn: all five of Mr. Bennet's daughters as well as two sons-in-law – the third, Mr. Denny, Lydia's second husband, being a military man away with his regiment. Mutual solace and the comfort of their mother were their common goals. Yet, even during this time of family unity, their natural pairings persisted – Jane with Elizabeth, Lydia and Kitty together, and Mr. Bingley with Mr. Darcy.

Once again, Mary felt herself the odd one out, accepted by all and yet the particular friend of none. It came as no surprise; it was always thus. Although she made no doubt her sisters loved her even as she loved each of them, their true commonality ran little further than their blood lines. None of the others shared her thirst for intellectual and musical accomplishment, and neither could she enter into their pursuits, her younger sisters' so trivial and the elders' now so thoroughly domestic. As for the men, they were something of an enigma to her, like another species altogether – vastly intriguing but far too foreign to trust oneself to completely. Perhaps if she had had a brother, she might have come to understand the sex better. As it was, Mary found little companionship there either.

Her chief consolation came from making herself useful. With her mother indisposed, Mary rightly appropriated the role of acting mistress of the house, seeing to it that the servants were supervised, the rooms orderly, family and visitors well fed, and every other practical need met. For her efforts, she might hope to be thanked but not truly esteemed. In that regard, she felt a special kinship with Martha from the Bible, whose worth she always considered unfairly disparaged. Although she counted it a very fine thing to sit reverently at the master's feet for a time, sooner or later somebody had to attend to the utilitarian as well. She had taken that role upon herself, allowing others leisure to weep alongside of their father's casket. Her own sorrows she reserved for solitary hours.

"Sister Mary," said Mr. Darcy from the doorway of the library, wresting her attention away from her private musings as she went about her business. "I was going to look for you. Would you be so good as to step in here for a moment?"

"Of course." She followed him thither, her curiosity to know what he had to tell her heightened by the supposition of its being in some manner connected with the documents he held. Within, she found Mr. Bingley as well, seated to one side of her father's desk. The sight of the empty chair behind it, where she had been used to seeing her father habitually situated, gave Mary fresh pangs.

Darcy moved as if to take Mr. Bennet's customary place before apparently thinking better of it and remaining where he was. "I am afraid this concerns the legal matters attending your father's death. Mr. Bingley and I will gladly undertake the duties involved if only you will set us off on the right course. I thought you might have some knowledge of Mr. Bennet's affairs – the whereabouts of his business ledgers and legal correspondence, for example. We have located these few items," he said, indicating the papers in his hand. "There must be more, however."

"We are sorry to disturb you at such a time, my dear," added Mr. Bingley. "It is only that there are a few importunate questions that will not wait. Your mother, you see, is in no state to guide us."

"No. No, indeed not," Mary agreed soberly. "Whatever I may do, I am at your service, gentlemen."

"Thank you," returned Mr. Darcy. "We will not keep you long. Please, do be seated, though," said he, pulling out her father's chair for her.

Mary understood it as a gesture of respect – a mark of confidence, an acknowledgment of her position of increased responsibility within the family. And perhaps she felt the compliment more deeply than she ought to have done. Nevertheless, with a dignified bearing she took the seat presented, perceiving that by doing so she laid claim, however temporarily, to a portion of her father's authority as well. It was a mantle she was prepared to shoulder by virtue of an

12

orderly mind (one better suited to business than usually thought befitting a female), a mind further schooled by conscientious study.

"I believe I can be of some use. Papa confided a great many things to me, especially toward the last. I flatter myself that his trust was not misplaced."

2
Sisterly Consolation

The next few days proceeded in much the same melancholy fashion common to all humanity. Death being no respecter of rank and privilege, it afflicted the Bennet household no less grievously than any other. They bore their pain, each one in his own style, as the customary rights and rituals attending Mr. Bennet's passing were conscientiously observed. Then they endured the comfort of their friends and neighbors with equal fortitude.

When all these well-meaning visitors had gone away, Mr. Bingley and Mr. Darcy also departed, traveling to London for the purpose of seeing the family's solicitor and settling Mr. Bennet's affairs.

That afternoon, Elizabeth took her turn attending her mother, who still insisted on keeping to her room.

"Perhaps, Lizzy, your clever husband will be able to discover something – something to our advantage – whilst he and Mr. Bingley are in town," said Mrs. Bennet in a rare moment of optimism. "With Mr. Collins out of the way these five or six years, it may be that the entail can be broken at last and Longbourn pass to Mr. Bennet's own poor daughters. Not so much for your sake or Jane's, mind you; neither one of you shall ever find yourself in want. And, you know, Kitty may yet get hold of a rich husband too. But think of Mary! Despite what she says, she cannot go on playing at being a governess forever. And with her father dead, how is her future to be secured? At the age of seven-and-twenty, she might as well take to wearing a cap, for any bloom she once possessed must have long gone off."

"I cannot agree with you about Mary, Mama. I think she is much improved in her looks this last two or three years, and the best may yet be ahead for her. It sometimes happens that a woman is handsomer at twenty-nine than she was ten years before. Furthermore, her manner has softened with the passage of time. She is now not so quick to judge or forever moralizing as she used to do. Have you not noticed it yourself?"

"Mary is a steady girl with a good head on her shoulders. However, I see little else that might serve to recommend her."

"Regardless of her personal prospects, none of you – Mary, Kitty, or yourself – shall lack anything in this world, so long as Mr. Darcy and I draw breath. As for any relief from the entail, though, your hopes are wholly unfounded, Mama. You know very well that Mr. Collins had a brother. We have been told that Longbourn shall simply pass to the younger sibling, now that the elder is deceased. There can be no doubt of it."

"Why should that be? Surely a daughter has more right to it than a younger brother to some sort of cousin!"

"I do not argue that it is fair. I simply mean that the death of Mr. Collins will make not the slightest bit of difference. If we girls could not inherit before, it will be the same now."

The door opened at this juncture, and Jane stepped in, saying, "Tea is ready, Mama. Will you not come down and take it with your family today?"

Mrs. Bennet sank deeper into her chair and closed her eyes, as if the exertions of the recent conversation had stolen her final ounce of strength. "Impossible," she groaned. "You must see how weak I am, Jane. I would faint dead away should I even attempt such a thing. No, no, you girls go on and join your sisters. Think nothing of me." She heaved a great sigh, and then added as an afterthought, "Only do tell Hill to bring my tray up as usual and... and that I especially asked for scones... with strawberry preserves, of course. I do believe that if anything can revive me, it must be scones and strawberry preserves."

Mrs. Hill, having already anticipated her mistress's instructions down to the last detail, entered the room at that moment carrying a tray set with, amongst other things, the very items wished for.

Jane and Elizabeth did as their mother bade them. They joined their sisters in the parlor, where Lydia and Kitty were already settled and Mary had taken charge of pouring the tea.

"Jane, you sit here," said Mary, indicating the chair to her right. "And Lizzy, on my other side, if you please."

Elizabeth received her instructions and her tea from her younger sister with composure, and with a spark of amusement. "Thank you, Mary," she said wryly. "I see that, as usual, you have everything well in hand. How efficient you are."

Mary nodded, acknowledging the compliment. "I believe it is a gift of nature, one which is of particular use in the current situation."

"Yes," agreed Elizabeth. "Mama could hardly have done without you these many days, I am sure. How good of the family at Netherfield to spare you so long."

"No doubt they are quite impatient for my return; they have come to depend on me so. Despite the inconvenience, however, Mr. Farnsworth cannot deny the higher claims of blood at such a time."

"How do the Netherfield children do?" asked Jane. "Is the younger girl still your favorite?"

Before Mary could respond, Lydia declared, "*I* should not hurry back to Netherfield for all its grandeur, not wearing your shoes at least, Mary. I think I should much rather suffer anything than be a servant, even in one of the finest houses in England."

With a decided glare, Mary rejoined, "A governess is *not* a common servant, whatever you may say. It is a perfectly genteel occupation and a position that commands respect, even esteem. Mr. Farnsworth has entrusted me with his children's education. That is proof of his good opinion."

"I see!" Lydia laughed mischievously and went on. "And I suppose he has the same high opinion of the gamekeeper's wife, whom he hired as wet nurse to his infants."

"Lydia!" cried Jane.

Elizabeth lifted up her eyes in amazement, but was too much oppressed to make any reply.

Kitty looked from face to face round the table and then offered in a conciliatory tone, "I daresay she meant no offense."

"Lord, no!" Lydia confirmed. "I am happy to allow that Mary is far more accomplished and quick witted than any old gamekeeper's wife. I only meant that it is all one to me – the office of governess no more tolerable than that of wet nurse. Do not pretend to be so shocked, Lizzy. You, of all people, should know how I feel about small children."

"I had depended on your opinion of them being improved over these five years by your own daughter!" said Elizabeth.

"Well, as these things go, I suppose Isabella is not really a bad sort of girl. Only, in so far as it is preventable, I certainly do not mean to have any more.

"Your husband may have something to say about that," advised Elizabeth.

"Lizzy is right," agreed Jane. "Surely Mr. Denny wishes to have a son. All men do, you know."

"That may well be," Lydia responded, "but it does not signify in the least, for Denny always gives me my own way in the end. And his mother is just as obliging, especially as regards the child. The woman fairly dotes on her, and she cannot tell me often enough how she looks on Isabella the same as her own grandchildren, though the girl is every inch her father's daughter. That is my one consolation – and my greatest sorrow – that I am, through Isabella, every day reminded of poor Wickham."

Mary held her tongue through the last, still feeling the cut of Lydia's belittling of her situation at Netherfield, as well as finding herself out of her depth in a discussion of husbands and offspring. She nevertheless had no very good opinion of her younger sister's attitude… or of her first husband either.

Mr. Wickham's conduct in life had been nothing short of infamous, yet Lydia persisted in holding him up as some sort of martyred hero, still to be mourned long after his death. Even with her limited experience, Mary counted herself a better judge of male character. She had no complaint against Mr. Denny, yet it was her other two brothers-in-law that now set the standard – a standard to which Mr. Wickham could never have risen, even should he have aspired to do so. As for her employer, Mr. Farnsworth, his true character was more difficult to develop.

~~ * ~~

Lydia, finding nothing to hold her at Longbourn, took leave of her grieving mother the following morning to return home to Plymouth. She embraced each of her sisters in turn on the stoop, and then climbed into the Bennets' carriage, which was to take her as far as London.

"Do write to me," she told Kitty through the open window, "and tell me what is to become of you. I am vastly curious to hear news of the heir, and how soon he shall arrive to turn you and Mama out onto the street."

Kitty's eyes grew wide with alarm.

"Of course, I am only joking," Lydia continued. "If you are flung out of this place, you are sure to come to ground somewhere far better. Jane or Lizzy will take you in, and I should feel no pity for you ending up at either Heatheridge or Pemberley. You have been used to spending half your time at one or other of those houses as it is."

"It would be a sad event nonetheless," Kitty repined. "Longbourn should have been my settled home until I married. I am only a visitor any place else, no matter how comfortable."

"Well then, I suppose you must hope the new owner is disposed to letting you and Mama stay on, though I shouldn't think it likely. Now, I must be off." With that, the youngest of the Bennet daughters waved cheerfully and was gone.

"Never mind, Kitty," said Jane, lightly resting her hands on her sister's sagging shoulders. "Lydia does not mean to be unkind. It is only her free and spirited way of speaking."

"You need not always be making excuses for her, Jane," said Mary. "We are, all of us, responsible for curbing our tongues when the occasion requires it. Yet it seems Lydia cannot be troubled to consider whom her careless words may injure."

When the carriage had traveled down the sweep and disappeared behind the hedgerow, they turned back into the house.

Elizabeth said, "I doubt Lydia can fully appreciate the attachment to Longbourn the rest of us feel, and thus the loss for losing it. When you think of it, she lived here fewer years than any of us, and has beer somewhat of a vagabond ever since. That life may suit her, whereas it never would me."

"Nor me," added Jane. "I can hardly bear being away from Heatheridge and my children, even for a few days."

Elizabeth echoed Jane's sentiment, and the two of them led the conversation in a decidedly domestic direction once again. It was not surprising that this should happen, Mary reminded herself, for they had seven children between them – Lizzy with her three sons, and Jane with two boys, two girls, and, according to early indications, another child on the way. Kitty, who spent weeks at a time in both households, could join in. Not Mary, however; she knew none of her nieces or nephews well, and had never even set eyes on Elizabeth's youngest.

"I had best go and sit with Mama," Mary said, excusing herself. "No doubt she is missing Lydia already."

3

The Heir

The following day, the watch began for the carriage that was to bring Mr. Darcy and Mr. Bingley, returned from London. It did come, and exactly when it might be reasonably looked for.

To Elizabeth and Jane, who were happy to see their husbands for their own sake, the event also meant they would the sooner be on their way back home to their families. For the rest, the anticipation of what the men might have to report predominated. Mrs. Bennet, feeling the import of the occasion, roused herself so much as to dress and venture downstairs, assisted by her two younger daughters.

They all gathered in the drawing room as soon as the men had had time to change from their traveling clothes and take a little refreshment. Mr. Darcy took his stand at the head of the room, before the hearth, whilst the others seated themselves, waiting in alert attendance upon his good pleasure. Even Mrs. Bennet held her peace, seeming in no hurry to demand the news from town. Silence was her friend. As long as the moment could be sustained, all things were still possible; every one of her darling wishes, no matter how ultimately unviable, still breathed. Yet she could not curb her curiosity and her tongue forever.

"Oh, Mr. Darcy, I can bear the suspense no longer!" she cried out. "What news do you bring, good or ill?"

"Forgive me, Madam," he answered, "but what is there of good to be expected?"

"The entail, of course! You must know that I have lived in the hope of Mr. Gerber discovering a way of escaping it. What do we pay him for, if not to turn the tide in our favor?"

"As with turning the tide, Mrs. Bennet, escaping the entail would require a miracle... or at the very least, an act of Parliament... and no such thing has occurred to spare Longbourn, I am sorry to say. Mr. Bennet's estate is just as entailed as it ever was, and now must legally pass, as we anticipated, into the hands of Mr. Collins's younger brother – a Mr. Tristan Collins. If there is any good news in the case, it is that he currently resides in the Americas, in a place called Virginia. Mr. Gerber is bound by law to notify him of his inheritance, and yet it will be some time – a few months at a minimum, I should think – before he could arrive to assert his rights. So you will have at least that long to make other arrangements."

"Then, all is lost forever!" Mrs. Bennet wailed before abandoning herself to a noisy fit of tears.

"There, there, Mama," offered Jane, patting her mother's hand. "This is nothing so very alarming, only what was to be expected. You shall always be well looked after. Have no fear."

When Mrs. Bennet had quieted some, Mr. Darcy went on to explain the rest of the information provided by the solicitor. There was nothing remarkable in it, only such limited provisions for Mr. Bennet's widow and daughters as had been known to them all along, and which would go no very great distance towards their comfort and keeping.

Unlike her mother, Mary heard the news with a brave face. She had never entertained even the slightest hope of a financial reprieve, nor did she particularly desire one. What difference would a larger dowry make for her now? Enough money might still have produced a marriage proposal, most likely one from a widowed old man with ten unruly children for her to look after. When compared to that unhappy scenario, however, she should infinitely prefer her current situation. After all, it was what she had chosen with her eyes wide open... over the strenuous objections of all her relations, some of whom had called it a lowering of herself and an embarrassment to the family.

Mary did not see honest employment as a degradation, though. In truth, she was proud that she had within herself the resources to make her own way in life. Her natural inclination for industry, study, and musical accomplishment had equipped her well for the occupation of governess. And surely there was sufficient consequence for any reasonable person in a job well done.

From these contemplations, Mary was called back to the room by her mother's sudden outburst.

"But, Mr. Darcy, you have failed to answer for us a most vital question!"

"I do beg your pardon, Madam; however, I am at a loss to understand on what point I could have been so negligent."

"About this Mr. Tristan Collins!" she said impatiently. "Well, sir, you have not yet told us if he is married or single."

Mr. Darcy could not resolve the mystery.

Mr. Bingley could not either, although he went so far as to share the intelligence that there was no record of Mr. Tristan Collins having taken a wife before emigrating as a comparative youth. "Yet I think it reasonable to assume that he might have done so since, once he established himself in America. He is a man of no less than thirty, you see, Mrs. Bennet, and must have wanted a wife by now."

Mrs. Bennet let the business drop, but Mary perceived that her silence did not betoken loss of interest, rather a mind fully engaged. Mama would have much more to say on the topic of Mr. Collins's marital status by and by. No doubt it would be the same scheme as before, only a different Mr. Collins; the heir to Longbourn must marry one of Mr. Bennet's daughters. Nothing else would do.

~~ * ~~

Mrs. Bennet retired to her room, leaving the others to ruminate over the events of the day and, in particular, the need to make some provision for the soon-to-be homeless Bennet females.

Mary, who could not allow herself to be classed amongst the helpless, spoke up. "I thank you all for your concern, but I believe I am not so much at a loss as to require your assistance. I shall do very well on my own, so no one need exert themselves on *my* account."

"It is as you say," agreed Mr. Darcy. "However, should the inclination or necessity ever arise, even in your case, you must know that you can rely on your family. That goes for your mother and sister as well."

"Yes, of course," said Mary. "That is very good of you, I am sure."

"Well, *I* am not too proud to accept your kindness, Mr. Darcy," Kitty rejoined, "or yours either, Mr. Bingley. I find that I can tolerate the charity of rich relations very well indeed. But what about Mama?"

"Mama must come to stay with us at Heatheridge," volunteered Jane, "at least temporarily."

"She can certainly visit us as well," said Elizabeth, "from time to time, that is. Still, I wonder if taking a house of her own would not be the best permanent arrangement."

"Her limited income would not support the letting of anything suitable," said Mr. Bingley.

"It would if supplemented," said Darcy. "The expense would be nothing, Charles. Perhaps an investment of three thousand pounds. We could spare so inconsiderable a sum with little inconvenience."

"And that would allow her to remain in the neighborhood of Longbourn," added Elizabeth, "with Mary and her friends nearby.

21

She might well prefer that to being uprooted only to live far away, as a perpetual guest in someone else's home."

What Mrs. Bennet might prefer was the subject of some further conjecture amongst the group, the various options being debated back and forth with eager interest by those most concerned. Would she best like the comforts of Heatheridge? Or perhaps the dower house at Pemberley? What about an establishment of her own in Meryton, Bath, or even London? Mary at last pointed out the obvious means of resolving the matter, that their mother must be applied to for her opinion. Yet little additional light was shed on the question by taking this measure. Mrs. Bennet foresaw insurmountable difficulties with every suggestion proffered, finding each one more detestable than the last, and ultimately discarding the lot as too loathsome to even admit contemplation.

~~ * ~~

The Darcys and the Bingleys made ready to take themselves off the following day, over the violent objections of Mrs. Bennet.

"It really is too cruel!" she told her two eldest. "Deserting me as though you had not a care in the world. I see how it will be. My trials shall soon be forgot. I shall be left all alone, nothing to do except to await the inevitable, being cast out into the gutter like so much rubbish."

"Oh, Mama!" cried Jane in distress. "You must not say such things."

"Particularly since not a word of it is true," declared Elizabeth. "Kitty will be with you, Mama, and Mary every Sunday. If any crisis should occur, the rest of us can be here in three or four days' time. As for having nothing to do, that is hardly the case either." She softened her tone, and laid a hand on Mrs. Bennet's arm. "Life goes on, and as soon as you can bear to, you really must begin collecting your things – that is to say, packing up whatever possessions you wish to take with you when the time comes."

This, not surprisingly, brought forth a new torrent of emotion from the ailing widow, who needed to be calmed and cajoled into tolerable order before her daughters could in good conscience finally depart. She was then assigned over to Mrs. Hill's patient ministrations, and Jane and Elizabeth made their way downstairs.

Mary then took this, her last chance, to correct a perceived wrong. Her conscience had been niggling at her the last two days, telling her that she should have taken more of an interest in her elder

sisters' concerns. Instead of bowing out of the conversation whenever it turned to domestic matters, she might have asked the
customary questions and listened with solicitude to their talk about
their offspring. Good manners called for this much, and her own
sense of what was due her sisters demanded it. Moreover, how could
she hope to maintain those family ties, which she valued more than
she cared to admit, if she herself were unwilling to make an effort?

She had paid her penance with Jane at an opportune moment the
day before, asking, "Am I right in thinking that the twins are five
years of age now?"

"Nearly six," said Jane, proudly. "I daresay you would get on
famously with little Charles, Mary, for he is grown into a great lover
of books, like yourself. I am afraid Frances Jane is a bit of a tomboy
instead, preferring to take her play out of doors or in the stables. Mrs.
Grayling is forever scolding her for muddying her frocks."

"Perhaps the girl will grow out of it," Mary suggested. "And the
other two children?"

"Oh, Phoebe is a proper lady already, though she is only four!
And John, the baby, has not yet revealed to us much of his future
character. They are, every one of them, so very dear." Jane daubed at
her eyes with the back of her hand. "And now it seems that God may
see fit to bless me with at least one more."

"Naturally you miss them, being away so long... all except this
new one, of course... whom you carry with you..." Mary trailed off
awkwardly.

"Yes." Jane smiled and reached out to squeeze her sister's hand.
"How kind you are to ask after them, Mary. I wish you all could
become better acquainted, but then, even in your present circumstances, you are not left without children to love. You must by now
have formed quite a fond attachment to the Netherfield family."

It had been simpler to go along with that assumption than to
attempt correcting it. There was at least a little truth in what Jane
said, after all. One could not spend more than three years with a
family without developing some kind of feeling for them. So what
purpose could it possibly serve to describe the true state of affairs,
the intricacies of which she did not fully understand herself? No
doubt in Jane's world children were always both dear and dearly
loved; their parents were always kind, patient, and benignly indul-
gent. In such a household, a governess's job must be simple indeed –
no divided loyalties, no competing priorities, no complications.
"Yes, of course," Mary had agreed, "I am quite attached."

Now, with one more act of reparation, her conscience would be satisfied. Though the Bingleys' smart carriage had just started off, the Darcys' equally excellent equipage was not yet made fully ready for departure, so Mary drew Elizabeth aside. "I regret that my obligations have left us with so little time to talk whilst you were here," she said.

"I regret it as well, for I would have liked to hear more about your situation at Netherfield. Does it still agree with you, Mary?"

"Every situation has its little vexations and grievances, I believe. Yet on the whole, I am satisfied. And it has allowed me to study music more seriously than I might have otherwise, which is a great pleasure to me."

"Oh, yes, how you have raved about your Monsieur Hubert! Do you suppose he could be persuaded into taking on a student as far north as Derbyshire? I thought perhaps five was a bit too young to commence music lessons, but Mr. Darcy insists that, as Bennet shows such an interest in the piano-forte, he should not be denied the advantage of early instruction. There is some justification for optimism, I suppose, since a good measure of natural talent can be found on both sides of the boy's family, with his Aunt Mary *and* his Aunt Georgiana being so musically inclined."

"I will be happy to propose the idea to Monsieur Hubert. I only wish I had been so fortunate as to have such a fine music master in my youth. How much more I might then have accomplished! But enough about me; I meant to ask after your children, Lizzy. I trust they are all three well and strong."

"I thank you, yes!" said Elizabeth, her countenance brightening at the enquiry.

"I am very glad to hear it."

"They are, thank heaven, fine, healthy boys," Elizabeth continued. "Bennet is quite the apple of his father's eye, and it is much the same with Edward and James. You see, Mary, I live in a household of men, and I must make the best of it. Fortunately, I would as soon sit atop a saddle these days as any other place, so I shall stand some chance of keeping up with them as they grow older." She turned her address to her husband, who had that moment entered the parlor. "There is nothing – or almost nothing – like the thrill of a good ride. Is not that your opinion as well, Mr. Darcy?"

"So I believe I have said on more than one occasion, my dear. Now, if you will make your good-byes, we can be on our way."

A lingering look passed between the two, and Elizabeth reached out to briefly rest a hand against the side of her husband's face.

Then, seeming to remember herself, she withdrew it again, embraced her sister, and said farewell.

Mary watched them go from the porch, conscious for the first time of a twinge of envy surfacing from somewhere deep within her soul. Never had she craved great wealth and its comfortable trappings; these things did not tempt her to covet her sister's situation. No, it was that stolen glimpse of tenderness she had seen upon Mr. Darcy's face when his usual mask of reserve dropped for a moment as he regarded his wife. What must it be like to be looked at in such a way by such a man? Mary could not help but wonder. She could only suppose that it was a thing very much to be prized.

A chill wind penetrated her shawl, reminding Mary where she was. She quickly discarded her musings as profitless, and returned to the house with her jaw firmly set. Tomorrow, at first light, she decided, she would take up her duties at Netherfield again. What must be done might as well be done at once.

4
Netherfield

"Oh, Miss Bennet!" Mrs. Brand, the housekeeper, burst forth in her high-pitched, thready voice upon seeing the governess entering the house. "What a relief that you are come back to us at last, and I do not care who hears me say it. We've not managed the children even tolerably well in your absence. Bless me, how troublesome they are sometimes! The girls are not too bad, but young Michael is always up to some pretty piece of mischief. I confess that I have very little notion what to do with him, and I daresay Miss Lavinia has even less. Well, never mind all that. How are things at Longbourn, my dear? How does your poor mother do?"

Although somewhat overpowered by this welcoming onslaught, Mary was nonetheless pleased to see Mrs. Brand, who was the closest thing to a friend she had at Netherfield. "I am sorry to report that Mama has not taken the change in her circumstances very well," she answered. "I thank you, though, for asking after her. Now, Mrs. Brand, I will go up to my bedchamber, if I may, before reporting to the schoolroom."

"Of course, of course," said the housekeeper. "You must be tired after your ordeal. Clinton will take your cases up. Clinton!" she called out.

"No, really, Mrs. Brand," Mary protested, "I am not the least bit tired, and I am quite capable of managing by myself."

"Nonsense, Miss. You are a gentleman's daughter, and you shall receive your due in this house as long as I have anything to say about it. Poor Mrs. Farnsworth, God rest her soul, always made sure of that, and I carry on in her stead. Besides, moving cases is a footman's job. What else has he got to do, I should like to know? Oh, there you are, Clinton. Do take Miss Bennet's things up for her."

The footman nodded his acknowledgement, and then allowed his hooded eyes to travel once over the governess as he turned to collect her luggage.

Mary followed several steps behind as he surmounted the wide, curving staircase and started down the dim corridor that accessed the family apartments. Her room was at the far end, adjacent to and ad-joining those of the Farnsworth children, the two girls on one side and the young master on the other.

Clinton opened the door and stepped back, giving Mary just enough leeway to pass by him and into her bedchamber. With his gloved hand, he motioned for her to do so.

Mary stopped where she stood and regarded the footman criti-cally. He was a well looking man of somewhere above thirty years of age, no doubt chosen for his position because of his superior height. Yet the elegant livery he wore could not disguise his humble origins or unrefined manners. "You may leave my things and go," she said. "I will not detain you from your other duties any longer."

"'Tain't no trouble, Miss," he said with a grin. "I'd be more'n happy to stay and help you unpack your dainties."

"Mind your place, man, and do as I say!"

"O'right, I'm goin'. Meant no offense, only that you can count on ol' Clinton if you needs anythin' else toted, or shifted, and such like."

Mary watched him go, then shut herself inside her room and looked about. It was just as she had left it – a very pleasant apart-ment, perhaps not as finely furnished as those belonging to the family, yet large and handsomely appointed nevertheless. The closets were adequate, the bed itself more than comfortable, and the view overlooked a green meadow where daffodils bloomed each spring. To either side of the window, her own collection of books, which she had brought with her from Longbourn, lined a low bank of shelves. Should these fail to satisfy her appetite during her few free hours, she could hope to be granted special permission to pick from the hun-dreds of volumes in the library downstairs, or to play the fine piano-forte that resided in the music room next door to it.

She could not have wished for anything more perfect than to be allowed to cloister herself in the welcoming seclusion of those two hallowed rooms, whiling away the hours unhurried and unmolested by the demands of others. Living as she did, surrounded by these intellectual delights, such imaginings did occasionally tempt her. It was pure fancy, however, for only a daughter of the house could ever expect such privileges.

Mary had not been given more than ten minutes to reacquaint herself with her surroundings when she was reminded of her true situation. The door from the young master's room swung wide into hers, and a stout boy of eight appeared.

"So you are come back," he stated flatly.

"Yes, Michael, as you see. But please recall that you are always to knock before entering a lady's room, even mine. Now, unless there is some dire emergency…"

Before she could finish, another door – the one directly opposite the first – opened as well, and two slight figures in yellow sprigged muslin issued through it. The taller one, a pretty dark-eyed girl of thirteen, announced from the doorway, "We heard a noise and came to discover what it was. Now I see it is only *you*, Miss Bennet. You stayed away so long that I thought perhaps you would never return."

"Of course I have returned, Gwendolyn," Mary answered evenly. "I always keep my obligations, as any lady should."

The other girl – her sister's inferior in beauty and by two years in age – pushed past and came to Mary's side. "Well, I for one am very glad of it, Miss! May we have a music lesson today?"

"By all means, Grace. I hope you have not neglected your practicing whilst I was away. Monsieur Hubert will not be pleased if you have."

"Oh, no, Miss! I practiced every day!"

"Good girl," said Mary, patting her shoulder. "Now then, we shall resume our regular studies directly, but you must allow me time to get my bearings first. So, return to what you were doing, all of you, and I will summon you shortly." With that, Mary began shooing the three children back whence they had come, closing the doors behind them.

There were no locks, of course, and hence no real privacy. In five minutes, her solitude might be interrupted once again, although she told herself this was no very great difference from her prior existence at Longbourn, where at any moment her mother or one of her sisters might break in upon her without so much as one word of apology. There, however, her modest bedchamber had belonged more exclusively to her than did this grander one, which was only designated for her temporary use.

Her services would not be wanted at Netherfield forever. Michael was to go away to Eton in the fall, and the girls were nearly grown. Employment of six or seven years more would be the utmost she could reasonably hope for. After that, she would be in search of a new situation. She could not expect to find anything half so convenient again – with a family of quality and in the very neighborhood of her home. Yet she was not at all afraid of being long unemployed. She knew there were places in town, offices where inquiry would soon produce something.

That was a long way off, however, and Mary resolved to think of it no more, quoting a memorized scripture to herself. *"Take therefore no thought for the morrow; for the morrow shall take thought for the things of itself. Sufficient unto the day is the evil thereof."*

~~ * ~~

Life at Netherfield settled once more into its customary pattern. Other than an hour or two in the evening, when they were usually suffered to enjoy their father's company, the three children were left chiefly to Miss Bennet's supervision. From Monday through Saturday, she not only oversaw their education, she took every meal and excursion with them as well. The mornings were reserved for academics – mathematics, geography, literature, a little Latin, and the modern languages – and the afternoons for outdoor exercise and the arts. Masters were engaged to periodically come to them from town, but it was the governess's office to provide rudimentary training in dance, drawing, and all forms of music.

Mr. Harrison Farnsworth's affairs kept him a good deal in London, so Mary saw little of him those first weeks back. This suited her well enough, as she could then attend to her duties without fear of falling under his critical eye. He unsettled her, as he seemed to do the rest of Netherfield's inmates to one degree or another.

By contrast, Mrs. Farnsworth had been a lenient, even indolent, mistress. Mary, upon first coming to the house, now nearly four years past, had mistaken the pale creature for at least five-and-thirty, though, as she later learnt, the lady fell far shy of that mark. No doubt the strain of having such a domineering husband – and also of having been brought five times to childbed with only three living offspring to show for her trouble – had taken its toll upon her constitution and nerves.

In those former days especially, the atmosphere at Netherfield altered perceptibly with the master's presence. An air of apprehension crept over the place from top to bottom, as if the house itself held its breath in anticipation of some unknown outburst or accident. Thus, it required nothing more than Mr. Farnsworth's suddenly coming into a room to start his wife and servants fidgeting and his children forgetting how to behave.

Mary had observed the phenomenon from her earliest days on the premises, and she could not help but feel fiercely sympathetic on Mrs. Farnsworth's account.

"So, this is the new governess," declared the lord and master at his first setting eyes on Mary those years ago.

Mr. Farnsworth was not an especially imposing man to look at, being only a little above the average in height and build, yet his autocratic tone made even this simple statement of fact sound like a challenge – daring her to deny the charge.

Rising to face him, Mary had only nodded curtly in response.

"Yes, my dear," his wife, who looked more frayed about the edges than usual, hastened to say. "This is Miss Bennet, Miss Mary Bennet from Longbourn. You will recall that I told you about her. She is a most accomplished and genteel young woman, and I am sure she will do very well by the children."

"*I* will be the judge of that, if you please, Madam."

"Naturally," Mrs. Farnsworth murmured, dropping her eyes to her lap, where her hands were tightly clasped.

A maid, who had come in with the tea tray, cringed as she set it down with more clatter than she intended.

"Must you make such an infernal racket?" Mr. Farnsworth barked, darting an eye in the direction of the offender.

"Sorry, sir," said the maid as she shrank from the room.

"The rest of you, out as well," he said, pointing to the door. "Mrs. Farnsworth, kindly take your children and go. I wish to speak to Miss Bennet."

Mr. Farnsworth had once been a captain in the Navy, so his military bearing did not surprise Mary. Whilst the others scrambled to obey, she studied her new employer, taking his features apart one by one – the bristling dark hair, the deliberately narrowed cobalt eyes, the hard set of his mouth, and the prematurely graying beard. The beard, she told herself with devilish satisfaction, had probably been grown by way of disguising what would ultimately prove to be a weak chin. Yes, that must be the case.

It was a trick she sometimes used to steady herself when confronted with an ominous problem, mentally dissecting it into a collection of smaller, more manageable bits. In the brutish case before her, she perceived one part tyrant and one part diffident boy, both covered over with a quantity of practiced intimidation. The gentleman did not appear so alarming under this analysis. He was formidable, not by true essence, she concluded. It was rather by considerable effort, as if he could only bolster his own confidence by cowering others. Judging from the prodigious scowl he wore, Mr. Farnsworth had next set himself the task of cowering her.

"Well, Miss Bennet," he commenced, slowly striding across the room with hands clasped behind his back and a cool, sideways gaze leveled at her. "Let us come to a right understanding at once. My wife may have engaged your services, but you shall stay or go according to *my* verdict. Is that clear?"

"Perfectly, sir."

"Good." He turned to retrace his steps. "I must say that I was none too pleased to hear of her selection. Although I know no harm of you personally, there certainly has been a good deal of talk about the Longbourn family in general throughout the neighborhood – not all of it to your credit, I might add. I understand there was some sort of scandal with one of your sisters several years back, and then there is the matter of your mother's low connections. What do you say to that?"

Being keenly conscious that this one conversation would likely determine the tenor for all their future dealings together, Mary had carefully weighed her answer. If she were too outspoken, she would lose her position altogether. Yet if she allowed herself to be subjugated, she would before long learn to loathe not only her employer, but her occupation and her own want of fortitude as well. Presently she straightened herself and replied.

"Sir, allow me to say first that you are most assuredly within your rights to do what you can to determine my fitness for tutoring your children. Your scruples do you credit, I am sure. However, I fail to see where your present line of enquiry is much relevant. All you need know on that head is that I have been brought up a gentleman's daughter. If you wish to interrogate me further concerning my own character, education, and accomplishments, however, I will be more than happy to supply you with the information you require. In truth, I would welcome the opportunity to do so."

Mr. Harrison Farnsworth drew up short and regarded the governess with a menacing glare of a long minute's duration. When she did not waver, he at last moved on in a new direction, both with his pacing of the room and in his mode of interview. He stated his expectations, which were very high. He warned of his tolerance for disobedience and disloyalty, which were exceptionally low. He reiterated her salary, which was equitable.

"And then there is the matter of my music lessons," Mary had reminded him. "I trust Mrs. Farnsworth has acquainted you with the arrangement we arrived at between ourselves."

"Mrs. Farnsworth did mention some such nonsense. I could not credit it, however. Music lessons for the governess? It is highly irregular. Why, I have never heard of such a preposterous idea!" he declared, pacing more furiously.

Mary had to consciously rein in her irritation. "Irregular it may be, sir, but certainly not preposterous. I was raised a gentleman's daughter, as I have said, and so I am still. The daughters of gentlemen often have the instruction of a music master. I understand you have engaged one of some renown for your own children – your sister's personal instructor, I am told. What reasonable objection can there be to allowing me to have a lesson following them? It will make me more fit to guide your children, and it can do you no possible harm. I am to use the instrument in the schoolroom for my practicing. And it is all arranged that I shall pay for my lessons out of my own salary, if that is what worries you."

"Huh! Did I say that I was worried about the trifling expense of it? No, it is the propriety of the arrangement I question, the efficiency of it. What are my children to do whilst you are closeted with Monsieur Hubert?"

"Your children, Mr. Farnsworth, are no longer infants who need constant attendance. Surely you do not mean to tell me that they are so unruly as to be impossible for the nursery maid to look after for one short hour. Otherwise, I begin to fear I may require more compensation for having the charge of such an unmanageable lot."

Again the imperious gentleman shot her a glare; again the governess remained unwavering under its force.

Just when Mary thought his mouth might be curling at one corner, Farnsworth brought his hand up to cover a cough. "Very well, Miss Bennet," he said afterward, "we shall give the arrangement a try." He coughed again before continuing sternly. "I warn you, though, should it interfere with your primary duties, I shall have no scruple whatsoever in putting an end to it. Do you understand me?"

A year and a half passed with hostilities in the household running just below the surface. The bad-tempered master blustered, and everybody else gave way. Then, following another unsuccessful lying-in, poor Mrs. Farnsworth was carried off by an infectious fever. The next Mary heard was that her husband had forsaken his country home in favor of London, and that he was sending his sister, Miss Lavinia Farnsworth, to act as mistress of Netherfield in place of his dead wife.

When he returned, he was quite altered. Much of the fight had gone out of him, and he began to make more of an effort with the children. Mary postulated that the change might be accounted for by a tormented conscience. Perhaps, she speculated, he finally felt proper remorse for having treated his wife so badly.

Mr. Farnsworth's new spirit of charity did not always extend as far as the governess. Yet from the beginning there had existed between them a tacit understanding, a wary truce born out of the healthy respect each felt for the peculiar strengths of the other. Mary was always careful to treat her employer with the deference his position demanded, and in return he generally refrained from practicing his manipulative arts on her, at least until recently.

5
Mrs. Bennet's Plan

On Sundays, Mary rested from her duties at Netherfield and returned to Longbourn to spend a few hours of liberty at her family home with her mother. According to their original arrangement, Mr. Farnsworth was obliged to send her off in one of his good carriages early in the morning, and then see to it that she was collected again at night. This particular Sunday in the middle of May was no different. Mary took her place with Kitty and Mrs. Bennet in their pew at Longbourn church, where the Netherfield carriage had set her down.

With their father having been gone for only five months, the sisters were both still garbed in full mourning, as was their mother next to them – Kitty in black crepe, and bombazine on the other two. For the widow and younger Miss Bennet, it constituted a dramatic departure from what had been their usual style. For Mary, it meant only a dimming of her dark governess's habit by one more degree, putting the light out entirely.

All through the service, Kitty fidgeted and sighed, singing the designated hymns less vociferously than usual, and attending to the sermon not at all. She had to be corrected by her sister more than once for moving amiss or losing her place in her prayer book.

"Are you unwell?" Mary demanded of her in a low voice as soon as they had done and made their way out into the churchyard. "Because otherwise I cannot account for your behavior in the least. I have often seen better self-command in a child of three."

"La! When I tell you my news, I daresay you will be sorry for taking that critical tone," rejoined Kitty, a fretful expression on her face. "It is a very great secret, and not for Mama's ears, so we shall have to look out for the first opportunity to get off by ourselves. Then we shall see if you do not think it worth an hour or two's agitation."

Mary, who suspected her sister of possessing nothing more than a bit of town gossip, did not press for more information.

Soon their mother finished her tête-à-tête with Mrs. Elkhorn and joined them for the brief walk to Longbourn. They proceeded rapidly, Mrs. Bennet setting the brisk pace.

"I declare, that lady would try the patience of a saint!" said she presently with an expression of disgust. "Every Sunday it is the same. 'Oh, my poor Mrs. Bennet, how ill you look.' Then she goes on to lament my 'unfortunate circumstances' in such melancholy terms as to make me grow quite distracted!"

"I suppose she only wishes to condole with you, Mama," suggested Mary. "She is a widow too, and should thereby understand better than most what you must be feeling."

"Then you suppose wrongly, Mary, for she has always been jealous of me, that I married so much better than she. Now she would see me fall back to her level and rejoice at it. Can you guess what she had the impudence to propose today? Hmm? Can you, Mary, Kitty?" Receiving no insightful speculations from her offspring, Mrs. Bennet hastened on. "Well then, she said that I had better start making inquiries for a cheap situation, and she actually dropped a hint that Mrs. Bell might have a room to let. As if I would ever consider such a thing!"

"What did you say to that, Mama?" asked Kitty. "I suppose you gave her a very sharp set down."

"I most certainly did! My words were perfectly cordial, mind, and yet my tone she could not mistake. I thanked her for her kind solicitude, but that I was in no immediate danger of sinking into poverty, not with two such wealthy sons-in-law. Then I let it drop, just in a casual way, what are the incomes of Mr. Darcy and Mr. Bingley. Well, she could make no answer there, for her Eleanor is only married to a curate, and she has still got Caroline on her hands. So that, I daresay, is the last I shall hear on the subject from Mrs. Elkhorn!"

Mrs. Bennet, savoring the recitation of this triumph, took an intermission as the three women covered the final portion of their passage home. Once inside the hall, however, her complacency seemed to falter. "Of course Mrs. Elkhorn has just the one daughter still unmarried, and I have two," she thought aloud whilst Mrs. Hill helped her off with her spencer. "I wonder that she did not mention it. It would be very like her, you know, to throw that in my face, and another time she may. Well, we shall soon remedy that, if only my plan might be lucky enough to succeed."

Mary and Kitty exchanged a speaking look. They had already had a month's worth of Sundays on the topic of Mrs. Bennet's "plan." After her husband's sudden demise, she had wasted no time in convincing herself that the heir to Longbourn would prove to be a single man of a most eligible aspect. To her way of thinking, it immediately followed that he must be in want of a wife, and that either Mary or Kitty ought to have him. By all that was natural and just, Mr. Tristan Collins was the rightful property of the one or other of her daughters.

"You assume far too much, Mama," Mary observed when the plan first came to light. "He may not even be single. As Mr. Bingley said, he is a man of thirty and has likely taken a wife by now."

"What? Marry an American! Have you lost your senses? From what I hear, there is nobody there but heathens and savages. What proper English gentleman would stoop so low? No, mark my words. He left England without a wife, and he shall surely return the same way. That is where *you* come in, Kitty."

"Me?" Kitty exclaimed with a violent start. "Why must *I* be the one who secures him, Mama? Mary is older and therefore has the higher claim."

"Yes, why must it be Kitty?" echoed Mary, hardly knowing why she said it.

It had then come out that Mrs. Bennet, having clearly consigned her elder daughter to the shelf, thought the younger, prettier one the only credible prospect for catching Mr. Collins. "Consider, Mary," she concluded, "if your sister can get him, then you and I will always have a home here at Longbourn. It is the best solution for us all; of that I am perfectly persuaded. It is unlucky, however, that we should be in mourning, for black is not very becoming, even on you, Kitty. Still, in another month, I think you girls may safely moderate your dress. That should do nicely. Of course the wedding will have to wait until a full year has elapsed, but that can be no great hardship I daresay."

It had since that day been quite a settled thing in Mrs. Bennet's mind, and every week since had brought forth from her lips further discourse on how her plan might best be accomplished. Indeed, her daughters began to dread every mention of Mr. Tristan Collins's name. However, all their considerable disinclination for the subject was insufficient to prevent its being canvassed again and again by their mother. Like a tune lodged firmly in her head to where she could think of nothing else, the tired refrain came out once more that Sunday in May. "Yes, if only my plan for Kitty and Mr. Collins might succeed," she said.

Meanwhile, Kitty impatiently awaited the opportunity to set her own ideas at work, ideas that were sure to sound a note of discord against her mother's unremitting theme. Although marriage was always her object, according to Kitty's way of thinking, being wed to anyone by the name of Collins could not possibly be agreeable. Her chance to set her escape in motion came directly after church with Mrs. Bennet's pronouncement that she would take a lie down until dinner, in consequence of a sudden headache.

"Come, Mary," said Kitty, taking up her sister's hand and pulling her toward the front door. "Let us leave Mama in peace and go out to the garden... to cut some flowers for the table."

"Yes, you girls go on," agreed Mrs. Bennet. "Take yourselves out of doors, and your noise with you, for I really cannot bear another sound. My head is very ill today."

Seeing that their mother truly wished them away, the Miss Bennets could not but oblige her. Venturing forth, consequently, they proceeded in silence along the gravel walk that led to the copse. Mary was determined to make no effort for conversation, still supposing her sister to have nothing more worthwhile than gossip to divulge.

Kitty willingly postponed beginning the conference a few minutes longer as well, scarcely knowing whether the keeping or the telling of her secret intelligence would prove the more harrowing. "Sit down, Mary, and prepare yourself," she said when they had reached that part of the garden where they were least likely to be interrupted.

After a pause and a sigh, Mary obeyed without comment, seating herself on the bench her sister indicated.

"Now you shall see why I am in such a flutter," Kitty said. She drew a packet of paper from her pocket and held it out to her sister. "Look what I have got."

Upon inspection, Mary discovered it to be a letter directed to her mother and written in a hand wholly unknown to her. "What is the meaning of this, Kitty? Who is this letter from, and why is it such a great secret?"

"It is from the heir to Longbourn – Mr. Tristan Collins! He has written from America, and it is a great secret because Mama has not yet read it. Nor must she! What a prodigious piece of luck it was that I came upon it first." Kitty held up a hand to forestall the anticipated protest. "I know you will say that I should not have taken it. But before you quote me a sermon, read the letter yourself and hear my proposal. Then, on the grounds of sisterly loyalty, you must come to

37

my aid, else before Michaelmas Mama will have me engaged to this stranger and forever miserable."

With this impassioned plea, Kitty sat down to wait in much perturbation. When her instructions were not immediately obeyed, she added, "You need not be afraid, Mary. There is nothing so very personal or private in it. I daresay Mama would have shown it to you herself, had she read it."

Mary looked grave, and yet she opened the letter.

Dear Madam,

I feel myself called upon by our relationship to condole with you on the grievous affliction you are now suffering under, of which I was only yesterday informed by a letter from your solicitor in London. I pray you will forgive me for introducing myself to your notice at this difficult time, and that you will not think my sympathy any less genuine for the awkwardness of our situation. I write chiefly to reassure you that I am very sensible of the severity of your loss, and that I mean to in no way add to your misery where it can be helped. Therefore, although I propose myself the satisfaction of coming to you without delay, I do not anticipate any need for you to vacate your comfortable abode at once. I ask only that you allow me to be a guest therein whilst we sort out between us what is best to be done. I travel alone, and so hope that my presence will not incommode your household unduly. I believe you will find that my wants and needs are simple, so I beseech you to make no special preparations for my coming. My intention is to follow this letter as soon as I am able to settle my business affairs, and I hope to arrive within three weeks of your receipt of the same. Until then, please convey my respectful compliments to all your family.

Tristan Collins, esquire

"Well? What do you think of it?" Kitty demanded.

"I think it is a very good letter – well composed and clearly expressed."

"Is that all you can say on the subject?" cried Kitty in exasperation. "How can you be so tiresome, Mary?"

"Very well, then. Let me look again."

Kitty rose to walk to and fro whilst her sister reread the short missive. Mary's second appraisal was more comprehensive and more gratifying to her sister's feelings.

"The content reveals nothing so very remarkable. It was always to be expected that he would come to inspect his property. This is only a little sooner than anticipated. As to the style of the letter, I must say that I am pleased with it. His generous sentiments do him credit, and they are elegantly conveyed." Mary took a moment to consider before adding one more point. "There *is* a certain something in his way of expressing himself, however. It is rather reminiscent of a person we used to know."

"Exactly! I can see this Mr. Tristan Collins now," said Kitty, evincing horror at the specter before her mind's eye. "The man is his brother to the very core, and he will be here in less than a month!"

6
Alternative

A vision out of the past likewise rose up before Mary's eyes. Yet her recollections of the former cleric of Hunsford were somewhat more charitable than her sister's. Although she flattered herself that her taste and judgment had since improved, there was a time when the former Mr. Collins – Mr. William Collins – had admittedly sparked her interest. He seemed to her then a serious, scholarly man with a comfortable home and an agreeable situation to offer. Being wife to a clergyman would have suited Mary's humble ambitions very well. And, considering the added satisfaction it would have given her to redeem the Longbourn estate for her family, she could not help feeling disappointed when Mr. Collins chose to bestow his affections elsewhere.

With the benefit of hindsight, however, she realized it was primarily the situation, not the man himself, that had attracted her. Yet she still believed she could have been happy with him, or at least content. In that respect, she fancied she was not so unlike the practical-minded Charlotte Lucas, to whom had gone both the husband and the cozy parsonage instead. Perhaps things might have turned out differently for Mr. Collins as well, had he chosen someone else for his wife. That could be said for any man or woman, she supposed. Marriage: how much of happiness or torment seemed bound up in that one, irrevocable act. The proof of it was everywhere about her to be seen.

Kitty called her back from these reflections. "Mary, are you listening? I prayed that Mama was wrong, and that he might turn out to be thoroughly married after all. But you see he says he travels alone and makes no mention of leaving family behind, only business. You must help me!"

"And what am I to do on the occasion? The man is coming; *I* cannot stop him. Besides, just because Mama has got it into her head that you will marry him, does not make it so. Mr. Collins may have something to say in the matter. Perhaps he is more interested in claiming his property than acquiring a wife. Or perhaps he will not find your charms as irresistible as you imagine. If worse comes to worse and he does make you an offer, you could always refuse him like Lizzy did the other Mr. Collins."

"I thought of that, but it will not do. I am not strong like Lizzy; I never was. And with Mama so determined, I cannot take the chance that my resolve may fail me in the end. No, it will be altogether safer if the situation can be avoided in the first place."

"Just how do you intend to manage that? Will you parade yourself before him as the most disagreeable creature in the world, or will you run away?" scoffed Mary.

"Yes, in a manner of speaking. I plan to take myself completely out of his road. Since Mama does not know Mr. Collins comes so soon, I shall persuade her to let me travel north to visit my sisters. I had a letter from Lizzy saying Mr. Darcy is now in London and will be stopping here before he returns to Pemberley. So it is easily done. Then I shall stay away as long as possible and try my best for someone else – anyone else. Meanwhile, you shall have Mr. Collins all to yourself."

"To myself? Do you imagine that I have designs on the man, then?"

"No, and yet you may happen to suit one another. At any rate, considering our differing views on the first Mr. Collins, it seems far more probable that you shall like his brother than that I should. Promise me that you will try for him, Mary, please."

"I will make no promise of the kind! I will be civil to the man, certainly, just as I would any other one of God's creatures. You must ask no more than that of me."

"Only one other thing. Will you at least swear not to let slip to Mama what I have told you?"

Mary pursed her lips, contemplating the question and the untenable position into which she had been placed. She had half a mind to march back into the house and hand the evidence over to her mother. After all, the letter was her rightful property. Yet, as little as she could condone being made an unwilling partner to subterfuge, she approved the idea of a coerced marriage even less. Kitty had her sincere sympathy there, and it seemed nothing worthwhile would be accomplished by reporting her misconduct. At length Mary answered, "If it all goes wrong, you alone must bear the blame, Kitty. I will take no share of it." She sighed. "But neither will I betray your confidence."

Kitty relaxed. "I knew I was right to trust you, and nothing will go wrong. You shall see."

"Hmm, I cannot help thinking you are quite mistaken there, and that I might pay the price for this misadventure in the end. Now then, what do you mean that I should do with this?" said Mary, waving the stolen letter before her sister's nose.

"Oh, heavens, I don't care. Keep it, burn it, or give it to Mama after I am gone. Say it had been misdirected at first. Whatever you think best. Just give me enough time to make good my escape."

~~ * ~~

With her sister's cooperation assured – limited though it might be – Kitty wasted no time applying for her mother's unwitting acquiescence to her plan as well. She made her request in form after dinner, asking for permission to travel to Pemberley when Mr. Darcy should be returning thither.

There was nothing odd in the request. Mrs. Bennet had very frequently – and very willingly – spared her fourth daughter from home to visit her sisters to the north, always with the hope that she would catch a rich husband for herself whilst she was away. It had seemed far more likely that such a thing should come to pass there, amongst the Bingleys' or the Darcys' acquaintance, than in the dull society of Longbourn and Meryton, where one could not expect to encounter anything superior to a penniless second son of a country squire. It had all come to naught, however, and the heir to Longbourn, who otherwise held no noble distinction and presumably little fortune, was all she had in view for Kitty now. Mrs. Bennet's permission was, therefore, more difficult to procure than expected.

"May I go, Mama?" asked Kitty again.

"There is nothing for you in Derbyshire, you know," said Mrs. Bennet. "Years of trying, and not a single offer to show for it. No, you had much better stay here and prepare for Mr. Collins's arrival. If my plan succeeds, this will be your home from now on, so you might as well get used to the fact that there will be no more of this traipsing about the countryside."

Kitty, whose spirits were about to fail her, made one last tearful attempt. "Very well. If that is what the future holds for me, then let this be my farewell tour. Allow me to visit Pemberley and Heatheridge one final time before taking up my duties here. You would not deny me this last request, would you, Mama?"

"Good gracious, child, the way you carry on, anyone would think you had a death sentence hanging over your head instead of a wedding. I am sure Mr. Collins is a fine, respectable young man, just like his brother was." Kitty sobbed all the louder. "And you will be lucky to get him. I see no occasion for all this wailing and blubbering. Still... if it means that much to you, I suppose you may as well go. I want you at your best – well rested and cheerful – when Mr. Collins arrives."

7
The Farnsworths

Kitty's design thus set into motion, the pact between the sisters was later sealed by an embrace and an expressive look exchanged as they parted. Mary then climbed into Mr. Farnsworth's comfortable carriage for the short drive back to Netherfield.

When underway, she drew Mr. Collins's letter from her reticule, where she had concealed it, and studied its contents again. One phrase caught her particular attention. *I travel alone.* Kitty was wrong to presume so much from that line; it could mean any number of things. If the man had a wife and a clutch of small children, it was not to be supposed that he would needlessly expose them to the risks of so long a sea voyage. No, one could not depend on his being single.

If he should be, though, what then? Mary's fancy was not permitted much of a meandering on that question. She very shortly called it back into line with the answer.

Even if Mr. Collins were discovered to be single, the next step in Kitty's logic was equally flawed. She had it worked out that Mr. Collins would be available for the asking, and that he would be so obliging as to marry whomsoever he was directed to – the same assumption their mother made, only with a different object. The idea that he might be made to care for herself, Mary all but dismissed. It was not that she underrated her own assets, only that they were of a type not as yet known to inspire romantic intentions.

As near as she could make out, young ladies were only considered desirable when they kept to the graces men had assigned them. They were allowed to be the fairer sex, and to excel in the arts of conversation and flirtation. These were hardly Mary's strong suits, however, as well she knew. According to her experience, a gentleman did not appreciate having his presumed superiority challenged in any other realm, even slightly.

Judging from the woman he had chosen to wed, Mr. Harrison Farnsworth was no different. Mrs. Farnsworth had been pretty enough and charming in a quiet sort of way, but she certainly had been no threat to her husband's authority, his strength of will, or to his mental prowess. Although Mary believed he had lately learnt to value her own abilities to a greater extent, it was only because they served his purpose in an altogether different role. He did not see her as a woman so much as an educator of his children. In that capacity, he could appreciate her talents. In that capacity, he had taken to consulting her and was even willing to be sometimes guided by her advice.

They had their moments of concord, she and her employer, and yet she could not depend on them. His moods were now so changeable that she never knew which person to expect, the old tyrant or the new man of enlightenment.

~~ * ~~

Two more weeks passed away, and two more Sundays at Longbourn. Kitty had made good her escape to the north, and Mary still held custody of the stolen letter from Mr. Tristan Collins. She had decided that delivering it after the fact, as her sister had proposed, would only involve her further by requiring lies which she feared she could neither tell convincingly nor reconcile with her conscience. Better to leave well enough alone, to simply let it be thought that the letter had been lost somewhere on its long journey.

"Mr. Farnsworth wishes to see you in the library, Miss," announced the butler upon her return to Netherfield Hall that Sunday night.

Mary was taken aback. A command appearance before her employer was not at all what she had intended that the rest of her evening should entail, but rather a book before her quiet fireside. "Very well, Haines," said she with a sigh. "I will just take my things up to my room first."

At that moment, Miss Lavinia Farnsworth bustled into the hall, holding her skirts and clucking her tongue. "No, Miss Bennet; that will not do. My brother was most insistent that you should come to him the instant you arrived. Now, give your things over to Clinton there, and go in at once."

"As you wish, then, Madam."

"It is as Mr. Farnsworth wishes, Miss Bennet."

Mary handed her coat and bag to the footman without further comment, and made her way to the library. At the massive mahogany door, she straightened her hair and smoothed her skirt before knocking.

"Enter," came the directive from the other side.

"You wished to see me, sir?" said Mary, pushing open the door.

Mr. Farnsworth sat in his usual place, behind the regally proportioned desk that stood in the exact center of the heavily draped and wood-paneled room. "Ah, Miss Bennet," he said, rising. He motioned her to a chair opposite himself. "Do come in and sit down. You must forgive me for summoning you at such a late hour, and on your off day too, but it could not be helped. I am for London early in the morning, and I needed to see you before I go."

Mary took the chair he offered her, glad that he appeared to be in a tolerably good humor. "Is it something urgent, sir? About the children?"

"Well, important if not urgent," he said, leaning against the edge of the desk with his arms crossed. "And it does concern the children, most particularly Michael."

"Michael, sir?"

"Yes, I wish you to excuse him from his music lessons, effective immediately, and you will tell your Monsieur Hubert the same when next he comes."

"Excuse him from studying music?" Mary repeated in some confusion. "But why?"

"Because he has requested it, and personally I see no reason that a boy in his situation…" He stopped and turned a sharp eye on Mary. "Look here, Miss Bennet, I hardly think I need to justify my decision. I have told you my wishes and that should be enough."

Mary stiffened. "Yes, sir, if those are your instructions, they will be carried out exactly."

"Just like that? What, no importunate questions or remonstration? You have no comment of any kind on the matter?"

"Nothing that could be the least bit relevant."

"This is a surprise. I thought sure we were in for a fight, but it seems I have at last hit upon a subject about which you profess to have no opinion."

"You mistake me, sir. It was not my intention to imply that I had no opinion, only that any opinion I may possess can have no material bearing on the case."

"Yes, I thought there was more. Now we are coming a little nearer the truth."

"The truth? The truth is that what I think does not signify in the least," said Mary, maintaining a calm exterior by force of will and with considerable difficulty. "As you have made abundantly clear, Mr. Farnsworth, *your* opinion is the only one that matters."

Farnsworth pushed off the desk and back to his feet, his eyes flashing. "Aha! There it is. I knew you disapproved."

"I did not say so, sir."

"Of course not. That would have been too straightforward, too honest, too much like a man would do. Instead you show me this…" He gestured at her with his hand. "…this dignified bearing, this martyred expression. I suppose this is your elegant little female way of driving home your point. This is how you choose to torture me."

"I do assure you, sir, that I have no pretensions whatever to that kind of elegance which consists in tormenting a respectable man."

"So you do not pretend to torment me?"

"No, sir."

"And yet you do. Hmm." He sank into the chair behind the desk again. "Very well, Miss Bennet, I must take you at your word, and you must take me at mine. Perhaps I have lately given the wrong impression, becoming too lax. I will by no means, however, brook any interference in the management of my children, not even from you. Have I made my position plainly understood?"

"I believe so, sir. There will be no more music lessons for Master Michael. Neither will there be any interference tolerated from me. And should you ever again desire to hear my opinion, you will ask for it. Does that correctly sum up your wishes?"

He looked heavenward and sighed. "What can I say to such a speech, Miss Bennet, except that you try my patience exceedingly?"

"Yes, sir. Will that be all, sir? I am really rather fatigued and I would like to retire."

As if she could not be soon enough removed from his sight, he covered his eyes with one hand and waved her off toward the door with the other.

The feeling was mutual. Mary left thinking him the most exasperating individual she had ever had the misfortune to encounter. He insisted on stirring up a fight where there wasn't one, and dragging insolence from her lips that she would otherwise have left unsaid. He claimed he would brook no insubordination, and yet he tempted her to it at every turn.

What was the point of the slow and careful progress they had made toward tolerance, understanding, and a good working relationship if it could all be undone in the space of a few minutes? And over such a ridiculous piece of business too. What was the man thinking of, cheating his son out of a solid foundation in music? Yes, she had an opinion on the subject, and another time perhaps he would get an earful of it… whether he asked for it or not.

~~ * ~~

Mr. Farnsworth was gone in the morning, leaving Mary only his children and his sister to deal with for the succeeding week.

Miss Lavinia Farnsworth always had a word of instruction or criticism to give, especially when the master was away. She politely withdrew to the shadows in his presence, but she became more and more emboldened by his every absence, as if she each time inherited another thin slice of his bravado and the duty to use it in his stead.

In her person, Miss Farnsworth *was* a younger, more delicate reflection of her brother – minus the beard – with the same strikingly juxtaposed dark hair and light eyes. Mary had befriended Lavinia when the lady arrived at Netherfield immediately after Mrs. Farnsworth's death. On the face of things, it was a natural pairing, the two being within a few years of each other in age, and from roughly the same social stratum. Mary felt a real compassion for her as well – a stranger to the house and forced by tragic circumstances to unexpectedly step into her sister-in-law's shoes.

Lavinia had welcomed the extended olive branch in the beginning. Later, however, she seemed embarrassed by the connection and was at great pains proving to everybody that Miss Bennet was nothing whatever to her. Mary always wondered if it had been the lady's brother who had put her off the friendship, not thinking a governess a suitable companion for his sister.

Nowadays, she made it her goal to stay out of Miss Farnsworth's way as completely as possible. Since Mary was always in the schoolroom – a place that apparently held no interest for the acting mistress of the house – it was easily done.

She stood on firmer ground with the children. Although Master Michael could be difficult and Miss Gwendolyn defiant of late, they were predictably so and not beyond Mary's ability to manage. Being acquainted with the deficiencies of their father and the early death of their mother, she could not be surprised by or even much resent their misbehavior. And Grace more than made up for the other members of the family. For her sake, Mary was prepared to put up with the faults and vagaries of all the rest.

Her other principal joy was her periodic music lesson, for which Mr. Farnsworth had ultimately refused to allow her to pay. Monsieur Hubert came once every fortnight and had students enough to fill an entire morning. Miss Farnsworth always took the first lesson, followed by the children in no particular order, and then lastly Mary.

The music master came according to his regular schedule the Tuesday Mr. Farnsworth was away. Mary reported to him an hour earlier than usual, at the end of Gwendolyn's time.

"Very good, Miss Farnsworth," said Monsieur Hubert with his familiar French accent, still prominent even after spending more than a dozen years exclusively in England. Although his looks were decidedly ordinary, even plain, he had a certain style that elevated him above any danger of being referred to as commonplace. "That will be all for today, I think. You must promise to practice more, however, or you will never be as accomplished as the other young ladies."

Gwendolyn rose from the instrument, bobbed her teacher a hurried curtsey, and left the room saying, "Yes, Monsieur."

The well-dressed man of five-and-thirty then turned his attention to Mary. "Ah, Miss Bennet!" he sang out, bringing his hands together in a gesture of mercurial delight. "Now I shall have the pleasure of hearing from my favorite pupil. You put all the others to shame."

"Bonjour, Monsieur," she said, smiling demurely and coming forward. Mary had no illusions. She assumed the music master must have many 'favorite' pupils, an idea which gave no offense. No one could dislike this man of gentle charm and grace, for there was a genuine warmth about him that melted away any irritation that might otherwise have sprung from his little excesses. "I suppose you have heard," she continued, "that Michael is to be excused henceforth."

"*Oui, oui*, so Miss Lavinia Farnsworth has informed me." He clucked his tongue and shook his head. "*Quel dommage*! It is ill-advised, *certainement*, but what can one do? Not that the boy showed much promise, you understand. Still, with time and hard work, something acceptable might have been achieved."

"My nephew would make you a more eager pupil, Monsieur Hubert. I have just had a letter from my sister, who is Mrs. Darcy of Pemberley in Derbyshire, reminding me to ask if you would consider taking the boy on. I know it is a long way to travel, but I am sure Mr. Darcy would be prepared to make it well worth your while."

"Ah, Derbyshire, you say, Miss Bennet. Divine country, that, simply divine! And I have heard of this place you call Pemberley. A very fine estate, I believe. Of what age is this child, your nephew?"

"He was five September last, and very eager to learn, I am told."

"Well, then, perhaps something might be arranged. For you, Miss Bennet, I will consider it. Now then, shall we begin?"

Mary did not need to be asked twice. She seated herself at the revered instrument and waited for further instructions.

"The scales, I think," said Monsieur Hubert. "Begin with your scales, and then we will move on to the Mozart."

Mary obediently commenced the methodical exercise with both hands, running her fingers up the keys for two octaves and then down again before moving on to the next scale in the sequence. She knew the prescribed progression well and had performed it a hundred times or more. Yet even this routine business, tedious to most, gave her exquisite pleasure. For this brief interval of time, once every other week, she could forget her responsibilities and become lost in the music. She could set aside the duties of a teacher and become the student instead. She could imagine herself a girl again – a talented and promising young lady with a bright future ahead... if only for that one hour.

8
Arrival

It was a Sunday when he first presented himself at Longbourn, and fortunately so, for thus Mary was on hand to support her mother through the crisis. The two ladies had been taking their ease after dinner when they heard a carriage approaching.

"It will only be my sister Phillips," said Mrs. Bennet, not bothering to lift her eyes from the bit of lace she was mending. "She said at church that she might drive over."

Mary, her mind alive to other possibilities, set aside her book at once. She knew very well that over three weeks had elapsed since the arrival of the letter from America. So the time was right and the important moment might well be at hand. Then Mrs. Hill corroborated what Mary's intuition already told her; coming into the sitting room, she announced the true identity of their visitor.

The effect on Mrs. Bennet was both stunning and immediate. She froze stock still, momentarily adopting both the color and character of a pillar of salt, before slowly coming back to life. "Mr. Tristan Collins?" she repeated, evincing her astonishment at the news. "He is here? Now?"

"Yes, ma'am," confirmed Mrs. Hill, "just this instant arrived all the way from America. Shall I show him in?"

"Are you mad, woman? I must have a moment to think. Lord bless me, how is this possible, Mary? We have had no card, no letter, no hint of his coming so soon."

Mary busied herself tidying the room, saying, "None of that matters now, Mama. He is come, and we must make the best of it. Let us not keep him waiting, as if he were unwelcome in his own house."

"*His* house?"

"Yes, for so it is, as well you know. It became his house the moment poor Papa died."

"I cannot bear it! I simply cannot bear it, that I should be forced to make way for this… this undeserving usurper!"

Mary hastened to her mother's side, urging her, "For heaven's sake, madam, speak lower. What advantage can it be to you to offend Mr. Collins? You will never recommend yourself – or your daughter – to him by so doing. Remember your plan, Mama."

"Yes, yes, the plan," said Mrs. Bennet with a little more composure and considerably less volume. "That is the thing to think of now. Mr. Collins must marry Kitty. Oh! But Kitty is gone off to her sisters. What bad luck! Well, she will be sent for and made to come home at once. In the meantime, I suppose we shall have to entertain Mr. Collins as well as may be. There was a time when I was considered quite the charmer, and you shall simply have to do your best too, Mary. I know this sort of thing is not really in your line. That cannot be helped now. We must each play our part to see that things turn out as they should." Mrs. Bennet took a deep breath to steady her nerves. "Hill, please show the gentleman in."

Mary was more prepared than her mother, and not nearly as surprised by so early an arrival of their cousin from America. Yet she too felt the need to steady herself for the first sight of this man whose person, situation, and manners had been the conjecture in nearly every recent discussion at Longbourn. Then, all at once, the suspense was over. Mrs. Hill opened the door, and the man so long speculated about, so high in everybody's interest, was actually before them.

Holding hat in hand, the distinguished young gentleman walked into the room and made a neat bow, saying, "Tristan Collins at your service."

Mrs. Bennet moved forward to greet him, extending her hand and smiling, her demeanor quite transformed from what it had been only moments earlier. "Ah, Mr. Collins, you are very welcome indeed. Did your wife sail with you from America?"

"What? Oh, no, Mrs. Bennet. I am not married."

Mrs. Bennet's countenance brightened still more. "What a shame that is, sir, for it strikes me that you are of a very good age for it."

The most pressing question already asked and answered, Mrs. Bennet proceeded to undertake the other necessary civilities as well. Mary was herself too much overcome to be of any assistance, for before her stood a most pleasingly featured man, and not at all like the one she had imagined.

"This is my middle daughter," said Mrs. Bennet. "Mary, come meet your cousin Mr. Collins."

They each took a step toward the other. "How do you do, Miss Bennet?" he said, smiling. "I cannot tell you how delighted I am to make your acquaintance."

"I thank you, sir," she said, bobbing a slight curtsey.

Mrs. Bennet continued. "I have four others, Mr. Collins, and they are the most agreeable girls you would ever care to meet, though I say it myself. Do let us sit down. Now, my eldest is Jane – Mrs. Bingley, that is… "

With her mother conducting the conversation all on her own, Mary had leisure to collect herself and take stock of their visitor. He was above middling height, with a spare frame – so unlike what his brother's had been – and with fairer coloring too. His features were not classically handsome, perhaps, but not very far off the mark either. The considerable powers of his person to recommend him were further augmented by a sincerity of expression and warmth of voice such as seemed certain proof of his amiability. There was something else too, something indefinable…

"Mary!" her mother was saying. "Mary, do try and pay attention. Now, I have just been telling Mr. Collins how sorry I am that more of the family was not here to greet him."

"Yes, you must pardon the paltry size of the welcoming party," said Mary. "You see, we had no idea of your coming so soon."

"Dear ladies, you owe me no apology and no special honors either. I am only distressed to learn that my letter should have gone astray, giving you no warning of my arrival."

"It is of no importance, sir. We are always ready to receive guests to Longbourn." Mary colored and stammered, "Oh! I… forgive me. I certainly do not mean that you are only a guest in this house, Mr. Collins. You are, of course, much more than that. It is we who… What I mean to say is that… that we stay here only by *your* kindness."

He laughed easily. "My dear Miss Bennet, there is no need for us to stand on ceremony, I trust. We are family, after all. If you had received my letter, you would know that I have no intention of throwing my weight about and casting you out into the cold. Your mother has endured enough hardship for one year, surely."

"You are very good, sir," said Mrs. Bennet.

"Yes, and not at all what I expected from your…" Mary left off clumsily, vexed with herself for letting her thoughts about his letter pass her lips too freely.

"Not at all like my brother? Is that what you were going to say, Miss Bennet?"

"No. Yes. I'm sorry."

"It is quite all right. Poor William. Did you know him well?"

"Not so well as we should have liked to," offered Mrs. Bennet. "He was a fine, respectable young man, with very noble intentions, I believe. Because of this awkward business with the entail, he naturally felt some responsibility toward this family. Did you know that he came to this house with the express purpose of choosing a wife from amongst Mr. Bennet's daughters? None of them was married at the time, you understand. I thought it an exceedingly good plan. However, in the end your brother went another way. And so... well, here we are."

"I trust you do not hold his choice against him, though, Mrs. Bennet."

"No indeed, sir, for one does not like to think ill of the dead. I am only saying that it was an excellent notion and surely one which would have satisfied the wishes of all concerned, had it come to pass."

Feeling uncomfortable with the direction her mother had carried the conversation, Mary interrupted. "Mr. Collins, you must be tired from your travels. Perhaps you would like to rest before supper. If so, you must not allow us to keep you sitting here talking."

"How kind you are, Miss Bennet. Yes, I think I would like that."

"Hill," Mary called out. "There you are, Mrs. Hill. Kindly show Mr. Collins to the guest room."

"Of course, Miss Mary," said Mrs. Hill. Then turning to Mr. Tristan Collins, she added, "This way, if you please, sir."

The gentleman was barely out of earshot when Mrs. Bennet began relating her opinion of him to her daughter: what a fine figure of a man he was; not ill-looking either; and so much more refined than expected of someone who had spent so many years away from all good society.

"And did you notice the expensive cut of his clothes?" she continued. "He must be a man of some fortune after all. What an excellent thing for Kitty! Yes, he will do very well. Was not it clever of me, Mary, to drop him that hint, just to get him thinking? Though he may never before have had any idea of finishing what his brother started, I daresay he will now, especially once he sets eyes on our Kitty."

Mrs. Bennet, well satisfied with this good beginning, took Mary's suggestion likewise, retiring to her own apartment until supper.

At last, Mary was alone with her thoughts and with the lively state of her emotions. She was by no means displeased with what she had thus far seen of her cousin. In truth, she agreed with her mother's assessment of his many advantages, excepting perhaps the idea that Kitty should necessarily be the beneficiary of them. After all, had not Kitty declared most emphatically that she wanted no part of Mr. Tristan Collins?

9
Mr. Tristan

Mary was still in the sitting room an hour later when Mr. Tristan returned. "Ah, there you are, Miss Bennet. I found that I was not so very tired after all. May I join you?"

"I should be glad if you would, Mr. Collins," said Mary, laying aside her book again. "I hope you find your room comfortable. You may, of course, have your choice of any in the house. It is your home now."

"Nonsense, no need to throw your well-organized household into upheaval on my account," he said, sitting down across from her. "I am very happily installed in the guest quarters, and there I shall remain until everything is settled."

Mary reflected a moment on his words before choosing to take the next logical step. "If I may be so bold, sir, may I ask what are your future plans for this house? It is not so much for myself that I wish to know; I reside primarily at Netherfield, an estate near here where I hold the position of governess. But provision will need to be made for my mother and my younger sister. With your coming sooner than expected, I am afraid no firm arrangements are yet in place."

"I appreciate your straightforwardness, Miss Bennet. We are all in a very awkward situation here, and we had best acknowledge it openly. As for my plans, I hardly know them myself. My life has been in America, as you are aware, and I still hold interests there – personal as well as business," he said thoughtfully. Mr. Collins then rose from his seat, stepped to the window, and gazed out at the western horizon before continuing. "I have been happy there... for the most part... yet I cannot say when, or even if, I shall ever return."

Mary felt certain there was more to the story, which perhaps her cousin would disclose in due course. For the time being, however, she had to be content with generalities. "What is it like... in America, I mean? One hears tales of all kinds of horrors."

"Horrors, Miss Bennet?" he said, turning to face her again and laughing good-humoredly. "Let me guess. You are envisioning something very primitive indeed – dense jungles inhabited only by wild animals, barbarians, and godless savages. Am I correct?"

"I cannot precisely say, sir. I prefer to depend on facts rather than imaginings. And, as I never before spoke to anybody who set foot in the new world, I have had very little opportunity to form an educated opinion."

"Quite right, Miss Bennet. I am pleased to hear that you place your confidence in what can be known by observation instead of on rumor and wild speculation. We could use a deal more of that philosophy, according to my view. I shall be happy to satisfy your intellectual curiosity on the subject of America. It is far too seldom that I find myself a singular expert on any topic." He peered once more out the window. "Can I persuade you to take our discussion into the garden? It is a fine day and, if you will not think it in bad taste for me to mention it, I should like to be made a little familiar with the grounds. In that field, *you* are the expert."

Assenting to his proposal, Mary accompanied her cousin on a walking tour of the small park belonging to Longbourn. She began by showing him the outbuildings at the rear: the poultry house; the stables, which shared a common roof with the dairy and cheese house; and the other barn, where the pigs and farm implements were kept. Then, from the top of a little knoll, she pointed out the orchard, the kitchen garden, and the approximate extent of the property. Along the way, she took care to draw attention to anything interesting or otherwise worthy of special note.

Mr. Collins observed all these, as well as the cultivated fields round about, with the strictest composure; nothing more animated than a mild compliment to their upkeep or a general nod of approval did he offer for any of the things he was shown.

Mary's natural pride in her lifelong home initially felt slighted by such cool restraint, thinking he was displeased by what he saw. Soon, however, she began to appreciate her cousin's forbearance in the proper light. Too much praise for Longbourn must have been more offensive to her than too little. Then it would seem as if Mr. Collins were congratulating himself over so fine an inheritance and counting the days until he could have it to himself.

They next passed through the little wilderness at the side of the lawn. Then the hermitage and the front flower patch were explored, followed by the walled garden. Mary had deliberately saved it for the last stop on their tour, as it was a particular favorite with her.

"I often come here to read," she said, taking a seat on one of the benches there. As her eyes revisited each familiar prospect – the moss-covered stone of the high walls; the canopy of quaking oak leaves overhead, waving at the bright sky; the gravel path underfoot and the slightly unkempt lawn; the sight of the house framed by the open gateway – she could not help thinking how very much she should regret not being able to come there ever again.

Netherfield had many beauties, and yet she had not allowed herself to become attached to them as she had her childhood home. She knew from the start that Netherfield was temporary, whereas it had seemed as if Longbourn would always be there waiting for her. It would not be, of course. In future, she would be admitted only at Mr. Collins's good pleasure.

"I can see why you do, Miss Bennet," he said, likewise sitting down. "It is a very pleasant spot. You are a great reader, I collect."

"I believe I am. I do not say it as an idle boast, but because books have been my constant companions from a tender age until this day. It is well that I like it, I suppose, for extensive reading is a necessity in my current vocation."

"Do your little charges share your thirst for knowledge? Are they good students who hang upon your every word? I ask because I well remember how resolutely I resisted my father's every attempt to instill in me an education. What fits I must have given him in those days! It was only later that I came to appreciate the value of instruction, and I like to think I have since made up for my former indolence."

"That is most commendable, sir. To answer your question, only one of my three pupils could be rightly called a true lover of learning. The other two get by with as little trouble about it as they can, although perhaps they will be converted in time as you were, Mr. Collins."

"Yes, you mustn't give up; there is hope even for the most reluctant student. What I could not abide as a child, I have since learnt to like exceedingly – mathematics, science, novels, histories, and even plays. The one thing I cannot quite make up my mind to enjoy is poetry. What about you, Miss Bennet? Are you fond of all kinds of verse – Shakespeare, Cowper, and the rest of that lot?"

"I am, decidedly so."

"I wish I were too. I read it a little as a duty, but it tells me nothing that does not vex and weary me. Will you now think the worse of your cousin for this admission? Has he confirmed for you what you already suspected – that he is a barbarian after all?"

"I would never say so."

"Ah, and yet you are thinking it."

Mary, flustered at not being sure if he spoke in jest or in earnest, answered with the simple truth. "Not at all. I was thinking that any man who can write as you do could never be thought a barbarian."

"Indeed? I thank you for the compliment, but you presume more than you know. Although I do compose a tolerably good letter – a talent you have had no opportunity to verify – the only other time I put pen to paper is to scribble entries into a business ledger. That will hardly serve to establish me as a gentleman."

It had been a stupid blunder on her part, which she now did her best to disguise. "You are correct, of course; I am in no position to judge. I only meant that, by the way you express yourself in speech, I assumed you would write at least as well."

"Now, there I must caution you, Miss Bennet. Trusting assumptions is nearly as perilous as depending on rumor and wild imaginings, something you said you never do."

Mary only nodded her assent and then turned the conversation to another line, reminding Mr. Tristan of her interest in hearing something of America.

Apparently pleased by the renewed request, Mr. Collins talked at some length on the subject. He began by assuring his cousin that, although there were vast, untamed regions farther west, the part of Virginia from whence he came was quite civilized indeed, the last of the red Indians having decamped decades earlier.

"I own a wheat farm, and some livestock on the side, which I have built up from modest beginnings. It is a sizable and rather profitable enterprise now, I am happy to say. I have left it all in the care of my good friend Calvin Beam. He and his sister…" Tristan trailed off.

"His sister?" said Mary, prompting him to continue.

"Yes, his sister. Polly is her name. They have the farm adjoining mine, and were some of the very first people I met when I arrived in the Shenandoah Valley, fresh from the boat, as you might say. They took me under their wings."

Mary waited for him to continue. When he did not, she volunteered, "It must have been difficult to leave such good friends behind in order to come here."

He seemed to remember himself and returned his attention to his companion. "True enough, Miss Bennet, but then sometimes one has to turn one's back on the past in order to make a new start. Do not you agree?"

"I hardly know how to answer you, Mr. Collins. I suppose I can envision circumstances that would make it necessary or desirable to begin again elsewhere. If that be your situation, however, do you mean to sell your holdings in America? To make a clean break of it?"

"That would no doubt be the sensible course of action, and yet I cannot countenance the idea so soon. Virginia still feels like home, and memories – whether good or bad – must make it painful to permanently part with one's home. Can you understand that, Miss Bennet?"

Mary stared back at him, suddenly confused, uncertain, and cut to the quick.

After a moment, he hastened on. "Oh, forgive me, my dear! What a dim-witted thing to say – to you of all people. Of course you would understand. Thanks to me, you understand all too well what it is to contemplate leaving your home forever!"

Mary could not keep a hint of bitterness from coloring her voice. "The difference being, sir, that you leave your home by choice, and we only by necessity." She rose to go. "Now, since you have had your tour of your new property, I trust you will excuse me."

Not waiting for a reply, Mary walked off in the direction of the house, feeling angry with herself as well as with her cousin. For months, she had schooled her mind to be entirely practical about this situation. She had vowed that her behavior would be civil, even cordial, to the inheritor of Longbourn. She had strictly charged her emotions not to interfere. And still she had failed in her resolve. This unexpected assault of sensibility was most unwelcome, and for inflicting it upon her, Mr. Tristan Collins must have the blame.

10
Vignettes

Mary was not obliged to encounter Mr. Tristan Collins again until supper, when Mrs. Bennet cheerfully occupied the preponderance of the gentleman's notice herself with a running narrative of her own clever devising. Her chief object – other than his general entertainment – seem to be to acquaint him with the names and situations of all the principal residents of the vicinity, and to save him the trouble of forming his own opinions by telling him in advance exactly what he ought to think of each of his new neighbors.

Mary remained aloof from the conversation, in so far as she was able. With only three persons present, however, she could not escape entirely. Although her mother ignored her well enough, Mr. Collins repeatedly made an effort to include her by directing questions and comments her way. He was, by these gentle attentions, trying to make up for the pain he had unintentionally inflicted earlier; Mary was sure of it, and that knowledge went a long way toward mollifying her resentment. Still, she was relieved when the carriage arrived to transport her back to Netherfield and her duties.

On the short journey, Mary took herself to task for her recent lapse, inwardly reciting all her usual maxims about invoking logic and exerting will over the ugly chaos that unrestrained emotion tended to produce. She could not admire such displays in others, and neither would she permit a similar laxity in herself. Since no quantity of worry or tears would alter that which could not be changed – a truth she had in recent months seen tested to the utmost by her own mother – it was much better to accept these things with forbearance. In that, there was at least a degree of dignity.

When she arrived at Netherfield with her self-control firmly reinstated, Mary left her things in the front hall temporarily to go in search of Mrs. Brand. She found the housekeeper below stairs, still at her work. "I just wanted you to know that I am back," she told her. "Is anything the matter?" she added, seeing the older woman in a state of apparent agitation.

"Oh, welcome home, Miss," said Mrs. Brand. "Have you had your supper?"

Mary nodded.

"Of course you have; I'm not thinking straight. The master just arrived this half hour past, and us not expecting him till the day after tomorrow."

"Mr. Farnsworth is returned from London?"

"That he is. Cook is fit to be tied, and Miss Lavinia is all in a tizzy herself for not having been given any notice either. Well, I guess he can come and go just as he pleases, being that this is his house. But bless me, it would be a considerable help to know what he is about sometimes."

"Well, Mr. Farnsworth shall just have to put up with things the way he finds them if he arrives without warning."

"Brave words, my dear. Would you like to be the one who tells him so to his face?"

"Not particularly, no."

"Nor would I, so there we are. He says jump, and we can only set to leaping about like a gang of rabbits with our wooly white tails on fire."

"I had best leave you to it then, Mrs. Brand. Goodnight."

"Goodnight, dearie, and watch your step on the way up. Master's in fine fettle."

Sound advice and Mary took care to heed it, surreptitiously retrieving her things from the hall and then taking the servants' stairs to minimize the chance of encountering Mr. Farnsworth along the way. Remembering the last scene between them before they parted, she wished to avoid another potentially unpleasant encounter at the end of what had been a long day. No doubt he would wish to speak to her after his absence, to hear an account of the children's progress, but tomorrow would surely be soon enough for that.

Seeing no one when she poked her head out from the stairs, Mary tiptoed down the hall and slipped into her bedchamber un-observed, closing the door softly behind her. Only then did she become aware that her heart was beating faster than it had any cause to do, as if she had barely escaped being molested by some fearsome beast. The thought brought a wry smile to her lips. Mr. Harrison Farnsworth did somewhat resemble a lumbering bear in manner, the way he prowled and growled about, and yet she should be ashamed to have him think her really afraid of him.

In any case, he had not been lying in wait for her as she had imagined. She had simply got caught up in her own game, sneaking about the house as if she had something to dread. Now that was silly, she admitted – infantile even, and it would not happen again.

Mary soon had opportunity to demonstrate the sincerity of her resolve, for she quickly discovered her reticule missing, presumably left behind in the front hall by accident. So down she went, this time using the main stairs and making no effort to conceal her presence. There it was, next to a potted plant where it had fallen unnoticed.

Mary stooped to retrieve the item.

"Ah, Miss Bennet. I was hoping to catch you."

And she was caught indeed.

~~*~~

Mary jumped at the first note of the baritone voice from behind. It was not Mr. Farnsworth, however, only the footman.

"Easy on, Miss Bennet," he said. "You are a might skittish to-night. Why, it's only ol' Clinton here, come to make himself useful."

"Good evening, Clinton. Yes, you did startle me, and as you see, there is nothing to be done. I have already taken up my things and just come back down to retrieve my reticule. Thank you, all the same."

"I suppose you know, then, that the master has returned from London. Quite unexpected, like, it were too. Very peculiar, if you ask me."

"Well, I did not ask, and it is not for you to question Mr. Farnsworth's comings and goings, Clinton," said Mary in the same firm voice she used to reprimand the children. "You should remember that."

"I do, Miss, and that's a fact. It has been my honor to serve in this house nigh on fifteen years, and I didn't rise to my current position by pokin' my nose in where it's not welcome... nor by failin' to comprehend a thing or two 'bout human nature neither. I keeps me eyes open, that's all. And I knows the master's wants and moods better 'n anyone. A body has got to be always lookin' about and noticin' things so as to foresee what's needed next. That's what makes a good servant: the knack of anticipation."

Mary glanced up at the footman's youthfully handsome face, towering above her, and she wondered if she had badly misjudged him all along. "That is quite an astute observation, Clinton," she said. "It might even be considered... profound."

"I think I have surprised you, Miss Bennet, which is not easily done." He winked at her and tapped his head with his forefinger. "I daresay there's more goin' on up here than you suspected."

"Possibly so, Clinton. Now, you really must excuse me. I am quite fatigued."

"Of course, Miss. Good night, Miss, and watch out for them bed bugs."

Making no reply, Mary turned to retrace her way up the stairs, conscious that the footman followed her with his eyes as she went. Then she heard his steps starting up the treads behind her, and she involuntarily quickened her pace.

A voice – it sounded like Miss Lavinia – rang out from down the corridor of the east wing of the house, summoning Clinton. After pausing a moment, he relented and went to answer the call of duty.

Upon achieving her own apartment once more, Mary shut herself inside and waited for her heartbeat to return to its normal rate. Although there seemed no more justification for anxiety this time than the last, the feeling stubbornly persisted, and it was some minutes before she felt quite herself again. When at last she did, she went to check on the children. Although Michael was already fast asleep, and Gwendolyn was settled quietly as well, Grace still had her candle burning and a book before her face.

Mary came over to kneel at the child's bedside. "What have I told you about reading late into the night, Gracie?" she whispered, gently removing the book from the girl's hands.

"Oh, but Miss, I was just coming to the good part," Grace protested.

Mary laid the book aside and with her fingers combed the loose strands of fawn-colored hair back from the girl's eyes. "It will keep till tomorrow, I promise you. You must get your rest so that you will be at your best for your lessons in the morning. You do not wish to be outdone by your brother and sister, do you?"

Grace's eyes grew wide. "No, Miss!"

"I thought not. Now, go to sleep." Mary blew out the candle and rose to leave.

"Miss?"

"Yes, Grace? What is it?"

"Nothing, just that I am glad you are come back."

Mary smiled to herself. "I was only gone for a day."

"I know, but I am still glad," the girl said as she rolled onto her side and closed her eyes.

Mary pulled up the coverlet, tucked it about the small form in the bed, and quietly retreated from the room.

Despite true weariness, Mary lay awake for an hour or more, pondering the singular event of the day – meeting the heir to Longbourn. On the whole, she had to admit to being fairly satisfied with him. That he would ultimately take her childhood home from her, she could not in her heart altogether forgive, though in her head she knew there was no logic to bearing such a grudge. If it had not been him, it would have been another. Then there was the chance that her mother's plan would succeed in keeping Longbourn within the family. Although Mary dared not entertain serious hopes for herself, there was always Kitty. And, come what may, at least Mr. Tristan Collins was a pleasant fellow.

By way of obvious contrast, Mr. Farnsworth then sprang to Mary's mind. Although he had his merits as well – sometimes less apparent than at others – "pleasant" was a word she would never think to apply to him. The term did not suit him at all, not even in his most favorable humors, and certainly not when the storm clouds gathered.

Fair weather or foul, however, she would see him on the morrow. Perhaps he had already put the squall that spoilt their last meeting out of his mind. It seemed likely enough, since the words and feelings of a governess could not be expected to leave a lasting impression on a man of Mr. Farnsworth's consequence. Though she flattered herself that she occupied a position significantly above the household's servants, the master himself might not always perceive the distinction.

~~*~~

Mary did not have long to wait next morning; before breakfast Mr. Farnsworth sent for her.

"Come," the familiar voice boomed out when she knocked on the library door.

"Good morning, Mr. Farnsworth, and welcome home," she said in her sunniest tone upon entering. "We did not look for you until Tuesday."

"Quite right, Miss Bennet. And depend on it, my sister has already taken me to task for catching her unawares. I hope you do not mean to scold me as well."

"Not at all, sir."

"Good. I called you in to make peace, and that would have started us off in the wrong direction entirely."

"I have not the pleasure of understanding you, sir. Make peace? Whatever for?"

"Ah, I see you are prepared to forget the little skirmish that took place on this very spot, when we were last in this room together."

"As you say, sir."

"Very well, then. Perhaps the less said about it the better. Now, how do the children do with their studies?"

Relieved to have sidestepped a renewal of hostilities, Mary willingly moved on to the new topic. Even here, though, a little diplomacy was needed.

Her first impulse when asked about the children was always to expound on Grace's rapid progress – the result of her natural gifts augmented by a superior outlook. But Mary was careful to mention Gwendolyn and Michael in as positive a light as she was able to shine in their direction. Neither of them lacked native intelligence; it was the want of proper application that prevented their excelling.

At eight, Michael still had time, and perhaps he would do better once he got to Eton. Or it could be that, like Mr. Tristan Collins, he would come to a proper appreciation for learning only later on. Either way, she had done what she could, and Michael's education would soon be in other hands.

As for Miss Gwendolyn, most likely she would never need to depend on her wits to make her way in life. Anybody could see she would be a beauty. All the unmistakable signs were there, even at thirteen. Her features were delicate and flawlessly regular, and a light yet womanly figure was clearly emerging to replace the awkwardness of youth. Her father would marry her off to a rich man who did not care if she could speak Italian or even keep household accounts.

"So, on the whole, you are pleased with their progress," Mr. Farnsworth summarized after hearing Mary's report. "You must hope that I am equally satisfied when I examine them myself. I shall question the children on a few of the points we discussed when I see them tonight."

11

In Good Company

Mr. Tristan Collins's new neighbors were not backward in their civilities. On only his second day at Longbourn, gentlemen of rank from the immediate vicinity commenced calling on him to pay their respects. The master of Netherfield was among the earliest of these.

His visit to Longbourn was soon the talk of the great house and beyond, with there being not a single servant or tradesman in the area that remained long in ignorance of it or in any doubt of what must follow. The call would soon be returned, and then a dinner (or an evening party, at the very least) must be given in honor of the new arrival.

Mr. Farnsworth, whatever his rumored propensities to the contrary in town, was known to keep almost no company in the country since his wife's death, and not that much before it. Had there been even a single ball or dinner party of any consequence at Netherfield in the last two years, the good people of Meryton would have easily divined it from the size of the orders to the butcher and wine merchant, and from the traffic of foreign carriages on the roads. Nothing much escaped their notice.

Among these good people, the general consensus developed that Mr. Farnsworth could not shirk his duty forever – in truth, that he could not reasonably hide behind the shield of mourning any longer. As owner of Netherfield Park, it was his responsibility to lead the way in local society. If his own conscience neglected to tell him so, his sister most assuredly did not. Thus being saved from the rigorous censure of the whole world, he did in fact issue the required invitations.

A dinner party it was to be, with the guest list pared down from the corpulent figure Miss Lavinia originally proposed to a character of the barest bones. On that point, Mr. Farnsworth was immovable. In addition to the guest of honor and his relations, Sir William Lucas, his lady, and two of his daughters were to attend, along with Mr. and Mrs. Cavanaugh. A brace of eligible young men were selected to even out their numbers, and to give the unattached young ladies someone to flirt with.

Those with invitations to the august event were soon judged by their neighbors to be the happiest creatures in the county, and those without the most unfortunate that ever lived. For nothing could be better than a dinner at Netherfield, except perhaps a ball.

Mary, upon learning that she was to be one of the lucky included, could not at first make up her mind to be pleased about it. Although she would have felt herself quite equal to attending a stately dinner anywhere else, to attend one at Netherfield, where she was also employed, seemed peculiarly awkward. How could she be the household's governess by day and its honored guest the same night? How could she follow Mr. Farnsworth's orders one moment, and dine with him as an equal the next?

It was an uncomfortable blurring of the lines. Social conventions existed for a reason, and within their well-defined strictures, one knew how to behave. There was security in it, and one ignored those boundaries at considerable peril. That was the untenable position of a governess, however – existing in some undefined middle ground between one class and another – so perhaps she had brought this upon herself.

Another Sunday visit home to Longbourn taught Mary one cause for joy in the matter. Mr. Tristan Collins would be at the dinner, and the more time she spent in his company, the better she liked it. As on the previous Sunday, when he had first arrived, the long afternoon afforded plenty of opportunity for conversation. Whilst Mrs. Bennet dominated, all Mary could observe of her cousin was the extent of his patience, which proved to be considerable. He bore with all the ill-judged officiousness of the mother, and heard all her silly remarks with forbearance and command of countenance. Then, as on the previous occasion, Mrs. Bennet did eventually take herself off.

"Mr. Collins, I hope you do not think me rude," she said at the conclusion of their afternoon meal, "but I feel one of my sick headaches coming on, and I must have a lie-down before it gets any worse. Please, do excuse me."

Mr. Collins rose when she did, saying, "Of course, my good lady."

"My daughter will be happy to entertain you in my absence. Mary, you will attend me for a few minutes first."

Mary did as she was bidden, following her mother from the room.

"Now, Mary," Mrs. Bennet whispered once upstairs. "I am leaving you alone with your cousin for a reason. Talk to him about whatever else you like, but you must take care to work your sister into the conversation and sing her praises a great deal. I have done what I can, and yet Mr. Collins might well think my opinion of Kitty prejudiced by maternal solicitude. He can have no reason to suspect *your* good opinion of her, however. And I wish him to be half in love with her by reputation before they ever meet. Do you understand me?"

"Yes, Mama." There was no point in arguing, however little Mary liked the task assigned to her. "Have you heard from Kitty to say when she is coming home?"

"Not a single word, which has vexed me greatly. Perhaps my letter has gone astray. The post seems to be alarmingly unreliable of late! At all events, they shall meet very soon, for Mr. Collins, as it turns out, plans to venture into Derbyshire himself in order to visit his sister. You remember Ruth Sanditon, do not you, Mary? Of course her name is something different now. What was it he told me? Thacker? No, Thornton! And she is wife to the rector of the parish under Mr. Darcy's patronage. So, you see, Mr. Collins will go and stay at Pemberley, and he shall be very often in Kitty's company. It will all work out exactly as I planned!"

Mary returned downstairs with her assignment and fresh topics for conversation. She found her cousin in the sitting room, on his feet and staring out the window. At the sound of her approach, he turned and quickly replaced his pensive look with an open smile. But in that brief glimpse of his unguarded expression, Mary had read much. She felt a rush of compassion for the man as she considered his position. He was away from all his friends and from the wide-open expanses of the new world, and now confined to a modestly proportioned manor house in a small village with only her mother for company. The walls must truly be closing in about him.

"I am sorry, Mr. Collins," she said instinctively.

"Why, Miss Bennet, whatever for?"

"Oh... perhaps for imposing myself on you," she answered, hardly knowing what she was saying. Mary looked about the undersized room as if seeing it for the first time – the outmoded furniture, the faded wallpaper peeling at the edges, the unnecessarily heavy draperies blocking what little sunlight managed to penetrate the overcast sky. "You have been cooped up in this house for a week with barely a moment to yourself since your arrival, I should imagine. And now, were it not for me, you would have had your chance for a little peace." Although it was an honest thought, Mary immediately reproached herself for speaking so freely to this man, who was still, she reminded herself, a relative stranger.

"I thank you for your sympathy so candidly expressed, Miss Bennet, but I have not suffered as badly as you suppose. I must keep my time and my mind occupied, and I am delighted that you are here to assist me. I so enjoyed our conversation last Sunday." He glanced once more out the window. "Perhaps we might safely venture out of doors again. Would that be agreeable to you, Miss Bennet? Or may I call you Mary? I am afraid I quickly lose patience with all this 'Missing' and 'Mister-ing' at every turn. Do not you?"

"We have only recently met, Mr. Collins."

"As cousins, the brief duration of our acquaintance should not signify. I have known of your existence all my life, and our people – two branches of the same family – have a long history together."

"Long, perhaps, but the association has not always been a happy one, I believe," she said, leading the way to the door.

"Quite right, Miss Mary – there, how is that for a suitable compromise? No doubt you refer to the dispute between our two fathers, which, sadly, was never resolved."

"Yes, never resolved and the origins never explained either, at least not to me. Papa refused to speak of it."

"I have only the vaguest knowledge of the business myself. *My* father was exceedingly long in his complaints but rather short on the details. I believe the gist of his quarrel with your father was this. He felt wronged by the manner in which their mutual grandmother settled her affairs. She was a woman of some means at the end, having outlived and inherited the assets of two husbands – my greatgrandfather first and then yours. Apparently the property of both was left to her in such a way that she could do as she pleased with it, and she chose – for what reason, I do not know – to bequeath most everything, including the Longbourn estate, to the son of her second family, your grandfather Bennet, instead of to mine."

"That would be highly irregular, and yet in no way my father's fault."

"Which is precisely my view of things. If anyone is to blame, it is the matriarch herself."

"Besides, the injustice is now corrected," said Mary in a satirical tone. "The estate has come over to the Collins side after all, thanks to the entail."

"Ironic, is it not? I think our granny entirely outfoxed herself there. Well, shall we walk towards Meryton? Though the shops will be closed, it is a charming village and it gives us a destination of sorts. Or are you too tired for such an undertaking, Miss Mary?"

"I am not tired in the least, Mr. Collins."

"Tristan," he corrected her

"Mr. Tristan, then. Still," with a glance at the sky, "I fear it will rain."

"Then we shall have to adopt a lively pace in order to return to Longbourn before it does. It will add adventure to the scheme."

Persuaded by his enthusiasm, Mary consented and they set off together at a brisk rate, as proposed. An easy silence rested between them some minutes as they gave themselves over to the enjoyment of the day, which, as Mr. Collins had suggested, held the tacit promise of adventure. The glowering nature of the sky lent a dramatic contrast to the occasional shaft of sunlight breaking through, and the air held a charge of anticipation at the threat of an approaching storm.

Remembering her mother's explicit instructions, Mary, almost regretfully, resumed their conversation. "I understand you have another, far grander destination in view, Mr. Tristan. I hear you are to visit Pemberley and to there meet with your sister as well as two of my own – my elder, Elizabeth, who is Mrs. Darcy, and my younger sister Kitty."

"You have heard correctly. I am for Derbyshire on Wednesday, the morning following this dinner party at Netherfield. As you might imagine, I am most anxious to see my dear sister Ruth again after so many years."

"Of course you are."

"And your mother was extremely insistent that I should stay at Pemberley whilst I am in the neighborhood. She has sent a letter on to your sister, and she assures me I will be most welcome. There is a good deal more room for guests at the great house than at the parsonage, Mrs. Bennet pointed out. She is thinking of my sister's comfort and my own, no doubt."

"No doubt." Mary pressed ahead with her assigned task. "I believe you will find both my sisters very amiable creatures."

"I am sure that I shall. Tell me; is either of them much like yourself?"

Mary could not contain an ironical little laugh at the idea. "Not one bit, I promise you, so you are bound to like them both exceedingly well. Elizabeth is considered spirited and witty, and Kitty exceptionally good-natured. What is more, they are both allowed to be very pretty."

71

"You are too modest of your own good qualities and accomplishments, Miss Mary. This commendation of your fair sisters is admirable, and yet it need not come at your own expense. I must say I admire you exceedingly – for having the wits and wherewithal to secure a highly respectable situation of your own, not depending on chance or wealthy relations to rescue you from unlucky circumstances." They walked on and, after a thoughtful pause, he added solemnly, "Besides, beauty is not what a prudent man values. It is a trap, and something *never* to be trusted."

Mary glanced sidelong at him but, seeing his grave expression, she knew not what reply to make. She therefore remained silent and returned her eyes to the road ahead. Still, she was pleased with the sentiment, which seemed to her a specimen of singular insight.

They were just passing the tree-lined lane for Lucas Lodge, when suddenly the clouds united over their heads, and a driving rain set full in their faces. There was only one thing to be done, to which the exigence of the moment gave more than usual propriety; it was that of running with all possible haste back the way from which they had come. Laughing, Mr. Tristan grasped Mary's hand without warning and compelled her along the road at a gallop. She held her skirt, put her head down, and raced along at his side, drawing deep draughts of the freshening air into her lungs as she went.

On they ran in unison, stride for stride. Neither of them proved fleet-footed enough to outstrip the rain, however, and they ended huddled together on the front porch of Longbourn, soaked clean through.

Too winded to speak, they could do nothing more for a long minute than breathe and stare at one another. Mary soon grew disconcerted by Mr. Tristan's proximity, and she averted her eyes to inspect the damage done to her exterior. Her half-boots were caked with dirt, and the hem of her charcoal-colored muslin was likewise muddied. She could imagine the rest. "I must look a sight," said she, cautiously lifting her eyes again to receive her cousin's opinion.

Tristan smiled down at her, drops of rain still caught in the tangled web of his pale eyelashes. "No more so than I, I would wager," he said, jovially. "Come now, Miss Mary, you mustn't take such a serious view of things. We have had our adventure after all, which I must say I enjoyed exceedingly. Will you not admit that you did as well?"

Before Mary could decide on an answer, Mrs. Hill opened the door and they were obliged to go inside.

12
A Step Forward

Mary retreated at once to her old bedchamber to change out of her wet clothes with the assistance of the household's young maid. "You shall have to see what you can do with these dirty things, Betsy," she told the girl. "I can wear something else for now, but I must be back in my customary attire before returning to Netherfield."

"Yes, Miss," said Betsy, who then began to rattle on about the sudden change in the weather, the misfortune of the two of them having been caught out in it, what her father always said about the risk of being struck by lightning, and other such nonsense.

Mary could not properly attend. Her mind turned back to the walk out with her cousin. It was not only the substance of their conversation that seemed to invite continued reflection. It was the exhilarating dash back to Longbourn in the rain.

Were she to answer Mr. Tristan's question honestly, she should tell him that she *had* enjoyed it... prodigiously, in fact. She could not recall when she had last indulged in the pure pleasure of a physical release. Yet she would probably be at great pains to avoid owning how it had thrilled her. Why? She could not have rightly explained, other than it was a natural aspect of her reserved manner and the staid life she had carefully constructed for herself. Still, she had never been more tempted to let down her guard than now, with this cousin whom she began to regard as a true friend.

Once rid of her wet outer garments, Mary went to the closet, where the things she had left behind when she took up her post at Netherfield remained. The soft prints and calicos she found there looked suddenly bright, almost gay, by contrast with the unvarying somber tones of her governess habit of the last few years. She scrutinized the some dozen gowns and chose a cheerful blue muslin that had been a favorite in her former life. With Betsy's help, Mary slipped it over her head and fastened it into place. Then she braved a look in the mirror. The gown was no doubt hopelessly out of fashion (as, she imagined, her sister Lydia would not have scrupled to point out), but at least she was presentable. A little attention to her mussed hair and she was ready to return downstairs.

Mrs. Bennet had not yet reappeared. However, Mr. Tristan, in fresh attire and with his wet hair neatly groomed, awaited her in the parlor.

"Ah, how well you look, Miss Mary," he said. "I see that you are none the worse for our little adventure. And no regrets, I trust?"

"Why should I have? There was nothing improper in it, was there?"

"Of course not! I only meant that I shouldn't think running headlong on a country lane through a downpour is really in your line – not your usual idea of amusement. You seem to be of a far more sedate tendency."

"Well, sir," she replied with a touch of indignation, "I think I have as much right to enjoy a little exercise and adventure as anybody. And I daresay if I can keep up with three lively children, I can certainly keep up with the likes of you."

"Well said, madam! I see I have underestimated you. That shall not occur again, I promise. And I am delighted to be proved wrong. It gives me reason to hope we shall share other adventures of a similar character in future. Do you ride, Miss Mary, or dance?"

"I am fully capable of both, I assure you, and yet rarely have the opportunity."

"I trust, my dear cousin, that shall not always be the case."

"I very much hope you are right, Mr. Tristan. Indeed, I look forward to it."

~~*~~

Mary returned to Netherfield that evening invigorated and refreshed – for her time away and for the knowledge that she would see her cousin again in only two days. She had surprised him – and herself – by owning how much she had enjoyed their shared escapade. In doing so, she felt as if she had passed an important milestone. To admit to a joy was to admit to vulnerability, and the voice of caution in her head always protested loudly against taking the smallest risk of that kind. This time, however, she was glad she had found the courage to ignore it.

Another cause for satisfaction was that she had done her duty with regard to her mother's demand for her to promote her sister's good qualities to Mr. Collins. She had indeed endeavored to do so, although she questioned to what effect. She also began to question if the two would even suit each other. The more she learnt of her cousin, the less likely she thought it. Kitty might initially find him appealing, with his good looks and genial nature. Still, that was no basis for a marriage. Besides, what would be in it for Mr. Tristan? There was no fortune to be gained. He did not prize beauty; he had said so himself. And he certainly would not find in Kitty the well-informed mind or the adventurous spirit he *did* seem to value. No, it would never do, and all their mother's machinations would come to naught in the end. In fact, a burgeoning hope in Mary's heart whispered that Mr. Tristan might more rightfully prefer herself.

Immediately upon reentering Netherfield house, Mary detected a heightened degree of activity. Usually by that time of night, the place was nearly silent. The family would have generally retired to their private apartments, and only a few servants – a scullery maid or two, and a couple of footmen – would still be actively about their duties. Instead, lights were ablaze all over the house and people scurried everywhere. Apparently, preparations had already begun for the dinner on Tuesday.

None of these efforts need concern her, Mary knew. A governess's job at such a time was simply to keep the children out of the way, which was in truth not vastly different from any other day. Except for their nightly visits with their father, the children were expected to be little seen and even less often heard.

Mary's only added chore in consideration of the special event would be to contrive something to wear to it. She could no longer claim deep mourning as an excuse for keeping strictly to her dark colors on a festive occasion. Yet there was no time or justification for ordering a new gown either. She would simply have to fashion something suitable from materials at hand. For that purpose, she had brought with her from Longbourn the best one of her old gowns and her entire store of haberdashery supplies for reworking it.

Upon achieving her room, Mary pulled the green pin-dotted muslin from her bag and evaluated it with a more critical eye. She could not approve of what she saw. Strange that she had never before noticed how desperately plain the garment was, not only by London standards but even when judged against the considerably lower mark set by women of local society. Perhaps if she shortened the sleeves and added a bit of lace at the neck it would be passable. Mary sighed and went to hang the gown, lest the wrinkles should set and make matters worse.

"You do not mean to wear that horrid thing to the dinner, do you?"

Mary instantly recognized the voice and tone of her eldest pupil. She carefully closed the door to the wardrobe before turning and answering. "Good evening, Gwendolyn. I did not hear you come in. As to my gown, it will do very well. A woman's beauty comes from within, from the quality of her mind and the purity of her character, not from outer adornments. You will find it says so quite particularly in the first letter of St. Peter."

"Spare me the sermon. I have had one already today in church, and that was quite enough." The girl, wearing only a nightdress, dropped into the chair beside the bookcase. She pulled a volume from the shelf and began idly paging through it.

"Is there something you wanted, Gwendolyn?" Mary asked.

"Wanted?" She said vaguely, flipping another page.

"Yes, why have you come in? You do not ordinarily prefer my room to yours."

"Ordinarily not. It is only that tonight my sister is being more than ordinarily annoying." Suddenly, she clapped the book shut and dropped it on the floor with a thud. "You would think that in a house of this size, there might be rooms enough that I could have a bedchamber to myself instead of being forced to share one with a child!"

Mary calmly picked up the book, returning it to its proper place on the shelf. "You are nearly a woman now, Gwendolyn, it is true. I suppose it is natural that you should feel the need for more privacy. Have you spoken to your father about this, or to your aunt?"

"I did ask Papa. He said I was just being silly, and that Grace would miss me if I were to have my own room."

Having no privacy herself at present – as exampled by her pupil's very presence – Mary could well relate to the girl's predicament. She then turned her mind back to when she was of the same age. Longbourn was a fraction the size of Netherfield, and yet she had not needed to share her bedchamber with anybody. It had in fact been her refuge, her one sanctuary. Especially when bad weather trapped them all indoors, it proved the only place in the house where she could go to be by herself – away from the silly talk of her mother and the wild behavior of her younger sisters, to be consoled by the more rational company of a book. The personalities in this case could not be compared to her own family, but the principal remained the same. "Would you like me to speak to your father for you?" Mary heard herself asking.

Gwendolyn hopped to her feet and clasped her hands together under her chin in a gesture of supplication. "Oh, would you, Miss?" she pleaded.

Mary already regretted making the offer, and yet could not retract it. "I will if you wish it, although I doubt that my opinion will carry much weight. Would you not rather speak to your Aunt Lavinia instead? She is acting mistress of this house, and your father is sure to take a hint from her more kindly than from me."

"She still thinks of me as a child and would not understand. But you do, Miss. I can see that you do."

"Very well, then. I will do what I can. You must not get your hopes up, though. As I said, I seem to have precious little influence with your father of late. Now, it is time for bed, so off you go."

To Mary's astonishment, the girl threw her arms about her, just for a moment, and then left without another word.

Perhaps she was making a little progress with Gwendolyn at last. Still, as much as she truly wished to succeed for her young charge's sake, Mary judged she would need to approach the topic with extreme caution in her next interview with the girl's father, which would likely be at least a few days off. Mr. Farnsworth might think her officious for even broaching a subject not strictly related to the children's education. She felt she had to try, however. In the meantime, she would turn the question over in her mind, hoping to hit upon the best strategy for attempting it. She desired that he would at least respect her views, even if he were unwilling to comply with her request. Yet it seemed far more likely he would entirely disregard her opinion or, worse still, berate her for daring to have one.

Before retiring to bed herself, Mary penned an overdue letter to Kitty, who had written the week before, asking for an assessment of Mr. Collins. Mary had not known how to best answer the question – still did not – and yet she had a responsibility to try. It was unfair to keep her sister in suspense any longer.

Dearest Kitty,

You must forgive me for not writing sooner. I needed some little time to form a proper opinion of our cousin before presuming to share it with anybody else. No doubt Mama's report has been most generous in its praise, but you must realize she would recommend the man to you (and you to him) even if he were only half a gentleman. Her determination to see you married to the heir to Longbourn has not abated in the least. And now she has secured lodgings for him at Pemberley when he comes soon to visit his sister, with the expectation that the two of you will be much thrown together during his stay.

I have done as you asked. I have made myself agreeable and entertained our cousin to the best of my abilities. In truth, it has been no hardship. Quite the reverse, for Mr. Tristan's company suits me very well, and I do flatter myself that he has likewise come to value my friendship. Our tastes and philosophies seem to coincide in nearly every particular. That does not mean you will like him, however. In fact, it is a rather strong argument against the idea, since what you and I admire is almost never the same thing.

Although I believe you will find our cousin outwardly not unappealing, you are so very, very different in all your inclinations and ways, that I consider it as quite impossible you should ever be tolerably happy together. Surely, you will both perceive this mutual incompatibility at once, and there will be no danger of an attachment forming on either side.

It will only remain for Mama to be dealt with when the time comes, and I think you may be easy on that head as well. Although you might feel yourself unequal to standing against her, I am certain Mr. Tristan is not a man to be bullied into an alliance against his will and against all common sense. Of course, it is possible that you have made great progress on your own side and none of this concerns you any longer. That would be by far the happiest conclusion. If you were to come home already engaged to somebody else, Mama could have nothing more to say.

I must close now for I have much to do tomorrow. Mr. Tristan is to be the honored guest at a dinner here at Netherfield on Tuesday, a dinner I am obliged to attend. So, I must scramble myself into something suitable to wear by then. How I wish you were here to assist me, for you are much cleverer about fashion than I shall ever be.

Do not hide yourself away in Derbyshire forever, Kitty. Once you see that it is quite safe, you must return to Longbourn, to your mother and sister who miss you.

With affection,
Mary

Mary reread the letter to be sure it would serve. The information it contained must relieve much of her sister's anxiety over Mr. Collins's coming, which was her primary purpose. Was she justified, however, in writing so sanguinely, as if there were no danger to any of them in the situation? Or was it merely wishful thinking on her part?

Mary carefully folded the two crisp sheets of paper, covered edge to edge in her tight, even hand. She dripped hot red wax across the edge of the flap and sank her monogrammed seal into it.

Only time would tell.

13
Wardrobe Woes

The next day, Mr. Farnsworth's three offspring worked quietly at their lessons round the child-sized table in the schoolroom. Their governess, dividing her time between them and an undertaking of her own, supervised from one of the chairs by the window, where the light was far better for working the fine stitches her project demanded. Mary had nearly finished attaching the lace to the neckline of her gown for the following night when she heard the door creak open. She looked up, expecting to see Jenny come from the kitchen with the tea things, but finding the tray in a pair of more refined hands instead.

"Why, Miss Farnsworth, this is quite a surprise," said Mary, rising at once and laying aside her work. "Here, do allow me to take that from you."

"Nonsense. I am quite capable of carrying a tea tray these twenty feet, I should think." And she did so, setting it down on the table next to Mary. "Good morning, children," she said, turning to them with an unenthused smile.

"Good morning, Aunt Lavinia," they answered in near-perfect unison before returning their attention to their assignments.

"Then you did not carry that heavy thing all the way from the kitchen?" Mary continued.

"Up three flights of stairs? Do be serious, Miss Bennet. I only took it from the maid when I met her in the passageway."

"Ah, I see. Will you be staying to take tea with me, then?"

"I did wish to speak to you, so perhaps I shall."

Mary removed her sewing from the other chair, so her guest could sit down, and draped the carefully reworked gown across her own lap.

"What have you there?" asked Lavinia.

"It is only a bit of sewing that I am working on in my spare moments – dressing up an old gown a little."

"Good lord! That cannot be what you intend to wear tomorrow night."

"I am afraid it is the best I own, so it will have to do," Mary said defensively, with a glance in Gwendolyn's direction. "I cannot see that it is any of your concern, Miss Farnsworth. As for me, devotion to finery is something I neither admire in others nor aspire to myself. I have the greatest dislike to the idea of being over-trimmed."

"Though you may not care what you look like, Miss Bennet, I most certainly do. As a member of this household, regardless of in what capacity, your appearance reflects on Mr. Farnsworth. I told him it was a mistake to include a governess at our table, but he claimed it was unavoidable, because of your relation to the guest of honor. I think you shall make him sorry he resolved on it."

"Miss Farnsworth, I doubt that your brother will even notice my gown, let alone be offended by its simplicity. It is so very ordinary as to quite blend into the background. And after all, is that not where you would prefer me to remain?"

Miss Farnsworth fixed Mary with an appraising gaze for a long minute. Then in a light, almost playful tone she said, "Perhaps you are right, Miss Bennet. It hardly signifies what a governess wears; no one will remark her presence in any event. So we shall say no more about your gown. Tea, Miss Bennet?"

"Yes, may I pour you some?"

"No! You must allow me," said Miss Farnsworth, rising to do the honors. When she took a step forward to hand a steaming cup to her companion, her toe seemed to catch on the rug and she lurched ahead. Although the lady quickly caught herself, avoiding a fall, the jolt caused the full cup to slide off its saucer and fly through the air. It landed squarely in Mary's lap, the black brew being instantly absorbed into the fabric of the pale green muslin garment that still rested there.

Mary jumped to her feet with a cry, and the sodden mass fell away before the hot liquid could soak through.

"Oh, how clumsy of me!" exclaimed Miss Farnsworth. "You might have been burned, and I bet your gown is ruined too."

Seeing the heap of stained and crumpled fabric on the floor, with bits of broken china scattered randomly about it, Mary's heart sank. "*Now* what am I to wear?" she asked herself aloud.

"I am quite certain that, under the circumstance, you had much rather not come to the dinner," said Miss Farnsworth. "I shall be happy to make your excuses to my brother. And you know your cousin shall not miss you, not when surrounded by the best company that can be had in the area."

Without waiting for Mary to recover enough from her shock to reply, Miss Farnsworth bustled from the schoolroom. She returned an hour later, however, with a sour expression on her countenance.

Mary looked up expectantly. "Yes, Miss Farnsworth, what is it? Did you come back for another cup of tea perhaps?"

"Very droll, Miss Bennet." She heaved a great sigh and then seemed resigned to get on with unpleasant business. "I am here because my brother has proposed a *happy* solution to your dilemma. Guessing that we are approximately the same size, he has kindly suggested that I might furnish you something to wear tomorrow night. Was that not clever of him to think of it?"

"I... it is very good of him, to be sure. But is the idea acceptable to you, Miss Farnsworth?"

"It seems I have no choice in the matter. So, if you would care to come by my rooms tomorrow – when you are finished with your duties, of course – then I shall see what can be done for you." As soon as Mary nodded her accord, the lady turned and hastened from the room again.

Mary knew not what to think of this development. There was a certain satisfaction that Miss Lavinia's efforts to exclude her from the party had failed. On the other hand, however uncomfortable that lady would be to loan the governess a gown, Mary suspected her own discomfort at borrowing one would be even greater. Yet they were both bound to obey Mr. Farnsworth's edict. At least it meant she would see Mr. Tristan again before he left for the north. In her estimation, that was worth a great deal.

~~*~~

Except for the hour spent with Monsieur Hubert in the music room, which occupied her completely, Mary's mind perpetually wandered the next day from her schoolroom duties to the prospect of the evening's special dinner, wavering between eager anticipation and dread at regular intervals. One moment, the imminent event seemed to hold all the promise of spring and Christmas rolled together, and she pictured herself emerging admired and triumphant. The next, she foresaw certain embarrassment and disaster. Nevertheless, she was determined to take courage and see it through. She had little choice.

When she had completed the day's lessons, Mary left the children in the nursery maid's charge and found her way to Miss

Lavinia's suite of rooms, as instructed. She paused long enough for two deep breaths and then knocked decisively.

The mistress's petite personal maid opened the door a few inches.

"Is that Miss Bennet?" Miss Farnsworth called from somewhere within.

"Yes, milady," the maid answered.

"Well, let her in, then, Hutchens," came the order.

The maid stepped back and pulled the door wide.

Taking three steps into the apartment, Mary had to stop and stare about herself. She had never entered the place before and could not have imagined what she found there.

Unlike the rest of the house, which was decorated with tasteful restraint, every surface of Miss Farnsworth's suite seemed smothered in excess. Set against a backdrop of bold, paisley-printed wallpaper, every window and piece of furniture lay shrouded in heavy brocade fabrics and weighed down by a congregation of guilt-framed paintings, porcelain figures, and trinkets of every description.

Miss Farnsworth remarked her guest's gaze and expression of amazement. "I collect that you are surprised by what you see, Miss Bennet. Magnificent, is it not?"

"Truly... stunning," Mary replied, still taking it all in.

Miss Farnsworth smiled in satisfaction. "I could not persuade my brother to let me help him with the rest of the house, but I was allowed to fit out these rooms to my own liking."

Only then did Mary notice how well her hostess looked. Although Miss Lavinia, much like her apartment, might have been criticized for being somewhat overly adorned – with all her lace, jewels, and elaborate hair design – the overall effect was not unpleasing.

"As you see, Miss Bennet, I am finished with my toilette. So I shall release my maid to you, that she might dress you and make you presentable, according to my brother's wishes."

"Make me presentable? Were those Mr. Farnsworth's words?"

"Yes, or some such. I cannot be troubled to remember every detail. Now, I have selected two very stylish gowns that you may choose between, and Hutchens will assist you." She waved them both off toward the dressing room and turned to depart. "I am needed downstairs."

Mary imagined Miss Farnsworth would wish to make her look as dowdy as possible with a gown nearly as plain as her own ruined muslin had been. She secretly hoped for exactly that. Something simple and modest would just suit her. She was unprepared, therefore, when Hutchens drew out a gown with a plunging neckline in a deep shade of rose red.

Mary gasped. "No, this will *never* do! Let me see the other one."

"Very well, Miss," said the maid, returning the first gown to its place in the large closet, and retrieving a second.

Mary despaired when she saw it. "Oh, dear," she sighed. "Are you certain, Hutchens, that these are the two your mistress meant for me to choose from?"

"Quite certain, Miss. Her instructions were very precise. She said you could have either one of these and a pair of gloves if you needed them. Then I am to arrange your hair. But on no account am I to show you anything different to wear."

"I understand."

Mary saw all too well what her adversary had in mind. Miss Farnsworth had known precisely how to most disconcert her. Other than being forced to appear in company completely naked, nothing could be more uncomfortable for her than by conspicuous dress drawing undue attention to herself.

There had been a time when she admittedly sought to do just that, to draw attention away from her more-handsome sisters unto herself. She could never hope to compete with them on the basis of looks, yet she had flattered herself that she excelled them all in music and intellectual pursuits. Pride had led her astray, pride that had accordingly brought on a proper humbling. She had learnt her lesson, although perhaps she had not learnt it well enough. For here, in the guise of a gown, had been given her yet another instrument of mortification.

The gown was not revealing, thank the Lord. And it was not a bold color either. It was in fact *many* colors, all jostling for attention in a fanciful plaid. The cloth might have looked well upholstering an armchair in this riotously patterned bedchamber, but made into a gown? Where had Miss Farnsworth found such a garment? Mary could hardly imagine the mistress of the house wearing it herself.

Inwardly groaning, Mary let the maid help her out of her governess's habit and into the dreadful plaid.

It fit, suspiciously enough, as if it had been made for her, Mary noticed, looking at her reflection in the glass. The bodice wanted neither more nor less than she had to fill it, and the plain lines of the skirt displayed her trim figure to some advantage. It was not altogether unbecoming, when she assessed the picture before her rationally. The fabric itself was... cheerful, she decided. Only the

84

application was questionable. But then, for all she knew, this *was* the latest fashion. At all events, it was much to be preferred to the brazen red one.

Hutchens expertly styled Mary's hair in a simple twist at the back of her head. Pleased, Mary thanked the maid and rose to go. It was time. She pinched a little color into cheeks white with fear, pulled on a pair of long gloves, straightened herself, and made her way downstairs to face her fate.

The footman Clinton was standing at his post in the front hall when Mary descended the stairs. "Well, what have we got here?" he said, taking in the view. "La! If it ain't the governess masqueradin' as a fine lady."

Mr. Farnsworth, just then emerging from the passageway, heard the comment. "That will be enough, Clinton. Please remember that tonight Miss Bennet is my guest at dinner, and as such, she is due all the respect of any other guest in this house. So I suggest you silence your uncivil tongue if you wish to keep your position."

Clinton had immediately snapped to attention. "Yes, sir. Sorry, sir," he said.

"Miss Bennet?" said Mr. Farnsworth, offering her his arm.

"Yes, uh… good evening, Mr. Farnsworth," she said, resting her gloved hand lightly on his sleeve with the greatest reluctance.

He steered her toward the drawing room.

"Thank you," she said.

"What for?"

"For coming to my rescue back there, with Clinton, I mean."

"That? No trouble at all." He then looked sideways at Mary, frowning as he studied her person. "Now, what the devil has that sister of mine got you wearing?"

14
The Netherfield Dinner

Halfway through dinner, Mary's cheeks were still burning. She could not meet Mr. Farnsworth's eye, nor his sister's, without seeing the amusement there. They were both laughing at her, at the way she was dressed and at her discomfort. Her colorful costume was *not* the latest fashion, then, for Mr. Farnsworth would surely know from all his time spent in London.

There was in fact not another plaid gown in the room; nothing but the finest chambrays and elegant silks with either no pattern at all or only the subtlest variation of shading. She must look a clown by comparison.

Thankfully, Sir William Lucas, her closest companion at table, was completely unaware of the joke. Mary pretended interest in his conversation as a way of hiding her own embarrassment. An occasional encouraging comment from her was all he required to keep him talking when once he began on his favorite topic – recounting his presentation at St. James's court.

As for Mr. Tristan, upon whom all her expectations for enjoyment had formerly depended, from him she had had a friendly greeting and a few smiles. But she had quite given up hope of deriving much pleasure beyond from his company that evening. As the eligible new gentleman in the neighborhood, he had quickly garnered the attention of every unattached female in the vicinity.

Maria and Henrietta Lucas thoroughly monopolized him in the drawing room before dinner, fawning over him so blatantly that Mary could not bear to watch. Now he was seated by Miss Farnsworth, who seemed to be making every effort to engage his interest to herself, which was surprising. Mary would have imagined that lady had her sights set much higher. Perhaps, however, with the advancing years, she could no longer afford to be too fastidious.

"Has that woman no shame?" Mrs. Bennet said in Mary's ear, when taking a break from her running conversation with Mr. Cavanaugh, who was on her other side. "It is perfectly disgraceful the way she throws herself at your cousin!"

"Perhaps Miss Farnsworth is simply trying to be polite, Mama. As hostess, she can hardly deny what is due Mr. Collins as honored guest."

"If that is mere politeness, I should be ashamed to witness her way of showing particular regard! No, she has set her cap at him, and at having Longbourn too. Mark my words, Mary. Well, it is a good thing he leaves for the north tomorrow. That is all I can say. Once he arrives at Pemberley and sees our Kitty, he shall soon forget all he left behind in Hertfordshire. There is no one here who can rival our darling girl for amiability and attractiveness of person."

The thought failed to cheer Mary, who could not help hoping Mr. Tristan would at least remember the time spent in *her* company. She certainly would not forget those hours, for they stood out in her mind as some of the pleasantest she had ever passed.

~~*~~

Who first proposed the plan, Mary was never sure. Probably it was one of the young men – Mr. Dunbar or Mr. Chambers – but when the whole group had reconvened after dinner, somebody suggested dancing. Soon the idea overtook them all and was quite a decided thing.

Their host did not actively promote the notion, nor did he do anything to discourage it. He leant back in his chair with one leg extended, tapping the fingers of both hands together in front of his chin. "You are my guests and may do as you please," Mr. Farnsworth said languidly.

"Then it is settled," said Mr. Dunbar, a confident young man with more air than might ordinarily be expected of a merchant's son. "Now, who will play for us? We cannot have a ball without some music."

Mr. Cavanaugh, a distinguished gentleman approaching his prime, spoke up. "Surely amongst all these accomplished young ladies, there must be more than one with sufficient musical talent. Miss Farnsworth, can we persuade you?"

"What? And give up the pleasure of dancing with you, sir? Upon my honor, I would not! Let us find a better candidate." She surveyed the company, her eyes inevitably alighting on Mary. "Ah, yes, Miss Bennet is by far the properest person for the job."

Mary hesitated.

"Come now, Miss Bennet," continued Miss Lavinia, slowly moving towards her. "Do not be coy. Monsieur Hubert is always

87

telling me what a superior musician you are. I think it high time I hear you for myself."

Mary felt the eyes of the whole company on her, looking to her expectantly.

"Surely, if you are accomplished enough to teach my nieces, playing a few simple tunes for us will be a trifling thing. You would not deny us that pleasure, would you? Not unless you mean to lead the dancing yourself."

To be spared further embarrassment at Miss Farnsworth's hands, Mary quickly consented. She withdrew to the corner of the room and took her place behind the piano-forte, where she and her plaid gown would be well hidden from view.

Anybody could see that the Miss Lucases were wild to dance with Mr. Tristan Collins, though they had to settle for the other two young men as that prize was first claimed by Miss Farnsworth. The Cavanaughs joined the small set as well, making four couple, and Mary played country dances for them for nearly an hour.

After Miss Farnsworth was obliged to give him up, Mr. Tristan danced with the other young ladies as well before finally approaching his cousin at the instrument. "Will you do me the very great honor of standing up with me, Miss Mary?" he said, holding out his hand to her. "I shall not be satisfied until you do, you know."

"Thank you, but I'm sure I am of much more use where I am, sir."

"Come away, Mr. Collins," called Miss Farnsworth. "Leave Miss Bennet to her work, and find a more ready partner here," she invited, indicating herself.

He remained as he was, however, turning his head to answer the lady whilst leaving his hand extended to Mary. "You are too kind, Miss Farnsworth, but I would very much like to see you take your turn at the instrument. In fact, if I dared be so bold, I would insist upon it."

"You heard the gentleman, Lavinia," said Mr. Farnsworth, now standing with arms crossed at the head of the room. "He is our special guest and we must indulge him in all things. Let us hear you play so that we may also have the pleasure of watching Miss Bennet dance. She has certainly earned a change."

Mary's embarrassment had deepened to an extreme during this exchange. She might indeed have wished for a few minutes with Mr. Tristan to herself. Not like this, however, not under the scrutiny of her employer as well as all her neighbors. Nevertheless, her cousin's hand still awaited her, and the encouraging expression of his countenance compelled her to take it. She rose without another thought.

"I have been looking forward to this chance all night," he said as he led her onto the floor. "In truth, since our last adventure, on Sunday, when you told me you were fully capable of dancing. Here is your opportunity to prove it."

"I shall do so, sir, but it seems rather unchivalrous of you to demand of me proof."

"I do not demand it, my dear cousin; I only eagerly desire it."

They took their places in the set, and the music began.

Through the first few minutes, Mary was acutely aware of those observing from the borders of the room. Mr. Farnsworth's gaze seemed particularly fierce, as if eager to pounce on any misstep she might make or to criticize her lack of style, which seemed patently unfair since he refused to dance himself.

Soon, however, her partner made her forget her detractors, and also made her reform her indifferent opinion of dancing. Mary had never before understood why other young people seemed so mad for it. Now, standing up opposite Mr. Tristan, it impressed her for the first time that the activity might deserve its widespread acclaim after all, that it indeed held the power to convey to its participants a brand of exquisite pleasure found nowhere else. The touch of his hand through her glove; the brush of her skirt across his boot tops; the falling away from each other with the implicit promise of coming back together again. Yes, there was a certain magic to it, a poetry in motion.

A resonant voice roused Mary from these musings.

"You prove yourself a fine dancer indeed," Mr. Tristan was saying. His words came in bits and phrases as the movements of the dance allowed. "And I enjoyed your playing as well... My admiration for your abilities grows day by day, Miss Mary, although... I believe there is at least one here tonight who does not share my high opinion of you." He nodded towards the figure now seated at the piano-forte.

Mary followed his gaze. "You are correct; Miss Farnsworth has set herself up as my severest critique... Or perhaps that honor goes to her brother."

"Oh, no. Forgive me for disagreeing, but you are quite mistaken there." They were parted again, causing another break in the conversation, and leaving Mary wondering what he meant, until Tristan was able to resume. "The brother speaks well enough of you;

I think it is only the sister who wishes you ill. Whatever did you do to deserve her censure?"

After circling round again, Mary answered, "I wish I knew. She is determined to see me punished for it, though, whatever my offence, forcing me to wear this silly gown this evening for a start."

"Is that so?" Stepping back to allow the other couples to pass between, Tristan appraised his partner. "Well, she has made a strategic error there," he said when they were reunited, "for I think yours by far the prettiest gown in the room, and very becoming on you."

Mary felt her cheeks warming under his praise, and she threw herself into the dance with even more enthusiasm. What did she care for Miss Farnsworth's opinion – or for her brother's either – when she had clearly earned the esteem of this man of superior worth? His approval on one side of the balance outweighed the sneers and belittlement of all the others combined. At that moment, she felt thoroughly content, even happy, perhaps more so than she had been in a very long time. And she wasted no more worry for her appearance or for her awkward situation.

At the finish of the first song, Mr. Tristan called for another and another, keeping Mary beside him as his partner to the end. When the guests at last prepared to depart, she had the opportunity for one more exchange with her cousin.

"So you leave for Derbyshire in the morning," she said, stating what they both knew to be true. "And how long shall you stop there, do you think?"

"Two or three weeks at the very least. Perhaps a month complete if my sister – or yours – does not grow weary of my company before then. Is there anything you would have me to carry to Pemberley for you?"

"No, nothing except my love for them all. For you, Mr. Tristan, I wish a safe journey." After a pause, Mary added, "And that you will not forsake your relations here in Hertfordshire forever."

"There is no danger of that, I promise you. I have enjoyed our time together, Miss Mary, more than I can say. And although we have had our dance together now, I am still waiting the chance to claim our ride. Until we meet again, then."

He took her hand, pressed it, and was on the point of carrying it to his lips when, from some fancy or other, he suddenly let it go. Why he should feel such a scruple, why he should change his mind when it was all but done, she could not perceive. The gallant intention, however, was indubitable, and it stayed with her long after the gentleman himself had gone.

15

The Play Is the Thing

Mary could not sleep for thinking of all that had passed that night, and her mind returned again and again to it the next day, even whilst she should have been fully engaged with her pupils. It had been a memorable evening, and one not to be soon recovered from. The awful plaid gown. The look of triumph on Miss Farnsworth's face, and the echoing amusement on her brother's. Her mother's praise of Kitty at dinner. Being forced to watch the other ladies dance and flirt with her cousin.

Yet all this misery seemed nearly swallowed up by the one redeeming aspect of the event – Mr. Tristan's marked attentions to herself at the last. Whilst dancing with him, she forgot to be embarrassed by her gown. When he bid her adieu, it was as if everybody else disappeared from view.

"Miss Bennet? Was that all right?" the girl asked.

"Yes, Grace, that was well done. Now it is your turn to read, Michael. Start where your sister left off, if you please."

Mary followed along as he began, but her attention soon drifted once more. By now, Mr. Tristan would be away, bound for Derbyshire. How she wished she could have gone with him – to continue in his excellent company, and also to see the families of her two older sisters. They were *her* true family as well – something Mary had thought of many times since her father's death.

She did not know her nieces and nephews as she ought. She spent her time and solicitude on somebody else's children in their place, children who could be taken from her care at a moment's notice upon their father's whim. An involuntary shudder quaked through her. Looking at her three students there gathered, Mary realized she had in fact become quite attached to them, just as Jane had suggested. Not only to Grace, but to Gwendolyn and Michael as well, irrespective of the trouble they gave. For all she might have imagined herself remaining aloof, it was simply untrue.

She could not have said how or when the change had occurred. The why of it was easier to develop. Who could look upon a motherless child and not be moved? Yet, when the time came, she would be expected to give them up entirely, to walk out of their lives forever. What a strange and unnatural position she had taken on as governess. She was now arguably closer to the Farnsworth children than anybody, yet she could never be considered a member of the family.

Mary called her attention back to the schoolroom, and gently corrected Michael on a difficult word. Then she turned to her oldest pupil. "Did you understand what your brother read just now, Gwendolyn?"

"How could I, when everybody in this play seems to talk and behave so very oddly?"

"Yes, they certainly do according to our modern ways. Shakespeare wrote his plays a long time ago when people spoke quite differently. You must also take into account that the story is set down in a kind of poetic style, which is considered very beautiful."

"All I can understand of it is that Juliet's father is being very cruel to her. She is only a little older than I am now, and he is going to force her into marrying some awful old man she barely knows."

"Very good, Gwendolyn. You have captured the essence of the scene even without comprehending every word. And such a situation is not all that unusual even now, except perhaps for the ages of those involved. A young lady often has little say in her own life, about whom she marries or anything else."

"But is that not mightily unfair?" Gwendolyn asked.

"A girl might hope to have a kind father with her best interests at heart. As to 'fair,' I cannot say, Gwen. I believe most people tend to judge things just and fair only when they have their own way. Yet, none of us is allowed to simply please ourselves. We all have a sworn duty to God, to our country, and to our families. No one can escape it."

"Not even the king, Miss?" asked Grace earnestly.

Michael added with a giggle. "Not even Father?"

"Not the king, or even your father, children. Now, let us return to the play and look once more at this last part. Perhaps we may decipher the meaning together. Michael, please read it out to us again, one line at a time."

Gwendolyn, though her situation was far from being as desperate as Juliet's, needed some help with her own father. Mary intended to keep her promise to speak on the girl's behalf at first opportunity. If Mr. Farnsworth did not summon her soon, then she would initiate a conference herself.

At week's end, however, the master did send for her. To her knowledge, there had been no crisis or upheaval, so Mary hoped it would be an ordinary meeting where she could introduce her business without tempers flaring.

And so it began.

Mr. Farnsworth greeted her when she entered the library and, after they both settled into their customary spots, he called for an account of his children's activities and progress, as usual. This Mary was happy to supply, taking her time and dwelling on the more positive aspects in her report. "And we have begun reading Shakespeare as well," she told him finally.

"Ah, Shakespeare. Very good." He leant back in his chair and clasped his hands behind his head. "Play or verse?"

"A play: Romeo and Juliet."

"I trust you know it turns out badly," he said in a wry tone.

"Of course, but I think the children are old enough to understand and appreciate the pathos. Or would you shield them from that sort of unpleasantness? I could select something else," Mary offered, wishing to keep the tenor of the meeting congenial.

Mr. Farnsworth did not answer immediately. Instead, he stared up at the ceiling, a glimmer of emotion flickering across his face like candlelight. "No, your play will do, Miss Bennet," he said in a more subdued voice. "Shielding my children from the reality of death is not something I have ever had within my power." Then he straightened himself and addressed Mary directly. "Now, was there anything else?"

Mary hesitated only a moment. "I did have one more subject I wished to discuss with you, sir. It is about Gwendolyn."

"Oh?"

"I promised her I would speak to you about her desire for her own bedchamber, separate from Grace, that is. She is a young lady now, and begins to feel the very natural need for more privacy. It seems to me quite a reasonable request, but she says you did not take the idea seriously when she proposed it."

"So, since I refused her, she has sent you as her emissary."

"I volunteered my help. That is all."

"And this request of hers. You think it entirely reasonable."

"I do, sir, although I know you may not credit my opinion."

"I confess that I am at a loss, Miss Bennet. Does this matter relate to the girl's education in some way? Because otherwise I fail to see where it is any of your concern."

She had come this far; there was no turning back. Mary drew a deep breath, and then pressed ahead. "Quite apart from my simple wish for her to be happy, Gwendolyn's health and state of mind *are* my business, Mr. Farnsworth, for they affect her ability to concentrate on her studies. In this case, I believe your daughter would be more content and better rested – and therefore more able to learn – were she to have her own bedchamber. In a house this size, accommodating her request cannot present the slightest inconvenience."

"You presume to tell me how to run my household as well," he said evenly, shooting Mary a challenging look.

Mary felt an answering defiance rising within her breast. "Am I now to shrink back and apologize?" she demanded recklessly. "Well, I did not run away when first you directed that glare at me, sir, the day we met, and neither shall I do so now. There is a stubbornness about me that never can bear to be frightened at the will of others. You may dismiss me if you wish, Mr. Farnsworth, but you cannot prevent me from having an opinion and speaking my mind."

"Obviously," he muttered. Harrison Farnsworth held her steady in his gaze a minute, a hint of his inscrutable thoughts in evidence behind his bright eyes. "Perhaps I should be grateful for that, Miss Bennet. We should not have one tolerably interesting conversation between us if you had no opinions and if I had always to be tiptoeing for fear of frightening you. Stimulating conversation is a luxury rare enough as it is. With whom can one discuss books? Who is capable of debating the latest scheme for social reform? That is what I should like to know."

Her employer's remarks caught Mary completely off guard. Could they be meant as a backhanded compliment to her? Impossible. Then what was he playing at? She must tread carefully to avoid being drawn into his game before she knew the rules. "Surely that is what your family and your London friends are meant to supply," she suggested. "They cannot all be ignorant."

He laughed. "You might be surprised. London society seems well versed in only one subject: London society. What a bore. As for my sister, although she does talk a great deal, I would hardly call it good conversation. However, she will serve if what I want is a lecture on etiquette or lady's fashion. And I am afraid my brother is no better. Though I am nearly forty, to him I shall always be an underling, an inferior creature, a child to be dismissed and whose opinions are not to be taken seriously."

"Much the way you see Gwendolyn," Mary pointed out.

"But she *is* a child!"

"She is thirteen, Mr. Farnsworth – old enough to be married in Shakespeare's day."

"And old enough to deserve her own bedchamber, I suppose you mean."

Mary simply nodded.

"Very well, Miss Bennet." He rose, signaling that the interview was drawing to a close. "You make a good case. I promise I will give the matter fair and genuine consideration. Are you satisfied?"

"Well enough for now, sir." Mary rose also, and turned to go.

"By the way," he said. "I meant to ask if you enjoyed yourself the other night."

She stopped and turned slowly back round to face him, expecting to see a mocking glint in his eye. There was something else in his countenance instead. Could it be concern? Perhaps he had not meant the comment as a taunt, then, yet it still called up a rush of awkward recollections to her mind and a flush of pink to her cheeks. "Did I enjoy myself?" she repeated, stalling for time. "Portions of the evening were pleasant to me, yes. I believe others enjoyed it far more, however."

"Your cousin, our guest of honor: I trust he is one to whom you refer."

"Yes, I believe Mr. Tristan Collins was very well pleased, although I was actually thinking more of your sister. Miss Farnsworth seemed to be laughing the whole night through."

"Much of it at your expense, I believe you mean – the dress and all."

Mary silently returned his gaze.

"I am truly sorry for that, Miss Bennet, and I have reprimanded Lavinia. I cannot imagine what she was thinking, to go to such lengths to discomfort you. She can have no reason to dislike you, can she?"

"I expect you know the answer to that question better than I do, Mr. Farnsworth."

16
Keeping Occupied

Longbourn house seemed strangely forlorn when Mary returned to it with Mrs. Bennet after church that Sunday. The rooms were silent and empty, with nothing to promise either adventure or novelty of any kind. Mr. Tristan, by his short residence there, had changed everything. He had become so much a part of the place that it felt as if something important were missing with him gone away again. Although the day was arguably no different from dozens of other Sundays past, the ordinary was suddenly more insipid and more impossible to bear, and the afternoon crawled miserably by as if dragging the weight of the world behind it.

Mary spent some time at her old spinet, which pleased her mother as much as herself. Then, following their dinner of pork and potatoes, the two ladies whiled away the remaining hours together in the front parlor, Miss Bennet with a book before her and Mrs. Bennet with chatter enough to be sure her daughter could make no headway in it.

"Did you notice Mrs. Plimpton's hat this morning?" Mrs. Bennet was saying. "Of course you did. How could anybody have missed seeing that mountain of fruit and feathers piled up to the sky? The woman must have had to bend over when coming through the doorway just to keep from knocking the thing off her head. Gauche – that is what I call it – gauche and irreligious to wear such an abomination to church. And it is not just my opinion. No one would dare say so, of course, but I make no doubt everybody was thinking the same thing."

Listening to her mother prattle on, Mary was reminded of what Mr. Farnsworth had said to her so recently. Stimulating conversation was a rare luxury indeed. At that moment she would have gladly exchanged her current circumstances for another confrontation with her employer. At least there she felt alive, invigorated even. Thinking back to what had transpired the day before, she could scarcely believe she had spoken so freely and not been dismissed. On the contrary, by the way he had responded, Mr. Farnsworth seemed to be giving her permission to do so again in future. It would be wise not to depend on it, however. Another day he might be less tolerant.

"Mary, did you hear me? Mary!"

"Yes, of course, Mama. Mrs. Plimpton's hat, feathers and fruit, an abomination," she said without looking up from her neglected book.

"Mercy, child! I had done with Mrs. Plimpton a good five minutes ago. Sometimes, Mary, I think you cannot be quite well, the way your mind wanders from what is going on about you. Mark my words; one of these days, it will get you into real trouble. If you become distracted whilst walking down the lane, you are just as likely as not to step out in front of a chaise traveling at breakneck speed. I daresay all your serious contemplation will not save you then."

Mary could think of no adequate rejoinder to this prediction of her own doom – nothing, at all events, that her mother would either understand or profit by. On such occasions, she had long since learnt, it was as well to be silent. And in that ensuing silence, she heard the means of her escape approaching. Mr. Farnsworth's carriage had come for her at last. She immediately caught up her things, kissed her mother's cheek, and flew out the door into the cool evening air, where she could breathe again.

~~*~~

One week passed by, and then two, with nothing but her private lesson with Monsieur Hubert to lend exceptional interest and pleasure. It was July now and the fine weather had arrived in Hertfordshire at last, enabling them all to spend more time out of doors, as they were this particular afternoon. Mary sat with Gwendolyn on a blanket spread beneath a gnarled, old oak, whilst her two younger charges played on the lawn.

As always, her duties at Netherfield kept her industriously employed, and yet Mary could not stay her mind from sometimes roaming north to Derbyshire, to Pemberley and all her friends there, wondering how they were getting on. So perhaps her mother was right after all; perhaps she was not entirely well. Judging by how often her thoughts returned to dwell on Mr. Tristan, for example, she had to admit suffering the effects of an emotional entanglement at the very least.

It was no accident either. After being exposed to Tristan's en-livening presence, she had deliberately chosen to step over the line,

97

to allow herself to consider the possibility that she could have a different kind of life, one that included him, that she might not be a governess forever after all.

The careful labor of a decade had been thus undone in only a few weeks' time, she realized. After so painstakingly boarding up the door to her heart against assault and sealing every crack, she had now flung wide a window. One moment, Mary gloried in the resulting quiet cataclysm – the air, the brightness, the expanse – and the next it thoroughly terrified her. The daylight had already flooded in, however; it refused to be gathered up and shut out again.

And it was not only Mr. Tristan that now had a claim on her heart, she knew, but also the Netherfield family.

Gwendolyn was quite an altered creature – her attitude in general and towards her governess in particular. Her father had ultimately given his consent for the requested change in bedchambers, and Mary had much of the credit for it. The improvement might only be temporary, and yet it pleased her to be on such good terms with the girl for as long as it lasted.

After observing Grace and Michael at their game of shuttlecock a few minutes more, Mary turned her attention to Gwendolyn, who was poised with a pensive aspect over a familiar book. "You have become quite a serious student of Shakespeare, I think," said Mary genially. "Or is it only Juliet and Romeo who have captured your imagination? I shouldn't be surprised if you had their play nearly memorized by now for how many times you have read it."

Gwendolyn looked up, squinting against the sun breaking through the leaf canopy overhead. "Are all Shakespeare's plays like this one? Are they all so beautifully tragic?"

"Nay, he wrote histories and farce as well, and I think you really should take some allowance of those in your daily study. Too much tragedy may be unsafe. I will choose something more cheerful for you from your father's library – *Twelfth Night*, perhaps. I daresay you will learn to like it as much as *Romeo and Juliet*, although for different reasons."

"I will try, but I do not see how anything else could be near as good."

Mary checked her watch. "Time for your ride," she told Gwendolyn. Then to the others she called the same news as she got to her feet. "Put your playthings up now, children. It is time we met your father at the stables.

"Hoorah!" shouted Michael, running to stow his racket in the cloth bag Mary held open for him.

Grace came more slowly. "Must I go, Miss Bennet? I had much rather stay here with you."

Mary collected Grace's things into the bag and cinched the drawstring tight. "Certainly you must go, Grace, and be grateful for your father's kindness. 'Tis not every day a girl has such a special invitation."

"Then will you come too?" Grace asked.

Mary laughed and took her hand. "No, *ma pauvre petite*. I have not been invited. Come along now, all of you. We must not keep your father waiting."

Michael needed no urging. He led the way, galloping down the grassy slope to where the stables were hidden behind a grove of elm trees. Four saddled horses stood at the ready when they reached their destination, and Mr. Farnsworth arrived only moments later.

"Good afternoon, sir," said Mary.

"Good afternoon, Miss Bennet," he answered, touching the brim of his hat. "Well, children, I hope you are ready for a good ride," he said in his customary dry tone. "I thought we might venture as far as Kirkfield today. What do you say?"

Michael cheered and Grace nodded dutifully. Gwendolyn said, "Father, may we take Miss Bennet along? It was Grace's particular wish that she should come with us."

Before he could answer, Mary protested, "No, Gwendolyn. It is not my place, and I really have no desire to intrude."

Ignoring her, Mr. Farnsworth answered his daughter's question. "Why not. You do ride, I presume, Miss Bennet."

"Yes, but…"

"Then it is settled," he said decisively.

Mary could only stare at him. The idea of a ride did not strike her as unpleasant in itself. In fact, ever since Mr. Tristan had suggested the possibility, she had been pleasurably anticipating when the chance might come. Yet this was not at all what she had in mind. She had imagined the outing would be made by her own free choice… and with a very different riding companion.

Observing her reaction, Mr. Farnsworth continued. "I see that the scheme is somewhat distasteful to you, Miss Bennet, and naturally I will not compel you to comply. You might consider it a favour, though, to me as much as to Grace."

"A favour to you, sir? How so?"

"Well… more of a convenience, really. I am overdue for a report from you about the children's progress, and you could give it to me along our way. Two birds, one stone, and all that. You must admit it is a fine day for riding."

He was correct on both counts, maddeningly so; the weather could not have been more obliging, and it would be an ideal opportunity to consult about the children. She could not even beg off because of her dress, for the gown she wore was as serviceable as any summer riding habit. Besides, Mary told herself, it was a chance to brush up on her skills, so that she might be in better form for another day and for that other, more pleasant riding partner.

"Very well, then," she said presently. "I will go if you wish it, although I must warn you that I am woefully out of practice."

"Never mind about that. We shall find you an accommodating mount and set a gentle pace." Mr. Farnsworth turned to the groom and gave orders as to which horse should be saddled for her. Then, eyeing his restless son, he told Mary, "Wait here with the girls, whilst Michael and I take a quick turn down the lane and back. Then we can all set off together."

Father and son climbed aboard their respective mounts – the man on a powerfully built bay and the boy on an appropriately sized pony. Michael used his crop to urge the pony into first a trot and then a reluctant canter, with his father matching his pace by his side.

Watching them ride off, Mary could feel her own excitement building for this next adventure. She only hoped she would not be sorry for agreeing to it.

17

Taken for a Ride

Mary was sorry almost immediately. The horse Mr. Farnsworth had assigned her – a little chestnut mare with a blaze of white like a thunderbolt down its face – was of lady-like proportions, and yet not of as placid a temperament as she might have hoped. The jaunty spring in the mare's step made it impossible for Mary to settle quietly into her seat at first, and a full mile passed by before horse and rider could agree upon who was in charge.

The only comfort was that Mr. Farnsworth took no notice of her struggle. Although he kept a watchful eye on the children, giving them occasional instructions or corrections, he all but ignored her as she battled along behind. Only when they were well down the road did he seem to remember that he also had the governess in tow.

Dropping back to join her, he asked, "How are you getting on with Arielle, Miss Bennet? I trust she is not too much for you to manage."

"I can manage, Mr. Farnsworth, although she is not so docile as you implied she would be."

"I said accommodating, if you remember, which is not necessarily the same thing. Would you rather be plodding along on an old nag who can barely put one foot in front of the other? Surely not! You have a bonny little mare here in Arielle, and now that you have mastered her, she will serve you well ever after."

"Ever after? I had not supposed I would be riding again anytime soon."

"That will depend largely upon you, I should think. Arielle is yours to command. I have no objection to your riding as often as you choose, with the children or on your own time. If I am unavailable, then a groom can escort you."

"That is very generous, Mr. Farnsworth, but quite irregular. A governess does not expect such privileges."

His face dropped into a scowl. "I care not a fig what is expected! I suppose I may do as I like with what belongs to me."

Did he mean his horses or his employees, Mary wondered. Probably both, which would make the gesture more about control than kindness. Either way, it opened possibilities. Perhaps when Mr. Tristan returned, they could have their ride together after all. That was something well worth looking forward to.

"Now, tell me how the children do with their studies," Mr. Farnsworth continued.

Gwendolyn had taken the point, with Michael and Grace following behind her in single file. Mary and Mr. Farnsworth now brought up the rear, riding side by side at a walking pace, making for comfortable conversation. The road was not a heavily traveled one, so they rarely met another soul along the way.

Since there was nothing of major significance, bad or good, to report, Mary kept her account of the children brief. Mr. Farnsworth seemed satisfied and soon enough moved on to a new topic. "So your amiable cousin has been some time in Derbyshire by now. That must be a great loss to your family, Miss Bennet."

"A loss to one part of my family and a gain to another. He is staying with my elder sister and in company with my younger, you know."

"Yes, when I heard where he was bound, I half expected you would ask to be one of the party. In all the time you have been in my employ, Miss Bennet, I can only recall you visiting your relations in the north twice. Have you no particular affection for them?"

"On the contrary, but I take my responsibilities to Netherfield very seriously. My time is not my own. As for making use of Mr. Tristan Collins's trip just now, I would not have presumed to ask for several weeks' leave only six months after abandoning my post when my father died."

"Several weeks, no, although perhaps two might have been arranged – might still be arranged."

"Forgive me, but how can that be?"

"I have a sister-in-law who resides in Stafford, the children's aunt on my late wife's side: Julia Bancroft. You must remember her. At all events, she has written me repeatedly, asking that the girls should come for a visit. I cannot take time away from my business to go myself. However, it does occur to me that you might. What if you were to see them safe to Staffordshire? Then, whilst Grace and Gwendolyn have a week with their aunt, you could take the carriage on from there to visit your own relations, collecting the girls again on the return. I would of course send a maid and manservant to accompany you. You would be quite safe, Miss Bennet."

"And what of Michael, sir? What is to become of him whilst I am away?"

Mr. Farnsworth narrowed his eyes at her. "You flatter yourself, Miss Bennet. I expect that – between myself, the nursery maids, Mrs. Brand, and my sister – we shall be able to fill the gaping void left by your absence."

Mary felt her cheeks begin to flame. "Of course. There can be no doubt of it," she mumbled.

"Then what do you say? Would you be interested in such an undertaking?"

Mary fought to regain her composure. Presently, she said, "Perhaps, and yet your proposal has taken me completely by surprise, Mr. Farnsworth. Might I not have a day or two to think it through before giving you my answer?"

"Very well, but it seems a perfect plan to me, benefiting one and all."

With a cluck of his tongue, Mr. Farnsworth sent his mount dancing obediently ahead, where he settled into the lead beside Gwendolyn. Mary did likewise, drawing abreast of Grace. Minute by minute, her confidence on Arielle grew, as did her satisfaction at having a mount with some life in her. Mr. Farnsworth had been right about that. A brief period of uneasiness, whilst earning the spirited mare's respect, was a small price to pay for all the hours of enjoyment that might then result.

They followed the road all the way to Kirkfield, and then headed home by another route – down trails and skirting farmers' fields – for the sake of variety. Once back inside Netherfield Park, Mr. Farnsworth set them all off on a final run for the stables. Starting from well behind, he then shot past them at a full gallop to arrive first.

Mary rounded the last turn with the children just in time to see the master drop neatly from the saddle and hand the reins over to a groom. He then helped his three children dismount, and lastly Mary. With his hands secure about her waist, he eased her to the ground only inches in front of him, being sure she had her balance before releasing his hold and stepping back. Had the service been rendered her by a nameless groom, Mary would have thought nothing of it. Coming from her employer, however, it seemed a singularly personal act.

"Come children," she said hastily. "Thank your father, and then back to the house to get cleaned up."

"Miss Bennet," said Mr. Farnsworth. "You will think about my proposal, won't you?"

"Sorry, what?"

"About taking the girls to visit their aunt in Staffordshire."

"Oh, yes, of course. I shall give the idea my immediate attention." With that, Mary turned and followed the children back toward the house.

They used the servants' entrance due to their disheveled appearance, and were met by Mrs. Brand. "Good heavens," she exclaimed. "What have we here? I declare, it must be a pack of beggar children come to my door for a crust of bread and a drink of water."

"No, Mrs. Brand! It is me, Michael," said the boy.

"Well so it is!" she said. "I did not recognize you, my lad, beneath all that dirt. Upstairs with you now, and the next time I see you, you had better look like a gentleman again instead of a ragamuffin. And you young ladies look near as bad. Off you go, then. Miss Bennet, you too?"

"Yes, me too, I am afraid."

"Well, you may be dusty from head to foot, but there are roses in your cheeks. So I daresay the air and exercise has done you more good than harm. Oh, and the post come whilst you were out. You shall find a letter waiting for you in your room."

"Thank you Mrs. Brand."

They all traipsed up two flights of back stairs and dispersed to their separate apartments. Although the children would have help with their toilette, Mary preferred to cope on her own. After washing and changing to a fresh but identical gown, she found her letter and settled into the chair by the window.

The hand on the direction was unmistakably Kitty's, and the missive bore the distinctive Pemberley seal. Mary broke it open at once and read.

My Dear Mary,

You must be in a state of mighty curiosity about how things go on here at Pemberley. First, I will tell you that we are all very well. With Elizabeth's little boys to entertain, I have not had one minute to become bored, even before the arrival of our charming cousin, and certainly not since.

I must say, Mary, that you have some very strange ideas about Mr. Tristan and about me, as you expressed them in your letter, saying that we surely would not like each other. You could hardly have been more wrong. He clearly likes me well enough, and I could not be more delighted with him. So, at last we have found one subject upon which you and I can agree.

Here is the only thing that gives me a little uneasiness. I am the one who told you to make yourself agreeable to our cousin, and now I am hoping you will not mind if I take over that office. I know Mr. Tristan has the highest opinion in the world of you, for he looks upon you quite as his own sister, and he mentions you with the greatest fondness. I trust, however, that it is on your side the same as it seems to be on his: only friendship.

You will think me very silly for how I have so quickly given up all my former prejudices, but I now think hearing myself called 'Mrs. Collins' might be an excellent thing indeed. I believe there is a real chance that I could end as mistress of Longbourn after all!

Have I shocked you, dear Mary? If so, I hope you will soon forgive and be happy for me. Pray, write to assure me that I have your blessing, for it may be still two weeks till I am come back to Longbourn.

Yours, etc.
Kitty

For Mary, a knife to her heart could not possibly have been more painful, although this missive seemed to her more like a stab in the back for the added element of betrayal in it. An unfamiliar rage welled up inside Mary. To think, her own sister had set herself up as a rival in the contest for Tristan's affection!

Or perhaps there was no contest at all. Perhaps she had only been deceiving herself when she thought her cousin admired her. *As his own sister... only friendship.* If these were truly his sentiments, then the battle might be lost already.

In any case, there was no time to lose. Before it was irrevocably too late, she must get herself to Derbyshire and see what, if anything, could be done. She darted from her chair, silently blessing Mr. Farnsworth for providing her the means to go. She would find her employer and, without revealing the real reason for it, accept his proposal at once.

18
Go North

With the weight of Mr. Farnsworth's support to expedite the arrangements, things were presently in line for an early departure. An express was immediately sent off to the aunt in Staffordshire, and two more to Jane and Elizabeth, to advise them that they were to expect guests. The trunks were soon packed and the necessary servants assigned for the journey. So on the morning of the second day, Gwendolyn and Grace were waving to their father as the coach pulled away, with their governess, a footman, two maids, a groom, and a coachman to accompany them.

As the crowded equipage moved ahead along the gravel sweep, Mary looked back at Netherfield's stately façade – and at her employer – with some sadness. For whatever the outcome of this expedition to the north, things would be altered when she returned. If she found that Mr. Collins did indeed care for her, her days as Netherfield's governess would be numbered. If he did not, it was her contentment with the position that she feared would be impossible to long sustain. Having once allowed herself to think of a wider happiness, the confines of a schoolroom would seem intolerable.

The hope she clung to – and it seemed a very reasonable one – was that Kitty might have misinterpreted their cousin's exceptional amiability as special regard. Of course, as Mary's logical mind told her, it was just as likely that she herself had been the one to fall into that error. When she saw Kitty and her cousin together, how they were with each other, she would know, but not before.

Gwendolyn and Grace were both in the merriest of humors as they set off, delighted with the prospect of new places to see and their favourite aunt to visit. They chattered almost incessantly about the views along the way and about their varied schemes for once they arrived. There would be a pair of rarely seen Bancroft cousins to entertain them, and a lake for boating. These were sure to make for hours of novelty and delight.

Mary could not join wholeheartedly in their high-spirited banter, but neither would she throw cold water on their pleasure by giving way to her own distress. She kept her feelings to herself, as she was so practiced at doing, and kept her mind as much as possible engaged with her current duties, rather than dwelling on what fate might await her in Derbyshire.

The coachman knew the route and had exacting instructions from the master about which inns to patronize along the way. Mary, however, had charge of the purse and of the girls, and she felt the responsibility most keenly. She felt the compliment that it represented as well. Mr. Farnsworth had placed his trust in her and, regardless of whatever else might come of this trip, she intended to prove herself worthy.

By the middle of the second day, even the enthusiasm of the young was flagging under the unfriendly elements of heat, dust, and constant jostling. It took the coachman's announcement that they had reached the town of Stafford to revive the weary travelers, who were then, after one last change of horses, obliged to press on the little distance that remained to their destination.

At Bancroft Hall, the girls were greeted like royalty by their aunt, and the needs of all the others attended to as well. Mary planned to remain only long enough to take some refreshment and see that her charges were comfortably settled before resuming her journey. The girls did not make it easy for her to depart, however, suddenly growing shy of their cousins and desirous of clinging to their governess's familiar presence. On the front steps, Mary briefly embraced each of them.

"Once I am out of sight, I daresay you will forget all about me for the fun you have in store with your cousins," she told them. "Your aunt is a very kind lady. Annie will be staying on with you here. And I shall return to collect you in a week's time, so there is nothing whatever to fear."

At that, she straightened herself and raised her chin with a tap of her fingers, demonstrating by her own posture what she expected from them. Then, with a last encouraging smile, Mary turned away and climbed into the carriage. She resisted the temptation to look back over her shoulder, to watch the diminutive figures on the front porch dwindle smaller and smaller till they faded from view altogether. A clean break would be easiest, and whatever happened next, she would see them again in a week.

"Not long now," she told Judy, the remaining maid, simply for something to say. "We shall break for the night at Heatheridge, with my sister Mrs. Bingley and her husband, before continuing on into Derbyshire."

"Very good, Miss," answered Judy.

Then they fell into a protracted silence, with only the noise of the road to fill the air between them. Mary would have much rather been alone, but Mr. Farnsworth had insisted on sending the second maid so that she would not be unaccompanied on the last leg of her journey. At least Judy, whom she barely knew, did not seem the chatty sort – not like Betsy at Longbourn. Mary was able to retreat unmolested to the privacy of her own thoughts.

An endless sea of green bounced and rolled along outside her window. It was beautiful country, especially with the trees dressed out in their summer finery. When she had last come this way, more than two years past, the bare bleakness of the December day had not shown the place off to best advantage. Yet it had been a happier occasion.

They had spent a very enjoyable Christmas, the whole family at Pemberley, not knowing it would be for the last time with all of them together. Darcy and Elizabeth had been the consummate host and hostess. Jane fairly glowed to be surrounded by all her loved ones, with her husband by her side. Papa – quite in his element – had made sardonic jokes at the expense of his two sons-in-law, tickled his six grandchildren silly, and savored every luxury Pemberley had to offer. Even Mama had set aside her customary frets and Lydia most of her mischief to be content for that brief season of delight.

Those days would never come again. Her family seemed to be all dispersing in different directions. Papa was gone forever and Mama left at loose ends. Lydia had flown off to Plymouth upon her pre-cipitous marriage to Mr. Denny. Jane and Elizabeth had their own growing families to occupy them here in the north, with Jane due to bring her fifth child into the world very soon. As for Kitty and herself, Mary wondered how they could possibly remain friends should they come to blows over Mr. Tristan. To win him at the expense of her own sister would sadly tarnish the victory; to lose them *both* would be unthinkable.

Upon first receiving Kitty's letter, it had appeared clear as crystal to Mary that she must act decisively, that she must intervene, that she must do something to secure her cousin to herself. Yet now that she was almost arrived, she had very little idea what – or even if – it ought to be attempted.

So deep in thought was Mary that she failed to notice the approach of Heatheridge until the house itself was immediately before her. Then the momentum of the carriage grinding to a halt nearly sent her sliding from her seat. Mary recovered herself and checked that her hair and hat were in order before exiting the carriage and making her way to the front door, which opened at once.

"Good evening, Miss Bennet," said the butler. He then directed a footman out to assist with the luggage. "You are expected," he continued. "Please make yourself comfortable, and I will notify the family that you are here." He pulled wide the richly paneled door of the drawing room for her.

Mary entered, discovering that the room was not unoccupied as she had supposed. "Mr. Darcy! What do you do here?" she asked in surprise.

19

Heatheridge

Darcy was already on his feet and coming forward to greet her. "Hello, Mary," he said, taking her hand briefly and bowing over it. "We have been expecting you, although I daresay you had not thought to see me here."

She immediately searched his face for signs of alarm, saying, "No, indeed. Has something happened? Jane?"

"Have no fear. Mrs. Bingley has been delivered of her child earlier than anticipated. That is all. And naturally Elizabeth wished to be with her."

Elizabeth herself hurried into the room then and embraced her sister. "Mary, how wonderful that you have come exactly now! You are just in time to see Jane's newest – another boy, born only a few hours ago."

Her sister's smile and animation went a long way toward dispelling Mary's worries. Still she asked, "Jane is well? And the baby?"

"Yes, very well. She will be so happy to see you. You must go up to her without delay."

"Oh, I would not wish to intrude at such a time. She will be tired."

"A little, perhaps. But she asked for you most particularly the moment she heard you had arrived, so you cannot refuse. Mr. Darcy, you will excuse us," said Elizabeth, taking Mary's arm.

Darcy acquiesced with a nod.

"You see, Mary, my husband is fond of no infants other than his own, and he would much rather sit here by himself. So come, let us leave him and go to Jane."

Elizabeth escorted Mary from the room and up the stairs. Then, as they approached the family bedchambers, a tumult erupted in the corridor. Four small and noisy bodies emerged through a doorway, followed by one larger: Mr. Bingley.

"Come along, children," he cajoled as he shepherded the brood before him. "You will see your mama and your baby brother again tomorrow. Now, however, it is time for your supper and for bed." He looked up and smiled. "Ah, Mary, there you are! Come say hello to your nieces and nephews before I take them off to the nursery."

Mary stepped forward to meet them.

"You remember the twins, Charles and Frances Jane," he said with obvious pride, tousling the ginger-colored hair on the heads of each in turn. "And Phoebe, who is… how old?" he asked the little girl.

"Four!" she shouted, displaying the corresponding number of digits.

"Quite right. And here is John," said Mr. Bingley, picking up the toddler, "whom we must now stop calling 'the baby,' I suppose. Say hello to your Aunt Mary, children."

They did, and Mary returned the greeting, remarking upon how much they had all grown since she last saw them. Then, with little John squirming in his arms, Mr. Bingley excused himself to continue down the corridor with his offspring in tow.

"Mr. Bingley seems to be… a very happy and patient father," said Mary.

"Oh, yes," agreed Elizabeth. "And a great deal more involved with his children than the average man. I think I must give him the nod even over Darcy on that score, for Mr. Bingley has no reserves to overcome." Elizabeth tapped softly on the door and then opened it. "Jane, dear, here is our sister Mary."

Mary went at once to Jane's bedside, kissing her cheek and then inspecting the small bundle in her arms. Mary had never seen a babe so newly born before, and she was quite at a loss for what to say on the subject. She could not call the red and wrinkled face beautiful; all she could politely mention was its size. "He is so very… small," she finished lamely.

Both her sisters laughed at this.

"For once, Jane, I think our more learned sister is at a loss for words," remarked Elizabeth.

"On the contrary, Lizzy," said Jane. "Mary is exactly right. 'Small' is by far the best word to describe little Christopher."

"So Christopher is his name?" asked Mary, leaning in for a closer look.

"I think so. We are trying it out to see if it suits him. Would you like to hold him, Mary?" Jane lifted the swaddled infant towards her. "You need not be afraid; you will not break him."

Mary cautiously took the sleeping child into her arms. "Why, he weighs no more than a kitten," she observed. "I would not have thought it possible."

111

"'Tis a miracle," Jane affirmed.

They all three fell quiet. What more was there to be said? Mary certainly had no inclination to argue the stated fact, not with what seemed like irrefutable evidence before her. She studied the flawlessly formed lips and nostrils, the barely visible fringe of golden lashes along the closed eyelids. When she pulled the swaddling cloth back a bit, a miniature hand came into view, each exquisite finger capped with a transparent nail, thin as a butterfly wing. What other than a miracle could account for such perfection?

Minute by minute, Mary grew more comfortable, and she even began to gently pat and rock her little bundle as she had so often seen other women do. All was well until the child started coming to life. The tiny body strained against its bindings, and the face grew crimson and contorted, finally erupting into a plaintive cry that broke the spell. Mary quickly handed the infant back to Jane.

"He is hungry," said the experienced mother as she untied the ribbon of her nightdress.

Mary averted her eyes and turned to Elizabeth. "Did not Kitty come here to Heatheridge with you?"

"No, she has not the nerves for the sickroom. Besides, I think she felt it would be impolite for *all* of us to abandon our houseguest."

"You mean our cousin, Mr. Tristan Collins," said Mary flatly. "So Kitty generously volunteered to stay on at Pemberley and... entertain him."

"Something like that," said Elizabeth with a sparkle in her eye. "Although I do not believe she considered it much of a sacrifice."

"No, I cannot suppose that she did."

Now, knowing that Kitty and Mr. Tristan were comparatively alone together there, Mary became more eager than before to get herself to Pemberley. Yet there was no question of traveling further that same night. Darkness was already closing in, and it would be unforgivably rude to fly off after so brief a stay with the Bingleys. She could do naught but stifle her worries, bide her time, and pray.

And pray she did when she retired to bed that night – prayed that Kitty and Tristan would not commit themselves hastily, that she would be in time to intervene if necessary, that she would know how to act when she arrived, and that God's will would be done. The last petition was only grudgingly offered, however, for even if it were God's will for her sister to have Mr. Tristan, Mary could not honestly desire it. Perhaps in time it might be possible. For the moment, though, she could not countenance accepting such an outcome graciously.

When Mary came down to breakfast the next day, she found Elizabeth already there.

"Good morning, Mary," said she. "Did you sleep well?"

"Tolerably well," Mary hedged, not wishing to reveal how long she had tossed and turned, or the reason for it. "I am never totally easy the first night in a new place."

"And yet you intend to press on to Pemberley today?"

"That is my plan, yes." Mary perused the excellent fare spread on the sideboard, and found nothing that could tempt her meager appetite. She settled for tea and toast.

"Then would you mind terribly taking an extra passenger with you?"

Mary gave Elizabeth a quizzical look and waited for an explanation.

"You see, I would like to stay another day or two with Jane, but Mr. Darcy is impatient to return home. If he can go with you, then I am free to travel in my own good time. You can spend a couple of days with Kitty, and I shall join you later. Would that be acceptable?"

"Your husband is very welcome to travel with me, of course. It is the only sensible solution." Mary tried to appear pleased when she made this answer, although inwardly she was thinking something entirely different. Three hours alone with Mr. Darcy? What in heaven's name would they find to talk about?

20

To Pemberley

Of course, she and Mr. Darcy would not be entirely alone. Judy, the maid, would be traveling in the coach with them. They would behave as if she were not there, though she would be always present. She would pretend not to hear, though she could not avoid being a silent witness to their every awkward attempt at conversation.

Her longstanding acquaintance with Mr. Farnsworth should have prepared Mary in some measure for this protracted confinement with Mr. Darcy, for it now struck her that the two men were not unlike in certain ways – the same powerful presence, the brooding and taciturn tendencies, for example. Yet with Mr. Farnsworth, Mary had the children in common. They were the starting point for nearly every verbal exchange between them. What did she have in common with Mr. Darcy? Only Elizabeth, and an appreciation for books and music. She supposed those topics would have to serve.

As Mary puzzled over how to begin, Mr. Darcy opened the dialogue himself. Five minutes down the road, he said, "This seems a very fine carriage. Your employer must be a gentleman of considerable means. Do you find him a just and principled man as well?"

"I am not in a position to judge his character on the whole, Mr. Darcy." It was true, and yet it had not stopped her from doing just that in the past, especially for his tyrannical outbursts of old. Still, a certain loyalty would never allow her to speak ill of him to others. "I can only tell you that Mr. Harrison Farnsworth has never been anything but honorable and scrupulously fair – even generous – to me personally." Also true, Mary realized.

"That speaks well of him. The proper measure of a man is not taken by how he treats his peers and betters, but in how he deals with those over whom he holds unconditional power – his wife, his children, his tenants, those in his service and employ. If he treats them fairly when he has no one except his own conscience to answer to, then he is honorable indeed. Outsiders do not know what goes on in another man's house, and yet his servants do. Therefore, it is *their* approbation that is most worth the earning. What praise is more valuable than the praise of an intelligent servant? I should much prefer it to the commendation of a lord."

"Truly? That is very well said, sir."

Mary was struck, not only by the laudable nature of his sentiment, but by its length. She could not recall hearing her brother-in-law ever speak so many words together before. He seemed to have exhausted his full supply at this, however, for not another did Mr. Darcy utter for a good half hour. The silence was not unpleasant. It was as if, having together already built a bulwark of conversation, they were entitled to rest comfortably in its protection for as long as they liked.

Another occasional smattering of talk erupted to punctuate the unvarying noise of wheel and hoof on roadway, the clank and jangle of harness. Mary asked if Mr. Darcy was expecting a good harvest from the tenant farms that year, which was followed by his brief answer in the affirmative. He asked whether she had found anything especially worth reading of late, whereupon Mary described her recent forays into Shakespeare with the Farnsworth children.

Ultimately, though, the rocking motion of the carriage, combined with Mary's lack of sleep the night before, did its work; she drifted off and did not wake again until the equipage slowed, indicating their arrival at Lambton. Then she knew it was only five miles more to Pemberley.

"May we stop at the first view of the house?" asked Mary when they entered the grounds of the estate. "I know it is a favorite prospect of my sister's, and I should very much like to see it again myself."

"If you wish," said Darcy. He watched for the place and signaled the driver to stop as they came out of the wood on an eminence twenty minutes later. "There it is."

Mary looked in the direction he indicated. "So handsomely situated," she said presently in admiration of the grand stone mansion on the opposite side of the valley. "The builder certainly knew what he was about when he chose the spot."

"Indeed," said Darcy. "I would never argue with you there. I have often blessed providence and my ancestor's foresight, for my family has benefited by them these several generations."

As they were gazing at the distant house, a pair of riders on horseback raced across the vast lawn between it and the lake – a gentleman and a lady, it appeared, although it was impossible to be certain of more than that from so far away.

"I wonder who they can be," Mary mused aloud.

"We shall soon find out, I should think," said Darcy, signaling the coachman to drive on.

They descended the hill, crossed the bridge, and drove to the door of Pemberley House. All the while, Mary's apprehension increased for what she should discover there, as well as her anxiety for how she should behave. Was it pure selfishness even to try for Mr. Collins, or was it truly an act of kindness if it spared Kitty the unhappiness of finding herself mismatched in marriage? Would anything she could do or say affect where Mr. Tristan chose to plant his affection? How far should she go to promote her own cause at the expense of her sister's? Since no answers presented themselves, Mary had to trust that her own conscience, as well as the behavior of the other two involved, would guide her rightly and rationally.

She did not have long to wait for the first test of this philosophy. Immediately upon alighting from the carriage, she saw Kitty and Mr. Tristan Collins approaching side-by-side on horseback, confirming that they were the two Mary had observed earlier. Their flushed complexions and high spirits bespoke either their enjoyment of the exercise or their pleasure at seeing the new arrivals – no telling which.

"Mary, how delightful!" Kitty exclaimed as she drew near. Tristan quickly slid from his saddle and then, with a firm hold about her waist, helped Kitty to dismount. "We were overjoyed when we received the message that you were coming," she said, embracing her sister.

"So good to see you again, Miss Mary," added Mr. Tristan with a bow and a smile. He then reached out to shake Mr. Darcy's hand, glancing into the carriage and saying, "Welcome home, sir. Your lovely wife is not is not with you, though?"

Mary was glad the others were momentarily occupied with Darcy's explanation and the civilities that followed, for she was at first too overcome to speak. Despite her determination to remain cool-headed, uninvited emotions had instantly assailed her. Tenderness and longing welled up within her breast upon seeing Tristan again. But when she turned to her sister, her rival, her chest tightened to the point of aching. For a moment, she felt as if the combined pressure would burst her heart wide open, and it seemed impossible that her companions should remain unaware of her painful inner turmoil.

Mary's senses were on edge as she watched Kitty and their cousin, alert for signs of intimacy between them. Their mutual affection she shortly verified. The rest was more difficult to judge.

Possibly there was more than friendship in the looks and pleasantries the two exchanged. There could be no doubt on her sister's side; Mary knew that from her letter. But was Kitty's love returned?

Reasserting some control, Mary joined the conversation as best she could, saying, "You two have been riding, I see."

"Yes, Miss Mary," said Mr. Tristan Collins. "Your sister was so good as to consent when I proposed the idea shortly after I arrived, and we have been several times since without yet exhausting all the beauties to be seen hereabouts. It is wonderful country, Derbyshire. Reminds me somewhat of my home in Virginia."

"So, Kitty, you are become a great rider as well," stated Mary. "This is rather sudden, is not it?"

"I suppose it is, for I would wager that I have been riding nearly as many times in the last few weeks as in the whole course of my life together before. I really cannot understand why I failed to appreciate the benefits of it sooner."

Mary struggled for some appropriate response. "Perhaps it is... the fine environs or better horses of Pemberley that have inspired this new passion. Longbourn can hardly compare."

"You wound me, Miss Mary," said Tristan, clapping his hand over his heart.

"How so, sir?"

"I had convinced myself it was my sterling company that your sister found so irresistible, but now you have unearthed the truth: merely horses and scenery. My pride may never recover from the blow."

Kitty laughed at this. Mary could not, for she knew that his idea was far nearer the truth than her own suggestion.

As the four of them ate and talked together that evening, Mary had further opportunity to observe the interaction between Mr. Tristan and her sister. There was no billing and cooing apparent, no overt sign of peculiar regard. But perhaps they were being careful to conceal it. What remained with Mary into the night was the first sight of them together – that picture of Kitty on horseback at Tristan's side, her countenance aglow with happiness.

All Mary could think of was that it ought to have been she herself in that place.

21
Heart to Heart

The next morning, Mary sought out Charlotte Collins, who was still employed at Pemberley as head housekeeper, to renew their acquaintance. "You should have joined us for dinner last night," Mary said, pressing her hand. "You would have been more than welcome."

"I know," Charlotte answered. "Elizabeth always invites me, and I do sometimes. But I thought I had better not on your first night here. Tomorrow perhaps."

Mary nodded in understanding. "You walk the same fine line here as I do at Netherfield – not a servant, and yet not quite family either. It sometimes makes it difficult for one to know how to behave. At least in your case, you can be sure that the master and mistress of the house are true friends and have your good at heart."

"Yes, there is no question of that. I am well satisfied with my position here, believe me, Mary. There is plenty to keep me occupied. I take a great deal of pride in my work. And I have many dear friends, here in this house and in the parish round about."

"And what do you think now you have met your brother-in-law?"

"I must admit he is not at all as I expected, not at all like my poor late husband. More like his sister Ruth, I suppose. At any rate, he is a most agreeable young man, and I am happy to know him."

The two women spent a few more minutes exchanging news and civilities before parting ways for the time being – Charlotte continuing with her duties and Mary joining the others in the breakfast room. Afterward, the men turned each to his own affairs. Mr. Darcy closeted himself in his study with his steward Mr. Adams, and Mr. Tristan rode off to Kympton parsonage to visit his sister again, leaving Mary and Kitty to themselves.

"Had you a pleasant trip from Hertfordshire?" Kitty asked a few minutes after they had settled together in one of Pemberley's spacious drawing rooms.

"Tolerable," Mary answered. "The roads were dry, although it is too great a distance for true comfort." She trailed off and then added, "As well you know, having made the trip many times yourself."

"Yes." After a considerable interval, Kitty continued. "And you said that Mama is well... and all those at Netherfield."

"Quite well, I assure you."

"Such good news you brought us about Jane," said Kitty presently, without looking at her sister. "Another boy."

"Christopher."

"Christopher?"

"That is what they plan to call him."

"Ah." Kitty sighed and pulled a pillow from behind her back, tossing the offending object aside.

Mary examined the brocade fabric on the settee most earnestly, tracing the intricate pattern over and again with her finger. She had never felt such awkwardness with her own sister before. Here they were, ensconced in the most comfortable room imaginable, and neither one of them could be easy, not whilst this unspoken question loomed between them. Yet Mary could not bring herself to open the topic.

"Take pity on me, Mary, for heaven's sake!" Kitty exclaimed at last. "You can guess how anxious I am to hear your reaction to what I told you in my letter. Do not keep me in suspense any longer."

Mary shot to her feet as if pulled up on puppet strings. "Let us go out into the garden first," she insisted. "I have a great desire to see it again."

"Surely not," Kitty objected, "for it looks like rain."

"We shall stay near the house, if you wish, but I simply must get out of doors." Mary felt she could better bear hearing whatever her sister might next tell her if she were out in the open. Should the news be bad, even the cavernous spaces of all Pemberley House would not contain enough air to revive her. "We can talk just as well there."

Kitty obeyed, and their conversation was suspended until they reached their destination. There they strolled by the China, Damask, and Gallica roses at the perimeter before entering the maze of precisely clipped hedges making up the heart of the formal knot garden.

"Well?" demanded Kitty, whose forbearance was utterly at an end.

Mary took a deep breath and plunged into the depths. "Very well then. I must tell you I was surprised, even a little alarmed by your letter, Kitty. The idea that, after all your protests, you should end by liking Mr. Collins seemed to me so incredible."

119

"You said yourself that you admire him."

"Yes, but when have you ever agreed with my opinion about what is good and valuable? In the past, you have liked nothing half so much as a red coat and a ball, whereas I have always preferred music and books. And to be already contemplating marriage, after so sort an acquaintance! How can that be prudent?"

"It is not time alone that determines intimacy, but also disposition. Seven years would be insufficient to make some people acquainted with each other, and seven days are more than enough for others. I know what I feel for Tristan. It is real and true; I have not invented it."

Mary perceived then that her sister was not to be easily discouraged. She was not to be talked out of her attachment to their cousin by bringing reason to bear. "I collect that this thing between you is serious, then," she said. "And you have no doubt of his returning your affection?"

"None whatever," Kitty declared with her chin raised. "Nothing could be clearer."

"I see." Mary gathered her courage. The next question was critical. What little remained of her hopes hung on its answer. "Tell me straight out, Kitty. Are you engaged to him?"

Kitty hesitated only a moment, and yet it seemed an eternity to Mary.

"No, we are not engaged, not exactly. I am still in mourning for Papa, after all." This much she stated without emotion. Then she turned pleading eyes on her sister. "Shall we have your blessing when we are? That is what I am desperate to know."

Now it was Mary's turn to take pause, and for longer than a moment. She bent her head and walked further into the maze of the knot garden, contemplating her response. Other than the fact that Tristan and Kitty were not finally engaged, she had learnt nothing encouraging. So what could she say now that was both kind and truthful? Mary chose her words with extreme circumspection. "As your sister, I want nothing other than what is best for you, Kitty. Should I become convinced that your marrying our cousin *is* the best thing, I shall wish you both very happy."

"Oh, thank you!" Apparently unaware of Mary's equivocation, Kitty spontaneously embraced her. "And please tell me you had not thought of marrying Tristan yourself. It was only friendship you felt for him."

A hysterical little laugh escaped Mary's lips. "What a question! How could I not at least have thought of marrying him when you yourself insisted that I should?" she demanded sharply.

Kitty gasped and looked appalled.

With a sigh, Mary turned away, crossed her arms, and studied the clouds hovering overhead. They had darkened considerably, just in the last minutes, and a deluge could not be far off now. There was nothing for it but to seek what shelter might be had and wait out the storm.

"Never mind that," Mary said presently. She placed her arm about Kitty's shoulders and ushered her toward the house. "That is all in the past... and with no harm done. I admit that, upon first meeting Mr. Tristan, I thought something more than friendship might not be unpleasant, especially if it would also benefit you and Mama. However..." Mary swallowed the bile that rose up in her throat before continuing. "However, it is not enough that a woman should find a gentleman agreeable. He must find her so as well. Then together they might hope to build something more substantial – a future. It seems that is to be *your* story, Kitty – yours and Mr. Tristan's."

"Oh, Mary, I can scarce believe it myself, that he should love me. It is too wonderful! He shall make you a very charming brother, I promise. You shall always be welcome to Longbourn."

"Yes... a very charming brother indeed. And what could I want for more than that?" Mary could feel her sister scrutinizing her and took care to keep her expression impassive. "You know my practical turn of mind, Kitty. I am hardly the romantic sort. You should not imagine that I lay awake pining over one man and then another."

"Of course not," Kitty answered, exhaling deeply. "Dear Mary, you are not at all the kind to fall in love, are you?"

"I never was. Perhaps it is not in my nature."

"Then you are safe. I see now I had no reason to worry for your heart."

"No, no reason at all." Mary continued putting one foot in front of the other without seeing where she was going, her features frozen in an unreadable mask.

Kitty, with her last scruple finally swept away, grew cheerful as a lark, and such was the brilliance of her felicity that it blinded her to every symptom of dullness and ill health in her sister.

121

When she had tarried with Kitty as long as she could bear, Mary pled a headache and retreated to her bedchamber with the vague idea of finding some bittersweet consolation in having a rare cry out. If any circumstance justified such an indulgence, this one surely did. Hope was at an end. Although the final word was yet to be written, her sister had left no room to doubt how matters would ultimately be settled.

No one but she would regret the outcome, Mary knew full well. It was what her mother had dreamt of from the start, and probably her sisters too. Kitty so obviously needed somebody to depend upon; whereas she... *She* had boasted to them all that she could, and would, look after herself. With chagrin, Mary recalled her exact words.

"I thank you for your concern, but I believe I am not so much at a loss as to require your assistance. I shall do very well on my own."

"What pride! What conceit! And what a just punishment, this!" she rebuked herself. She had written her own sentence, and now, 'on her own' she always would be, without even a sister to confide in. To be required to eat the unpalatable fruit of her own vanity was no more than what she deserved. She, who had clearly valued her talents too highly, who had often disdained her supposedly weaker sisters, who had flattered herself into thinking her cousin cared for her... "Oh, what an unappealing portrait is now before me!"

Going to the mirror, Mary took a long, hard look at herself. Her physical image was no more promising than the picture she had just glimpsed of her character.

Having by then worked herself up for it, Mary fell prostrate on the bed and waited for the tears to come. They would not. She willed, she demanded, she pleaded for them to come. Nothing. Perhaps, she ruefully considered, all those years of forced banishment had finally driven them off for good, and they would visit her no more.

Ten minutes later, eyes still dry and feeling quite ridiculous, Mary got up and sharply tugged her clothing back into order. Very well, then, she thought, she would return to her stoic way. Her brief departure from it had only brought her grief in any case. The important thing now was to determine how to proceed. One must go on; one simply had no choice.

She went to the window and stood gazing out over the lawn and the lake for a long while. The storm clouds had come and then gone just as quickly. Now, in the heat of the midday sun, little stirred out of doors except the light itself, its merciless rays breaking up every shadow and glaring off the face of the water. Nothing could hide from their harsh scrutiny, which laid bare the real nature of every object. Refusing to look at it would not change the truth.

It was perfectly clear to Mary what she must do, and there would be no room for complaint or compromise. She felt it to be her duty to try to overcome all that was excessive, all that bordered on selfishness, in her affection for Tristan. To call or to fancy it a loss, a disappointment, would be a presumption for which she had not words strong enough to satisfy her own humility. To think of him as Kitty might be justified in thinking would be insanity. To her, he could be nothing under any circumstances, nothing dearer than a brother.

~~*~~

Now that she had learnt what she had come to Derbyshire for, Mary would as soon have quitted the place at once. Of course, that was impossible without explanations she would be much too mortified to give. The best she could contrive was an early departure on the excuse of spending an extra day at Heatheridge before collecting her charges and returning home. Until then, she was trapped at Pemberley, trapped in an earthly paradise that would yield to her no benefit, where she must continually witness the happiness of others, though it meant the ruination of her own.

It made her heart ache to see Tristan now, not because he had changed toward her, but because he was exactly the same – just as amiable and kind as before, both reminding Mary what she had lost, and proving once and for all that any partiality he had seemed to show for her was entirely in her own imagination. Did he not demonstrate every bit as much regard for Elizabeth when she returned the next day, and also for Kitty?

Even worse, however, was bearing with Kitty's exaltations as she expounded upon the manifold attractions of the man she regarded as her future husband. It appeared the only thing standing between

123

her and utter bliss was that Mr. Tristan Collins was not yet at liberty to declare his intentions to the world. Their mutual attachment could not be officially announced until a few months hence, when Kitty's year of mourning had at last come to an end.

"In the meantime," Kitty explained, "we are obliged to be discreet. We must hide the real extent of our affection, although I believe that at least Elizabeth may suspect it. But with you, dear Mary, I may be entirely open. What a blessing it is to have a sister who shares my secret and can rejoice with me in my private happiness!"

Mary told herself that it was not Kitty's fault; she had no clue that every word in praise of Tristan or in celebration of their love grated like a sharp stone ground into her already wounded soul. Oh, why had she ever been so foolish as to put off her armor, to lay aside her shield? Now it was too late; the damage was done.

Mary found some refuge from these assaults in the familiar world of the schoolroom and nursery. There she could both escape Kitty's triumph and distract herself with the antics of Elizabeth's three sons. After all, getting better acquainted with her nephews had been a secondary goal for coming north.

No governess had yet been engaged, since the eldest, Master Bennet, was not yet six. A nurse and an under nurse had the charge of the children when they were not with either of their parents. Mary willingly volunteered her services as well. If her family members thought it odd that she should prefer spending so many hours with her nephews rather than with them, they did not say so.

Little James, at the tender age of two, needed only to be held and have stories read to him to keep him happy all the day long. Four-year-old Edward could not sit still for reading or codling of any kind. He was constantly in motion, and constantly making his younger brother cry by stealing away his toys. He would not mind the nurse, and Mary had little success with him either.

However, she discovered young Bennet Darcy to be a quiet, serious boy, bright and eager to learn – so different from Edward and from her own reluctant pupil Michael. Mary therefore took it upon herself to advance his knowledge of numbers and words, the basics of which he had already mastered, and to teach him such little songs and rhymes as she had attempted to impart to the Netherfield children at a similar age.

These, Mary had the satisfaction in hearing the boy recite for the company of an evening. On the third night after her arrival, Bennet stood before them in the drawing room and, with a little prompting from his aunt, produced the following in a small, yet confident voice:

124

The Grand old Duke of York,
He had ten thousand men.
He marched them up to the top of the hill,
And he marched them down again.
When they were up, they were up.
And when they were down, they were down.
And when they were only halfway up,
They were neither up nor down.

The five adults, friends and relations all, applauded the boy's efforts enthusiastically. Mary nodded her approval.

Mr. Tristan Collins cried, "Bravo!" and Kitty echoed the same.

"That was delightful," exclaimed Elizabeth. "What a clever boy you are, Bennet, and your aunt is a very clever teacher. Well done, Mary."

Mary smiled. "It was nothing; he is a clever boy, just as you say."

"Have it your way, Mary, but I think we will be very fortunate to find someone half as qualified when we go to hire a governess."

"Come here, son," said Mr. Darcy, and Bennet obeyed. "That was a very good rhyme. Do you know what it means?" The child shook his head. "It is about a battle that took place a very long time ago."

"Really now, Mr. Darcy," Elizabeth censured him mildly. "Do let the boy enjoy his rhyme without making a dull, old history lesson out of it. He is only five, after all."

"Never too young to learn," Darcy said. "Mary will support me. These old nursery rhymes, many of them have some basis in history. I believe this one refers to the defeat of Richard – the War of the Roses, fifteenth century. Is it not so?"

"Yes, you are correct, Mr. Darcy," said Mary, "although I had not attempted to impart all these details to Bennet. Learning the rhyme seemed challenging enough for the moment."

"Precisely," said Elizabeth, with an arch look at her husband. Turning her attention to the boy again, she continued. "Bennet, dear, you have entertained us well. Now it is time to say your good-nights."

Accordingly, the boy shook his father's hand and Mr. Tristan's, and then he kissed his two aunts and mother on their offered cheeks.

Elizabeth would not be satisfied with that, however, and she bundled her first born into a tight embrace. "Off you go, and sleep well," she then said, sending the boy to the nurse, who waited to one side. Elizabeth's eyes followed him till he was out the door and gone. She then turned to her companions. "So, who shall we hear from next? Mary, do save us by playing something. Otherwise, I fear Mr. Darcy will insist on resuming our history lesson, and that would never do. I feel far too gay for lessons of any kind tonight."

23
No Reprieve

The next day being Sunday, they all made the trek from Pemberley to the church at Kympton, the parish for which Mr. Darcy had the patronage. There they heard the sermon of Mr. Thornton, and afterward spoke outside the church with him and with his wife Ruth, Mr. Tristan's sister.

"How good to see you again, Miss Bennet," said the woman with a gentle smile. She had a very pleasing aspect, an infant in her arms, and a shy toddler hiding behind her skirts.

"And you as well," said Mary. "Your family has grown since last I saw you."

"Very true. Our bashful boy Duncan is now three, and this is our little Bess, born only two months past." She leant forward and uncovered the child's face for Mary to see.

"My congratulations. She is a fine, healthy-looking infant, Mrs. Thornton."

"Yes, God has been very good to us."

Had Mary still been imagining a future with Tristan, meeting his sister and her husband again would now have taken on special significance, in the expectation that these would one day be her relations as well. A fresh pang coursed through her, for Mary felt instinctively that she could have liked this lady very much.

Kitty then joined them, and, by her familiar manner of greeting Mrs. Thornton, it was immediately apparent that a relationship of some degree of intimacy existed between them, as was to be expected. At once feeling like an intruder, Mary invented a reason to move on, slowly making her way toward the carriage.

"Are you quite well, Sister Mary?" said Mr. Darcy, coming to her side and placing a supporting hand at her elbow. "You do look rather done in."

"Thank you for your concern, Mr. Darcy, but it is nothing. I am only a little over warm in the sun. I will just wait in the carriage, if I might."

"Certainly. Allow me to escort you." They walked on toward an oak tree, in the shade of which the carriage and horses rested, and he presently said, "I fear you are not enjoying your stay with us as much as your sister and I had hoped. Is there any exertion we can make for your comfort? Anything at all? You have only to say the word and it is done."

"You are too kind, sir, and your hospitality is flawless, as usual. Please do not worry yourself on my account. I assure you, I am quite content." Mary was on the verge of confessing to him her desire to depart a day early, when Kitty came dashing up on her other side.

"What do you think, Mary?" she began cheerfully. "I have just hit upon an idea that you are sure to like exceedingly. I cannot imagine why no one thought of it before, for it is quite clearly the best plan in the world."

"Is it really? Then do tell me."

"You leave Pemberley in two days' time. Is that not so?"

Mary hesitated. "Yes… that was my original plan."

"Well, then, what say I return to Longbourn with you? And Mr. Tristan too. What could be more perfect? We shall be such a cheerful party!"

Mary's mind raced to find a way out. "It… It is an excellent plan, Kitty, to be sure, although far too generous. I know how you love it here at Pemberley. I have no choice other than to go, but you and Mr. Tristan must not cut short your stay on my account." Grasping at straws, she added, "Besides, I am not at all certain there will be room in Mr. Farnsworth's carriage. As it is, I have Gwendolyn and Grace, all their luggage, and two maids as well."

"Oh! You think Mr. Farnsworth would object, then?" Kitty asked, as if she had heard nothing else her sister said. "I would not wish to be seen as taking unfair advantage."

It was a tempting excuse, and yet Mary could not in good conscience make Mr. Farnsworth the villain of the piece. "No, Kitty, I am quite certain he would not see it as an imposition."

"Then it is settled! Mr. Tristan will ride his own horse or sit on the box, and that great coach you came in will certainly hold the other six of us. Why, the Farnsworth girls are not even full grown. So unless the second maid – whom I have not seen – is prodigiously fat, one can only imagine how comfortable we shall be. As for leaving Pemberley, I believe it is high time I took myself out from under foot. Do not you think so, Mr. Darcy?"

"You are welcome to stay as long as you like," said he, "both of you, and Mr. Collins as well, of course."

"Thank you, kind sir," said Kitty, bobbing a slight curtsey in a spirit of fun. She then glanced over her shoulder in the direction of Mr. Tristan. "I believe I already have what I came for, though."

~~*~~

Mary thought no more of quitting Pemberley early. Now it would make no difference if she stayed or went, for her troubles were determined to cling to her either way.

Craving at least a brief respite, she came downstairs early the next day, mindful that Kitty and Elizabeth rarely made an appearance before ten o'clock, and even Mr. Tristan was inclined to breakfast late. She counted Mr. Darcy, should she happen to come upon him, as the least problematic, for he would likely be as reluctant for conversation as she was herself.

Had she not known where to go, her nose could have easily been her guide, for the spicy smell of baked ham and the aroma of fresh biscuits wafted in the air. Mary inhaled deeply and, picturing herself sitting down blissfully alone to an enjoyable meal, she entered the breakfast room. She then drew up short just inside the doorway, arrested by the sight before her. For there was Tristan Collins, smartly dressed and standing at the sideboard, dishing a serving of kippers onto his plate.

He looked up and smiled. "Would you like some?" he asked, offering the portion to Mary instead.

Retreat was impossible.

"Ah, Mr. Tristan, I had not thought to see you here so early." She waved off the kippers, took a plate, and turned her earnest attention to the selection on the sideboard.

He laughed. "You cannot be more surprised at it than I am myself. It was Mr. Darcy's idea, you see. He promised me a spot of fishing, but only if I can be ready by eight. Trout breakfast early too, apparently."

"Then that explains it."

"What is your excuse, Miss Mary? I thought all fashionable ladies insisted on sleeping until at least nine."

"I suppose they do. I cannot say, for I am not to be classed amongst them. I must be up early every day, ahead of the children in my charge."

"Yes, but there are no children in your charge at Pemberley, Miss Mary. You are on holiday, and you might indulge yourself in the decadent luxury of an additional hour's sleep, if you wished."

Mary replaced the lid to the silver porridge tureen with a clatter. "It is, perhaps, more prudent not to indulge oneself too much with pleasures one has no right to keep. It only makes it more painful when those pleasant things must be given up. Surely, you must see that," said Mary, with a tone of challenge.

Their eyes met and held for a long moment. A look of consciousness crossed Tristan's face. His customary jocularity fell away, replaced by a somberness of countenance that Mary had seen him take on some once or twice before.

"There is some truth in what you say, Miss Mary. Yet to never experience the good, for fear that it will one day be taken from you – what kind of way is that to live?"

They were clearly, neither one of them, any longer speaking of something as trifling as an extra hour's sleep. Mary was certain of thus much. She was far less certain what exactly he *did* have on his mind, or whether he could read hers.

With Tristan's question still hanging in the air betwixt them, she saved herself the trouble of responding by deciding it was rhetorical – that he had asked it without wanting or expecting an answer. As she had none to offer in any case, she returned to the business of breakfast.

They continued in silence some minutes, sitting six feet apart at the same table and both entirely focused on dissecting and rearranging the food on the plates before them.

Presently, however, Tristan set down his fork and glanced sidelong at Mary. "I am sorry," he said in a low voice.

Mary steadied her nerves and schooled her features into an expression of mild curiosity before looking at him. "Sorry? What do you mean, sir? Have you done something for which you need to repent?"

"I believe I must have, for you do seem displeased with me. I noticed it almost as soon as you arrived at Pemberley. My esteem for you is most sincere, Miss Mary, and I place a high value on your friendship. So, if I have offended or injured you in any way, I am truly sorry."

Mary stood abruptly, nearly knocking over her chair. "I thank you for your compliments, Mr. Collins. I also thank you for your apology, although it is entirely unnecessary, I assure you. Now, you really must excuse me; I could not possibly eat another bite." Leaving her breakfast unfinished and her companion unenlightened, Mary quit the room.

24
Returning Home

The party for Longbourn prepared to quit Pemberley the following morning, the farewells taking place in the entry hall instead of out of doors due to inclement weather. A heavy rain had begun at dawn and showed no sign of subsiding. The dark skies promised a wet passage to Heatheridge – their first day's destination – and Mary's mood was decidedly gray as well.

Under these gloomy auspices, the parting took place and the journey began. Although her stay at Pemberley had turned out far less agreeable than she had hoped, Mary did not quit the place without feelings of regret. Looking back at the great house once more as the carriage drew away, she could not deny its appeal. The sincere hospitality found within its walls, the daily comforts afforded by a family with a generous income, the vast expanse of natural beauty out of doors, and the tasteful elegance in: all these were reasons to lament leaving.

Her chief regret, however, was the loss of the Pemberley family itself. She had now become acquainted with her Darcy nephews, forming an attachment to Bennet especially. She had enjoyed seeing Elizabeth well settled into motherhood, and what a different model of the office she made from their *own* mother. And her relations with Mr. Darcy continued to improve with each additional exposure. Mary had discovered that she could abide his presence composedly, almost cheerfully, after all. The little awkwardness that remained between them was nothing compared to what she would face on the three-day journey ahead.

~~*~~

They came and went without incident from Heatheridge and Bancroft Hall in turn. Then the three uncomfortable days predicted stretched into five with the great misfortune of the carriage breaking down, causing them to limp along for miles and miles before reaching the next town with a coaching inn, where repairs could be undertaken.

Kitty's continual presence did not trouble Mary as much, or at least not in the same way, as she had supposed it would. Since they were seldom alone together, Kitty could rarely loose her tongue to expound on her secret passion for Mr. Tristan Collins and their plans together. However, she did made an irksome habit of conspicuously watching him out the carriage window as he rode alongside.

"Is not our cousin a fine horseman, Mary?" she asked on more than one occasion.

Mary simply agreed with her the first time, ignored the question the second, but could not keep silent when it came still again. They had collected Grace and Gwendolyn by then, so she asked them, "What do you say, girls? Is Mr. Collins the finest horseman you have ever observed? I think not. In fact, I believe your own father is a bolder rider and much more comfortable in the saddle." This was nothing more than what Mary had already been thinking.

"Well," rejoined Kitty, "I cannot answer for that. I see no reason to compare the two in any case."

"You opened the subject yourself. I was simply offering an opinion to further the discussion. Yet perhaps you are right, Kitty. It is an unfair comparison. After all, Mr. Farnsworth rides nearly every day, whereas Mr. Collins may not have had the same opportunity, being so occupied with his farm in Virginia. He may have been obliged to spend more time working the ground and less on the back of a horse."

Kitty never returned to the topic of Mr. Tristan's riding again.

Mary had tried telling herself she should be happy for Kitty, and that she must draw her own comfort from the fact that she had done her solemn duty. For that one moment at least – when faced with the choice whether or not to spoil her sister's joy by revealing her own ruined aspirations – her finer impulses had prevailed. Upon further reflection, however, Mary had begun to question her noble response and nearly everything else, including Kitty's claims to Tristan Collins.

A person of integrity would never tamper with a solemn engagement. That was not the case here, however. And really, other than Kitty's own assertions, what evidence was there to establish a definite attachment between the two? Nothing that Mary could perceive or recall. An ember of hope flared to life. What she had taken for discretion on Tristan's part could just as reasonably be interpreted as indifference. And had he not continued to show the same affectionate regard for herself as he had at Longbourn? The more Mary considered it, the more she became convinced that it was at least possible that Kitty was the one who had deceived herself, and that the contest for Tristan's heart was not yet fully decided. No, she would not give up on him just yet.

From that point on, Mary made more effort to be civil to Tristan – civil and a good deal more, to her sister's obvious consternation.

~~*~~

The Farnsworth girls proved an invaluable resource as the friction between the Bennet sisters increased day by day and mile by mile. Mary hardly knew how they would have managed through the long hours of confinement without Grace and Gwendolyn. She kept them talking about their games and adventures with their Bancroft cousins, and the many little kindnesses of their aunt. Mary had brought her Shakespeare with her as well, and all four of them took turns reading aloud from it to pass the time.

Although not without taxing every resource of patience and comfort, Mary and her companions survived the ordeal and arrived in Hertfordshire with all their limbs and faculties intact.

The carriage stopped briefly at Longbourn to unburden itself of Kitty and her belongings. Mr. Tristan Collins dismounted immediately to lend assistance, and Mrs. Bennet came rushing out to greet them.

"Oh, thank the Lord you are safe!" she exclaimed. "When I did not see Mary in church, I thought sure the carriage had been overset or some other terrible calamity had occurred. How good you are, Mr. Collins, to ride escort. And Kitty, I must say it is high time you returned home. I hope you found your long stay at Pemberley worthwhile."

"Very worthwhile," she said with a coy smile, taking Tristan's hand to alight from the carriage.

"I am glad to hear it. You must tell me all about it over tea. Perhaps the young ladies would care to come in for some refreshment," Mrs. Bennet said with a nod to the Farnsworth girls.

"No, Mama," replied Mary. "We may not stay. Their father will be anxious for their safe return since our arrival is overdue. We must continue on to Netherfield without delay."

The footman folded up the step and closed the door so they could get underway again. Mary glanced back as they moved off, and then wished that she had not. Now the picture left in her mind was that of

Kitty close by Mr. Tristan's side, standing in front of what might be their home together in the future. Should Longbourn and Mr. Tristan both to fall to her sister in the end, Mary did not know which of the three she should regret the loss of most. For lost to her they surely would be then.

25

Rest Disturbed

A reception party quickly assembled at Netherfield upon their arrival – half a dozen servants, and then the master himself strode forward to hand the ladies out of the carriage.

Mr. Farnsworth stiffly embraced Gwendolyn and Grace in turn as they alighted. Then he offered his assistance to Mary. "Welcome home, Miss Bennet," he said sternly. "It is good to have you all returned... *late* but well, it appears. I will want an accounting from you presently."

"Yes, sir. I can explain the delay."

"And you shall, but not right now." He turned from her to rejoin his daughters, softening his tone with them. "Now, girls, let us go in. I want to hear all about your travels, and about your cousins at Bancroft."

Mrs. Brand said to Mary, "Never mind, Dearie. The master will be himself again afore long. He has been half out of his wits these last two days, a' waiting and a' worrying. Off his food and everything. Now all's turned out well, he shall soon rally, I expect."

"Thank you, Mrs. Brand. I am sure you are right."

Mary was not at all sure, nor could she be bothered to care at that moment. A sudden weariness had overtaken her, and she could not get to her own chamber quickly enough. Once there, she prayed she would not be disturbed. Solitude, precious solitude: that was what she desperately craved after so many days in constant company. No more putting on a front for others. No more pretending that all was well when it might never be so again. Mary shut herself in, dropped fully clothed onto her bed, and was asleep within minutes.

It was dusk when she at last awoke, and it took her a moment to remember where she was. When her eyes cleared and could focus, she let out a muffled shriek at seeing the shape of a man, five feet away and silhouetted against the dim light of the window.

"You mustn't take on so, Miss. 'Tis only me."

Mary recognized the voice and her fears were a little allayed. "What do you do here, Clinton?" she asked cautiously as she swung her feet to the floor.

"I brung up your trunk for you, see, and then I just stayed to watch over you a minute. You was laid out so comfortable like."

A chill raced across Mary's shoulders and down her arms, and she could feel the hairs on the back of her neck prickle. She was careful, however, that her voice should remain calm. "I did not hear you knock."

"I let myself in real quiet like, so as not to disturb you. I figured you might be asleep, and so you was."

"Nevertheless, you should have knocked and waited for an answer. Please go now, Clinton. You have completed your task, and I thank you."

"Well, if you're sure there ain't nothin' else I can do for you."

"Nothing at all."

He hesitated, and for a moment Mary thought he might not obey. But then he turned and left her. When the door was shut between them, Mary closed her eyes and exhaled. What was the man thinking, coming into her room like that, uninvited? How long had he been standing there, and what were his intentions? In the poor light, reading his expression had been impossible. Perhaps he meant no harm, although this was not the first time he had behaved improperly towards her.

Mary wondered if she should speak to someone about it, that someone of necessity being Miss Farnsworth. She hated to get Clinton in trouble unnecessarily. After all, nothing untoward had actually happened. On the other hand, she dared not wait until it did before taking action. It also occurred to Mary that if he were this forward with her, Clinton might well be harassing other female members of the household more overtly, girls who had less standing and little chance of protecting themselves. Perhaps she ought to speak out in their defense if not in her own. After debating the question back and forth in her mind the whole evening, Mary ultimately decided to report the incident to Miss Farnsworth first thing in the morning.

"You caught him looking at you?" said Lavinia Farnsworth from behind the ornate desk where she managed her correspondence. "Well, that is hardly a crime."

Mary stood opposite, with her hands clasped behind her back. "It was the circumstances that made it improper, Madam, not the fact that he was looking at me. He was in my bedchamber without leave, watching me sleep! Does that not strike you as odd? And as I said, this is not the first time something like this has happened."

"So you have therefore concluded what? That Clinton is in love with you, or that he intends to murder you in your bed? Which is it? Really, Miss Bennet, what a fevered imagination you must have. Perhaps you should be flattered rather than offended; I daresay it is not every day that a man pays you so much attention."

Mary felt her face growing warm, half in embarrassment and half in bitter annoyance. "I do not consider this a joking matter, Miss Farnsworth, and I would appreciate it if you did not either."

"Very well; have it your own way. I will see to it that Haines speaks to the man, but more than that I will not do. You said yourself that he has yet to lay a finger on you. And if I were to dismiss every servant who looked at another sideways or uttered an impertinent remark, there should soon be no one left to do our bidding."

"Please…"

"That will be all, Miss Bennet! Now, I suggest you return to the schoolroom, where you belong… and where I trust you will be unable to tempt anybody else to misbehave."

Not trusting herself to speak, Mary gave a curt nod and left without saying another word. There was no more to be done at present. Should something more serious occur, she would not hesitate to bypass the acting mistress of the house and go straight to the master. To do so now, however, would only make of Miss Farnsworth a more violent enemy without cause.

Mary did indeed return to the schoolroom and took some comfort in the familiar surroundings there. Grace was eager enough to resume her studies. Michael, not surprisingly, was more difficult to reign in after being largely left to his own devises for over a week. But Gwendolyn was the mystery.

On their journey home from Staffordshire, Mary had noticed in her oldest pupil periods of distraction and seeming wistfulness. Now, however, she was positively melancholy, moping about and unable to take an interest in anything save Shakespeare. She had taken up a copy of his sonnets upon their return and refused to part with it, even during their period of outdoor exercise that afternoon. When Mary insisted that she walk rather than sit in the shade, Gwendolyn simply took her book of verse with her, alternately studying it and staring at the sky, paying no attention to where she was going. Mary could not help worrying she would end by stumbling into a ditch or briar patch.

"It is Phillip Bancroft," Grace presently volunteered in explanation.

Mary had again turned her watchful eye from Michael, who was scaling the lower limbs of his favorite tree, back to his wandering eldest sister. "Phillip Bancroft?" she repeated.

"Yes, he is our second cousin on our uncle's side, and he came to visit whilst we were staying at Bancroft Hall. Gwendolyn began behaving very silly the moment she set eyes on him, and then she told me she is in love."

"Is that so? And of what age is this young man?"

"Two-and-twenty! And the book he likes best in all the world is Shakespeare's sonnets. He read out his favorite one to us the second night he was there. Gwen looked nigh on to fainting by the time he had finished."

"Ah, I see."

"It is completely ridiculous, of course. He is far too old for her."

"For the time being, yes, but perhaps not in another four or five years. She will be a beauty then, and old enough for a gentleman still in his twenties to consider."

Grace rolled her eyes and made a sound of disgust. "Do not tell me we shall have to put up with *this*..." She gestured to her sister. "...this dreadful mooning about for another four or five years!"

Mary had to smile at the girl's dramatics, which were so unlike her usual reserved self. "I fear you may, my dear Grace. Young ladies of your sister's age and older are often prone to such nonsense. You must be thankful, then, that you have only one sister. Pity me, for I lived with four." Thinking back, Mary recalled all too well her own disgust at Kitty and Lydia's wild enthusiasm over every man in regimentals, and how Jane had for months suffered love-sickness in her own quiet way. At last, belatedly and painfully, she had now herself acquired some empathy for their affliction.

26
Confidentially Speaking

All day she had expected his summons; all day she had prepared herself to give an accounting of the trip to Stafford-shire – a financial accounting as well as the explanation for their delayed return. Finally, after she had taken her evening meal with the children in the nursery, the call came.

Mary resolutely made her way downstairs to meet with her employer in the library, as she had done so many times before. She found him, however, not in his usual place, at the desk that dominated the center of the room, but instead sunk deep into one of the leather armchairs near the window.

He turned his eyes from the twilight without, half rose, and attempted a smile. "Do come and sit here, Miss Bennet," he said, indicating the mate to his own chair. "I am far too tired for formalities tonight. I hope you do not mind."

"Not at all, sir," she answered, crossing the room to take the proffered seat as he settled back into his own. "This chair will do as well for me as any other." Mary handed him the large envelope she had brought with her.

"What is this?" he asked, absently taking it from her.

"It is a ledger documenting all the expenses from the journey to Staffordshire, sir, along with the funds that remain. As for our delayed return, I can explain."

"Never mind all that," he said, tossing the envelope aside. "The girls told me about the breakdown. Not your fault, obviously, and that is not why I sent for you." He sighed wearily. "No, the truth is, I need someone to talk to, and you are the only creature in this household upon whom I can absolutely rely for an honest, intelligent opinion. You *will* be honest with me, won't you, Mary?"

"Of course, sir, if I can. But are you sure I am the properest person to consult? Surely Miss Farnsworth would..."

He interrupted. "Miss Farnsworth will not serve. You understand as well as I do that she has limited capacity for serious contemplations."

"I would beg to differ with you, sir. I believe…"

"Miss Bennet!" he interrupted again in a tone of exasperation.

Mary silenced herself at once and waited for him to continue.

"I did not invite you here to debate my sister's merits. I am simply asking for your assistance. That is all. You must trust me to know my own business, and to know that Miss Farnsworth is not the one who can help me now."

"Yes. I beg your pardon, sir. How may I be of assistance?"

His taut expression relaxed. "Ah, that is better. Now, I will speak plainly. The situation is this. Miss Agatha Browning – do you know the lady I mean? Yes, of course, you do. You will have seen her in Meryton. Apothecary's daughter."

Mary nodded.

"I barely know the woman, and yet apparently she has put it about the neighborhood that I have made romantic overtures to her, raising certain expectations. Well, her father came to see me whilst you were away, wishing to know my intentions. Of course I told him there was nothing in it, and that my affections were engaged else-where. Still, he could make things damned unpleasant if he chooses – not just for me, but for Miss Farnsworth and the children – saying I have used his daughter ill. I think what he really wants is money. Beastly nuisance, I know, but there it is."

As he spoke, Mary felt the color rising hot into her cheeks, and when he finished, she asked, "Sir, what can you mean by telling me all this?"

"Have I shocked you? Indeed, I would not have thought it. You are hardly a child. Surely you know that these kinds of things do occur. Why should not we speak of them frankly?"

"But why to me, sir? What has any of this to do with me?"

"Do not you see, Mary? No, of course you do not. Your modesty prevents you from acknowledging half your own worth or how much I have come to rely on your opinions." Leaning forward, he regarded her with an entreating look. "You are the only one I *can* speak to about this matter. Being neither a servant nor a member of the family, you have a unique position of objectivity in this household. Furthermore, I believe you are fully capable of considering such a delicate matter with common sense and discretion. Most importantly, though, you have the good of this family, especially the children, in view. Is it not so? Have I overstated the case or misjudged your loyalty?"

Mary hardly knew what to say or do. Had her pride allowed it, she might have flown from the room, but above all, a sense of dignity must be maintained. She did not wish anyone, least of all Mr. Harrison Farnsworth, to think her naïve or unsophisticated. Besides, her concern for the Farnsworth family was sincere. In that much, he was correct.

"I see that I have overwhelmed you," he said. "Forgive me, Miss Bennet, for burdening you with my problems. Perhaps I have presumed too much upon our growing friendship." He rose abruptly and crossed the room to stare into the empty fire grate.

Mary stayed where she was, rooted to her chair with her gaze resting on Mr. Farnsworth's back. Much could be read there, if one knew where to look, how to interpret the drooping line of the shoulders, the head bowed down by care.

"Mr. Farnsworth," she began cautiously. "I admit that I *was* momentarily overcome by what you disclosed. Now that I have had time to consider, however..." He turned, and Mary saw the hopeful expression on his face. "...perhaps we might discuss the problem openly and rationally, as you suggest."

"Excellent," he said, coming toward her again with renewed vigor. He sat once more in the chair facing her, this time forward and at attention. "Now then, what is your opinion of this ticklish situation? What would you advise me to do about it?"

"Sir, I confess that I am surprised at your being in any doubt. To me, it seems perfectly obvious."

"So I suspected it would, which is why I have asked you. I am too caught up in the middle of the thing to see it clearly."

"I suppose that is the explanation. At all events, I shall tell you what you must already know yourself. If you have not behaved improperly toward this lady, then you must not pay her father damages as if you had. To do so would only confirm your guilt in the eyes of some, and lay yourself open for others attempting the same. My guess is that Mr. Browning will go away quietly, for to spread rumors would damage his daughter far more than it would you in the end."

"Yes, right you are, Mary. I cannot give in to blackmail, for that is what it amounts to, in truth. What can be done to prevent such gossip and speculation in future, though? That is perhaps the larger question."

Mary chose her words carefully. "I think, sir, that a gentleman in his prime – one with a fortune and no wife – will always be a topic of interest to the local population, if you will excuse my saying so. Perhaps..." Mary stopped herself from finishing the thought aloud.

"What is it, Miss Bennet?"

"It is nothing, sir. Not my place to say."

"No, do go on, please. I give you leave to say whatever is on your mind. In fact, I insist on hearing it."

"Yes, sir. Then forgive me if my opinions seem too pert, but it strikes me that the quickest way to put an end to false speculation would be to let the truth be known. You said your affection is engaged elsewhere – a lady of your London acquaintance, no doubt. Well then, why hide it? Bring her to Netherfield. Parade her in public. Give the local gossips some truth to spread instead of leaving them to make up lies."

"Now you sound like Lavinia. She thinks it is high time I marry again – someone high born and moneyed, by her prescription." He rose and took up his habit of pacing once more.

"Sir, I would never presume to go so far as that!"

"You would not, but my sister does. And she may be right. Mrs. Farnsworth has been gone nearly two years now, and the children should have a mother," he concluded.

Mary dared not break in upon his thoughtful silence. She sat patiently and most uncomfortably by, wondering that she had allowed herself to become embroiled in such an awkward conversation. Although her regular conferences with Mr. Farnsworth had lately taken on a more familiar, less business-like tone – a change that left her feeling vaguely uneasy – this was far and away the most personal subject raised by him yet. He seemed genuinely desirous of her opinions and friendship, yet she could not help wondering if under the surface he was toying with her. Was this some kind of game to him, and she his pawn?

She knew how to behave toward the authoritarian employer of the last three years. She could not say the same for the one of the last several months, who increasingly treated with casual disregard the lines that had heretofore guided all their dealings together.

Lost in her own contemplations, Mary started at the sound of Mr. Farnsworth's bold voice resuming the conversation.

"Do you know, I think you are absolutely right!" said he with an intensity of a character Mary could not decipher. "I shall give a house party here at Netherfield and invite all my friends, including the lady we were alluding to. We shall have dancing and merriment the likes of which this place has not seen in some time. Although, as to dancing, I am sadly out of practice. I shall make a bloody shambles of the business unless you help me, Mary. You must give me lessons, starting right here this minute," he said, holding out his hand to her."

"Me? Oh, no, I could not!"

"I have seen you dance, remember? That night when you looked so happy in Mr. Collins's arms. So it is no good pleading want of ability."

"Then I shall plead want of propriety, sir... and the lateness of the hour. You said yourself that you were tired."

"Propriety be damned. Are we two children who need a chaperone? And as for being tired, I feel suddenly revived by the idea of dancing with you. Come now, Miss Bennet," he commanded, his hand still extended to receive hers. "You teach my children; why not their father? Would you have me embarrassed in front of my guests ... and my lady?"

Ignoring his question and his hand, Mary pushed out of her chair and made straight for the door. Before she reached it, however, she heard him laughing.

"Another time, then," he called after her. "Make no doubt about it, Mary; another time, and you *shall* dance with me."

27

Complications

Mary could hear his derisive laughter echoing in her ears all the way back to her bedchamber. So he *was* toying with her after all.

And what about his sad story of Miss Browning? Was that only a ruse to draw her into some elaborate game? No. She discarded the idea at once. Whatever else Mr. Harrison Farnsworth might be capable of, Mary could not believe he would sully the names of a respectable lady and her father for his own amusement. It appeared she herself was his only intended victim, and she could not imagine what she had done to deserve such treatment.

Mary was hurt and embarrassed, but more than that, she was bitterly disappointed in him. She had thought Mr. Farnsworth's brutish ways a thing of the past. The blow of his wife's death had seemed to soften his manner, made him gentler with his children and more sympathetic to the others. On a more personal level, Mary had been convinced that they had forged a bond of mutual respect, even tenuous friendship, between them. Apparently, she had been grossly mistaken.

Sunday now became the single object upon which Mary set all her store for gratification. To see her cousin again, and to avoid her employer in the meantime: these were her solemn goals. All hope of the latter seemed at an end, however, when Mr. Farnsworth sent a note up to the schoolroom Friday morning, advising her that he desired that she and the children should go riding with him that afternoon.

She thought of making some excuse. The note was phrased just loosely enough that, coming from some other man, it might be interpreted as a request instead of a command. But Mr. Farnsworth, she reminded herself, did not make suggestions; he gave orders, and he was accustomed to having them obeyed as if he were still a captain in the Navy. In the end, Mary decided it would draw less attention to herself, and therefore less discomfort, if she simply did what was expected of her. With the children along, it seemed unlikely that she would be forced into any awkward conversations similar to the one the other night.

Michael was always eager for a ride, especially with his father. Grace was happy because Mary was going too. This time it was Gwendolyn who complained, preferring to stay behind in the company of her poetry, but she was also aware how futile attempting to cry off would be. So, Mary and her charges dutifully donned their riding clothes and assembled at the stables by the appointed time. Their five horses were saddled and waiting as well. Instead of Mr. Farnsworth coming, however, at ten minutes after the hour another note from him arrived. It was directed to the governess in his bold, careless hand.

Miss Bennet,

I have just this minute received an urgent message, summoning me to town on business that cannot be postponed. Please instruct that someone should bring my horse round to the front of the house at once. You and the children must continue on as planned, taking a groom along for safety's sake. My disappointment at not being able to join you on this occasion is only assuaged by the thought that we shall keep our appointment another time. You shall ride with me again, Miss Bennet. H.F.

Mary's thoughts upon reading the brief missive were all in celebration of her reprieve. That Mr. Farnsworth should be taken off at the very moment when she expected to have to see him again, and that he should in all probability be kept away from Netherfield for several days following, could be nothing other than the sweetest stroke of good fortune.

Michael was all disappointment, however, and the quality of this second ride suffered undeniably for his father's absence. Mary could not fill Mr. Farnsworth's place for leading the expedition; she did not know the best routes to take, nor did she possess his knack for making discoveries round every corner and behind every hedge. Even the horses seemed to sense the difference – that nothing remarkable would be required of them that day – and they settled into a plodding pace from which no amount of coaxing could dislodge them. The result was a calmer albeit far less interesting afternoon.

If Friday failed to supply its full measure of stimulation, Sunday more than made up for it. Mary arrived at Longbourn church that morning, fifteen minutes before the commencement of the service, to find the gathered congregation a-hum with news of strangers in their midst. Mrs. Bennet, who was no doubt the source of these reports, quickly provided her daughter with all the necessary information as well.

"Friends of Mr. Collins from America!" she told Mary. "A brother and sister by the name of Beam – Mr. Calvin and Miss Polly Beam. Perhaps you have heard your cousin speak of them. They took a notion to follow Mr. Collins here to England, and so they have! They are both this minute at Longbourn with him, drinking tea and sitting in our front parlor. What do you think of that, Mary?"

"This is most surprising. I do remember Mr. Collins speaking of some particular friends in Virginia – neighbors also, they were. But what could have possessed them to travel so far to see him again so soon?"

"That is the very question I would wish to ask them myself – that and how long they intend to stay – although I should hope that I know better than to do so. It might be indelicate in my position for me to make such inquiries, and yet I cannot help wishing Mr. Tristan Collins would."

"I suppose he must be pleased to see his friends."

"I daresay he is, although I believe he was as surprised as anyone else that they had come. Nevertheless, we have made room for them, and you shall meet them for yourself after church. They declined my invitation to come along this morning – which I must say vexed me greatly – claiming to be too tired from their travels. I suppose I shall have to be content to wait until tomorrow to introduce them to our local society. We are all bidden to your aunt Phillips's house then for supper and cards. Everybody's curiosity will have been vastly increased by suspense, I daresay, so I can at least think of that whilst I am waiting."

"Really, Mama! Are they such oddities that people will throng to get a look at them?"

"They are Americans, Mary, born and bred! Not simply English returned to their native country like your cousin."

"Do you mean to say that they are red Indians, Mama?"

"Certainly not! Do you suppose I would stay two minutes, let alone two days, in the same house as bloodthirsty savages who are as likely to slit my throat as look at me? Good gracious, no. Their father was English right enough; so I understand. No doubt he saw to it they were raised to have *some* manners, but still I shudder to think what must have been lacking in their upbringing. Their mother came from France, after all, which may account for Miss Beam's looks as well as the airs she takes on, as if she imagines herself a very fine lady instead of the next thing to a heathen. And her coming just now, before your sister has had a chance to secure Mr. Collins, is very unlucky. I do not like the way Miss Beam looks at him, not one bit. Kitty had better watch out for that one, and so I have told her!" It was then time to go in, so Mrs. Bennet was forced to leave off her tales of the newcomers.

Mary could barely be civil to her fellow parishioners as they all made their way into the church, so thoroughly was her mind occupied with the information her mother had imparted about Mr. and Miss Beam, and with what she herself could recall of Mr. Tristan's remarks about the pair. They owned the farm adjoining his in Virginia – she was certain of that much – and that they had treated him kindly when he first arrived in that place.

There must have been some kind of unpleasantness thereafter, because the conversation had moved on to the desirability of making a fresh start. Whether or not the unpleasantness had anything to do with the Beams, however, Mary had no way of knowing. She only remembered Tristan's expression when he spoke of it – the shadow that flitted across his determinedly cheerful countenance. Yet he had left his holdings in Calvin Beam's care.

And now here they were, come nearly halfway round the world to see their friend again. Was it excessive affection that brought them, Mary wondered, or some other pressing matter? Her mother had already marked Miss Beam out as a rival to Kitty, and thus to herself as well. Although Mary would not credit half her mother's opinions, the idea of a lovers' quarrel and going to great lengths to repair it would explain the facts.

The first hymn was just beginning when Mary sat down in the pew next to her sister. Kitty said nothing; she only smiled in a way that evoked the idea of a wistful apology. Mary answered with an equally conciliatory look. She did not wish to quarrel. And if there really were a threat from the outside, it would be well for the Bennet sisters to close ranks against the interloper.

28

The Americans

Mr. Calvin Beam's sun-bleached hair and ruddy complexion portrayed a young man accustomed to a life lived much out of doors, and, despite Mrs. Bennet's disparagement of his origins, he also possessed every mark of a well-bred, civilized gentleman. Under normal circumstances, Mary would have been curious to learn more about him. In this case, however, it was his sister that immediately captured and held her attention – not because she was a devastating beauty, for she was less than that, but because of the striking resemblance she bore to her own sister Kitty.

"How do you do, Miss Beam?" Mary said as she surreptitiously examined the woman's face upon first seeing her at Longbourn after church.

The features were not exact, of course; Miss Beam's jaw line was squarer and her nose a bit shorter. But the fawn-colored hair and the large, gentle brown eyes were nearly identical, giving the same appealing impression of a vulnerable innocent begging for love and protection.

"Tolerably well, I thank you," said Miss Beam in a soft voice. "Although an ocean crossing is not something to be quickly recovered from, I find."

"I should think not!" exclaimed Mrs. Bennet as they all six settled together in the drawing room – she with her two daughters on one settee, the American brother and sister the other, and Tristan Collins in an armchair. "Nothing less than the sharp point of a sword could persuade me to submit myself to such a punishment. I wonder that you should have done so voluntarily, Miss Beam, as delicate as you seem to be."

The lady looked unsure how to respond.

Calvin Beam came to her rescue. "Although my sister may appear delicate, Mrs. Bennet, her health is every bit as robust as mine, and she never shies away from a challenge. Besides, we have long wanted to see England, and this seemed the perfect opportunity, with our friend here to guide us at this particular juncture."

"There was no hurry, though," said Kitty. "Mr. Collins will be here at Longbourn to receive visitors for years to come."

Now it was Calvin Beam's turn to look confused. He regarded his friend. "Are you firmly decided on staying, then, Triss? We had hoped you might be returning to Virginia with us in the end."

All eyes rested expectantly on Mr. Tristan Collins.

"Not irrevocably decided, no. I am torn, as you might well imagine, between my ties on this side of the Atlantic and those on the other. I only wish I could unite all the benefits of both in one place, but of course that is quite impossible."

"Yes, quite impossible," repeated Miss Beam. "You shall have to choose between the two."

"I am well aware of that, Miss Beam, believe me." Tristan's eyes darted from person to person about the room, and then ultimately dropped to the floor.

A silence followed, one which Mrs. Bennet soon rushed to fill. "Well, whilst you are here in England, Miss Beam, you must make the most of your opportunity. There are many beauties and wonders in the countryside round about, and should you be inclined to travel far and wide, I would be happy to advise you on what is worth seeing. But I daresay you have plenty of lakes and mountains where you come from. No, London is where you must go; London must by no means be missed. You will not find its equal anywhere, especially in the colonies."

"Mama," whispered Mary, "they are not 'the colonies' anymore."

"Ah, yes, I keep forgetting. What I meant to say is that there can be nothing in your young country to equal the history and culture of London."

"I am sure you are correct, Mrs. Bennet," replied Calvin Beam. "Nothing in America can pretend to match London's historic edifices, although we do flatter ourselves that we are not totally deficient in culture."

A civil yet spirited debate continued, primarily between these two, comparing the merits of English tradition and American innovation.

Mary could attend to it but little, so thoroughly occupied was she observing the faces round the room and listening to what was *not* being said. Her mother had been right, she shortly concluded. There had been something more than friendship between Mr. Tristan and Miss Polly Beam, and it was entirely possible the lady had come with the hope of rekindling it. Miss Beam was clearly trying to catch

Tristan's eye. Kitty alternated between also looking to him for a sign of reassurance and staring daggers at Miss Beam. The man himself avoided them both and feigned interest in the conversation going forward amongst the others. Finally, he settled his troubled gaze on Mary. She returned it with one intended to convey understanding and compassion.

That would be her advantage, she decided right then and there. Where the others made demands of Tristan, she would not. When her rivals pressed him for a decision, she would be patient. She would prove her value in being a listening ear, a sympathetic friend, a true and unselfish heart. She would not criticize Kitty or Miss Beam; she would rise above. Then, after the other two had exhausted themselves in a series of unbecoming skirmishes, she would still be standing, tall and untarnished, to take the prize.

"Mrs. Bennet," said Mr. Collins suddenly, interrupting another one of her long speeches. "I feel the need for some exercise before dinner. What would you advise? Have you no more lanes hereabouts in which I may lose my way?"

"By all means, Mr. Collins. Do take your friends and walk to Oakham Mount. It is a nice long walk, and you have never seen the view. Kitty will be happy to show you the way."

"It may do very well for me and for my strong friend Mr. Beam," replied Tristan, "but I am sure it will be too much for the ladies."

"It is not too much for me," declared Kitty, getting to her feet at once. "I have made the trek several times before, and I am not the least bit tired."

"Nor am I," said Miss Beam, also rising. "I should very much like to see this view."

"Then you may as well go too, Mary," said Mrs. Bennet. "I shall have a little nap whilst you young people are out. Mind you are not gone too long, though. Cook will have her nose out of joint for a fortnight if her famous fish stew is ruined."

"I shall just dash upstairs and change to my boots," said Kitty. "Mary, will you help me?"

Since changing footwear was hardly a two-person job, Mary perceived that what her sister actually desired was a word with her in private. Being curious what Kitty had to say, she willingly went.

"Is this not the most upsetting development, Mary?" Kitty began in hushed tones when the door was closed. "What were these people thinking to arrive here unannounced and uninvited? The brother is not too bad, I suppose, except that he is always putting his sister forward. But that Miss Beam! She cannot take her eyes of our cousin Tristan, and we have not had a moment to ourselves since she arrived."

"I gather there is some history between the two. What does Mr. Collins tell you about it?"

"Very little. As I say, we have barely had a moment for a private conversation, not with *her* always lurking about. And I think he does not wish to worry me by letting on that there was ever anything serious between them."

"You *are* worried, though. You see this Miss Beam as a threat to your position."

"No, not as a threat. She is no more to me than an irritating nuisance, an insect buzzing in my ear. I certainly have no reason to fear her, and yet you must see how uncomfortable she makes our dear Tristan."

"There is something else odd about her too," Mary said tentatively. "Do not you think so?"

"What do you mean by odd?"

"Surely you cannot have failed to notice her looks, how much she resembles you."

"Resembles me? Miss Beam?"

"Why, yes, I was immediately struck by the similarity! Do you not think it remarkable?"

"I see no very strong likeness, but it would not be so surprising if there were. Some men prefer tall, fair girls and others those of shorter stature with brown hair and eyes. What of it? The point is this, Mary, that you must assist me to get Mr. and Miss Beam out of the way so that I can talk to Tristan alone."

"What would you have me do? Shall I push them off the cliff whilst they are admiring the view?"

"Do be serious, Mary! I simply want you distract them, to engage them in conversation, to walk ahead with them when I hang back with Tristan. Do you suppose you can do that much for me?"

Mary thought a moment. "I shall do as you ask if you will return the favor."

"What? You wish to have time alone with Tristan as well? What can you possibly have to say to him that will not admit being overheard?"

"An apology," declared Mary, giving Kitty an even look. "I said something rude to him at Pemberley and I am determined to make him an apology today. My conscience demands that I beg his pardon, and yet my vanity insists that there be no witnesses."

Kitty studied her before answering. "Very well, then," she said slowly. "We shall work as a team. You shall have your turn, and I must have mine."

29
Admiring a View

It was not easy, but Mary did manage to attach both Mr. and Miss Beam to herself for most of the walk up to Oakham Mount. Feigning absolute ignorance about the new world and an equally absolute urgency to remedy the situation, she soon entangled the brother and sister in a web of questions so dense that it required the better part of an hour to extract themselves from it.

Kitty, meanwhile, followed along behind on the arm of Mr. Tristan Collins, talking with him in tones too subtle to decipher at any distance. Mary for a long while resisted glancing back at them, both to avoid torturing herself and to avoid drawing Miss Beam's attention thither. That lady's eyes were sure to wander to the view at the rear at least once in every five minutes as it was.

Finally, Mary did look back, hoping to receive a signal from her sister that she could at last free her captives. Kitty gave her a stern glare instead. So Mary soldiered on a few minutes more until she ran out of questions to ask and out of patience with Kitty's demands. She then thanked the Beams for all their helpful information. "You must forgive me for monopolizing your time," she told them. "I have such an insatiable thirst for knowledge that I could not seem to help myself."

"That is quite all right, Miss Bennet," said Calvin Beam. "I admire your dedication to learning as well as teaching. With all the knowledge you have accumulated, you must be a very valuable asset to your students." He then stopped and turned, and his sister did as well. "Come along, you two," he called. "I have never seen such dawdlers. Are you so out of breath?"

"Not out of breath," Tristan answered. "We are only in less of a great hurry than you three seem to be. It is not a race, you know."

They finished the assent reunited as one group, and stood to admire the view several minutes. Mary pointed out the principal landmarks visible from that vantage point – a portion of the village of Meryton, the London road, Miller's pond, and the house and park of Netherfield. After providing this service, she withdrew a little, taking Kitty with her. "I hope you are satisfied," she whispered.

"You could have kept them away a little longer," Kitty returned in hushed tones.

"I should like to see you do half so well for me."

Kitty frowned. "Did you notice how Miss Bean fastened herself onto Tristan like a leach just now, the moment my back was turned?"

"You cannot blame her; she has no way of knowing that you consider him your private property. Perhaps someone ought to warn her off."

Miss Beam was no longer gazing down at the bucolic scene in the valley below, but up at Mr. Tristan Collins's handsome face instead, listening intently to his opinion on what constituted a truly picturesque view. "Please excuse me from making any comment," she said when he had finished. "I know nothing of the picturesque."

"As for me, Triss," Mr. Beam chimed in, "you must be satisfied with such admiration as I can honestly give. I call it a very fine country – the hills are steep, the woods seem full of fine timber, and the valley looks comfortable and snug – with rich meadows and several neat farm houses scattered here and there. It exactly answers my idea of a fine country, because it unites beauty and utility."

"And I daresay it is a picturesque one too, because you admire it," added Miss Beam with a warm smile at Tristan.

"Yes, indeed." said Kitty for her sister's ears alone. "Perhaps someone should warn her off."

When everybody had got their fill of seeing what could be achieved from the top of a hill, Kitty suggested they should start back, and she claimed Miss Beam as her walking companion. She failed to account for Mr. Beam, however, who then joined Mary and Tristan in a second informal group. As the two men conversed, Mary cast about for some scheme to dispose of the unwanted spare. She had nearly given up hope of having one minute alone with Tristan when Mr. Beam himself provided the solution.

"Oh, bother," he said in disgust, stopping in his tracks. "I have somehow managed to get a sharp pebble into my boot, and it is cutting into my flesh like broken glass. I cannot go on until I have shifted it." He limped off toward a boulder that would serve for a seat whilst he accomplished the operation.

"We shall wait for you," said Tristan.

"No, no, there is no sense in that, old boy. You and Miss Bennet go on and I shall catch you up presently."

"Very well," said Tristan. He offered his arm to Mary and they resumed their descent of the hill, albeit more slowly.

Not knowing how long Mr. Beam would be elsewhere occupied, Mary wasted no time. "Mr. Tristan," she began, "I am glad that we have a moment alone, for there is something very particular I wish to say to you."

"You mustn't look so grave, dear Mary. Surely it cannot be anything as dire as all that."

"Not dire perhaps, but a serious subject nonetheless. I wanted to apologize for somewhat of my conduct at Pemberley and on the journey home. I believe I behaved in a rather uncharitable manner toward you, and I am sorry for it. Will you forgive me?"

"It is already forgiven and forgotten, my dear cousin. I could clearly comprehend that something had got the better of you, stolen away your usual good nature as it were. I was only distressed by the impression that I might unknowingly have been the cause of it."

"No, it was something else entirely."

"You said 'was.' I trust that means your trouble is now all in the past."

"It will be if you say that we are still friends, Cousin Tristan."

"Of course we are," he said, patting her hand as it rested on the sleeve of his coat. "We are more than friends. We are...uh... Why, we are family as well, are we not?"

"That we are." They walked on in silence for a minute before Mary broached a new topic, watching for his reaction as she did so. "You must have been surprised by the arrival of your friends from America – surprised and pleased."

"Naturally," he said with a smile that looked a little forced, "at least once I ascertained that all was well – with them and with my holdings. When I left Virginia, I had no idea of ever seeing them again, at least not this side of the Atlantic."

"So they had not told you about their earnest desire to see England, then."

"No, it must have been a notion that came upon them quite recently. One may develop a sudden interest in a place one has heard a great deal about, I suppose, especially when one has a friend there to visit."

"Undoubtedly. Would you permit me to make an observation, though?"

"Please, speak freely."

"Well, I cannot help thinking that the unexpected presence of the Beams has placed you in a rather... awkward position." He started to

155

say something but Mary held up her free hand to stop him. "No, you owe me no explanations, and indeed I desire none. I merely meant to tell you that if ever you are in need of a sympathetic ear, an impartial confidante, I hope you will feel at liberty to come to me. As your true friend, I will hear whatever you like. I will tell you exactly what I think."

"My goodness! I hardly know what to say, Miss Mary. Your kindness has quite overwhelmed me."

Calvin Beam, walking now without a limp, rejoined them at that moment, putting an end to their brief tête-à-tête. Although Mary could have wished for more time, she was satisfied. She had accomplished what she had set out to do. She had made her position clear. She had put her association with Mr. Tristan Collins back on solid footing. And what was more, she had done so without sacrificing her dignity.

He could no longer be in any doubt of possessing her steadfast respect and affection. What he ultimately chose to do about it was out of her hands. She would trust to him, to God, and to the full measure of time to decide the matter rightly. She would not throw herself at him. She refused to make a spectacle as if she had taken complete leave of her senses. If that was what was required to win the man, Mary felt she had much rather let one of the other two have him, for that would mean he was not worth the price after all.

30

Company Coming

Once returned to Netherfield, Mary did her best to put those at Longbourn out of her mind. There was nothing more she could do about that situation at present. The family drama between Mr. Tristan Collins, Kitty, and Miss Beam would have to carry on without her for another week, at least without her physical presence. She had to hope that her existence would not be entirely forgotten, though, that some lingering impression remained to keep her prospects alive.

As usual, Mary's work with the Farnsworth children kept her much occupied the next day. They had started with mathematics that morning and had just moved on to geography when Clinton came into the schoolroom to say that Mary's presence was required downstairs.

"Miss Farnsworth it is who wants you," he told her. "Said as I should fetch you right away."

"Very well, Clinton," Mary replied. "You have delivered your message and may go. I know my way and will come directly."

"I think I had better wait for you. Miss Farnsworth told me…"

"And now *I* am telling you to go on ahead without me," Mary interrupted. "I do not require an escort, and I will be there the more quickly if you leave me now to settle the children. Do you understand me?"

"'Course I do; I ain't no dunce, you know. Only you mustn't dawdle. Miss F. has got herself worked up into quite a pucker."

When he had gone, Mary gave Gwendolyn, Grace, and Michael each an assignment to work on in her absence, and then she hastened down to the entry hall. There she found all the upper servants gathered in silence before Miss Farnsworth. That lady held in her hand what appeared to be a letter, and she was doing a fair imitation of her brother, scowling and pacing an abbreviated route in front of the doorway.

She looked up when Mary came down the stairs. "Ah, I see Miss Bennet has deigned to join us, so now we may begin," she said, coming to a standstill. "I have called you all here to apprise you of Mr. Farnsworth's plans, that you may begin making ready immediately." She waved the letter in the air for emphasis. "He will be returning from London on Wednesday, and not alone. He is bringing with him a large party of friends, who will be staying for no less than a week. There will be feasting, and dancing, and everything in the way of the best entertainment."

A low murmuring broke out amongst the servants at this momentous news.

"It goes without saying that your master will expect everyone and everything here at Netherfield to be in peak form," Miss Farnsworth continued, "to do him proud before his guests. There is much work to be done in preparation and not a moment to lose. Cook, I will want to see your menu plans this afternoon without fail. Mrs. Brand, I must consult with you immediately. The rest of you, with the exception of Miss Bennet, may go and get busy about your duties at once. That is all for now."

A hum of chatter surged and then died away again as the others dispersed, leaving Mary, Mrs. Brand, and Miss Farnsworth behind in the hall.

"Miss Bennet," said Miss Farnsworth with obvious hostility.

"Yes, Madam?"

"You may be wondering what any of this has to do with you. And so am I, in truth. All I do know is that I have been charged by my brother to give you *this*." She shook a sealed note at Mary, as if it were conclusive evidence of some crime. "If there is anything in it that at all pertains to my preparations, I trust you will bring it to my attention. What my brother could have to say to *you* that merits a private correspondence, I am sure I cannot imagine. Go now, for I have more important matters to discuss with Mrs. Brand."

Mrs. Brand gave Mary a sympathetic look, but she could say nothing with the mistress present. Mary had no wish to linger in any case. Her curiosity to know the contents of the note from Mr. Farnsworth was at least equal to that which it had excited in his sister. She hurried back upstairs with her prize, going to her bedchamber instead of returning to the schoolroom, to read the missive in private. Carrying it to the pool of light streaming in through the window, she broke the seal and read.

Miss Mary Bennet,

I hope you do not find my writing to you to be presumptuous. I know that some might consider it improper for me, a single gentle-

man, to correspond directly with you, a single lady. Such privileges are generally reserved for engaged couples, I believe. I should have allowed my sister to relay this message were I altogether certain she would do so properly. In light of past events, however, I had no such assurances. Furthermore, I thought that, under the guise of our professional relationship, I might be permitted this minor liberty.

You will have learnt by now that I have adopted your advice, just as I said I would. We shall give the local gossips some truth to talk about as you recommended, for I am indeed inviting my friends to Netherfield for dancing and general merriment. My particular wish is that you should be counted amongst the guests – for the entire week or at least at the ball to be held Thursday night. That is the purpose for my writing to you now, to personally invite you. You shall be introduced as the daughter of a local gentleman, which indeed you are, as you have more than once reminded me. There will be no mention made of your current occupation unless you yourself chose to divulge it.

Miss Farnsworth will not approve, of course, which is why I did not entrust to her the task of telling you all this. She will, however, abide by my wishes when she has no choice. Show her the pertinent portion of this letter and she will provide you with anything you may need to be properly attired – <u>your</u> choice from her best gowns this time, not hers. I promised myself that one day I would dance with you, Miss Bennet. Please do not disappoint me.

Yours, etc.
Harrison Farnsworth

Mary sat some minutes staring at the confident strokes of black ink scrawled on the single sheet of paper, silently digesting the meaning of the words they conveyed. She was astounded – and extremely flattered – that Mr. Farnsworth should invite her to be his guest at the house party. For a moment she even pictured herself fitted out like a proper lady and proudly escorted to the dance floor on Mr. Farnsworth's steady arm. The letter clearly stated that was what he desired. And on the face of things his tone sounded sincere and gracious enough – very little of his former autocratic tendencies in evidence.

And yet something inside her would not allow Mary to trust it. Much could be concealed on a written page, after all, and it was possible to put more than one construction on the words of the author.

She read the letter again, imagining that Mr. Farnsworth himself was present. This time, hearing the words as from his own mouth, there was no sincerity or graciousness. Mary saw only cavalier diversion in his eyes and heard only derision in his voice, as she had at the close of their last meeting, when he laughed at her. How much different was the effect of this second perusal! How quickly it put an end to any pleasant feelings of gratification… and to every idea of accepting the invitation.

Under the best of circumstances, with Mr. Farnsworth's full loyalty and regard, a party amongst *the ton* would be no very pleasant prospect for her. How much worse, then, to know herself to be at a severe disadvantage going in. Despite what he promised in his letter, it was sure to come out that she was merely the governess in that house. Then the jokes would begin. Mary shuddered at the thought.

No, she would certainly not attend only to be laughed at again, to be made the object of Miss Farnsworth's insults and Mr. Farnsworth's sport. It was out of the question even to consider it.

Had there been a fire in the grate, Mary would have tossed the offensive note straight in. As it was, she took the great satisfaction of ruthlessly tearing it to shreds before discarding it.

~~*~~

Mary carefully kept to the schoolroom and to the company of the Farnsworth children as much as possible after that. However, she made a brief but happy exception when Monsieur Hubert arrived the next morning. Miss Farnsworth sent a message to the nursery saying that she could not under the circumstances spare the time to take her turn, and that Gwendolyn should report directly to the music room in her place. Grace followed, and then, with all three children settled at their geography assignments, Mary lightheartedly flew downstairs.

"Ah, Miss Bennet, a pleasure, as always!" said Monsieur Hubert upon her entrance. "My favorite pupil is, like the sweet after a meal, reserved for last again today."

"Really, Monsieur, you should not say such things; it is too much flattery."

"*Mais non*! I tell you nothing more than what is the truth. There is no need to dissemble, therefore. A lady should be able to hear and acknowledge her merits with dignity. No embarrassment, Miss Bennet! And no more protests either! That is my command. Now, how have you been getting on with Monsieur Beethoven, hmm?"

As usual, Monsieur Hubert and the magic of music carried all Mary's troubles away. For that one hour, the house party and Mr. Farnsworth's upsetting letter retreated to a distant corner of her mind, where they could be as completely forgotten as yesterday's dirty dishes.

Alas, it was only a temporary reprieve. When Mary returned to the schoolroom, Gwendolyn made it difficult for her to keep at bay thoughts of the coming event. The girl had caught the excitement of the thing and could form neither an opinion nor a sentence concerning anything else in the intervening days. Even though it was unlikely she should catch much more than a glimpse of the party's splendor, the anticipation of its going forward in her vicinity was enough to feed every one of her burgeoning notions of romance.

"Oh, how I wish I were old enough to be there!" she exclaimed Tuesday afternoon whilst they were taking their airing out of doors.

Mary had started off at a brisk pace with the children, taking a circular lane on the property that she had discovered made an excellent path for exercise. Michael and Grace had scampered on ahead, but Gwen hung back with Mary, speculation about the coming party on her mind.

"Do you suppose Papa might allow me to attend the ball on Thursday night?" she asked.

"I think not, my dear Gwen," Mary answered. "You are far too young. Perhaps when you are sixteen or seventeen. No doubt there will be many other opportunities, now that your father has decided to entertain at Netherfield again."

"If I could only be there to watch, I should be satisfied. Well, almost satisfied. I used to love to watch my father and mother dancing," the girl added, dropping both her gaze and her voice.

"Really? You must have been very young. How long ago was this?" Mary asked gently.

"It was before we came to Netherfield, when Mama was still strong. We lived in town then, and we often had parties with dancing. Mama loved to give parties, and I sometimes slipped down from the nursery to watch. I would have been seven or eight, I suppose, for I was nine when we came here."

"And did both your mother and father like to dance then?"

"Oh, yes! Sometimes they did not even wait for a ball. Papa would pull my mother to her feet of a sudden and sweep her round the room with no real music to dance by – just him humming a tune. I wonder whom he will dance with on Thursday."

"I could not even guess, Gwen." Mary only knew that it would not be herself.

Gwendolyn chattered on, but Mary was too lost in her own thoughts to properly attend. She could not get this new picture of her employer out of her head – Mr. Farnsworth dancing gaily with his poor wife as if they, neither one of them, had a care in the world. The poignant portrait intrigued her, and yet the people in it were un-recognizable as those she had met upon first coming to Longbourn – he dictatorial and cold, she frail and defeated. Mary had not imagined there had ever been much affection, let alone joy, in the Farnsworths' marriage. At least there had been precious little evidence of it by the time she knew them. What could have happened to change them both so severely?

31
Observing a Ball

Since the schoolroom windows overlooked the gravel sweep at the front of the house, Mary and the children could hear every carriage as it approached on Wednesday. Mr. Farnsworth's own carriage arrived first, an hour before any of the others. Presently he came up to see his children, embracing each of the girls and shaking hands with his young son. Then he turned to Mary.

"Hello, Miss Bennet," he said. "You are well, I hope."

"Yes, sir, very well indeed."

"Excellent! I trust I shall be seeing you again soon, downstairs tomorrow evening if not before," he said with a significant look. Then he gave a slight bow and left the room.

He had not waited for an answer because he was confident that she would come. Mary concluded thus much from his manner and his tone. Accustomed to having his own way, Mr. Farnsworth expected this occasion to be no different than any other. He expected *her* to be no different than any other. Perhaps she ought to have called him back and undeceived him at once. Instead, she had let the correct moment for doing so slip by with him none the wiser.

"What did Papa mean?" Grace asked. "Why should you see him again soon?"

"I cannot say, Grace. Perhaps he means to send for me to discuss your progress, so we had best get back to our studies."

Very little progress was made that day, however. The children ran to the windows every time they heard another carriage, and they strained to see who was alighting from it. Michael was sure to call out something about the horses or the style of the carriage, and Gwendolyn something about the lady who emerged from it. Mary could not blame them; it was the most singular event to take place at Netherfield in years, and it was only natural they should be excited.

For her part, Mary wished only to stay as much out of the way as possible. It was a big house, and there seemed little chance of her coming across the master or any of his guests as long as she kept to a governess's province – her own chamber, the children's quarters, the schoolroom, and the back staircase. When they went out of doors, they would come and go as inconspicuously as possible and stay far from the house and stables. Her plan worked flawlessly the rest of that day and all the next. Mary's difficulty came on Thursday evening.

"Please say yes, Miss Bennet." Gwendolyn peered up at her with beseeching eyes to match her tone of voice. "I swear I will go alone if I must, but I had much rather you went with me."

The ball was well underway downstairs, and the lively music filtered up to the nursery, where they were taking their supper. Mary hesitated, torn between an earnest desire to accommodate the girl's request to observe the dancing and her own to go nowhere near it.

Gwen continued. "We shall not be seen, if that is what worries you. And in any case, I daresay Papa would not mind in the least."

"I am by no means assured of that, Gwen." He might not mind his daughter spying on the party. The uncooperative governess was quite another thing. Still, if they were careful...

"Please, Miss. I must be allowed to watch, just for a few minutes, or I think I shall simply burst!"

"Compose yourself, Gwendolyn. Wild and uncontrolled behavior will not serve. If we are to attempt this, I must be certain that you are able to conduct yourself with caution and decorum."

The girl's eyes popped wide with excitement, but she stifled any further outburst, covering her mouth with both hands. After a minute of inward jubilation, she became tolerably calm once more.

"That is better," said Mary. "Now finish your supper, and then we shall have a brief look downstairs. You must promise to be discreet. I should not wish your father or any of his guests to ever have an idea that we had been near the place. Do you understand?"

"Oh, yes, Miss! Thank you, Miss! I will be very good and very quiet. You shall see."

"Remember," Mary said when they were ready to start down, "we can only stay a few minutes. You must do nothing to draw attention to our presence. And you must be prepared to retreat at my command should anybody come in our direction. Agreed?"

Gwendolyn nodded vigorously.

"Very well, then."

They used the back stairs to avoid any chance encounters and emerged in the corridor that led to the far end of the largest drawing room. Mary knew that was the one which had been given over as a ballroom, now and in the past. She could not help momentarily thinking with horror of the first and only other Netherfield ball that she had been present for, then as a proper guest. What a spectacle her family had made of themselves that night! And she had unwittingly done her part. This time, however, she would not be putting herself forward to be humiliated; she would be hiding in the shadows, quite literally.

Taking Gwen's hand, Mary led her down the dimly lit passageway, which was ordinarily used only by servants. She slowed as they approached the first of two doorways opening to the drawing room. The music swelled, and Mary could glimpse the musicians applying themselves just inside. She could picture the rest of the scene even before confirming it by sight.

Mary took care to position Gwen at the edge of the doorway and just short of the shaft of light spilling through it. She stood directly behind with her hands on the girl's shoulders to be sure she would not stray. There they had an unobstructed view with very little possibility of being seen themselves.

As Mary had imagined, the great crystal chandeliers and more than a dozen wall sconces were ablaze with the glow of tall, tapered, wax candles, their light reflecting off every mirrored, metal, and glass surface. A set of elegantly coiffed and attired dancers glided through their prescribed patterns down the center of the room with clusters of onlookers lingering about the edges, the crowd composed of those who had come from London augmented by a select number of the local gentry. A few of these faces Mary recognized at a glance, but they could not fasten her attention. Nor could any of the strangers from town. There was only one person, somewhere in that room, who held any interest whatsoever for Mary, the one person she both cared and dreaded to see: Mr. Farnsworth. Would he be enjoying himself, she wondered? Would he be dancing? And with whom? Would he even have noticed that she had not accepted his disingenuous invitation?

Then she saw him, and at the same time so did Gwendolyn. "Look!" the girl whispered. "There is Papa! But who is that lady he is dancing with?"

"I do not know her," answered Mary in a hushed voice. "Someone of your father's London acquaintance, I expect."

"She is very elegant, is not she? And very beautiful."

"Yes. And very young," Mary added, almost to herself. The lady was undoubtedly all that and more. Was this the woman Mr. Farnsworth had meant when he had said his affections were engaged? Would this mere girl, probably less than half his age, be the next mistress of Netherfield?

165

Turning her attention to Mr. Farnsworth himself, Mary noted that his evening clothes suited him well, giving him a rather regal bearing. Yet it was not his appearance but his dancing that especially struck her. He had professed to be sadly out of practice, and she had pitied him for it. Yet the man before her now looked as much at ease on the dance floor as ever he had on the back of a horse.

Before Mary could dwell long on that inconsistency, the dance concluded. It left Mr. Farnsworth and his partner at the end of the set nearest the musicians, and thus also nearest to the doorway where the two spies were concealed. When he turned in their direction, Mary instinctively drew back deeper into the shadows, pulling Gwen with her. Gwen, however, strained against her grasp and broke free, momentarily stepping into the light before resuming her previous position.

In that instant, her father had seen her, and he came swiftly toward the door.

Mary gasped. "Away, Gwen!" she said softy but urgently, her feet already in motion. "We must away."

They were down the corridor in a trice and had almost reached the stairs when Mr. Farnsworth's voice rang out. "Gwendolyn, stay where you are! You too, Miss Bennet."

Mary froze in her tracks and then turned to face her employer, shielding Gwen behind her skirts. "Mr. Farnsworth," she said, holding her chin high.

"Miss Bennet. What is this, then? You refuse an invitation to come in the front door like a lady, so I find you skulking at the rear like a servant or a common thief."

Mary ignored the charge and said, "Your daughter wished to watch some of the dancing. I saw no harm in that, sir."

"Is this true, Gwen?"

The girl stepped forward. "Yes, Papa. I should certainly have come on my own had I not been able to persuade Miss Bennet. I heard the music and it reminded me of when you used to dance with Mama."

His expression faltered and then quickly recovered. "Very well," he told his daughter. "You got what you came for, and we shall say no more about it. Run along up to bed now. I wish to have a word with Miss Bennet."

"Do not be angry with her, Papa," Gwendolyn pleaded. "It was all my idea."

"Yes, yes, never mind that now," he said. "Off you go."

Gwendolyn did as she was told, disappearing up the stairs.

Mary stood her ground when Mr. Farnsworth took a step toward her.

"This was not where I had hoped to see you tonight, Miss Bennet," he said deliberately. "You did not accept my invitation to join the party, and I cannot help wondering why. I am not accustomed to having my invitations go unacknowledged."

Mary faced straight ahead, refusing to meet his eyes. "Sorry if I disappointed you, sir. I was perplexed by your invitation, and I could not imagine you meant it sincerely. In any case, I would have found it quite uncomfortable to accept with so many people here that I do not know."

"You know me," he said in a low rumble.

"Do I?" she said defiantly, looking straight at him now. She saw at once by his reaction that she ought not to have said it. She had felt cornered; that was her excuse. She was being called on the carpet as if she were a naughty child caught stealing sweets.

Mr. Farnsworth began to pace a constricted arc about her, hands behind his back and looking very grim. "For the record, Miss Bennet, I rarely say anything I do not mean, and I would never put falsehoods into writing. As for the cause of your discomfort, now there you have *me* puzzled, but we shall have to discuss it another time. I must return to my guests – those persons who *did* see fit to accept my invitation. You understand."

"Yes, I believe I understand you perfectly."

He turned on his heel to go and then wheeled back toward her again. "Oh, Miss Bennet, one more thing. I have arranged an excursion to St. Albans tomorrow for the entire party, weather permitting, and I will be taking the children with me. Would you be good enough to see to it that they are ready at ten o'clock sharp? Be not alarmed, Madam, by any apprehension that I shall renew my offer for you to join us; I would not wish to be accused of placing you in uncomfortable circumstances again. And just to prove I harbor no ill will for this little misunderstanding, you may take the balance of tomorrow to do with as you please. Consider it a present, a small token of my sincere esteem." He made a curt bow and then left her.

Considering the tone of cutting sarcasm Mr. Farnsworth had risen to during this speech, it was difficult to believe he felt anything like sincere esteem for her, no more than she had been accurate in saying she understood him perfectly. For Mary did not understand him in the least.

32
Unexpected Holiday

When she returned upstairs that night, Mary told the three Farnsworth children that they were to accompany their father and his friends on the next day's excursion. Not surprisingly, Gwendolyn burst into raptures, thrilled at being included in such a social highlight. Although dancing would have been better, an outing in fine carriages would do nearly as well.

Michael cared nothing for the society of London ladies and gentlemen; it was the adventure of the expedition that appealed to his boyish sensibilities. "I shall ask Papa if I may sit on the box, so that I can keep a watch out for highwaymen!" he proclaimed.

Grace, being shy and retiring by nature, did not wish to go at all. "All those people, and me not knowing anyone!" she worried aloud.

Mary could well appreciate her feelings. Had she not just plead the same excuse herself? And how much worse at age eleven. "You shall undoubtedly ride with your father, your brother, and your sister, and perhaps one or two others at most. Now, there is nothing frightening in that, is there?"

"I do not see why Papa should want us with him. He certainly would not miss me with so many other people to keep him company."

"He is proud of you, I should think, and he wants to show you off to his friends a bit. So you must not disappoint him; you must behave like two ladies and a young gentleman in order to make a good impression on your father's guests." One of them in particular, perhaps, Mary added to herself. It was only logical that Mr. Farnsworth should wish to introduce his offspring to his perspective bride. That, undoubtedly, was the real purpose of this outing.

After seeing the children safely to their beds, Mary prepared to retire to her own, beginning by placing an armchair in front of the door that gave onto the outside corridor. She had taken to doing this the day she found Clinton in her room, watching her as she slept. It would probably not stop anybody from forcing his way in, were he truly determined, but at least she hoped the noise would afford her some warning.

As little as she liked to dwell on that possibility, the next subject that sprang to her mind was no more pleasant: Mr. Farnsworth.

Mary commenced the nightly ritual of taking down her hair. She removed the pins that had bound it tightly to the top of her head all day long, and braced for the painful prickling sensation in her scalp as it fell about her shoulders. Then she began brushing it her customary one hundred times. As she counted, however, the slow and methodical stroking evolved into something more like passionate flailing.

It infuriated her that she could never seem to keep her dealings with Mr. Farnsworth on an even keel for more than a week at a stretch. One day she thought they had settled into a comfortable working relationship, and the next it was all overthrown. She could not make him out, which was a frustration in itself, an insult to her intelligence. And the more she tried to decipher his behavior, the less sense it made.

The most maddeningly inexplicable part about it, however, was that she should care at all what Mr. Farnsworth said, what he did, or what he thought of her. Why should any of it matter? He did not frighten her, and she was able to avoid him most of the time. If the situation became completely insupportable – should the new Mrs. Farnsworth be more difficult to bear than the present acting mistress of the house, for an example – she could always leave.

Ever since visiting Pemberley, Mary had been turning over in her mind the idea that she could make a very comfortable home for herself there if necessary, offering her services as governess to her young nephews. She had every reason to think such an offer would be welcome. Had not Elizabeth said that they should be fortunate to find anyone half so qualified?

For a moment, Mary imagined herself soaring free – free to fly from her current troublesome situation and come to rest at Pemberley. But to break with the Farnsworth family completely? To never see the children – or their father – again? The thought was almost more than Mary could bear, and it brought her crashing back to earth again. No, if she were to go anywhere, it had much better be Longbourn. As mistress of that house, she could see as much or as little of her Netherfield neighbors as she liked.

As Mary climbed into bed and pulled the covers snugly up under her chin, she reminded herself that tomorrow would be a holiday for her. 'Do as you like,' Mr. Farnsworth had said. Very well, then. What appealed most to her was to forget her employer, at least temporarily, and spend time in the company of someone far easier to get along with. Mary therefore earnestly tried to replace every thought of Mr. Farnsworth with an image of Mr. Tristan Collins.

Even before falling asleep she had formulated her plan, and upon first waking she reviewed it to be sure it still appeared sound in the clear light of day. The more she considered it, though, the more excellent a scheme it seemed.

Mary could feel a flutter of excitement building inside her chest as she dressed. She did not own a proper riding habit, so she once again chose the gown that had served as the most suitable substitute. Then, after breakfasting with the children and seeing them down the front stairs to meet their father, Mary slipped out the back way and across the lawn to the stables.

"Will you please saddle Arielle for me?" she asked the first boy she met with there.

"Yes, Miss," he said and trotted off down the passageway between the double row of box stalls.

Two other young men, one of whom she recognized as the groom who had assisted her before, then came from the direction of the house. "Did you need something, Miss Bennet?" the familiar face asked.

"I just sent the boy to saddle Arielle for me."

"Johnny," the first young man told the other groom, "you had best check on Charlie and then saddle another horse for me." Turning back to Mary, he continued, "I must ride with you, Miss. Master said you was never to go off unescorted."

"I see," Mary replied coolly, although it was not this man that annoyed her. It was the one who had given the order. It appeared that even his 'do as you like' had its limitations. "Very well," she said. "I suppose I ought to know your name then."

"It's William, Miss."

"So tell me, William, have the carriages got off all right?" she inquired, supposing that to be the reason he had been needed up at the house.

"They have indeed. It looked like a very merry party. A pity you could not go along, if you will excuse me sayin' so."

"I have my own little excursion planned. You can see me as far as Longbourn. I am meeting a friend there, and he will bring me back safe. That should satisfy Mr. Farnsworth's requirements."

In a few minutes more they were underway, and the distance itself was only three miles. Upon arrival at Longbourn, Mary rode past the house. Seeing no one there to either help or greet her, she continued on to the small stables – a fraction of the size of those at Netherfield – whereupon she dismounted with William's help, and then promptly dismissed him. Although he was none too willing to go, Mary was so firm that she gave him no choice.

Mr. Jeffers – the man who served as Longbourn's single coach-man, groom, and stable hand – was nowhere to be found. And then she noticed the vacant carriage house with its door standing ajar. Leaving Arielle in an empty box, Mary hastened to the house.

"Oh, Hill, there you are," she said, meeting the housekeeper immediately upon entering. "I saw the carriage was missing. Have they all gone out, then?"

"Yes, Miss Mary, all except Miss Kitty, I believe. Mrs. Bennet and the others left for Meryton, oh, it must be an hour past by now. But Miss Kitty, who was feeling unwell, took herself off to bed instead."

"Do you know if Mama intends to be gone long?"

"I shouldn't think so. Mrs. Bennet wished to give Mr. and Miss Beam a tour of the village, and how long could that take? There is not much to it, after all. I should think they will all be back within the hour, if you should care to wait, Miss."

Mary sighed. "Yes, there is nothing else to be done, I suppose." Thinking a minute, she added, "I shall just go up to my old room, Hill. There was something I had meant to look for in that trunk of mine, and I might as well do it now as another time."

"Very good, Miss."

With the last puff of wind now fully escaped from her sails, Mary mounted the stairs in no particular hurry. This was not at all the way she had pictured the day going forward. She was to have glided gracefully up to Longbourn, alone. Mr. Tristan, perceiving her presence, would have observed her approach, remembered his promise to go riding with her, and dashed out to meet her. Before any of the others could even think of joining them, they would have been off on another delightful adventure together. It would no doubt have been hours before they returned, having become entirely caught up in the pleasure of each other's company, and perhaps by then an understanding between them would have been secured. Now, though...

Passing the closed door to Kitty's bedchamber, Mary paused, de-ciding she should look in on her ailing sister. Not wishing to wake her, she omitted knocking and noiselessly eased the door open. Though the curtains had been drawn, and the room was dark, Mary at once sensed something was not as it should be. There were mur-

murings where there should have been silence, movement where there should have been none. As her eyes adjusted to the lack of light, Mary saw – not Kitty asleep in bed as she had expected, but Kitty in a state of partial undress and standing in the passionate embrace of a man. The man was none other than Tristan Collins.

33

Elucidation

Mary cried out in horror and then fled down the stairs and out of the house. She ran not knowing where she was going, her only thought to escape the dreadful picture now seared into her brain. It was a nightmare; it had to be. The only other explanation was that Kitty – dear, vulnerable Kitty – had gone the way of their sister Lydia, not waited for benefit of marriage to part with her maidenhood. That it should be to Mr. Tristan and not some other man that Kitty had chosen to sacrifice all now seemed of limited importance.

If only time could be wound back an hour, Mary's addled mind suggested by way of a solution. If only she had never taken it into her head to make a surprise visit to Longbourn! She turned toward the stables. She must undo what had been done; she must get back in the saddle and return to Netherfield before anything else occurred to verify that what she had seen was real.

Although Arielle was ready and waiting, there was no one to help Mary mount. She was looking about for something to climb on top of when she heard her name being called out. It was Kitty's voice, and it threw Mary into a state of panic. She had to get away; the last person she wished to confront at that moment was her fallen sister. She did not know if she would ever be able to look her in the face again, much less so soon.

"Oh, Mary! There you are," said Kitty flying into the stables out of breath.

Mary looked past her for a way of escape, but there was none.

"Dear, Mary," Kitty continued, coming toward her with her arms outstretched. "What a shock I have given you! You must allow me to explain."

"I want none of your explanations. Now let me pass."

"I will not!" said Kitty, taking hold of Mary's arms. "You shall not go away thinking there was anything improper in what you saw. Tristan and I... well, it is not what it appeared."

Mary pulled free of her grasp. "A man and a woman alone, behind a closed door in a darkened room, with... I need not go on; you know what you were doing. How can that not be improper?"

"Because, my dear sister, Tristan and I are husband and wife. We are married."

"Married!"

"Yes, I am sorry for your finding out in such a way. Still, it is better you should know the truth now than to continue in ignorance and misapprehension."

Mary leant back against the wall that formed the outside of Arielle's stall and slid slowly down to sit in the hay at its base. She was too weak to stand, and too stunned to speak. She simply gaped at her sister and waited helplessly for whatever would come next.

Kitty lowered herself to sit alongside Mary. "We eloped, you see, to Gretna Green when everybody left us alone at Pemberley for three days to attend Jane. We snuck off and back again, and no one the wiser. You will think it imprudent, I daresay. And perhaps we should have waited for the year of mourning to be done and then married at Longbourn Church in front of all our friends. We had planned it so ourselves, until we found that we loved each other too ardently to keep apart for all those months. So we were secretly married instead, with the intention of waiting until the proper time to announce it. Now you know all, Mary. Can you forgive us?"

Mary could not answer. She needed more time – much more time – to adjust her disordered thinking, to extract this hard new truth from the agreeable fiction she had been used to believing.

"Say something, Mary. I know this has come as a shock, but you did tell me at Pemberley that you would wish us happy when the time came."

"And *you* said at Pemberley that you were not engaged!"

"It was the truth, for we were not engaged but married when you asked."

"Too late, then," Mary muttered with hands to her face. "It was always too late."

"Too late?" Kitty repeated. "Too late for what?"

Mary trembled with pent-up emotion. She wanted to scream at her sister or rage at the world in general. Instead, she was obliged to sit sedately and produce a plausible response. "I was thinking about ... about poor Miss Beam," Mary finally choked out. "She came all this way and tried so hard, but she never had a chance, did she?"

"Miss Beam! You must not feel sorry for her. She *did* have her chance, in truth, and squandered it."

"Oh, I see. Tristan has told you this?"

"On Sunday, when you did such a fine job of distracting the others. He said there was a time when he liked her very much, and he might have married her then if she had given him any encouragement. Miss Beam, however, had set her cap at a richer man, one who has apparently since thrown her over. So now, upon her brother's urging, she has come crawling back to Tristan. Although, as you say, it is too late, and so Tristan has privately told Mr. Calvin Beam. They are to clear out tomorrow and back to America. I say good riddance to them too!"

"You have won the prize, Kitty. You could afford to be a little more charitable to the losers." Another thought struck Mary. "Does Mama know any of this?"

"No! We dare not tell her."

"Why not? She might be angry to have been cheated out of another wedding, but she would forgive you soon enough when she realizes that both Mr. Collins and Longbourn are secure."

"I daresay she would! No, it is not for fear of her anger; it is for fear that she will be incapable of keeping our marriage to herself. First it would be our aunt Phillips, and then Lady Lucas. Before the week is out the whole parish and beyond will know it. And we should still like to wait until January before announcing anything. We thought we could visit my aunt and uncle in Gracechurch Street this winter and return home married, as if the ceremony had taken place in London. For my part, I would as soon tell the world this minute, but Tristan is anxious to establish a good name for himself in this neighborhood. He wishes everything to appear right and proper, with no disrespect to the memory of our late, honoured father, may God rest his soul."

Calmer now, Mary advised, "That being the case, you had better pray not to be blessed with a child too soon. The common folk round about may not be exceptionally bright, but I would wager they can, every one of them, count to nine."

Kitty blushed profusely and laughed. With bittersweet feelings, Mary embraced her sister and wished her happy. There was clearly nothing else to be done.

"Now, dearest Mary," Kitty continued, after they released each other. "If you are sufficiently recovered from your shock, you must come back into the house. Tristan is as worried about you as I was. So, let me intreat you to say and look every thing that may set his heart at ease, and incline him to be satisfied that you are pleased with the match."

"You must allow me a few minutes alone to compose myself first." Mary got to her feet, and her sister did likewise.

"Very well, if you promise not to fly off again."

Mary offered a reassuring smile. "I will be along presently, Kitty. I might just take a turn in the garden first."

With a look of pure contentment, Kitty scampered off – back to her house and to her husband, their ownership being now irrevocably established.

Mary's own smile faded as soon as her sister left her and cold reality came home. It was over. The time had come to face that truth squarely. The impossible dream she had been clinging to had proved genuinely impossible after all. She had resolved once before to give Tristan up, and now it had to be done in earnest. Henceforth, he was her brother and nothing more. And there was an end to it.

Before Mary had summoned enough courage to return to the house and face her cousin, she heard and then saw Mrs. Bennet's carriage approaching up the gravel sweep. Her heart sank within her. There could be no more delay. Now, exertion was indispensably necessary, and she struggled so resolutely against the oppression of her feelings, that her success was speedy and for the time complete.

Being thankful that she had no tears to betray her true state of mind, Mary feigned cheerfulness and greeted the three persons alighting from the carriage – Mr. Beam first, who then assisted Mrs. Bennet and Miss Beam out. Then, turning to Mr. Jeffers on the box, Mary asked him to attend to Arielle as soon as he was able.

"Well, Mary," said Mrs. Bennet. "What do you think? We have been to Meryton, where I have acquainted our American friends with all the comforts and conveniences an English village can afford. And what do you do here? I never expect to see you at Longbourn any time but Sunday."

"I was given an unexpected holiday," Mary explained as they all proceeded into the house. "Mr. Farnsworth has taken the children with him on an outing."

"Oh, yes!" Mrs. Bennet exclaimed, her voice rising with excitement. "The goings on at Netherfield – that is the subject on everybody's lips in Meryton. Mrs. Elkhorn said she had seen ever so many fine carriages bound in that direction on the London road. My sister Phillips heard from the butcher that Mrs. Nicholls had come from Netherfield on Monday to order in a vast quantity of meat for Wednesday, and a good deal more for Saturday. It is also said that musicians were brought in for a ball last night. But I suppose you have observed little of the business yourself, Mary. What a shame, for it must have been a grand affair. Since I was not invited, I should very much have liked to be a mouse in the corner – to behold the splendor, and to see if the master was dancing and with whom. They say he has done it all to impress a lady, and that there might be a new Mrs. Farnsworth before long."

With such fresh and interesting fodder for discussion, Mrs. Bennet was able to carry the preponderance of the conversation through until dinner and beyond. Mary was called upon primarily to contribute what factual information she could supply from her first-hand knowledge of Netherfield. The rest Mrs. Bennet was perfectly content to leave to the authority of her own speculation. Mr. Beam served as a useful foil, providing just enough conversation to encourage and sustain her efforts. The others, for their various reasons, contributed little.

For once, Mary was glad for her mother's facility for talking, and she could not even be bothered to care about her lack of sense and decorum. Along with the clock in the hall, she was just marking time, waiting in suspense until she could go, and the less attention paid her the better. Directly after dinner she made her excuses.

"I must be getting back," she told them all upon their repairing to the drawing room. "Mr. Beam, Miss Beam, since I will not be seeing you again before you sail, I wish you a safe and comfortable journey home. Now, if you will pardon me, I shall take my leave."

Miss Beam nodded, and the gentlemen rose when Mary did.

"So good to have met you, Miss Bennet," said Mr. Beam, taking her hand and bowing over it.

"You came on horseback, I understand, Miss Mary," said Tristan.

"I did."

"Then you must allow me to accompany you back to Netherfield."

"I thank you, sir, but I assure you it is entirely unnecessary. I am perfectly capable of traveling the three miles on my own."

"I insist," he said. "It will be my honor and my pleasure." With this he escorted her from the room, and they both made their way to the stables.

Little more passed between them until they were mounted and underway. Even then, Mary did not know where or how to begin, so great was her discomfiture at being alone with her cousin after all that had occurred. She was embarrassed for what she had seen and found out that day, but still more so for what she had said to him the previous Sunday. Had he understood, or at least suspected, her feelings and wishes? Had he pitied her or, worse yet, laughed at her behind her back for her pathetic illusions? Mortifying. Mary could only hope he had been as blind to her desires as she had been to his, and she waited for him to reveal the truth of the matter by what he said next.

178

"This is a time for redeeming promises made," said Tristan, once they had passed beyond the boundaries of Longbourn Park.

His remark was not at all what Mary had expected. "How do you mean, sir?" she inquired.

"I promised myself that we would one day have a ride together. Have you forgotten?"

"Oh, yes, perhaps I had," she lied.

"I am not surprised; no doubt the idea was far more significant to me than it could possibly have been to you. Then, more recently, you generously promised to be my confidante, if I should need one – that you would hear whatever I should wish to say, and tell me exactly what you thought. Those were your very words, which I took as a clear proof of your sincere and impartial friendship. I hope what has happened has not changed that. Your continued friendship means a great deal to me, Mary – and more now too, for we are brother and sister."

"True, I did promise it… out of friendship, as you say, and because of my general inclination to be of use wherever I can. The situation is somewhat altered now, however. I now know what I did not then. You have a wife, sir, and she must be your primary confidante."

"Very well said. Then I shall simply ask you this. Tell me what you honestly think of my having married your sister. Can you be happy for us, and will you forgive the shock we gave you earlier today?"

"It is my Christian duty to forgive, Mr. Collins, and I do so willingly. As for my being happy for you and Kitty, that I trust will come in time. I cannot think it prudent for you to have entered into wedlock so precipitously. But when your marriage proves to be a blessing to yourselves and to others, how could I refuse to be delighted for it as well?"

"I see I shall have to be satisfied with that for now. It is an awkward beginning, I concede, and yet I wish you to believe there will be no reason for anybody to repine over what we have done. I shall make it my life's work to see that your sister is happy. Your mother will be cared for as well; she need never leave her home if she does not wish to."

"That is admirable indeed, Mr. Collins, especially the latter part. Not every man would be prepared to practice forbearance to such a degree, even for a wife that he loves."

"We all have our little foibles, Miss Mary," he said chuckling, "and your mother is certainly no exception. Fortunately, I seem to

179

have been blessed with a more patient nature than most. I am not quickly provoked by the follies of others. And I believe Kitty will be easier having her mother close at hand; that is reason enough. You know her best, though, my dear sister. Is there anything else you can suggest I do for my wife's comfort, or for your family's peace of mind?"

"No, Mr. Collins. You seem to have thought of everything."

They rode along in silence for a considerable time, the discomfort between them a little eased for their already having gracefully covered the necessary ground. Mary still did not know with certainty what Tristan might have suspected of her amorous intentions – and most probably she never would – although, after this first test, it at least appeared unlikely he would ever allude to comprehending anything of the sort. That was some relief.

At Tristan's suggestion, they prodded their mounts into first a canter and then finally a full gallop over the last mile to Netherfield. With the warm breeze blowing across her cheeks and whistling past her ears, Mary could not help but feel some of that same exhilaration she had originally expected from when they would at last have their ride together. In fact, she was laughing by the time they reined in their horses at the entrance to the stables.

Tristan slid to the ground first and then helped Mary dismount from Arielle. At that moment, Mr. Farnsworth emerged from the doorway of the stables.

"Ah, Mr. Collins," he said stiffly. "Thank you for returning Miss Bennet, but I can take over from here. We need not detain you any longer."

"It has been my pleasure, believe me, Mr. Farnsworth. It was good of you to spare Mary today."

"Can I give you a leg up, then?"

"No need," answered Tristan, throwing himself atop his horse and swinging into position. "Good day, Cousin Mary," he said, tipping his hat before riding away.

Once her cousin was a little down the lane, Mary turned to her employer. "That was rude of you, sir."

"Was it?" he said absently, turning Arielle over to a groom.

"You know very well it was," Mary scolded, starting toward the house. "You practically warned Mr. Collins off your land."

Mr. Farnsworth fell into step beside her. "Perhaps I am not feeling sociable today. What do you say to that?"

"I say is a great pity, for you have a house full of guests. Did your expedition fail to live up to expectations, Mr. Farnsworth? Is that what has put you in such a foul mood?"

"Me? In a foul mood? Never. I am only a little concerned for one of the carriage horses, which has come up lame. That is why you found me in the stables rather than with my guests. Oh, I hope you did not think I waited there in compliment to you, Miss Bennet."

"Not at all. Why on earth should I?"

"No reason, really." After a moment he continued sardonically, "So it is for your beloved cousin that you have thrown me over, I suppose."

"What?"

"No doubt you are his favorite as well. I see how it is."

It was too much – salt in a fresh wound. "No, Mr. Farnsworth! You see nothing, for there is nothing to be seen. Only a blind person or a fool could suppose that Mr. Tristan Collins thought of me in that way, that he could ever have preferred..." Mary broke off and strode purposefully away from him toward the service entrance, a place the master of the house would hardly dare to follow.

35

Change in the Air

With guests in the house, the Farnsworth children did not go down to take their supper with their father as they often did. They ate in the nursery instead that evening, and Mary with them. At least with the children, there was no question of awkwardness or embarrassment for her. They could know nothing of her humiliation that day, nothing of her disappointed hopes. In fact, her three young friends seemed her only consolation. Whilst they were still in her charge, she had companionship, useful employment, and some measure of purpose to each day.

"How was your outing to St. Albans, children?" Mary asked when she joined them, taking care to sound cheerful. They all started talking at once. "Patience," she cautioned. "One at a time. Gwen, you first. Was it everything you had hoped for?"

"Oh, yes… and no. The picnic was delightful and the cathedral was very pretty."

"That all sounds promising. Was it the company that let you down then?"

The girl nodded. "They are fine ladies and gentlemen, to be sure, but they did not have much of anything interesting to say for themselves. And they could not be bothered to talk to me at all."

"Ah, yes, people will often disappoint us, especially if our expectations are too high. I daresay that was the problem here. You expected society folk to be special, and they turned out to be only ordinary people with airs and fine clothes. And Michael, did you have an adventure today?"

"It was a very dull ride there, for Papa would not let me sit on the box. He said I could on the way home if I behaved. So I tried my best, even though there were so many places to explore that it was difficult for me to be good."

"And did you succeed? Were you allowed to ride home on the box?"

"Yes! Papa said I behaved well enough so that I could. There were no highwaymen after all, but I did see a fox and a barn on fire."

"A barn on fire? Oh, my!"

"Well, it was only some smoke in the distance, but I thought it must be a barn on fire."

"Aha. So you had an adventure after all. What about you, Grace? Tell me about your day. Was it as fearful as you supposed it would be?"

"No, Miss. It was just as you said. We rode in the carriage with Papa, and nobody required me to do or say very much at all."

"I am glad. Did anyone else ride with you?"

"Yes, Miss Hawkins and Mrs. Candleford."

Mary looked enquiringly at Gwendolyn.

"Miss June Hawkins is the lady we saw dancing with Papa, and Mrs. Candleford is her aunt, who came along as her chaperone."

"I see," said Mary. "Miss Hawkins must be a very special friend if your father invited her to dance and also to ride in his carriage."

"I suppose so," answered Gwen. "She did very often smile at Papa. And he must know her father, for they talked about him a great deal. He owns a bank in London."

That made perfect sense, thought Mary. Miss Hawkins was pretty, young, with desirable family connections and probably fortune too, and yet someone who would likely never dare challenge Mr. Farnsworth's authority. "And did you children like Miss Hawkins?" she asked.

Gwen shrugged and Michael had no opinion either.

"I thought she was very silly," said Grace. "She kept laughing when there was nothing the least bit funny."

"Well, I am sure there are worse faults a person could have," said Mary. "The main thing is that if your father likes her, you three must make an effort to like her as well."

"Why must we?" asked Michael.

"Because it is quite possible she will be spending a great deal of time here at Netherfield in the future, and you will all need to get on together."

~~*~~

Mary wished only to drop away into the gulf of oblivious sleep that night. Instead, she lay awake a long while against her will, held hostage by her muddled thoughts. She wondered how things would evolve at Longbourn. Would she ever be able to visit there comfortably again, or would she always feel like a jealous fool in the presence of her sister and brother-in-law? Would Mr. Farnsworth really marry this Miss Hawkins? If so, what kind of changes would that bring to Netherfield and how should she deal with them?

Her logical mind insisted she should sort these questions out according to degree of urgency, project the likely outcomes, and plan reasonable strategies for dealing with the unpleasantness ahead. This self-assigned task soon proved impossible, however. Emotion insisted on playing a part, and it steadfastly refused to obey any of Mary's sensible directions.

Thus, her painful contemplations continued into the next day unresolved. Although the morning was fully given over to the children's studies, the afternoon afforded Mary enough leisure to revisit her troubles again. She gave in to the children's bidding that, on account of the exceptionally fine weather, they could just as easily have their Latin lesson out of doors, using the occasion to review the names of the various flora and fauna they met with there. Once finished, she freed them for taking what kind of exercise they should prefer. Michael made straight for his favorite climbing tree, and the girls organized a game of shuttlecock between them, leaving Mary little to do but keep watch, and no one to talk to other than herself as she strolled about.

"Tristan is gone," her practical side declared, "and you had better get used to the idea at once."

Emotion argued back. "Let me be. Have you no sympathy? I have suffered a great tragedy, and I must be allowed to grieve my loss."

"Bah! How can you lose something you never possessed? Surely you knew all along it was impossible."

"No! I did think he might could love me… at least at the start."

"The evidence to the contrary has been mounting ever since you received Kitty's letter from Pemberley. She tried to warn you; you refused to listen. If you are miserable over Mr. Tristan now, you have only yourself to blame."

Mary waited for the answering argument, and yet her emotions were strangely silent. She did not feel nearly as miserable over Tristan as she had expected – foolish, embarrassed, mightily disappointed, but not desperately miserable. Perhaps reason was right, that at some deeper level she had known ever since Kitty's letter that he was lost to her, and perhaps she had begun letting go of that hope even then.

A cursory check of the children confirmed all was well – the girls still at their game and Michael now halfway up his tree.

No, when she analyzed her current unhappiness, it seemed to relate as much to the loss of her sister as the loss of Mr. Tristan Collins. By her marriage, Kitty had, in a manner of speaking, deserted her. Although their contrasting characters prevented any especial closeness, they had shared a sympathetic bond in being both left uncomfortably unmarried the past five years, long after the others had wed. Now, that single cord of commonality between them had been broken, and Mary felt set adrift.

Other changes were in the works as well, as Mary was reminded when she gazed toward the back of the house. The noise of voices and laughter had drawn her attention to where Mr. Farnsworth and some of his guests had gathered in the shade of the expansive portico, there to drink lemonade and enjoy the warm August air.

Miss Hawkins was beside him again. If she became the new mistress of Netherfield – and all signs pointed in that direction – what revolutionary alterations would it bring? Miss Farnsworth would soon be gone, her services no longer required. This Mary could not lament, unless the lady who replaced her as mistress of the house proved to be even more difficult to get along with. But what of Mr. Farnsworth himself? Mary supposed he would be very much occupied with his young wife. Would he then spend less time in London, or more? Would he neglect his children, or steal them away to form a cozy family life with his new wife? Would he then allow that lady to manage the children and no longer consult with their governess himself?

For reasons she could not rightly comprehend, Mary's heart weighed heavily within her chest as she considered this last point. Surely she should be glad to be spared those often worrisome confrontations with her employer. But the truth was that, however exasperating her dealings with Mr. Farnsworth might sometimes be, she should miss them if they ceased altogether. On an endless sea of routine and sameness, he was the brambly island that gave interest to the otherwise lifeless horizon. Although that island was protected by rocky shoals upon which one might easily shipwreck, Mary still had the sense that the reward awaiting the successful navigator could make the risk of nearer approach worth taking.

As Mary's thoughts had rambled farther afield, so had her feet. When she at last came to herself, it was with a shock for forgetting her duty. Next, a bolt of alarm struck home at a sudden but sure premonition of some imminent danger. She instantly swung round to locate the children. With relief, she saw the girls safe and sound. They had quit their game and were coming to join her. Then she remembered Michael... Michael, who when last she saw him was *halfway up a tree!*

36

Falling Down

In her mind, she saw him falling – falling slowly, as if in a dream, his features contorted in terror. "Michael, be careful!" Mary shouted as she wheeled in his direction. But it was too late; he had already lost his grip. His small body came tumbling down from a height of fifteen feet, brutally striking two lower branches and then falling lifelessly to the ground with a muffled thud.

For a moment, Mary could do nothing but stare in horror. Her brain rejected what she saw, her feet refused to move, and her voice caught in her throat. Then, as if someone had pushed her from behind, she lurched forward, running toward the boy's crumpled form.

Michael lay still as a corpse, and Mary felt the press of what seemed like bands of iron tightening round her chest. She dropped to her knees beside the boy, and for a long, horrifying minute feared there was no breath left in his body. Taking up his limp hand, she rubbed it and murmured his name again and again, all the while searching for some proof that life persisted.

"He is dead!" cried Gwendolyn as she and her sister arrived on the scene. "Our brother is dead!"

"No!" Mary assured her. "He still breathes, but we must get help for him at once. Now listen to me, Gwen. Hurry to the stables and send someone for the surgeon immediately. Can you do that?" Mary directed a steadying look at the girl, who then nodded and dashed off. "Grace, you had better go get your father."

The last instruction was entirely unnecessary, however, for Mr. Farnsworth was already halfway across the lawn, his attention having been drawn by the commotion. "Good God! What has happened?" he demanded as he flew to the spot. The big man knelt and at once caught his little son up in his arms.

"He fell," said Mary, knowing the words to be both needless and woefully inadequate to describe the catastrophe. "I am so very sorry, Mr. Farnsworth."

"What am I to do now? Is there no one to help me?" Mr. Farnsworth cried out as if all his own strength were gone.

The look of anguish on his face was more than Mary could bear. "I have sent for the surgeon. He will know what to do. In the meantime, let us take Michael into the house, perhaps to one of the small parlors on the main floor."

"Yes," he agreed. "Yes, of course. I must get him inside."

"Very gently now," Mary added in a soothing tone as Mr. Farnsworth got to his feet with his son cradled against his body.

Carefully, they made their way back toward the house, Mary at Mr. Farnsworth's side with one hand at his back, ushering him forward, and the other resting gently on Michael's head. Miss Farnsworth and some of the houseguests converged on them to lend their help or hysteria, according to their natural abilities, and Mary soon found herself crowded out by the encircling throng. Mr. Farnsworth paid no attention to anyone. He continued on as if in a daze, his countenance ashen and drawn.

Left behind and thus prevented from ministering to Michael, Mary turned her efforts to his sisters. Grace, who had trailed after, softly sobbing, Mary gathered into a tight embrace at once. Gwendolyn presently came hurrying back from the direction of the stables.

"Has someone already gone for the surgeon?" Mary asked her.

"Yes, William went at once. When I told him what had happened, he did not even take time to saddle a horse – just put a bridle on Jasper, flung himself on his back, and galloped off for town. Will Michael be all right, Miss?"

"We must pray that he is. We must all pray very diligently."

It was with much perturbation of spirit that Mary returned to the nursery. She did her best to console the girls, and yet her thoughts were elsewhere, in a different part of the house with Michael and his father. If only she had paid more attention, they might not be suffering now! If only she had been more devoted to her duty instead of worrying about her own trivial problems, that dear boy might still be well and happy. Oh, what she would give to see him scampering up the stairs that moment, to hear his mischievous laughter echoing in the corridor! Would that sweet music ever come to her ears again?

From the window, Mary observed the surgeon's arrival barely twenty minutes after the accident. Then later, when she judged he would have had time to render some kind of opinion in the case, she left Gwendolyn and Grace, quietly settled with their books, and ventured down the back stairs to see what could be learnt by discreet enquiry.

Mary emerged noiselessly into the service passageway on the main level and crept toward the entry hall, hoping to meet with an opportunity for news there. Although she would not have dreamt of imposing on Mr. Farnsworth at such a time, she thought she might find something out from his sister or one of the servants. Instead, she overheard a conversation that stopped her in her tracks, one going forward between two ladies – Miss Hawkins and an older woman, soon discovered to be her aunt, Mrs. Candleford. Although they were only a few feet away from Mary, with their backs to her, they had obviously not detected her presence just behind the protruding wall.

"The outlook seems very grim," said Miss Hawkins in low tones. "The surgeon thinks that even if the child lives, he will likely never be quite right again."

"In what way?" asked Mrs. Candleford, leaning a little closer.

"No one can say when the brain has been affected. He could be weak in the head, unable to walk, or possibly without sense or feeling altogether."

"The boy is his father's heir too. If he were to die..."

"Hush, Aunt! We must trust it will not come to that!"

"Do not pretend to be so shocked, my dear. When something like this occurs, the mind leaps ahead to the obvious conclusion unbidden. What is a tragedy for one person often becomes an opportunity for another."

"I daresay you are right, and yet it is far too soon to be making plans of that sort. I am not Mrs. Farnsworth yet, you know."

"Soon you will be, however, and perhaps now *your* son... Well, you understand me."

"Yes, Auntie, I take your meaning, but I shall not spend my time spinning a future from what may never be. For now, I must be content with what is within my control. And you can be sure that when I am lady of this house, there will be many changes made. The first order of business will be to find a proper boarding school for the two daughters. I will not have them always underfoot."

"Ah, and what of the governess? Your future husband may be well satisfied with the current arrangement."

"He may have been in the past, but everything is altered now. After all, this accident is entirely that incompetent governess's fault. If Mr. Farnsworth cannot see it for himself, than I will use my influence to make sure he comes to that conclusion in the end. Once the governess is gone, it is only a small step to the idea of boarding school for the girls, and for the boy as well, of course... if he lives."

"I see what you mean, my dear June. You shall make quick work of it too. I would wager that before long you shall be leading the old codger about by the nose and have him thanking you for it into the bargain."

Miss Hawkins laughed behind her gloved hand. "Aunt, you really mustn't say such things. You shall make me sound quite heartless, or calculating at the very least."

"Nothing of the sort, my dear! It is simply the natural order of things. A man likes to think he is having his own way, but any woman worth her salt will learn to master him without him even being aware of it. So it was with your uncle, may God rest his soul, and your Mr. Farnsworth will be no different. I assure you he will be happier in the end being told what to do, as long as you let it seem that it was all his own idea."

Mary slipped back down the corridor. She had got what she came for... and far more. Her own future at Netherfield looked bleak, and yet it was for little Michael that her heart bled – Michael and his poor father. *A grim outlook... never right again, even if he lives*, which he quite possibly would not, according to what she had overheard.

The heavy bands about Mary's chest constricted a few degrees tighter so that she found it nearly impossible to breathe as she slowly climbed the stairs. She deserved to lose her position even if Michael recovered. If, God forbid, he did not, she deserved much worse.

37
Awaiting Word

An expectant hush had descended on the whole house immediately after Michael's accident, and it deepened into a deathly stillness the following day after most of the guests, by ones and twos, departed Netherfield. The party, which had been intended to last a full week, clearly could not continue without its host, who now had no thought for anything beyond his son.

Mr. Farnsworth did not send for his daughters or for Mary, which was not surprising. Mary would hardly have expected to hear from him unless it was to send her packing, and she had very little idea what she would have said to him if she could. How could she adequately apologize for what had happened? Nothing she might say could possibly comfort a man in the depths of despair over his dying son. Still, that is what she longed to be able to do – to lend some effectual aid or comfort, to ease Mr. Farnsworth's pain, and to tell him how very, very sorry she was.

It seemed the only service she could render him was to look after his daughters better than she had his son, to keep them safe and console them in their distress. Even as she did so, however, she reminded herself that she must soon be prepared to give them up – give *all* of them up. That knowledge drove the knife a little deeper.

She remained closeted with Grace and Gwen all day, their single source of news coming from the servants whose duties brought them to the nursery. The only information they could convey, however, was that the surgeon had come and gone twice that day. Finally, Mary determined to risk another foray downstairs, this time making the head housekeeper her object. Mrs. Brand's responsibilities gave her access to every part of the estate, and not much escaped that lady's notice. If anybody beyond the family would know what was happening with Michael, it would be Mrs. Brand.

Mary found her in her workroom and closed the door behind her.

Mrs. Brand came round from behind her table and held her hands out, saying, "Oh, my dear girl, what you must be suffering!"

"Say nothing of that," answered Mary, taking both Mrs. Brand's proffered hands for a moment. "It has been my own doing, and I ought to feel it. What grieves me is that others are suffering for my sins."

"Now, now, Miss, you mustn't take on so. 'Tis a hard blow and no denying. I do not see as how you could have prevented it, though. Boys will climb trees and sometimes they fall is all."

"You are too kind, Mrs. Brand, but I am prepared to take the blame. My only worry now is for the boy. How does he do? What have you heard? I must know, although I dread it at the same time."

"Sit down, my dear, and take some tea with me. It will do us both good." The housekeeper directed Mary to a straight-backed chair and poured them each a cup. "I will tell you what little I know, which is this. The poor boy is alive but still out of his senses. The surgeon do say it could go either way. He may yet recover with most of his faculties intact, or... or he may not. There simply be no way of knowing yet."

"Surely there must be something the doctor can do for him, something that should be attempted. We cannot sit idly by, waiting for Michael to die!"

"Depend on it, Miss Bennet. Everything that can be done for the lad has been done. The master will have seen to that. The rest is in the Lord's hands, I reckon, so there's no use making yourself ill by fretting."

They sat quietly together a few minutes, Mary pondering what she had learnt thus far before addressing her other pressing question. "Mrs. Brand," she began presently. "Tell me about Mr. Farnsworth. How is he bearing up?"

Mrs. Brand frowned and shook her head. "I must say the master looks very bad to me, Miss. In one of the blackest moods I ever did see, and I have been with him nigh on fifteen years now. He refuses to leave the parlor where they have Michael laid out, not for food nor rest, and I hardly know as to which he will wear out first – himself or the patch of carpet where he paces up and down."

Mary stayed another ten minutes out of sheer politeness, but she was not fit company for anyone. Although she had entertained no very high hopes that it could be otherwise, the housekeeper's report had confirmed Mary's fears. Michael and his father were suffering most cruelly, and there was nothing she or anybody else could do about it.

It was with a heavy heart that Mary began ascending the stairs again, paying a self-imposed penance with each step upward by listening to the accuser's measured words, beating in time to her footfalls. "How... could... you... have... been... so... careless?" he whispered in her ear as she climbed. Mary submitted to the punishment as just and right. "Look... what... your... incompetence... has... wrought. Have... you... not... done... enough... harm?" She was completely in the prosecutor's power now, and he drove her on with another harsh word for every stair. "Leave... this... place... at... once. No... one... wants... you... here. Not... after... what... you... have... done."

When Mary at last came out of the stairs into the passageway, she looked about herself in confusion. Something was not right. The corridor was too narrow and the ceiling too low. Things were familiar, and yet not quite as they should be. Then she realized her mistake; in her distracted state of mind, she had come up one floor too far and emerged in the servants' quarters – the *male* servants' quarters. Quickly spinning round to return the way she had come, she ran straight into Clinton.

"Well, well, what have we here?" he said in a taunting voice.

"Excuse me," said Mary, moving to slip by him.

He blocked her way with his long arm. "Goin' so soon, Miss Bennet? Why, I won't hear of it."

"I am sorry to have bothered you, Clinton. I came this way by mistake. Now please let me pass."

"No need to pretend with me, you know. I shouldn't tell a soul you come to visit ole Clinton." With his left hand already resting on the wall in front of Mary, he then brought the right up behind to block any retreat. "You are in enough trouble as it is, from what I hear."

She was effectively trapped against the wall with the large man looming over her.

"No need to be shy," he continued. "Just give us a little kiss." Suddenly forcing his body against Mary, Clinton at the same time dropped his mouth over hers.

Mary struggled against him, but she was no match for his superior strength. And she had no air in her lungs with which to scream for help; his weight had pressed it from her.

"'Tain't no use fighting, Mary," he grunted when he finally finished with what he had termed a kiss.

Her mouth momentarily free, Mary gulped for air and tried to scream. Nothing more than a plaintive squeak emerged.

"I shall have you now, and nothin' you can do about it." Clinton covered her mouth with his hand and began dragging her through the nearest doorway.

"What's this then?" boomed out a male voice from the far end of the corridor.

Clinton's grasp faltered and Mary broke free. She fled without a backward glance and flew down the stairs, her heart pounding in her ears. On she ran, not daring to slacken her pace until she was secure in her own bedchamber with the door barricaded. Adding her own weight to the heavy chair she had used, Mary fought to catch her breath as her mind raced for what to do next.

Was she safe now or would Clinton risk coming after her again? Would his actions be reported, whereupon Clinton would rightfully be turned from the house? Or had it appeared to the witness that she was just as much to blame? She could inform on the unsavory incident herself. But to whom could she go, especially with the household still reeling from the shock of Michael's accident? No. No one could be expected to worry themselves about the governess's complaint at such a time, or to take seriously her wild tale of a footman's peccadillo.

There was only one thing to do, much as it pained Mary to admit it.

38
Farewell

Although Mary knew she might have to leave Netherfield eventually, she had not expected the necessity to arise so abruptly or by such means. In truth, she had hoped it would never come at all. Yet now her immediate departure was imperative. She could not stay another day in the same house as her assailant, and she would not under any circumstances appeal to the only person who could have saved her. Mr. Farnsworth – should he even be inclined to assist her – had trouble and heartache enough of his own.

Unconsciously, Mary adopted his habit of pacing, taking six strides toward the window of her room and then six back, over and over again as she considered what to do next. She was far too agitated to sit still with so much hanging in the balance and no plan for how to proceed.

Where should she go, and by what means? She would be welcome to Longbourn, but that would not serve. Kitty and Tristan were there, Mary remembered with a fresh flush of embarrassment. Besides, it was too near to Netherfield. What she wanted was to leave her old life behind completely, to get away and make a fresh start. It must be a clean and decisive break too, if she were to bear it. No parting scenes or emotional good byes. She wished to be long gone before anyone in the house knew of it, and off to someplace safe, where she would not constantly be seeing and hearing of those now forever lost to her. It must be Pemberley, she concluded. There she would take her sanctuary; there she would in some manner come to terms with what had happened.

With her destination decided, Mary soon had the rest satisfactorily worked out in her mind. Leaving Netherfield would be the simplest business in the world to manage… and at the same time, the hardest thing she had ever done.

Whether it was the thought of departure or the accumulated trauma of the last few days, Mary could not be certain. But when she sat down to her next task, the tears finally began to flow – slowly at first and then with a vengeance. She had no more than headed her letter with the words "Dear Mr. Farnsworth" when the dam that had held them in check so long suddenly could not contain another drop, and the flood burst forth.

She wept for the broken man downstairs keeping vigil by the half-dead body of his son. She wept for poor Michael, once so full of high spirits and mischief, and for the wretched mischance that had been his undoing. She wept for the girls, who were now having the carefully reestablished order in their lives overthrown again. And she wept for herself as well, for her loss... and for how low she had sunk, this very act being proof of the complete collapse of her former strongholds. Of all the emotions she had so fastidiously avoided in years past, self-pity was the most abhorrent and the last to overtake her.

She had striven against it in her youth, when she had first comprehended her insurmountable disadvantages by comparison with her sisters – "hopelessly ill-favored in person and temperament," as her mother and others had branded her. Self-pity had not conquered her then. On the contrary, she had made such cruel characterizations a rallying cry for building up her strengths, her accomplishments, and her defenses against further attack. Now, however, she could no longer secretly harbor any claim to superiority of character or even salvage her self-respect. All was at an end; all was lost.

It was no good attempting to write when she could no longer see through the rivers that ran before her eyes, when sobs racked her body so that her hand could no longer steady the pen. Mary abandoned the letter and gave herself over to her sorrows completely, curling up on her bed and crying into her pillow until she fell asleep, exhausted.

It was some time later when a hand shook her shoulder. "Miss Bennet," someone said softly, rousing her. "Are you well?"

Mary recognized the voice as belonging to Gwendolyn, and she opened her eyes to find Grace also alongside her bed. "What?" she asked, still not fully awake.

"Are you well, Miss?" Gwen repeated. "We wondered when you did not return, and so we came to find you. It is time for our supper."

Mary sat up and rubbed her face with both hands to clear the cobwebs. "Oh, yes, girls. I was only a little tired, but I had not meant to fall asleep. Give me a moment to tidy myself, and I will be along directly."

Again, just as with the recent situation at Longbourn, Mary was required to exert herself mightily in hiding how much her feelings were oppressed by what had occurred... and for what lay ahead.

Sitting down to supper with the Farnsworth girls, it was impossible to forget that this would be their last meal together, or to ignore the empty chair where Michael should have been.

She looked about the pleasant room where she had spent a large share of the last four years and attempted to commit the details to memory – the cheerful wallpaper, the toys and games they had employed at play, the furniture perfectly proportioned to fit the children who used it. Then Mary's eyes greedily took in the faces beside her one last time – first Grace on her right and then Gwendolyn on her left, both now become so dear to her.

Mary set her fork down and got to her feet, saying, "I am sorry, girls. I'm afraid I am not well after all. I think I shall return to my bed and make an early night of it."

Gwen and Grace both rose from the table to say their good nights. Instead of the light embrace and perfunctory kiss they customarily exchanged with their governess, however, Mary held them both tightly to herself for a long while. "I want you to know how very proud you have made me," she told them. "You are both becoming fine young ladies, and I know I can depend on you to carry on as such... whatever happens."

"Why are you crying, Miss?" asked Grace, looking up into Mary's eyes, where the tears had begun to pool once more.

"She is thinking of Michael," Gwen answered for her.

"Yes," confirmed Mary, releasing the girls and crouching down to Grace's level. "Life is full of unexpected turns, and we must do the best we can when we meet with one. Whatever happens, you must be strong for each other and for your father. Will you remember that for me?" The girls nodded, and then Mary left them to hurry back to her own room.

Once there, she steadied herself and set to work packing together the few belongings she intended to take with her. She would have to travel light and hope to retrieve the rest of her things at some later date. For now, a couple of gowns, her personal items, and perhaps two or three of her most precious books would have to do. And money: she could not travel without money. Fortunately, she had been frugal, setting much of her salary aside each month. Now that nest egg would buy her freedom, giving her the means to make her escape.

When she had finished all her other preparations and could think of no way to avoid it, Mary returned to the letter which she had barely begun two hours before. With a heavy sigh, she sat down to commence the task again, taking care over every word.

Dear Mr. Farnsworth,

By the time you read this, I will have gone from Netherfield forever. Due to what has happened in the last two days (of which you know only part), I must resign my position as governess effective immediately, thereby saving you the trouble of telling me my services are no longer required.

There are no words adequate to express my sorrow over what has occurred, for which I hold myself chiefly responsible. I can only promise my continued prayers for Michael's recovery and offer my profound apologies to you, sir, that I failed in my duty to protect him from harm. I also, by my immediate departure, hope to spare you the inconvenience of ever setting eyes on me again, a circumstance which you would most understandably wish to avoid. Toward that end, I mean to accept a position that I have been offered with a reputable family in London, and I will take up residence there immediately.

I do ask your attention one minute more, however, for I must now speak out on behalf of your daughters' welfare. When I am gone, the thought may occur that, instead of hiring a new governess, you should consider boarding school for the girls. I implore you to reject the idea, should it ever be suggested. Gwendolyn and Grace have lost their mother, and now I must leave them too. Do not take their home and their father from them as well, I beg you.

You will say that I have already forfeited any right to an interest in your family's affairs, and yet I find that the attachment of four years' duration is not so easily broken. With my very sincere regard and regrets,

Miss Mary Bennet

Mary reread the finished letter. It seemed so woefully inadequate, and yet what more could she have said that would not be offensive? Should she have told him that she had come to care for his children as if they were her own? Should she have admitted that she would miss him as well, that leaving Netherfield would be no less excruciating than cutting off her right arm? No, it would be selfish, unseemly, and rude to demand his sympathy by citing her own pain at such a time. She should not even think of it. And as for the one falsehood she had told, it seemed a necessary deviation, her only protection against unwanted discovery.

Mary abruptly folded and sealed the letter. Then there was nothing more to do but wait.

39

Escape

Mary waited for the familiar sounds and stirrings of the house to still for the night, and then she waited one hour longer. Only then did she deem it safe to embark upon her night errand. She believed she could leave the house in the morning without arousing any undue suspicion, but not if she were carrying a bag packed for traveling. So the bag, she had determined, would have to leave the house beforehand, under cover of darkness.

Down the corridor and stairs Mary crept with it, wincing at every creaking floorboard and every squeaking hinge. There was a tolerable moon to light her way once she attained the garden. From there she stole into the wood beyond the stables and looked for an appropriate hiding spot – someplace secure from the eyes of passersby yet easily accessible to herself. She ignored the haunting call of the owl above and the various rustlings in the brush. She could not afford to be squeamish at this juncture; everything depended on her carrying her mission through without faltering.

After prowling about in the shadowy undergrowth near the lane some minutes, Mary came upon the very thing: the stump of a large, long-fallen tree, now made nurse to a tangle of new growth. It would, she reasoned, provide adequate cover, and the raised situation would make retrieving her bag from horseback far more convenient. She burrowed the article in amongst the concealing thicket atop the stump, took careful notice of the exact location, and then hurried back toward the house.

She paused on the lawn to look at Netherfield House once more. In the morning, there would be no time to stop and bid farewell to what had been her home for over four years, and Jane and Mr. Bingley's before that. This moonlight aspect would have to serve. The pale stone seemed to glow slightly, even in the dimness, but all the windows were black, all save one. A light burned in the room where Michael lay with his young soul suspended halfway between life and death. This was as she would have expected, for Mary knew a continuous vigil was kept for him there. Never was he left unattended by night or by day.

Mary instinctively drew back into the shrubbery when a figure – unmistakably a man – appeared at the window. Then, looking once more, she recognized him. The silhouetted form belonged to the master of the house. Mr. Farnsworth himself was keeping watch over his son that night. Mary felt her throat tightening and the sting of tears in her eyes. She had not thought to see him ever again, and now this imperfect portrait would be her parting view – imperfect as to the illumination of his person, but perhaps the most accurate as to the character of the man. For all his faults and vagaries, she would ultimately remember Mr. Farnsworth as a man of uprightness and proper feeling.

She was content to remain in that attitude as long as he was within view, daring not to stir herself whilst there was any chance he might see her. Having already accomplished her assignment, she was in no hurry. It seemed they both had the long hours of the night to pass in waiting and expectancy. For Mary, the morning would bring departure and moving on; for Mr. Farnsworth, she prayed God it would bring some relief of anxiety in the form of Michael's improvement.

~~*~~

Mary had little sleep that night – only so much as she could collect between two o'clock and half past the hour of six, fully dressed and sitting in an armchair. She had returned to her room without incident in the middle of the night, and now meant to be off as soon as possible. It was several miles to the nearest coaching inn, and she wished to arrive in good time, with the hope of securing a seat on the first respectable vehicle traveling north.

Although she had intended to tell no one she was going, she found she must make one exception. Mrs. Brand was as sound and trustworthy a person as Mary had ever come across, and she knew her secret would be safe with her. Mrs. Brand also kept early hours, so at seven Mary made her way down to the housekeeper's workroom.

"Mrs. Brand," Mary said, knocking and opening the door at the same time. "May I speak to you?"

Mrs. Brand looked up in surprise. "Mercy, child, but you gave me a start! What brings you to see me so early in the morning? Nothing amiss, I pray."

"No, nothing seriously amiss. I have come to bid you good bye; that is all."

"Good bye, you say. What is it you are about, Miss? You do not mean to leave Netherfield, do you?"

"Yes, almost this moment, Mrs. Brand, and you must not try to dissuade me. I am determined to go directly. I have said nothing about it to anybody. It would only be giving trouble needlessly. But I am certain that my leaving is the right and necessary thing after all that has happened."

"Oh, no, you must not go away because you blame yourself for the business with Michael. No one else will, and besides, the young ladies need you."

"My good woman, it is enough for you to know that I have very sound reasons for going. And now I must ask your assistance on three important points."

"I still say as there can be no occasion for your leaving, Missy, but I will do for you whatever I can."

"Thank you, Mrs. Brand. First, I ask that you keep my departure quiet as long as possible, only speaking of it when I am missed." Mary then handed her the letter she had written. "Give this to Mr. Farnsworth whenever you think best." The housekeeper nodded, and Mary went on. "Secondly, would you see to it that the rest of my belongings are transported to Longbourn whenever it is convenient?"

"Yes, Miss."

"Very good. The other thing I require of you – and this must be guarded in the strictest confidence – is that you write to me periodically to keep me informed of Master Michael's condition. I shall always regret the part I played in his terrible fall, but I will rest somewhat easier when I know he is out of danger. God forbid there will be any other outcome in the case, although I must be told that as well, should it occur. Will you undertake to do this for me?"

"Yes, that I will, Miss. Where am I to send the letters? Where are you bound?"

"Pemberley. Direct your letters to the great house at Pemberley, in Derbyshire."

After engaging for these arrangements, Mrs. Brand made one final try at overthrowing the need for them, offering such arguments as seemed to her most likely to persuade Mary against her planned course of action. It was all for naught, however, and Mary, suspecting the woman quite capable of conjuring up tears to carry her point, quickly took leave.

Only one obstacle remained between herself and a fair escape, and it again required a degree of stealth and subterfuge beyond what Mary ordinarily had any cause to employ. But her desperation to be away gave her boldness. Taking no notice of the wild beating of her own heart, she strolled across the dew-covered lawn as if it were the most commonplace thing in the world for her to be taking a turn in the garden at that hour. From there, unchallenged, she made her way down the incline and past the grove to the entrance of the stables. It was early, yet she knew there would be somebody about to help her.

Approaching the doorway, Mary first met with the earthy scents of hay and horses. "Hello," she called out. There was the muffled sound of approaching footsteps. "Ah, William, good. Please saddle Arielle for me," she said with as much calm assurance as she could muster.

The groom regarded her quizzically and did not at once obey.

"Arielle, please." she repeated. "I am in a bit of a hurry too, so could you…" Mary motioned him on his way.

He stood his ground. "This is quite irregular, Miss. What can be taking you out at this hour, if you do not mind my asking?"

"I'm afraid I rather do mind, William. You have instructions from Mr. Farnsworth to make Arielle available to me whenever I wish. Is that not correct?"

"It is, Miss. But the master also say as I am not to allow you to go off on your own. Will you be needing me to accompany you wherever you are bound?"

"That will not necessary. My cousin Mr. Collins – you saw him the other day, remember? He is meeting me for another ride. I expect him any minute. So, if you would be so good as to ready my horse?"

William gave her one more measured look, and then slowly turned to do as he had been bidden, coming back ten minutes later with Arielle and leading her outside. He looked about and seeing no Mr. Collins, he said, "Has your party been detained?"

"Perhaps he has," answered Mary. "I believe I hear him coming now, though. Help me into the saddle." After he had done so, Mary added, "Ah, yes. I see my cousin approaching. I shall just ride out to meet him. Thank you, William."

"Wait, Miss…" William protested.

Mary did not remain to hear more. She pulled Arielle's head round and urged the mare down the lane at a canter, soon reaching the bend and passing out of sight of the stables. Then it was the work of only a minute to locate and retrieve her bag. Even if William should raise an alarm over her unorthodox behaviour, which Mary considered unlikely, she would be long gone before a pursuit could be mounted. And why would anybody follow her? She was not a thief who must be run to ground. Other than one of Mr. Farnsworth's many horses, which would promptly be returned to him, Mary took nothing with her that would be missed. Neither did she leave any tangible remnant of herself behind to be long remembered.

40
Miles to Go

Her plan had worked to perfection. She had come away unnoticed and unmissed. She had left Arielle at the inn, paying for someone to see the mare home to her owner. She had then procured a seat on a northbound post chaise that same afternoon. And just before departing, she had sent a brief note of explanation off to her mother.

Now the jostling coach carried her steadily towards her destination and away from the past. Every few minutes another mile was added to the measure of all that divided her from her former life – from Netherfield and its family, from her own relations at Longbourn, and from what she had thought would be her life's work – raising up and educating the Farnsworth children.

Perhaps she should have been relieved to be safely away, and one part of her was. Perhaps she should also have been excited by the adventure she was in the midst of and the new challenge that lay ahead. Alas, she could not be. Although Pemberley exceeded Netherfield Park in every way, and the children there were her own flesh and blood, it would not feel like home to her. In due course, the painful memories would surely subside and new affections might grow to supplant the old attachments. That could take years, however, and how was she to get on in the meantime?

Mary surreptitiously surveyed her fellow passengers – a well-looking young man that she took to be some sort of tradesman, and two rather dowdy women in their middle years, probably sisters from the way they carried on together. None of them seemed to have a care in the world. They could be off on holiday for all the calm smiles of the one and the merry chatter of the other two.

Their good spirits rankled Mary unreasonably, and she turned away from the sight to gaze out the window instead. There, however, she found the broad summer sky likewise inconveniently cheerful. Only the dappled gray clouds skirting the western horizon gave her hope of something more appropriately melancholy in the offing.

After her collapse at Netherfield, she had given herself tacit permission to dwell a while longer in the darkness of her anguish, to thoroughly wallow in the mire of her misery for a limited period. Self-control must be reestablished by the time she reached Pemberley. Until then, however, she was free to feel the full extent of her pain, and to not add the need for exertion to the awful weight of it. When tears came, she let them flow. What did she care for the curious stares of her temporary companions? She would never see them again, and they could be nothing to her.

Instead of vexing her, the long, inconvenient journey was in fact her ally. It gave her time – time to grieve and then recover in part. When the road was rough and dirty, it merely coincided with her uncomfortable frame of mind. And although the accommodations at the inns where she stayed were decidedly below standard, she uttered no complaint. If she could not remain in the great house where she had left her heart, what did it matter where she laid her head?

~~*~~

Mary was three nights on the road. Then on the forth day, she hired a trap and driver to take her the final leg of her travels, using those last hours to compose herself and plan what explanation she would give to her sister for her unheralded appearance at Pemberley. At half past three in the afternoon, she arrived and was admitted by the butler, who directed her to wait in the drawing room whilst he alerted his mistress.

"Mary, how wonderful!" Elizabeth cried coming to her a few minutes later. "I could not believe it when Henderson told me you were here." After embracing Mary, Elizabeth held her at arm's length again and scrutinized her face. "Oh, my dear, you look very ill. What has happened?"

"Be not alarmed. All is well at Longbourn," said Mary, reading her sister's thoughts. "And I am tolerably well also. I have decided to leave my post at Netherfield; that is all."

Elizabeth gasped a little at this and drew Mary to a sofa, where they both sat down. "Now tell me what this is all about. I thought you were content at Netherfield. You have said so yourself on more than one occasion."

"Yes, I was content, but the situation is irreversibly altered now, making it impossible for me to stay." Mary continued by giving her rehearsed account of Michael's fall and Clinton's advances, only just managing to do so without shedding tears.

"My dear, you take far too much responsibility upon yourself," responded Elizabeth when Mary had done. "No sensible person will hold you responsible for the boy's fall, and you are certainly not to blame for the other business! You might yet set things right. Would not Mr. Farnsworth give you a fair hearing, once his son is on the road to recovery?"

Mary's throat tightened and she struggled for self-command. "God grant that Michael will pull through this, but as for Mr. Farnsworth... Well, he is a good man, an honorable man, I believe, and yet one of demanding standards and a somewhat resentful temper. I am by no means assured of his forgiveness, even if the boy makes a full recovery. Besides, Mr. Farnsworth is contemplating a new marriage, and his intended bride has no use for governesses. No, there is no future for me at Netherfield. I must start afresh elsewhere. I rather hoped I might find a place here at Pemberley, Elizabeth. If you and Mr. Darcy will have me, I thought I might make myself useful with the children."

"Oh, my goodness, Bennet would love it! He has not stopped talking of his Aunt Mary since you were here the last time, reciting his poem and playing the little ditty you taught him on the pianoforte. And I can speak for my husband as well as myself; we would be delighted to have you staying. Still, there is no need to work for your keep. As you know, Kitty remained with us for weeks at a time without being the least bit useful!"

Elizabeth laughed, but her attempt to lighten the mood was lost on Mary. Kitty's name only reminded her of another source of grief, one which she could not acknowledge or explain to Elizabeth. "Thank you," said Mary. "If I stay, though, I must have some occupation. There is dignity and consolation in work."

"Now you begin to sound like Charlotte, which is not a bad thing. I would be lost without her efficient help, and I daresay you will prove yourself just as indispensable to this household in time, Mary. You are most welcome here, and you may stay on your own terms for as long as you like." They both rose and embraced again. "And Mr. Darcy will tell you the same. I know it."

Mary started as the man himself entered the room at that moment, saying, "Why, hello, Sister Mary. Very good to see you again so soon." Then, turning to his wife, he asked, "What is it precisely you have foreseen that I shall tell your sister?"

She smiled up at him. "That she may stay with us as long as she likes, of course. Am I correct?"

"Entirely, my dear, as is usually the case."

"There, did I not tell you, Mary. Of course you shall stay. It is all decided," concluded Elizabeth brightly.

206

Mary thanked them profusely and then left to settle once more into the same bedchamber she had so recently inhabited.

When she had gone, Darcy turned to his wife. "I meant what I said, that you were entirely correct in supposing I should wish to welcome your sister here. But what is the occasion for her needing our help? What brings her to Pemberley, and to stay apparently?"

"She says she wants to make a fresh start, to be of service here with the children. She has resigned her post at Netherfield, upset by the Farnsworth boy's taking a bad tumble from a tree, for which she believes she will be blamed, and by some funny business with an impertinent footman. Although I cannot help thinking there is more to the story than what she is telling, for she is clearly distraught, brokenhearted even. Did you not notice her drawn expression and sallow skin? These are things she could not hide. And at one moment, I would swear she was on the point of tears. If it were Lydia or Kitty, I would not be so concerned; rarely a day would pass without one of them falling victim to some crisis – real or imagined. But this is Mary we are speaking of – steady and stoic Mary, who never betrays a hint of emotion to anybody, not even when Papa died."

"What is it that you suspect, then?"

"I hardly know. I have never seen her like this before. It strikes me that it cannot be the loss of her position alone that has reduced her to such a state."

"Perhaps she places more store by her abilities as a governess than you or I can imagine. With no home or family of her own to occupy her, it does not seem unreasonable to me that she should be devastated by the loss of the employment that constituted her one source of pride and satisfaction."

"With no home or family," Elizabeth repeated thoughtfully. "Yes, there is something in what you say, my love. For in losing her position at Netherfield she has perhaps lost far more – her adopted home and family of four years are gone with it."

41

Lessons and Letters

Mary had not fooled herself into thinking it would be easy to begin again, and it was not. The process might have been helped along if she could have kept busier, but the Darcy children were of less than ideal ages for that. Bennet, who turned six the first week she was at Pemberley, was a ready learner, yet even he could not be expected to sit for a full day of lessons. And very little of an educational nature could be done for his brothers, Edward being too contrary minded and James too young.

As a result, Mary was left with more vacant hours to fill than she believed wise. For when she could find no occupation for her hands, her mind worked on, canvassing the dangerous ground once more. It tortured her with regrets for past events at Netherfield, and taunted her with what might be going forward there at present – Michael's unknown condition, how Mr. Farnsworth and the girls fared, if Miss Hawkins continued to make her influence felt. Most perilous of all, however, was the question of whether or not her own absence was regretted. Did anybody there lament the loss of her? Every time the idea occurred, Mary chastised herself for allowing such a vain thought to enter her head. She should not, must not, flatter herself by supposing Mr. Farnsworth or any of the others were missing her the way she continued to suffer over them.

Although Pemberley's excellent library and the well-appointed music room provided some useful distraction from such unprofitable tendencies of mind, nothing seemed to keep them at bay for long. And when Mary applied to Elizabeth for the suggestion of some other useful occupation, her sister was sure to say, "For heaven's sake, take your ease, Mary! You have worked hard for years, and you have surely earned a rest."

It was kindly meant, as were the other efforts made for her comfort and diversion. But the kindness Mary appreciated most was the respect shown for her wish to keep her private business to herself. There was no officiousness. There were no importunate questions asked. Since the day of her first arriving, Elizabeth had not once pressed her for further explanations, and Mr. Darcy never alluded to the past. They both soon treated her as an established member of the household, and her presence at Pemberley as if they could not recall that it had ever been otherwise.

Charlotte Collins also proved herself a great friend in those early weeks. She, more than Elizabeth, could understand Mary's need to keep busy, and, in her position as housekeeper, she was also more able to help. "I was lost when I had to leave Hunsford parsonage after Mr. Collins died," she told Mary. "I had a great need to be doing something, and it was only after I came to Pemberley that I felt truly useful again."

"Yes, exactly!" answered Mary. "Work is a great tonic."

"I quite agree. Come to me when you are at loose ends, Mary. I will find an odd job for you. In a place this size, there is always something that needs doing."

For this and other considerations shown her, Mary felt she could not have chosen a better place of refuge. Yet there was one unanticipated drawback to Pemberley, and that was the person of Mr. Darcy himself.

Mary had been struck some once or twice before by a certain similarity between her former employer and her current host – not so much in physical description as in various mannerisms and in the commanding presence they each seemed to innately possess. When either man entered a room, all eyes instinctively turned towards him in expectation. Other people unconsciously took from him their cue for what was important and how to behave.

In the past, this likeness had been nothing more than a point of casual interest and slight amusement. Now, however, it was an ever-present, ever-painful reminder. Mary could not see Mr. Darcy or hear him speak without Mr. Farnsworth abruptly being recalled to her mind. It was in the purposefulness of his stride, the tenor of his voice, the steady intensity of his look. If she had come to Pemberley to forget Netherfield, and more particularly its master, then she had come to the wrong place.

~~*~~

With equal parts of hope and dread, Mary watched the post for news from Mrs. Brand. Instead, the first letter from Hertfordshire was in her mother's disorderly hand.

Dear Mary,

What on earth can you mean by going off like this, with only that short message to inform me of your plans at the last minute? I daresay your sister Elizabeth is very pleased for your company, but you might have given a little consideration to the rest of us. Kitty is beside herself with worry over you, and I cannot be entirely easy in the manner of your going – sneaking off like a thief in the night and traveling post, as we are given to suppose. And what are we to think of your insistence on secrecy? Have you committed a crime or are you on the run for your life?

You have left a fine mess behind you at Netherfield too. Opinions hereabouts are pretty much divided over whether you were dismissed from your position or voluntarily deserted your duty. There is not much honor in either case. And when I think of that poor boy, lying there, still out of his wits... Well, it seems a very hard thing that you should have abandoned the family at such a time.

My only consolation is that Kitty and your cousin seem to be in a fair way of falling in love with each other. I observe their progress daily, and I have the very sanguine expectation of something good developing there as soon as may be. My little comments about finding another place to live are always met with Mr. Collins saying, "I shall hear no more talk of moving out, my dear lady," or some such thing. That can only be interpreted one way. You know that long before he had ever set one foot on the grounds, I predicted he would marry Kitty. Once they are settled together here at Longbourn as man and wife, I truly shall have nothing left to wish for!

Be of what use you can to your sister, Mary, and do have the courtesy to send us a more credible letter without delay. In it, perhaps you will be so good as to provide some explanation for your rash behaviour and give a more thorough account of your plans. I daresay you owe us that much.

Yours, etc.

These maternal solicitudes failed to provide much comfort for the one to whom they were addressed. Nevertheless, out of duty, Mary did write to her mother, although she well knew that the meager contents of her letter would not much gratify Mrs. Bennet's curiosity, no more than Mrs. Bennet's missive had answered all Mary's questions about the situation at Netherfield. All she learned was that Michael was, at that point, still unconscious... unconscious, but alive.

Mrs. Brand's first letter arrived a week later, bringing information in a more direct line, and yet with little additional satisfaction. Michael was much the same, with no symptoms better or worse than before. Her next, ten days following, was more encouraging, however. The patient now enjoyed brief intervals of sense and consciousness, and this had given rise to a cautious optimism amongst his doctors, and consequently the family as well. They had been told that a speedy cure must not be hoped, but everything was going on as well as the nature of the case admitted.

This news did more to strengthen Mary's spirits and bolster her courage than anything else in all creation could have. It was an answered prayer, and should Michael fully recover, Mary felt she would be cast down no longer. If God would only restore the boy to his father, whole and hearty, she would promise not to grieve over any of the rest.

~~*~~

Two more months went by, and a third and then a fourth letter came from Mrs. Brand. The last one gave this welcome account of the culmination of the boy's progress towards recovery:

"...I wish you could be here to see it, Miss Mary. It is like an awful black cloud is finally lifting and the light flooding back into the house at last. The young master is now apt to talk a body's arm off as not. And the best of it is that all fear for his spine seems at an end. Doctor says he should be up and walking before too much longer. I declare, when Michael wriggled his little toes for me, it was the prettiest sight I ever beheld. You can imagine, then, how the boy's father must feel..."

Yes, Mary could imagine, just as if she were at Netherfield again – Michael's cheerful energy reasserting itself; seeing the boy wiggle his ten pink toes; Mr. Farnsworth's broad smile, liberated at last from long months of anxiety.

Tears quietly slid down Mary's cheeks, and she was glad she did not have to hide them, having gained the seclusion of her own room before opening her prized letter. Although she, like Mrs. Brand, wished she could be at Netherfield to witness these happy sights, she remembered her promise, and her tears were tears of gratitude, not self-pity. With a new lightness of spirit she shared the good report on Michael with Elizabeth an hour later.

211

"Oh, that is excellent news, Mary!" said she in response. "You must be so relieved after having this worry pressing on your mind for so many weeks."

"Naturally, but it is not primarily for myself that I rejoice. I no longer have a share in that family's fortunes. It is for Mr. Farnsworth's sake, and for his children, that I am most gratified." She would not repine, yet the concerns of Netherfield and its citizens remained strong in Mary's heart and consciousness. This she could not help.

Whenever Mary chanced to think of Longbourn, however, she noted that an extraordinary revolution in her feelings had occurred over the past three months. With the initial shock of Kitty and Tristan's secret marriage long since worn away, nothing remained of her anger and surprisingly little of that disappointment which had seemed so all encompassing at the time. Other events had quickly overshadowed it and thrown it into a proper light. Their marriage was a settled thing, and she had learnt to admit it. Mary could not even bring herself to any longer wish the couple unhappy, as she had first done to her shame.

What unpleasant sensations lingered mostly stemmed from her own unbecoming behaviour in the case, and in an odd sort of wonderment that she had ever fancied herself so much in love with her cousin. Mr. Tristan was very agreeable; there was no denying it. On further reflection, however, he was far less well matched to herself than she had once supposed. He was not intellectual or musical; he did not appreciate poetry; and she had never seen proof that he possessed the capacity for much in the way of serious contemplations. What adventures they had shared were of the physical rather than the metaphysical variety, and one without the other was incomplete.

It now struck Mary that perhaps it was just as with the first Mr. Collins. Although Tristan was unquestionably favored with many more natural gifts than his elder brother, it might still have been as much the situation he offered as the man himself that she had been so taken with. She had once again clutched at the unexpected chance to become the wife of a respectable gentleman and, in so doing, being the one who redeemed Longbourn for her family. If it had been foolish for her to think of it, then Kitty must have a share of the blame, for she was the one who had first proposed the idea. It might never have occurred to Mary otherwise.

Even should this not be the full and honest truth of the matter, it was an explanation Mary could accept with grace, and one which she thought wise to actively cultivate. It seemed to her that folly could be recovered from much more readily than rejection and betrayal at the hands of one's own relations. And, the more she considered the subject, it seemed by far the most logical explanation for what had occurred and the change in her feelings since. She now told herself it would be quite possible that she could meet Tristan and Kitty again without any serious mortification or resentment. It was a bold assertion soon to be tested.

42
Surprising News

Mary had sufficient warning of their coming, since the plan for again gathering a large family party to Pemberley for Christmas had been proposed more than two months before the day arrived. The Gardiners from London and the three from Longbourn were all to spend at least a fortnight, and the Bingleys would drive over from Heatheridge some once or twice for a few days at a time. This number would naturally be augmented on occasion by the Thorntons and other local friends.

Darcy and Elizabeth had been to visit all the Fitzwilliam clan in early October and had hoped to entice those they held dearest to return the visit at Christmas. However, owing to the joyously anticipated arrival of their second child before the year was out, Georgiana and the colonel were forced to decline.

Lydia, made newly unwell by the same cause but with a far less cheerful outlook, was also obliged to send regrets on behalf of herself and her expanding family.

"So, Denny has caught up with her at last," said Elizabeth with a mischievous grin upon reading the letter that announced this news. She and Mary were alone in the breakfast room, finishing their meal. "I am glad for him. And at least Lydia has a doting mama-in-law to help her, so perhaps she will not be so cast down this time as she was the first."

"Do you hope for more children yourself, Elizabeth?" asked Mary.

Elizabeth smiled wistfully. "I would not trade my three boys for anything in the world, but I do sometimes wish for a daughter as well." After a pause, she continued. "Mary, would you mind it very much if I asked you something of a rather personal nature?"

Mary looked sideways at her sister. "It depends entirely on what exactly you wish to know. You may ask questions which I shall not choose to answer."

"Fair enough. And you must know that only sincere concern would prompt me to ask in the first place. It is just that I have often wondered if you are much grieved by the fact that you do not have a husband and children of your own? I know you find your work fulfilling, and you have always seemed so fiercely independent that I hoped you were not regretting it in the least. And of course, it may yet happen."

Mary did not respond at first, being entirely occupied with cutting the crust off from her bread in a very precise manner. Then she said, "No, I am not much pained by the lack of something I have never possessed. I believe it is only the loss of something one has become very much attached to that has the power to break a person. The same would be true for you, I am sure. Although you may harbor some regret over not having a daughter, the loss of the three children and the husband you already adore – or any one of them – would be a thousand times worse. Do not you agree?"

Elizabeth shuddered. "Have mercy, Mary! Do not even speak of it! I cannot bear to think of such a calamity. I should never survive."

"I disagree," said Mary, with a distant look in her eyes. "You would suffer terribly, yes, yet you would go on living day by day because you had no other choice. People do it all the time." She then remembered herself and gave her sister an apologetic smile. "But God forbid *you* should ever be faced with such a trial, Elizabeth."

"Yes, pray God forbids it indeed! Now, may we please talk of something more cheerful?"

Although the conversation had subsequently taken an upsetting turn, Elizabeth was at least tolerably reassured by her sister's answer to her original question. It seemed there was no need to worry for Mary on that head. Only later did Elizabeth realize that, far from being the disavowal of serious pain that she had initially taken it for, Mary's statement could just as easily have been a veiled declaration of a profound grief.

~~*~~

If Mary regretted having had no opportunity for a husband and children of her own, as her sister had feared, the situation was soon unexpectedly altered.

Monsieur Hubert, who had at last been coaxed to Pemberley by Mr. Darcy's persistence and generosity, had been astonished on his first visit there that November to find not one but two students awaiting him. "Ah, Miss Bennet! *Quelle surprise!*" he exclaimed upon his first seeing Mary. "You cannot imagine how extremely delighted I am to find you here. You disappeared without a word, and no one at Netherfield could tell me where you had gone."

"Yes, I am very sorry for having had no chance to inform you, Monsieur. The change came about rather abruptly," Mary explained. "But now I hope we can go on just as before."

And they had from that day. Monsieur Hubert came once a fort-night, just as Mary was accustomed to at Netherfield. Bennet always had the first lesson and Mary the second. As in the past, the music master was warm and solicitous in his manner to her. As in the past, Mary enjoyed their time together more than almost anything else. And now there was the added possibility of hearing news from him of the Netherfield family. Although Mary had quickly sworn him to silence as to her whereabouts, the silence did not apply in both direc-tions. In fact, she encouraged him to speak of Netherfield at every reasonable opportunity.

"Well, you perhaps have not heard, Miss Bennet," he told her one time. "The boy Michael has nearly recovered his strength. He came in to listen to his sisters' lessons when I was there a week ago, and we shared a few words together. I would not be surprised if he should return to the instrument when he is fully recovered. It often takes something shocking, even grave, to teach us what is impor-tant."

Another time he said, "That Miss Lavinia Farnsworth! She is hopeless! Even *I* can do nothing with her. Always I am saying to her, 'Why cannot you be more like Miss Bennet?' But it does no good. She has no taste and no true feeling for music. I think Mr. Farns-worth is wasting his money on that one. The daughters, I can be of use to, not the sister."

By far the most startling communication he ever related, how-ever, carried no news of Netherfield at all. On his most recent visit to Pemberley, in the middle of December, he spoke purely of his own sentiments. Then it was that, at the close of Mary's lesson, Monsieur Hubert had flung himself at her feet and grasped her hand as desper-ately as if it were a lifeline thrown a drowning man.

"Monsieur!" Mary cried in alarm at being thus attacked. "What is the meaning of this?"

"Oh, my darling, do you not know? Have you failed to perceive how much I admire and love you? You alone have captured both my heart and my soul, and I can hide my true feelings no longer. I am a lost man, Miss Bennet, unless you will save me. Will you not take pity on me now, I beg you, and agree to be my wife?"

216

Mary was dumbstruck by so violent and unexpected a declaration. She could not utter a single syllable for fully half a minute, during which time her mind raced to assess this new information. Simultaneously, Monsieur Hubert's lips rushed to further his suit.

"We will be so happy, my dear Mary. I know it. We think alike, you and I. We speak the same language. Together we will make beautiful music and poetry – only music and poetry... and perhaps children who will inherit the best of these abilities."

"Wait, Monsieur," interrupted Mary, regaining her power of speech. "You forget that I have made no answer, nor indeed can I at this minute. Your declaration has taken me completely by surprise."

"*Mais, oui*! The surprise, it is a welcome one, *non*?"

Mary hesitated. "No, I mean yes. Certainly I am flattered, Monsieur, flattered and honoured. More than that I cannot say at present. It is an idea I never before considered."

"Ah, yes of course, my angel. Your modesty, it has naturally prevented such a happy possibility from entering your head. But now you must think of it. You must take all the time you need to decide. I trust that then you will come to the right conclusion. One can only see how content we shall be together. I am not a rich man, it is true, and yet I can give you a good home – in London, or Hertfordshire if you prefer – and the benefit of some of the best society available.

"One thing more, my dearest Mary. I see that you value your independence, and I admire you for it. That need not change so much when we are married. You shall be free to manage the household as you see fit, to accompany me on my travels or to stay at home, just as you please. I think you will find that I make very few demands on you. Only say yes, and I am the happiest man that ever lived."

Mary could not help being moved. "You pay me a very high compliment indeed, Monsieur. I am overwhelmed by your generosity. Still, I must have time to carefully consider."

"But, of course. I am also a patient man. You will give me your answer when I return in January, yes?"

"Yes, I will," promised Mary.

At this, he smiled the smile of a confident man and tenderly brushed his lips and moustache across the back of her hand. He bowed his way from the room and left the house. Then looking back and espying her at the window, he kissed his own hand to her as a parting salute before entering his carriage and driving away.

It was impossible, of course, or so she thought at first. She did not love Monsieur Hubert – not in a romantic sort of way at least –

and it was only out of delicacy of feeling that she had promised to think about his proposal at all.

That he should love her was astonishing... and also highly gratifying, Mary had to admit. One could not help feeling much for such a man, the first (and apparently the only) who had ever conceived the notion of choosing her for a wife. What was it that he saw in her that all the others had missed? Had he been able to look past her plain exterior to an inner landscape that was pleasing to his esthetic eye? Was he truly able to prefer the qualities of the mind over the more base attractions of the physical form? That must be the case, Mary reasoned, which proved him a man superior to most... and perhaps the best man for her, in the end? What would life be like being married to a music master?

"It is likely to be the best offer I ever receive," she told Elizabeth the following day, when she decided to confide in her. "Very possibly my *only* offer. I am now eight-and-twenty, and I must be practical."

"Ask Charlotte about making the practical choice, if you must. See if she regrets compromising everything for the sake of a comfortable home. You must not ask me, Mary, not unless you wish to be talked out of it. You know my sentiments – that there is nothing more loathsome, more repugnant than the idea of marrying a man one does not love. Do anything rather than marry without affection!"

"But I *do* have affection for Monsieur Hubert," replied Mary, prompted to argue the other side of the case out of a sense of fairness. "Perhaps love would follow, as it often does, I believe."

"Will you stake your happiness, your entire future on it?"

"I only said I would consider his offer, and that is what I am doing – considering all the possibilities. You can trust me to behave rationally, Lizzy. Have I not always done so?"

"Be that as it may, Mary, your rational mind might not be your best counselor this time, for who can by power of reason alone account for the ways of love?"

43
Christmas Guests

The entire company from the south arrived at once, the Gardiners having traveled first from London to Longbourn, and then from there on to Derbyshire in tandem with the Bennets' carriage containing Mrs. Bennet, Kitty, and Mr. Tristan Collins. Hearing the commotion, Mary prepared herself and then came downstairs to face them.

The four Gardiner children, now more than half grown, issued through the door first, followed by their parents. All these were warmly received by Elizabeth. "Mr. Darcy has ridden off on an errand of business," she was saying as Mary arrived on the scene. "But he will be delighted to welcome you when he very shortly returns. And here is Mary."

Mary was soon swallowed up by the little band of travelers and their cheerful greetings. When she emerged again, the others had come in as well.

"So, there you are, Mary," said Mrs. Bennet. "I had begun to despair of ever seeing *you* again. You seem well enough, though, for all your dramatics and ill-judged exploits. We have carried your trunk with us from Longbourn too, just as you asked, though I could little understand your need of such trifles as it contains when you have your sister's hospitality and this entire estate at your disposal. I daresay the library here has a copy of every book ever printed, and yet you could not be content without having your own poor volumes returned to you."

"Thank you, Mama. I am pleased to see you as well."

Mary then turned to where Kitty and Mr. Tristan waited to greet her. There was a moment of awkwardness, each of the three acutely conscious of events – though now nearly four months past – that had played out between them at their last meeting. Perceiving that the other two waited to be guided by her actions, Mary broke the tension by embracing her sister and then offering her hand and a tepid smile to Tristan. "I am happy you have come," said she. "I am glad to see you again… both of you." And, much to her own surprise, she found that it was very nearly true.

"I am delighted to see you looking so well," said Tristan.

"Oh, Mary, you cannot imagine how worried I have been for you," said Kitty, sinking her voice and glancing about. "Going away so very abruptly as you did, and so soon after... Well, I hoped we... that is to say, I hoped the shock Tristan and I gave you is not to blame."

"You may put that ridiculous idea out of your mind at once, Kitty. It was simply time for a change, as I explained in my letter. I am needed here at Pemberley now."

"So I must have told your sister a dozen times," said Tristan. "'Mary has a life of her own and knows how to go about it,' said I. 'She is not so much at a loss for direction as to be ruled by *our* paltry little affairs.' And if I might add, Miss Mary, your nephews are fortunate indeed to have such a kind and capable aunt come to look out for their education."

Mary acknowledged the handsome compliment with a slight inclination of her head. Tristan then moved off to greet his hostess whilst Mary continued with a private word for Kitty. "You do not go to London this winter as you had proposed?" she asked.

Kitty shook her head. "We had expected to stay with my aunt and uncle, if you recall, which became impossible once we discovered they intended to come here for Christmas. But then we thought that three weeks in Derbyshire would do as well for us as three weeks in London. We could have returned to Hertfordshire married and hopefully no one the wiser. That was the plan. The year of mourning for Papa is nearly gone, you know."

"Yes, impossible as it is to believe."

"It would seem but a month or two, except for all that has happened. I am sure a year ago I never had any idea of being married by now to my cousin, whom I had not once set eyes on before! How strangely these things do turn out! And another thing you should know, Mary... "

Mr. Darcy came in just then, accompanied by his dogs, and a clamor of human and canine voices erupted, putting a swift end to the whispered tête-à-tête between the two sisters.

There it was again. Mary felt the now-familiar lurch of her heart at her brother-in-law's sudden appearing. In her mind's eye, it was Mr. Farnsworth who strode into the hall. For that moment, it was Mr. Farnsworth who stopped less than three feet from her, and Mr. Farnsworth who effortlessly took command of the room.

"Excellent!" Darcy declared above the din. "I am gratified to see you have all arrived safely, and sorry I was not here to receive you properly." Turning to Mr. Gardiner and shaking his hand, he continued, "You must have made good time, sir. We did not look for you until at least two hours hence. Mr. Collins, very good to have you with us again." And in like manner he greeted them all – with a bow, a firm shake of the hand, a confident word, a gesture of regard.

However Mary might try to put Netherfield's master out of her mind, it was useless with this powerful reminder ever before her in the form of Mr. Darcy.

~~*~~

Mr. Tristan's presence Mary soon learnt to endure with tolerable equanimity. Although he and Kitty still concealed their real situation, they now made very little secret of their mutual regard. No one with eyes and an ounce of sense could doubt their strong attachment, certainly no one at Pemberley that Christmas, for they were rarely out of each other's company when they could be in it. And if an excuse existed for them to get off by themselves to the garden or library, they were sure to find it. None of this was lost on the others, as their significant looks and knowing comments clearly attested.

Mrs. Gardiner, one morning in the drawing room, nodded toward the couple talking close together by the fire. "What do you think of it?" she asked of Mary and Elizabeth with a conspiratorial smile. "A most suitable connection everybody must consider it – but I think it might be a very happy one as well. One can only sympathize that they are kept waiting. Better that they should be allowed to marry at once."

Mary smiled pleasantly and said nothing.

Elizabeth was more forthcoming, agreeing with her aunt in all respects and prophesying that it would not be long before they heard something definite from the young lovers.

Not surprisingly, Mrs. Bennet was the most vocal on this topic, wasting no opportunity to expound on her felicity, and on her satisfaction at foreseeing the match, to anybody who would listen. Cornering Mary on one occasion, she began anew. "You see how it is with your sister and Mr. Tristan. It is exactly as I planned it all those months ago. Oh, I am so happy! Kitty will be mistress of Longbourn, and there shall be no occasion for me moving out. Of course, I would not wish to be in their way once they are married. All newlyweds need a bit of privacy. I might stay a month at Heatheridge with your sister Jane, or perhaps I will have a holiday at

Brighton and go sea-bathing. Have you never heard me say before that a little sea-bathing would set me up forever?"

"Yes, Mama, and I recall the circumstances all too well," Mary said gravely.

"You make allusions to Lydia's trip to Brighton, I suppose, which never did her any harm in the end. Or the rest of us either, for that matter. Elizabeth and Jane married exceedingly well despite all that, and now Kitty is on the brink of an excellent match as well. When news of her engagement becomes known in Meryton, it may have a very telling effect, for people do say that the expectation of one wedding is enough to bring on another. Perhaps Mr. Farnsworth's plans will move forward again, now his son is on the mend. It was entirely fitting that he should have set aside thoughts of matrimony whilst the boy lay at death's door, but there can be no occasion for postponing any longer."

Feigning nonchalance, Mary asked, "So, is it quite a settled thing that he is to marry again?"

"Oh, yes, my dear. I am surprised you are not better informed. One hears of it everywhere these days. He is engaged to a Miss Haystack, or Harcourt, or some such name."

"Could it be Hawkins, Miss June Hawkins?"

"Very likely so. I do not recall exactly, but it is said she is young and beautiful, and of course rich – the daughter of a friend of his. It was all settled between them months ago. The only wonder was, what they could be waiting for, till the business with the boy happened; then indeed it was clear enough that they must wait till he was sufficiently recovered. And so he is now."

"Have you ever spoken to Mr. Farnsworth yourself, Mama, on this or any other topic, since I came away? Or have you had any kind of correspondence from him?"

"Heavens, no! Why should Mr. Farnsworth want to write to me, pray? And he almost never leaves the house anymore, I am told, not since his son fell ill. Although I daresay that cannot last; he is sure to take an interest in the outside world again soon. He had better, for his new wife will not take kindly to being shut up in that big house. A bride must have her due, you know – parties and visits and all manner of merrymaking. Do you think I shall be invited to the wedding? I will be quite cut up if I am not. It is sure to be a grand affair, and I would not miss it for the world. I always say, there is nothing I like so much as a high tone wedding."

Mary told herself that her mother's information might proceed from nothing more than the false witness of idle gossip. However, with no better authority available, there seemed little reason for skepticism, little justification for supposing the prevailing public theory incorrect in this case. After all, she had seen the evidence with her own eyes before she had come away and arrived at the same conclusion.

Mary brightened when she considered that Mrs. Brand must surely know the truth, and in her letters she had made no mention of any such extraordinary announcement in the offing. But then that good lady had only contracted for reporting one kind of news. She could have no reason to suppose that a development on the romantic front would be of more than passing interest to Mary.

In fact, it was of very keen interest to her indeed. Whilst everybody at Pemberley seemed consumed with Kitty and Tristan's developing situation, Mary's own thoughts dwelt more and more on the distressing possibility of a different alliance afar off in Hertfordshire.

The holiday itself began with a trip to Kympton for church. Later, back at Pemberley, much was made of the Christmas dinner and of the children's enjoyment – all twelve Bingley, Darcy, and Gardiner offspring – and of the special little treats and traditions established within the family to commemorate the occasion. Mary was called upon to render the day all the more festive by employing her musical abilities, playing a number of yuletide hymns and popular tunes on the piano-forte.

That evening, after the children were all tucked quietly into their beds and the adults were assembled in one of the drawing rooms, Mr. Tristan Collins cleared his throat noisily as he rose to his feet, capturing the attention of the rest, as he no doubt intended. Other conversations fell away, and everybody turned towards him with heightened expectations.

"Excuse me for interrupting," said Tristan. "I have something important I must say to all of you, and now seems as good a time as any." He looked at Kitty and received an encouraging nod.

"Go ahead, Mr. Collins," said Elizabeth with a hint of merriment in her eye. "We are an eager audience."

For a moment, Tristan bowed his head in thought before proceeding with deliberation. "First, I must thank you all for welcoming me so graciously. I do not mind telling you now that I came to Longbourn with a measure of trepidation, uncertain of what kind of reception awaited me. After all, there was the longstanding disagreement between the two branches of our family to consider, as well as the more unforgivable business of the entail. You might have rightfully resented my intrusion into your lives, and especially into your home. Instead, I was shown kindness and affability at every turn. I was made to feel one of the family from the very moment of my first arriving," he declared with a smile at Mary, "and all the more so since."

Here again he rested his affectionate gaze on his secret wife. "I am certain, moreover, that none of you will be surprised to learn that

I have developed feelings of a very tender nature for one member of the Bennet family in particular, one who fortunately returns my regard. Now, with you all assembled here, and with the year of mourning for her late, honored father having nearly passed, Kitty and I had wished to take this opportunity to announce our engagement."

A gratifying chorus of congratulations poured forth as each one of the company hurried to register his or her approbation, beginning with the eager but barely intelligible expostulations of Mrs. Bennet. She squealed exactly like a schoolgirl and clapped her hands together before exclaiming, "Oh, I am so very, very happy! But then I always knew how it would be!"

"This is excellent news indeed!" said Mr. Gardiner at the same time.

"Congratulations, my good fellow," said Mr. Bingley next, shaking Tristan's hand. "You could not have made a better choice."

"I am so very pleased for you, dear Kitty," added Jane, "for both of you."

"Lovely, lovely," said Mrs. Gardiner. "This is just as it should be."

Mr. Darcy wished them both joy.

Kitty looked radiantly happy, if a bit embarrassed.

Mary, who was sitting beside her, put an arm about Kitty's shoulders in a half embrace. "So happy," she said, in a more subdued tone than the rest.

Then Mr. Tristan held up his hands to try to stem the premature tide of well-wishing. "One moment, if you please," he was saying as he attempted to quiet them. "If I could have your attention again, there is just one more thing." When the commotion had died down sufficiently, he continued. "There is something else. I said we had wished to announce our engagement, but now it seems we shall have to do more than that, for it appears that Kitty is... That is to say..." Tristan paused and then blurted the rest out in rapid fashion. "Since Kitty appears to be in a family way, you ought to know that we have in fact been secretly married since August."

This news had the opposite effect of the original announcement, resulting in somewhat of a stunned silence. Kitty leapt to fill the void. "It is true," she said. "We fell in love nearly as soon as we set eyes on one another. And we *did* intend to wait until I was out of mourning, but..."

Elizabeth burst out laughing. "But instead you ran off to Gretna Green at your first opportunity!"

"How did you know, Lizzy?" a shocked Kitty inquired.

"Yes, how?" asked Tristan. "You were away at Heatheridge at the time."

Darcy evenly answered in place of his wife. "You should not suppose us to be uninformed about what takes place here even in our absence. No doubt you charged the servants to keep your secret for you. They are a fiercely loyal group, however – loyal to me, that is."

"Yes," agreed Elizabeth, having got her mirth tolerably under control. "With the information they supplied, as well as the way you both had been behaving, it was easy enough to add two and two together and make four."

Mrs. Bennet suddenly found her voice and turned on her daughter. "You are married?"

"Yes, Mama," confirmed Kitty.

"All this time?" continued Mrs. Bennet. "Married! And... and under the same roof. Oh, my goodness gracious! And not telling me! Sneaking round behind my back and... carrying on as if..."

"Yes, Madam," said Tristan. "I am sorry, but I'm afraid there *has* been a certain amount of carrying on behind your back."

"Obviously," muttered Darcy.

"Who else knew of this?" demanded Mrs. Bennet. "Am I the only one kept in the dark?"

"We have told no one except Mary, Mama," cried Kitty, "and we had no choice with her for she discovered us... That is, she walked in when we were..."

All attention turned to Mary, who squirmed with discomfort.

"Oh, good heavens!" exclaimed Mrs. Bennet. "Where are my salts? Somebody fetch me my salts else I shall surely faint." She proceeded to slump sideways in her chair, casting anxious eyes heavenward.

"Now, now, my dear sister," said Mr. Gardiner with calm authority as he came to Mrs. Bennet's side. "There is no need for hysterics. I am sure it was not as bad as that, was it, Mary?" Mary shook her head resolutely. "See there. No harm has been done, so dry your eyes. All that has happened is that you have had your most cherished wish granted even sooner than you hoped for. What is it that you have wanted more than anything these many years if not to see one of your daughters married to the heir to Longbourn? Rejoice then, my dear Fanny, for God has been very good to you!"

By more sentiments of a similarly reassuring nature, along with the bracing effects of an application or two of her salts, Mrs. Bennet was eventually made to see that the situation was not so disagreeable after all. Not only had the wished-for union taken place, but with any luck, a male child of that union was already on the way to securing the Longbourn estate for another generation. All things considered, and despite being cheated out of a wedding in front of her Meryton friends, Mrs. Bennet had to admit there was much with which she might console herself.

No one else pretended to be much shocked by the more surprising aspects of the couple's announcement. Even Mary barely blinked at the prospect of acquiring another niece or nephew sooner than expected. And she could have predicted what would happen next. The men rallied round Mr. Tristan, shaking his hand and soundly clapping him on the back, to mark his officially joining the family. Similarly, Jane and Elizabeth enveloped Kitty, welcoming her into their sisterhood of the married and congratulating her on her imminent entrée to the fellowship of young mothers.

More so than ever now, Mary found herself on the outside, looking in.

45

Contemplations

As the celebration of the newlyweds' nuptials continued all about her, Mary told herself she was not jealous – not really – and in some respects that assertion was perfectly true. Although she might envy Kitty her happiness, she did not envy Kitty her husband. Looking at her open-faced cousin now, she judged that marriage to him would most probably have been pleasant enough – simply and uncomplicatedly pleasant. Whereas marriage to Mr. Farnsworth... Mary felt a hot blush flood her face as she considered it. That would be altogether different. *He* was a passionate man, for better or for worse. Whatever else it might entail, Mary surmised that having him for a husband would never be dull.

"Are you feeling quite well, Mary?" asked Mrs. Bennet after she had taken the place beside her daughter, which Kitty had lately vacated to join her other two sisters. "You are very quiet, and I must say that you are looking a little flushed as well. I hope you are not coming down with some ailment. With so many children in the house, there is sure to be some sickness or fever close at hand."

"I am well, Mama – just a little overheated. That is all. I will move further away from the fire, if I may. Excuse me."

"By all means, my dear. It will be cooler nearer the windows, but there may be a draught. Take care you do not catch a chill."

Mary did go to the windows, glad for an excuse to at least temporarily separate herself from the rest of the group. It took too much exertion for her to affect the air of excited pleasure most of the others apparently felt so sincerely. Moreover, her own thoughts were far away.

Gazing out into the night, Mary could just make out the faded gray of the lawn below, guarded by a few sentinel trees, as it fell away toward the inky blackness of the lake. The filtered moonlight's poor illumination rendered every familiar article in ghostly guise, or was it something else that made it all look so peculiarly eerie? Ah, it had begun to snow, she then realized. For the moment, it was only a sugar dusting, but doubtless by daybreak everything would be wearing a full coat of winter white.

"It is snowing," she informed the others.

Kitty, who had always been particularly enamored of snow, came bounding excitedly to the window. A few of the others followed more sedately. "How thrilled the children will be when they wake in the morning!" remarked Jane.

Without stirring, Mrs. Bennet said, "I for one am not surprised. I can always tell it will snow by how my rheumatism comes on. Oh, such pains and spasms as I have suffered all the day long! But then I never like to complain."

"I thought there was something in the smell of the air today that hinted at snow," said Mr. Gardiner.

As her companions lost interest and moved back to the fireside, Mary remained at the window and likewise reverted to her prior occupation. Her mind returned to Mr. Farnsworth, and how she had seen him venture out on horseback into a foot of snow the previous winter, entirely undaunted. He had made a striking picture – an imposing man, darkly clad, atop an equally dusky-colored horse, the two moving as one out into the lonely white landscape. She remembered feeling a passing and yet powerful desire to join Mr. Farnsworth, to ride out with him, although she had no conscious thought at the time as to why that might be. Now Mary understood it in its proper light. She must have been in a fair way to falling in love with him even then. Was it snowing at Netherfield now, she wondered?

At length, the family party broke up for the night, and everybody retreated to their own bedchambers, with one important alteration from the night before. No one said a word about it, of course, yet it was understood by all that Mr. and Mrs. Tristan Collins would, for the first time, be openly retiring together instead of apart.

They were all paired off now, Mary acknowledged with a pang, as alone she entered her own bedchamber – all her sisters. And whilst she could honestly say that she did not covet the mate of any one of them, Mary could not declare the same for the lovely and fortunate Miss Hawkins. She could not help imagining the joy she herself might have found in the arms of that lady's chosen partner, had circumstances been different.

Even had there been no other woman in the case, however, Mr. Farnsworth would hardly have thought of her in a romantic way. If he reflected on her at all, it was as a person who had once been in his employ, an inferior person, a lowly governess who had caused him and his family great harm, a person who should be forgot as soon as could be.

It was useless speculation to think that things might have turned out differently – worse than useless, in truth. "Useless" implied that nothing more grievous than wasted time would come of it, whereas the true price to pay would be far higher. Should she continue indulging in romantic fantasies about Mr. Harrison Farnsworth, Mary knew she would never be at peace again, never come to terms with the limited option she did have available.

The only offer before her was Monsieur Hubert's. That is what she ought to be considering. It was not a comparison between him and some ideal man; it was a choice between Monsieur Hubert and no husband at all, Monsieur Hubert and being a governess forever.

She had originally taken up the occupation of her own free will; no one had forced her. And for a long time she had been entirely satisfied with her decision, satisfied and proud that she had the wherewithal to carry it off. The work had been enjoyable for the most part, and also the feelings of worth and independence that earning her own bread had engendered. True, there would always be an employer to answer to, but no man was a governess's master, not in the total and irrevocable sense marriage represented. She retained her ultimate autonomy. At the very least, a governess still possessed the liberty to walk away, and so she herself had done.

Why now this discontent? If she had been happy as a governess before, could she not expect to be happy again, especially at Pemberley working under the most accommodating conditions imaginable? Why then did she still feel restless and dissatisfied? Mary realized that she had already answered her own question. It was the indulgence of unrealistic fantasies that had worked the evil, and it had to stop. Once such thoughts were banished for good, there was every reason to think she could be content with her life again – as a governess or perhaps in a marriage of convenience, either one. It only remained for her to decide between the two, and she had a week left to do it.

~~*~~

Elizabeth's opinion on the subject, Mary already had, but, as her sister had pointed out, Charlotte's might be the more relevant one. Mary decided she would seek it out.

"I do understand your situation, Mary," said Charlotte Collins upon first being applied to. "It is remarkably similar to mine some years back. I was nearly the exact same age when Mr. Collins proposed, and my prospects were likewise limited. I certainly had no reason to aspire to making a better match. It was either take him or be a dependent spinster all my days, so it seemed."

"What would you advise me, then?"

"Oh, heavens! I am no expert on marriage, and I would not presume to advise you for the world."

"Then allow me to put it to you another way. If you had it to do over, would you make the same choice? With the benefit of hindsight, would you marry Mr. Collins again?"

"What a question! Perhaps it is as well that none of us is given such a chance. There will be various ruts and pitfalls along whatever road one chooses. I daresay none of us should ever be content if we were always thinking about how we might have taken a different path."

Mary struggled to keep her impatience in check. "Yes, of course, but would you not agree that we should be foolish indeed to hazard our own mistakes when we might have easily avoided them by learning from the wisdom of those who have gone before us? That is what I have in view by asking you these things, Charlotte – to benefit from your experience. Surely you would not deprive me of that chance."

"Very well, Mary. I shall do my best by you." Charlotte took a moment to consider before answering. "This much I believe I may tell you without disrespect to my late husband. Most days, I was quite content with my decision to accept his proposal. After all, I had made it with eyes wide open. I did not expect (nor indeed was I to find) grand passion in my marriage, or even the sweet consolation of a likeminded partner. I had asked only for a comfortable home and the claims to reputation marriage can provide. These things I achieved, thanks to Mr. Collins. The more irksome aspects of the arrangement I dealt with as well as I might."

"And did you never suffer any serious melancholy over it, any painful regrets?"

"Melancholy? No, but then I suppose it is not in my nature. I believe I possess the happy knack of being content in whatever situation I find myself. I do admit there were times in our short marriage when I experienced a certain kind of regret. I regretted that I could not love and respect my husband as is a wife's duty. And I regretted that there could never be a true oneness of thought or spirit between us. It was not so much that I felt sorry for myself, you understand; for as I have said, I entered into the arrangement with eyes wide open. It is more that I recognized how far short we fell of the ideal God intended."

"That is true of every person and every human endeavor," rejoined Mary.

"Precisely so, which is why I was not in the least surprised by it nor even very much discouraged. It is all in one's expectations, I think. If one expects perfect bliss in marriage, one will always be disappointed. By contrast, if one's expectations are kept within reasonable proportions…"

"Kept low, in other words," Mary interjected.

Charlotte gave an assenting nod. "…then one will never be let down, only sometimes pleasantly surprised when things turn out better than anticipated."

"So you do not regret your marriage."

"No." Charlotte then allowed herself a half smile. "But neither do I much regret its being over. The position I now occupy suits me far better."

Over the course of the next few days, Mary thought long and hard about what Charlotte had said to her. Their situations – Charlotte's then and her own now – were indeed similar. In addition, Mary had always seen a likeness between Charlotte and herself – the practical turn of their minds, and their mutual satisfaction in being usefully employed – which made her opinion even more valuable.

Yet there were important differences in their respective cases as well. For one, she did not consider Monsieur Hubert to be entirely lacking the makings of a good husband. He certainly had the advantage over what Charlotte's spouse had been. Monsieur Hubert was someone Mary held in high regard, someone she would be able to wholeheartedly respect if not love. And there was a far greater basis for oneness of mind and spirit between them as well, considering their common devotion to music and poetry. So perhaps it was not so unthinkable.

On the other hand, Mary was not certain she could lower her expectations to the degree that Charlotte recommended. Perhaps once upon a time she might have, when all she had upon which to base her ideas of the connubial union was the hopelessly flawed example set by her own parents. Since then, better ideas had been awakened, and the glimpse of happier possibilities had forever changed her views. She had seen both Jane and Elizabeth vastly contented in marriage. And lately she had begun to picture herself equally well matched in Mr. Harrison Farnsworth. Could she really put all that aside again to marry Monsieur Hubert?

46
Decision Time

Through resolution of character and hours of internal debate, Mary reached a decision by the day of Monsieur Hubert's expected return the first week of January. She knew what she would do, what she must do, and yet there was a kind trepidation to the idea that the course of her life would soon be unalterably fixed.

For a decade, one unanswered question had been lurking in a little-attended corner of her subconscious mind. Would she ever receive an offer of marriage, eligible or otherwise? The unacknowledged question had been there right along, but it had seemed as if she had, years past, missed her only reasonable chance. Now fate had stepped in. Fate had seen fit to give her one last opportunity. Was it a kindness or a cruel joke that at the age of eight-and-twenty she was finally receiving a proposal? She would give her answer not knowing which.

It should have been a relief to at least have matters settled once and for all. And yet, as uncomfortable as not knowing had been, that very uncertainty had held a ray of hope, the merest whisper of a better life ahead. Now other possibilities would be banished forever.

But perhaps Monsieur Hubert would not come today.

Snow had been falling off and on for the better part of a week. What was a long journey under the best of conditions might now have been rendered impossible. He was already more than two hours late as Mary watched out the window of the nursery, and she had nearly made up her mind that he had been turned back by the weather when his carriage came into view.

She swallowed hard and then called out to her nephew, who was building a fortress out of wooden blocks on the other side of the room. "Bennet, Monsieur Hubert is come. You had better go down and get ready to have your lesson after all." The boy cheered, abandoned his unfinished edifice, and hurried out the door.

The carriage stopped abreast of the front entrance, and the neatly groomed, mustachioed music master stepped lightly out. He smiled as he donned his beaver hat and took in the façade of the house, which included the high window where Mary sat observing him. Showing no indication that he had seen her there, he gave some instruction to the coachman and disappeared from view in the direction of the door.

Bennet would have his lesson first, as always, and then Mary knew it would be her turn to go to Monsieur Hubert. Only this time, she expected, they would not have a proper lesson, but instead a discussion about the future – *their* future... together. It still surprised her to think of it, although she had had three weeks to accustom herself to the idea. Was she mad to think of accepting him? Sometimes she wondered, and yet that is exactly what she was prepared to do if he answered certain remaining questions to her satisfaction.

What her torturous deliberations had really come down to was that she could no longer imagine herself being satisfied as governess to someone else's children, an expendable appendage to someone else's family, not when there was still the possibility that she might have her own – a husband and children that she could become attached to without the risk of being obliged to give them up at some future point in time. She had learnt that much at Netherfield – that she must never again attempt to love by halves. Without knowingly consenting to it, her *whole* heart had become entangled, fully given over to the Farnsworth family, and it still bled every day at being torn away from them. Months of separation had not stemmed the tide of that grief, and she refused to expose herself to that kind of pain again.

She was perhaps safer at Pemberley. Even if for some reason the children were ultimately removed from her charge, they could not be removed from her family. She would see them from time to time, watch them grow up from a distance, and yet they would never be fully hers either. Monsieur Hubert offered her what no one else had – the chance for a home and family of her very own – and she found that in the end she could not pass it by.

Mary left the window and turned her attentions to amusing her four-year-old nephew. She began to read him a story, and then, when he lost interest, she offered him the use of the blocks recently abandoned by his elder brother. After he had worked away at these for a few minutes, she asked him, "Are you building a wall, Edward? Or is it a castle?"

"Not a castle. A church."

"Ah, that is a very good idea. Is a church your favorite kind of building, then?"

"A church has a high steeple," the boy said as he added another block to his growing tower.

"Yes, indeed," agreed Mary. "And do you especially like to build something tall?"

Little Edward nodded. "So I can smash it down again." With a yell, he fiercely swept away the foundation of the building with his dimpled hand and sent all the blocks clattering across the floor.

The door to the nursery opened at the same time, admitting the child's mother. "Good heavens," exclaimed Elizabeth. "What a racket! Ah, Edward. I might have known. Jenny," she continued, addressing the nursery maid cheerfully. "I must steal my sister away for a while. You can manage on your own, I trust."

The maid said that she could manage very well.

"Excellent. Mary, come with me," said Elizabeth most insistently, holding out her hand.

Mary followed her sister from the room without protest. "What is it?" she asked outside. "Can I do something for you?"

"You can indeed," said Elizabeth, hurrying her down the corridor. "You can indulge me in my determination to see that you should take some air today. See how the weather has cleared," she added, gesturing toward the large Palladian window above the stairs, through which the sun was streaming. "You need some exercise to put a little color in your cheeks, Mary. You have been far too long confined inside. It is not healthy."

"Exercise? Now?"

"Of course! I heard you say only this morning that you fancied a turn out of doors, and this clearing may not last. Now, go to your apartment and get properly dressed at once – heavy boots and that blue coat you look so well in. Although the weather is fair for the moment, it is by no means warm."

They had by this time reached the door to Mary's bedchamber. "Wait," she said. "I do not understand you, Lizzy. Why are you so determined to get me out of doors? And what about Monsieur Hubert? He will be expecting me in less than half an hour, so there is not time for a walk."

"Have no worry. I will keep Monsieur busy for you when Bennet is through." Elizabeth hesitated for a moment, and then continued brightly, "The truth is that I have had a sudden inclination to take a music lesson myself, and I would be much obliged if you would be so kind as to step aside for me, just this once."

"But…"

"No more objections, Mary. My mind is quite made up, and I will brook no refusal. You simply must humor me in this. It will be for the best, I promise you."

Still somewhat mystified, Mary did as she was told; she entered her rooms and set about making the necessary alterations to her attire. If her sister wished to take a more serious interest in music, *she* would certainly not be the one to discourage it. And it was also true that she had desired an opportunity to take a tour out of doors. It might be the very thing needed to give her courage, she thought – to clear her mind and sharpen her resolve. No doubt Monsieur Hubert would be waiting when she returned. A little delay would make no difference. He would not come all this way without seeing her, without hearing the answer he had been promised.

An inexplicable anticipation built within Mary as she prepared for her outing – almost an urgency. On the surface, the stark winter picture out her window looked inhospitable, yet somehow it was, in a deeper way, fiercely compelling. It called to her. It invited her to inhale deeply of its bracing air, to feel its enlivening chill penetrating her lungs. She saw herself, not strolling, but running to embrace the cold landscape, to fly with abandon across the snow and away from the confines of the house, if only for a little while.

Down the stairs she skipped. Elizabeth was waiting in the front hall, her eyes sparkling with the same kind of animation Mary herself was feeling at that moment.

"Off you go, then," said Elizabeth, smiling mischievously. "Take as long as you like; I will manage things here."

"Thank you, Lizzy. I still am not certain why you thought of it but... I am ever so glad you did." Impulsively, Mary kissed Elizabeth on the cheek. She quickly donned her fur-lined gloves and pulled her woolen hat down over her ears. Then she opened the door and stepped out onto the porch, straight into the presence of Mr. Farnsworth.

Mary's heart leapt within her chest and her stomach became likewise unruly. A dozen questions sprang to her mind at once. Mr. Farnsworth at Pemberley? Was it really he? What was he doing there? How had he found her? And what could he mean by coming so far? Could it be he wished to tell her she was forgiven for Michael's fall, to let her know the boy had recovered? Or was it possible he wanted her to return to being governess at Netherfield, as she had longed for every day since she left the place?

But Mary said none of these things. She simply stared at Mr. Farnsworth, unbelieving, whilst her sister quietly closed the door behind her.

"Hello, Mary," he said, warmly returning her gaze.

"Mr. Farnsworth," she answered in little more than a whisper.

"Thank you for agreeing to see me. Shall we walk?" He motioned with his outstretched hand that Mary should lead the way. "Your sister said you were wanting a turn in the garden."

Mechanically, Mary started off. "Did she?"

"Yes. Mrs. Darcy has been most helpful."

They moved down the steps together and in the direction of the lake. Although the walk had been largely cleared of snow, the frozen remnants crunched with every footfall. At length, Mary recovered her manners and her power of speech enough to enquire, "You are well, I trust, sir? And the children also?"

"We are, thank you. It has been a trying time, though. For you as well, I think. I worried when you went away so abruptly, under duress it seemed, and without giving any specifics about where you were going and how you were to live. London is a big place, and all my inquiries after you led me nowhere. Now I know why, of course, for I take it you have been here all along."

"I am sorry that you should have wasted any thought for me at such a time."

"Michael is nearly recovered now, thank God. He is up and walking and will soon be terrorizing the staff like before, I daresay. But perhaps you have already heard."

"Yes, through Mrs. Brand, and you cannot imagine how pleased and relieved I was for the news. Was it she who also told where I had gone? I had not thought her so untrustworthy."

"Mrs. Brand? No, she said not a word. It was through quite another source that I was informed of your true whereabouts… and less than a week ago, else I would have come sooner." He received a quizzical look from his companion. "It was by your sister's information. Mrs. Darcy wrote me."

"Elizabeth! She wrote to you? Why on earth should she do that?"

"That is something you shall have to ask her yourself. I am only very grateful that she did." They had come to the edge of the lake and both paused to take in the view out across it to the rambling meadows beyond. The air was clear with only a wisp of mist hovering above the face of the water. "I have long desired to see this place, and it is every bit as beautiful as I had heard."

"Still, I am sorry you have had the trouble of such a long journey, and in bad weather too. It was generous of you to come when a letter might have served as well to tell me of Michael's recovered health."

"A letter could never have said the things I wish to say to you, Miss Bennet."

"Let me speak first, sir, please. You must allow me to tell you again how very sorry I am about Michael's accident. Naturally, I take full responsibility. And even if you can somehow forgive me, I shall never forgive myself."

"For what? For allowing a boy to climb a tree? How could you have known what would happen?"

"'Tis a governess's job. I should have been able to foresee the danger and prevent it."

"Then you have an exceedingly high opinion of a governess's abilities!"

"What?"

"Oh, never mind, Miss Bennet. Another time perhaps we shall debate which one of us has the greater share of guilt where Michael is concerned. The material point is this. I knew my son liked to climb trees, and I did not forbid it. So you were not responsible for enforcing a rule that did not exist. That is the plain truth of the matter, and I will listen to no further argument on the topic."

Mary had been fully prepared to battle on in proof of her own guilt. However, when she considered Mr. Farnsworth's statement, she could find no fault with it, no error in logic by which to attack it. She therefore had no choice but to give up the campaign. "Very well, then, tell me how the girls do. I have missed them so. I hope you have not been persuaded to send them away to school."

"No, indeed! I have no clue where you ever got the idea into your head that I might. Michael, of course, must go to Eton eventually, but not until he is stronger. He will do very well with the new governess for another year at least."

Mary's heart sank. "The new governess," she repeated dully.

"Oh, did not I say? Yes, I have engaged a Miss Ellington. She comes highly recommended and seems to be getting on quite well with the girls. Even Michael likes her."

"I see," said Mary. It was all she could manage. She started away from him, down the path.

Farnsworth hurried to follow. "Are you not pleased for them, Miss Bennet? To know that your former pupils are in capable hands?"

"Pleased?" She knew she ought to be. "Oh, yes, that is excellent news, only..." She broke off, uncertain how to continue.

"Yes, Miss Bennet. Only what?" he asked eagerly.

Deciding she had nothing to lose, Mary continued. "Only why are you here, then, if not to ask me to return to Netherfield?"

"Oh, but I *am* here to ask you to return, Mary, only not as the governess. I am come to offer you an entirely different position."

Mary stopped in her tracks and held her breath until she should hear more, a small, hopeful voice whispering one explanation – one glorious possibility, although she dared not believe it. She had made the mistake before of seeing love where there was none; she would not skip ahead only to be tripped up and humiliated again.

All Mr. Farnsworth's natural bravado deserted him, and he suddenly seemed more like an uncertain youth. He dropped his eyes, turned, and retreated a few paces. "It was dreadful when you went away," he said finally.

"Michael's accident," added Mary. "Yes, a terrible time for you, for *all* of you."

"It was." He let that thought rest a moment. Then he returned to face her. "Yet that is just the thing, you see. I realized then, more than ever before, that I needed someone beside me, someone I could confide in and depend on – a woman I loved. Do you understand me, Mary?"

So that was it, she thought. He had come to tell her he was getting married. "Miss Hawkins, I suppose."

Farnsworth looked confused. "Miss Hawkins! How did she enter into this conversation?"

"I understood that... Well, if not she, then you must mean... you must mean your sister; you needed Miss Farnsworth beside you."

"No! Blast it all, Mary, sometimes you can be the most exasperating female! Must I spell it out for you? It was not my sister that I wanted when Michael fell ill, and certainly not some feather-brained girl just out of the schoolroom."

Mary's irritation flared at his arrogant tone. "Who, then?" she demanded. "And there is no need to shout at me."

"Well, if you must know, it was you, confound it! *You* were the one I wanted to share my troubles with... and you were the first one I wanted to tell when Michael opened his eyes again. Look, Miss Bennet, I know I am an old fool and a despot besides, but here's the thing. I love you, and I would rather quarrel with you for the rest of my life than go one day without you again. So what do you say? Will you marry me?"

Mary's annoyance instantly dissolved, replaced by shock of the pleasantest variety. It was not the most romantic proposal, to be sure; however, there could be no doubt of its honesty and strength of feeling.

"Sorry," Farnsworth added quietly. "I had something much more elegant and complimentary planned."

Still in somewhat of a daze, Mary said, "It is quite all right, sir. I... I appreciate your straightforwardness, and I do not desire flattery in any case."

"Then tell me what you think of the idea."

Mary drew a deep breath of the frosty air to give her time to collect her thoughts. "I am very sensible of the high compliment you pay me, Mr. Farnsworth," she continued. "Indeed, I am quite overwhelmed by it. But if I accept your proposal, what will your smart London friends say – oh, and your poor sister! – when they discover you are to marry the governess? They will surely regard it as nothing short of infamous."

"They will do no such thing or they are no friends of mine! And that goes for my addle-brained sister as well. They shall, every one of them, recognize you as a lady of quality – would already know you to be such if you had allowed me to introduce you at the house party ball."

240

Mary glanced at him in surprise. It was a long time since she had thought of that event. Michael's accident immediately following had overshadowed everything that had gone before. How different must be her interpretation of that incident now, in light of Mr. Farnsworth's proposal. "Then you really did wish me to come?"

"Of course. I said so, did I not?"

"Forgive me, but I believed..." She shook her head. "Well, never mind what I believed."

"You suspected me of ulterior motives, I suppose. Is that why you declined? Look here, Mary. I admit I enjoy a lively verbal joust as much as a good game of chess, especially with a worthy partner. In the end, though, I am a plainspoken man and you can take me at my word. I invited you because I wanted you to come and enjoy yourself. I was desirous that you should meet my friends, that they should meet you... and that we might dance together. I even swallowed my pride so far as to take a private dancing lesson in London, since you declined the office of teaching me, so that I might not injure you or embarrass myself at the ball. You cannot imagine my disappointment when you refused to come."

"I am sorry now that I did."

"Well, despite all that, I had no intention of giving you up. I was determined to battle on as long as there was any hope left to me, although lately I must confess to being rather afraid of coming in a distant third in the contest for your affection."

Mary laughed at the absurdity embodied in the idea of as many as three men vying for her heart at once. "The contest for my affection, you say! Then where are your rivals, sir? Point them out for me, if you will."

"One, I know for a certainty, has already declared himself, and I believe he is this minute awaiting you in the music room."

Mary felt a stab of conscience at needing to be reminded that her dear music master waited, even now, in hopeful anticipation of her answer to his proposal. To Mr. Farnsworth she said, "Your amaze me, sir. How do you purport to know this?"

"Here again, your sister has been most helpful. As for the other ... contender. At one time at least, I rather imagined you had become quite attached to your cousin Mr. Collins. It drove me insane with jealousy to think of it, which is when I first knew that I had lost my heart to you. And now the man has been here at Pemberley with you for more than a fortnight, I believe. Has he come in ahead of me as well?"

"Ah! Mr. Collins. Yes, there is some truth to what you say. However, you will be pleased to hear that that gentleman has very honorably retired from the field of battle. He has in fact, sometime past, taken himself out of the running altogether by secretly marrying my sister Kitty."

"Indeed? Well, this is very good news!" Farnsworth said, rubbing his hands together. "I shall be happy to wish them joy."

"As for Monsieur Hubert," Mary said solemnly. "He is a dear man and a true friend. I have in fact been entertaining his suit most earnestly."

Mary paused and hazarded a look at her companion, who stood in motionless suspense. In his familiar, well-seasoned visage she discovered all she needed to know. There she saw sincerity and hope. There she saw wisdom and intelligence. There she saw humor and passion. Simply put, she saw the face of the man she loved, the man who, inexplicably and according to his own fervent declaration, also loved her.

In that moment, the heaviness she had been carrying so long slid from her shoulders like snow from tree branches. Her limbs felt suddenly lighter, and it seemed as if her back could straighten properly for the first time in months. Mary felt herself smiling. She could not help it, despite the passing thought of her music master's forthcoming disappointment.

"Upon further reflection, however," she continued. "I am not certain that dear Monsieur Hubert would suit me any better than Mr. Collins would have. You see, Mr. Farnsworth, both your supposed rivals are far too agreeable. Since they were sure to always give me my way, I could never have had a respectable argument with either one of them. And I believe *I* enjoy a 'lively verbal joust' as much as you do."

Amusement briefly tugged at the corner of Mr. Farnsworth's mouth, and then his expression grew serious again. He held Mary by the shoulders and searched her face. "My dear, although I am just selfish enough to marry you anyway, I would like to believe I could make you happy. Is it possible that you could love me after all? Will you have me, faults and foul temper into the bargain? Will you come back to Netherfield and be my wife, and mother to my children?"

A vestige of Mary's old, guarded ways momentarily asserted itself. It told her to answer reservedly – to accept him, yes, but not to admit how much she cared. Once he knew how broken she had been without him, how lost she would certainly be again should he ever forsake her, he would always possess a fundamental power over her.

She knew this instinctively, and just as instinctively she resisted putting herself in that kind of peril.

"Well?" he prompted nervously. "Do you have an answer for me, Mary, or do you need more time?"

"No!" she exclaimed, jolted out of her reverie.

"No? Is that your answer?" He looked horrified at the prospect.

"Yes... I... I mean no." Mary shook herself and tried again. "No, I do not need more time and... and yes, I will marry you, Mr. Farnsworth, happily."

A mixture of powerful emotions played across his face – surprise, gratitude, and overpowering joy, it appeared. The sight spoke more profoundly than words, and Mary was well satisfied.

"Then you must call me Harrison," Farnsworth said matter-of-factly when he had regained mastery of himself. He drew Mary's gloved hand through to rest on his arm, and they started slowly down the path again. "But are you certain, absolutely certain?" he asked after a minute, turning to look at her.

Mary nodded. "There can be no doubt of it. I do love you... with all my heart, for I have been truly miserable without you these months, without you and the children. Nothing will make me happier than to become your wife." Unaccountably, she began to cry, and once begun, could not stop.

Farnsworth pulled Mary close so that her cheek rested against his chest and her tears soaked into the rough fibers of his great coat. "There, there," he said awkwardly. "If that be the case, my dear, you might start by trying to look the tiniest bit happy now, else no one will ever believe you."

Mary sobbed all the louder.

"Forgive me," she said minutes later, drawing back slightly and blotting her face with the handkerchief Farnsworth had provided her. "I am not usually prone to fits of crying; at least I never used to be."

"No need to apologize. This has been a tumultuous year for you, beginning with your father's death. These kinds of things cannot help leaving an impression on a person, or so they ought to do."

"But I despise excessive sentiment. It is a weakness." She looked up then and saw that his own eyes glistened with unshed tears.

He took both her hands in his. "If sentiment is a weakness, my dear Mary, then I think it is one of which you need not be ashamed. I believe it may be why I fell in love with you, in truth."

"Indeed? How so?"

"Well, I already had great respect for your strength of character and intellect. Then, every now and again, I would catch a glimpse of the person who had let her protective armor slip just a bit; the one who risked all to stand up for my children, even against their own father, and yet was vulnerable herself; the one who might need something I had to offer after all."

Mary felt a tremendous welling up of love and tenderness as she studied the face of her newly betrothed, only inches from her own. Love, yes, but there was something more too – a yearning, a desire for intimacy beyond what she had ever experienced before. She found herself inwardly straining towards an anticipated oneness with this man. Drawing a fraction closer to him, she tilted her head to one side.

Farnsworth understood and bent his mouth to hers in a gentle kiss.

The first brush of his soft lips sent a delicious shiver all through Mary's body, and she unconsciously responded with added fervor, pressing more tightly against him. A tide of longing she had not known existed released in that moment, washing over her in a bittersweet blend of anguish and rapture – anguish for what had been missing all these years, and rapture that it was finally to be hers. *He* was finally to be hers: Mr. Harrison Farnsworth. It was too much to fathom, too wonderful to believe. Mary could not contain her emotions, and as they kissed again, quiet tears flowed once more.

48

Important Communications

They had wandered far along the path that bordered the lake and the stream at its outlet when Mary broke the pensive silence with a question. "Harrison, do you think the children will approve of our plans to wed? Will they be happy to have a new mother... to have *me* as their new mother?"

He turned to her with a broad grin. "You need have no worries on that head, my dear. I told the children what I hoped to accomplish by coming here, and I received a very enthusiastic endorsement of the plan from each one."

So gratified was Mary at hearing this that she could only return his smile with shining eyes.

"What about your family, Mary? Is there anybody I should speak to or ask for your hand?"

"I am of age and may do as I please. Perhaps you might speak to Mr. Darcy, though, just as a courtesy. I count him as an elder brother, and with Papa gone..."

"Yes, of course. He may well be sorry to see you go from Pemberley. And yet he will have no one to blame but his own wife, for it was Mrs. Darcy's letter that brought me here. I nearly went mad searching for you in London after Michael recovered. You cannot imagine what a relief it was to at last receive some news of you."

"That is a letter I would very much like to see for myself."

"Then you shall," he said, reaching into his coat pocket.

Mary accepted the missive from his hand and read.

To Mr. H. Farnsworth
Netherfield Hall, Hertfordshire

Dear Sir,
   When you know my purpose, I trust you will forgive my taking the liberty of writing to you. I believe (and my husband concurs with me) that you would wish to be made aware of certain facts relating to my sister, Miss Mary Bennet, late of your employ. I expect you

have long been concerned for her well-being and whereabouts after she quit Netherfield so abruptly. Should that in fact be the case, allow me to set your mind at rest. Mary is safe with us here at Pemberley. It may also interest you to know that my sister has recently received an offer of marriage from a respected musical gentleman of our common acquaintance, the acceptance of which she is earnestly considering at this moment. Unless something or someone should intervene, the next time you see Mary, I rather expect you will be greeting her as Madam Hubert.

Yours sincerely,
Mrs. E. Darcy

P.S. – Should you ever happen to be traveling in Derbyshire, Mr. Darcy and I would be delighted to receive you to Pemberley. My sister has always spoken so highly of you that we have long been desirous of making your better acquaintance.

"It seems I have much for which to thank my sister," said Mary, refolding the letter and returning it to its owner.

"I am deeply indebted to her as well. Were it not for her timely information, I might have come too late. Did you indeed intend to accept Monsieur Hubert? Never mind," he continued quickly. "It is none of my affair and it no longer matters."

"We should be getting back to the house," said Mary. "Although I would much prefer to stay out here, alone with you, Monsieur deserves an answer. I owe him that much."

"Yes, of course. My gain is his loss, poor fellow."

The lovers languidly made their way back toward the house, their progress slowed by their mutual reluctance to bring the cherished interval to an end. Every picturesque prospect or natural curiosity along their way served as an excuse for delay, for conversation, for another coming together in fervent embrace. But at last, they were on the very porch and could not forestall their entrance into the house any longer.

"Oh, there you are," said Elizabeth, coming into the hall at the sound of the door. She looked from one to the other of them with a gleam in her eye and a satisfied smile. "Had you a pleasant walk, Mary?" she said archly.

Mary dropped her escort's arm and blushed – very becomingly, as Mr. Farnsworth noticed.

Elizabeth continued. "Yes, I thought a little exercise would put some color into your cheeks, and now I see that I was right."

"You are a wise woman, Mrs. Darcy," said Mr. Farnsworth. "The turn in the garden has done us both a world of good, I believe, and I thank you most sincerely for suggesting it. Now, might I have a word with your husband, if he is at liberty?"

"Of course! What an excellent notion! You will find him in his library. Henderson will show you the way. Mary, you must come with me and warm yourself in front of the fire."

After a glance back at Mr. Farnsworth's retreating form, Mary followed her sister to the saloon, which was one of the family's favorite rooms. There, the failing daylight was supplemented by a cheerful fire casting a warm glow throughout.

"Sit here with me," said Elizabeth, leading her sister to the sofa facing the hearth. "Now, explain yourself. What has happened? I can see by your countenance that you are not in the same frame of mind as you were earlier today. Tell me, then, will you be leaving us after all?"

"Oh, Lizzy!" gasped Mary. "I owe you my happiness. Your letter... Well, my goodness. How did you know?"

Elizabeth laughed and clapped her hands. "Do you mean I was right? Has he proposed?"

Mary nodded. "He has indeed, though I can scarce believe it. Oh, that he should love me, of all people! It is too fantastical. Can you imagine me as mistress of Netherfield?"

"And why not, I should like to know?" exclaimed Elizabeth indignantly. "You undervalue yourself, Mary. You are as worthy of a fine house and a fine husband as any lady I know, and more worthy than some. Why should you not have your chance?"

"But I still do not understand how you came to send that letter, Lizzy, how you knew the truth."

"I suppose I did not know the *whole* truth, although I could plainly see your half of it. As for Mr. Farnsworth, I just had to go on faith. I expected that if he cared for you, he would know how to act on my information."

"And if he did not?"

Elizabeth shrugged. "Well, if he did not, then my letter would have done no harm. Are you very angry with me for sending it? It was a violation of your confidence, I freely admit."

"Oh! When I think how differently things might have transpired had you not sent that blessed letter, Lizzy! Why, by now I might have been engaged to Monsieur Hubert instead! Where is he, by the way?"

"Gone. I told him you had been called away on urgent business and that I could not be certain when you would be at home again. I did offer myself as a pupil in your place, with the possibility that you might yet return in time to see him. He had no patience for my poor performance, however, and I cannot say that I much blame him. After hearing me, he suggested that, '*Perhaps your son, Mrs. Darcy, he inherits his musical talent from his father, oui?*'" Elizabeth laughed heartily. "Poor man. I daresay this day has not turned out at all as he had hoped. In any event, Monsieur Hubert will be staying the night at the inn at Lambton. He said he must depart by noon tomorrow to keep his next appointment, and he begs that you would send him some word before then."

"Yes, I shall. I hope he will not be so very disappointed. Oh, and I hope he will consent to still being my teacher. Do you suppose he is the kind of man who would hold a grudge against me?"

"Perhaps you would like to reconsider your decision then, Mary," her sister teased. "A good music master is very difficult to come by. In fact, I begin to regret that I ever championed Mr. Farnsworth's cause. Should Monsieur Hubert get wind of it, I may be obliged to find a new instructor for my children as well. What a great nuisance that would be."

~~*~~

Mary, who knew that her next duty was to relate the good news to her mother, was glad to learn from her sister that she had gone up to her own apartment only a half hour before. Mary followed her there and made the important communication. The effect was most extraordinary; for on first hearing it, Mrs. Bennet sat quite still and unable to utter a syllable. Nor was it under many minutes that she could comprehend what she heard. She began at length to recover, to fidget about in her chair, to get up, sit down again, wonder, and bless herself.

"Good gracious! Lord bless me! Is this really true? You are to marry Mr. Farnsworth? Can it be possible? Of all my daughters, I never would have expected it to be *you* who ended as mistress of Netherfield. You must forgive my underestimating you, my dear. And never to say a word about it until now. How sly you are. Oh my! What fine horses and carriages you will have, Mary, and what pin-money! I begin to feel quite sorry to Kitty, for she will be nothing to you after all. And what if Mr. Farnsworth is a little gray? He is very well set up and must leave you a rich widow when the time comes."

"Mama!" Mary cried in horror.

"Well, never mind that. It will be years and years from now, I daresay. Mr. Farnsworth seems to have a strong enough constitution. But a young wife, you know, could be overtaxing to a man of his age. You must remember to be careful."

"Please, Mama."

"Oh, I am so very happy! All five daughters married: it is more than I had ever dared to hope for. I cannot wait to tell my sister Phillips – and that snobbish Mrs. Elkhorn – about you and about Kitty both. Everybody will have to congratulate me on my good fortune. And, thanks to you, Mary, we shall yet have one more wedding from Longbourn!"

Over the course of the evening, Mary received the best wishes of the other members of her family as well. They, though likewise surprised and pleased by the news of her engagement to Mr. Farnsworth, were better able to govern their behavior and temper their effusions of delight. For this, Mary was grateful. As indisputably happy as she was, she could not help also feeling embarrassed at occupying the foreign position as the center of attention.

She was glad, therefore, for the chance to steal away for a few minutes alone with Mr. Farnsworth.

"Your family seems pleased with our news," he said.

"Of course they are pleased. Not one of them expected me ever to marry at all, let alone so well. And they cannot help liking you, Mr. Farnsworth."

"Harrison, remember?"

"Harrison, then. Oh, how strange that sounds, for I have been used to calling you something else for nearly five years. It is a fine name, though. Why is it that you did not pass it on to your son?"

A shadow flitted across his face. "It was my wife's doing; she chose the name for her own reasons. But that is a story for another day. I wish to think only of agreeable things tonight, my darling, like how soon I can make you my bride." He gathered her into his embrace and bent her back to kiss her.

Yes, Mary thought as she relaxed into his arms, only agreeable things tonight.

When Mary awoke next morning, she was a few minutes remembering all that had transpired the day before, and few minutes more being convinced that her happy recollections were genuine. Still, until she saw him again, she did not feel as if she could fully trust the fact that Mr. Farnsworth – Harrison, she corrected herself – loved her, was solemnly pledged to marry her, and that he would soon carry her home to Netherfield.

Before she went in search of her betrothed, however, she determined to dispatch a piece of business less enjoyable and yet just as necessary. She therefore took up paper to pen a note to Monsieur Hubert. Although it was not an easy letter to write, Mary did it without flinching, brought the sealed packet downstairs with her, and had it sent straightaway to the inn at Lambton. Later she might learn how its recipient took the news – if he would still be her music instructor though he could not be her husband. For now, however, all she could think of was finding Harrison Farnsworth.

He was in the breakfast room, and his face lit up when he saw her. Starting out of his chair, he said, "Good morning."

"Yes, it is," she agreed, staring back at him from the doorway.

Presently he continued, "I thought we might ride together today, if the weather holds. I have so much to talk to you about, Mary, so much I must tell you."

"I should enjoy a ride above all things." She dropped her eyes self-consciously and set about filling her plate, suddenly realizing how hungry she was.

"A ride?" said Kitty, entering the room with her husband at that same moment. "What a splendid idea. Tristan and I shall go with you, and perhaps Lizzy and Mr. Darcy will as well. We shall make a party of it. After all, we must not leave the two of you unchaperoned, must we?"

"I am convinced that 'unchaperoned' is exactly what they had in mind, my dear," Tristan told Kitty. "Nevertheless, a bracing ride would be just the thing to clear away the cobwebs. We have been all too long confined indoors." To the others he added, "Have no fear, though. We shall be certain to take a wrong turn and lose ourselves at the first opportunity. If anybody can be sympathetic to the evils of a want of privacy, it is I."

Mr. Tristan Collins was as good as his word. Although they began as a riding party of four (Elizabeth and Mr. Darcy declining to join them), they shortly divided into a pair of twosomes, Kitty and Tristan veering off toward the hills whilst Mary and Mr. Farnsworth continued down the trail by the stream. Mary took the lead and set a brisk pace, enjoying the feel of the powerful animal moving beneath her and the cold air whipping past her cheeks. The knowledge that the man she loved rode just behind her completed her idea of happiness.

When the trail widened out enough to admit two riders abreast, she slowed her horse and waited for her companion to draw along-side. "What was it that you wished to tell me, Harrison?" Mary called out, taking pleasure in hearing his name roll off her tongue. "We are alone now, and this is your chance."

A distant peal of thunder rumbled somewhere off to the west.

Farnsworth reined in his horse to the walking pace of hers. "I want you to know all – everything about me, Mary. If we are to be happy together, there can be no secrets or deceit between us."

"I quite agree. My life is an open book; there is nothing you may not know, and very little of which you are not already aware, I should think."

"It is quite a different thing with me, however. I am ten years older, and I had a life before coming to Hertfordshire, which you can have little knowledge of." His tone was very grave. "It is better that you should hear these things now, before we are married, in case it will make a difference in the way you feel."

A tremor of uneasiness trickled down Mary's spine. "You begin to frighten me, Harrison. Is there something in your past, some horrible scandal or indiscretion that you mean to confess to me?"

"Indiscretion, certainly. Scandal? That too, if it had become widely known, which thankfully it did not. How horrible the business is, you shall be the judge. Be patient and I will tell you the whole story."

Mary said no more. She drew a deep breath and sat a little straighter in the saddle, bracing herself for what was to come. Half an hour before, she would have said that nothing could have shaken her confidence in Mr. Farnsworth, and yet now she trembled with dread for what he might say. Could that happiness which she had waited so long to taste be swept away from her lips the very next day? Surely not; it would be too cruel.

For a long moment, Mr. Farnsworth remained silent as well, looking afar off into the distance as they rode apace down the path. "The trouble erupted six years ago," he began. "No, I must go farther back." He sighed and a weary expression came over his countenance. "As you may know, I made my fortune years ago in the war, as a captain in His Majesty's Navy, a fortune which enabled me to marry where I wished and to set myself up in London in some kind of style. We were happy in those early years, Constance and I – just the two of us at first, and then with the added blessing of our daughters. The only point of contention between us was my necessary absences at sea. Constance hated being left alone at home, and she begged me to resign my commission. 'Out of the question,' I told her. It was my career, after all, and one I was well suited to. So I came home whenever I could, and kept promising to retire before long. Then about ten years ago, I was put ashore earlier than expected after a voyage and came home to surprise my wife." He paused.

"She must have been… delighted to see you," Mary said tentatively.

"Shocked, more like. I discovered her there, at our London house, in the arms of an old acquaintance – a man who had been a lieutenant under my first command, and who had been more than once a guest in my home. Constance denied everything, of course. They both did. She claimed Ekhart had come strictly as a friend in time of need, a shoulder to cry on. You see, she had just lost what would have been our third child – a boy. And *I* was not there to comfort her, as she pointed out."

Again, Farnsworth paused, but Mary dared not venture any remark on this aspect of the story. Instead, she observed, "The sky is darkening. Perhaps we should start back. We can cross here and take the shorter way home."

He nodded without comment, and then continued his narrative after the horses had picked their way through the cold, hock-deep water to the other side. "I made some discrete inquiries, and the two of them had been seen keeping company about town, but nothing too alarming. Constance continued to plead her innocence, and in the end, I decided to believe her. I wanted to, of course. No man likes to think himself a cuckold. I hoped we could put the unfortunate business behind us and go on as before. Then, when Michael came along a year and a half later, it seemed we had succeeded in doing so. With our family growing, I made good on my promise to retire, and all was well again. Those were happy days. We laughed, we played with the children, we entertained, and we danced with no thought for the past."

Mary glanced sidelong at him and saw his wistful smile before it faded. "Happy days," she repeated.

"Yes... until Ekhart turned up again. I thought him long gone to Scotland, and then I happened upon him at my club one night, losing at cards and drinking heavily. Apparently, he had been at it some time, for he was in rather rough shape. He spied me and demanded that, in homage to our past service in arms together, I advance him twenty pounds to settle his debts. It may not surprise you to learn that I refused his request. From there his behavior deteriorated rapidly until I was conscripted – along with another gentleman, a fine fellow by the name of Talbot – to remove the troublemaker from the premises. None too willingly, he came along, stumbling and cursing all the way to his rooms at a boarding house, where we prepared to leave him to sleep off his foul mood. Before we went, however, Ekhart turned on me and fired the fatal shot. He said I should not look down my nose at him, for he would have the last laugh, since the heir to my estate..." He took a deep breath and let it out again in a cloud of steam. "The heir to my estate was his own bastard son."

Mary gasped in spite of herself. "Michael?" she whispered.

Mr. Farnsworth nodded solemnly. "You may imagine what I felt and how I acted. I flew at the man and nearly tore him limb from limb. Were it not for Talbot being there to restrain me, I might have murdered a man that night. Does that shock you, Mary?"

Mary did not know how to answer.

"Never mind; it is not a fair question to put to you."

"Did you believe what this man said, about Michael, I mean?"

"When I later considered his assertion rationally, I realized that there was just enough uncertainty about the date of conception as to cast into doubt whether I had been at home or away at the time. And then there was Constance's insistence that the child be named Michael – Ekhart's given name. So, yes, I did believe it, and I acted accordingly. If I was to be miserable, I was determined I should not be the only one. I took my wife away from her home in town and from the society she loved, all but imprisoning her at Netherfield whilst I hobnobbed in London to spite her. And what is worse, I shunned the boy; I withheld the merest kindness from him, my own flesh and blood."

"Yes, he *is* your flesh and blood! Surely no one who has seen the strong resemblance between the two of you could deny it!"

"Clear enough in the boy of nine, I grant you, but it was not so obvious in the two-year-old infant. Michael is my son; I am as certain of that as anything in this world. Even were he not, however, he had done nothing to deserve what I gave him: my contempt... and more. Shall I tell you the worst, Mary? Or do you already despise me?"

They had come up the rise, out of the wood to an open meadow. A heavy dampness permeated the air, and Mary noticed the first drops of rain spotting her cloak. "I... I do not despise you, sir."

"And yet your faith in me is shaken by this news. I see it plainly written on your face."

"No," Mary said with far more conviction than she felt. "These are difficult things to hear. Still, I trust I shall understand you better for it in the end."

"Then I do not regret speaking, and I will be bold to tell you one thing more so that my conscience may be clear, whatever else comes of it." Farnsworth brought his horse round and stopped so that he was facing Mary, and as close to her as the situation allowed. He reached for her hand, held it, and studied it, as if to give himself an excuse for not meeting her eyes. In a voice thick with emotion he said, "When I thought... When I thought Michael was a different man's child... God forgive me, but I secretly hoped he would not live to inherit my estate. I prayed for another son to take his place, one that I could be sure was mine." Farnsworth lifted his anguished face to look at Mary. "*This* is the guilt I carry with me always."

Mary could say nothing for the distress his words had engendered within her. Her eyes stung with tears, and a choking sob issued from somewhere deep within her chest. It sickened her to think this man had ever been brought so low as to wish his own son harm.

"I see you understand the gravity of what I have told you, Mary. You cannot think any worse of me for it than I do myself, however. And I assure you I have been sorely punished. The sons I wanted were born dead, and then their mother – whom I still loved, despite everything – was carried off as well. Finally, when I had begun to regain some hope for the future, to think about the possibility of a new life with you, it seemed I would lose Michael too, in delayed fulfillment of my horrid wish. I thank God that He saw fit to give me back my son, and also that I had had an opportunity to make my peace with Constance before she passed from this life." He paused. "But what about you, Mary? Will you really consent to unite yourself to the black-hearted villain you see before you now? Knowing what you do, can you still love me?"

50
Teacher, Know Thyself

As the rain began pouring down in earnest, a crack of thunder broke directly overhead. Mary screamed, and her mount bolted forward, racing across the field for home. She did nothing to restrain the animal, only held tight and allowed it to chart its own course. She welcomed the icy drops striking her face and the wind roaring in her ears, as if their force might overpower all other unpleasantness, as if the shock of Harrison Farnsworth's confession could be outdistanced if only she flew fast enough.

Another minute and they had reached the stables, where Mary quickly slid from the saddle and consigned her mare over to a groom before dashing away again.

Mr. Farnsworth, who had been hard upon Mary's heels the whole way, finally overtook her on foot. "Wait!" he implored her, coming round in front and taking hold of her shoulders. "I have bared my soul to you, Mary. Have you nothing to say in response?"

"The rain!" she cried out. "We must go in. And I *must* be allowed to think before answering!"

Mary broke free and ran on to the house. Once inside, she hurried to her own room and closed the door, pausing there to steady her nerves and stay her trembling hands. She needed time – time alone to digest what she had just learnt and to reconcile herself to the altered state of affairs if possible.

Wishing she could shed all her worries with as little effort, she then began peeling away her damp clothing, simply letting it fall to the floor where she stood. Once dry and redressed, she settled herself at her dressing table and regarded the troubled face she saw in the glass, the one that had looked so serenely content only a few hours before. Her mind still reeled with all that Harrison had told her concerning his past, his marriage, his dead wife, and his relationship to his son.

This new information explained much about what Mary had observed when first she came to Netherfield. Now the palpable tension she had noticed in the household made sense, as well as Mr.

Farnsworth's behavior to his wife and son. She could even understand – at least in part – what he had suffered at the hands of others
and by the punishment of his own conscience. But did his latterly
remorse erase the vindictiveness of which he had admitted being
guilty?

A few years earlier, she would have had no difficulty judging
such a case, and no scruple doing so either. She would have con-
demned them both, husband and wife, with hardly a second thought.

Things had seemed simpler then, before the clear demarcations
she had drawn between right and wrong were thoroughly tested. True
right and wrong were still what they had always been, of course;
only her sympathy for those who sometimes found themselves over
the line had changed. Her former prejudices had been stripped away,
and she had more understanding of the powerful forces that pushed
and pulled at the vulnerable hearts of men.

Experience had been her teacher. Her unforeseen attachment to
the Farnsworth children, her silent grief over her father's death, her
ambition and infatuation for Mr. Tristan Collins, her animosity towards her own sister for coming between them, her painful banishment from Netherfield, and the final realization of her desperate
love for Mr. Farnsworth: each one of these had stripped away
another layer of the armor that had long kept her untouched by
commonplace emotional turmoil.

In the past, she had been able to moralize over the infamous sins
of others with superior self-satisfaction, both because she had maintained a degree of detachment from their plights, and because she
had never been tempted to such behavior herself. Could she say the
same now?

There was a knock at the door, and Elizabeth entered a moment
later. "Oh, there you are, dearest," she said coming over to where
Mary still sat at her dressing table. Elizabeth studied her sister's
reflection in the mirror, saying, "Is anything the matter? I spied Mr.
Farnsworth treading to and fro on the gravel out in the rain, looking
very worried. And I see you are currently wearing a similar expression."

"Oh! Is he still out in the rain?" Mary crossed immediately to the
window and looked down. There, through the wavy, water-streaked
pane, she saw his distorted form – now paused, and now resuming
his purposeful march to nowhere in particular.

"I called to him," said Elizabeth, "urging him to come in, but he
would not. He says he is waiting for a word from you."

Mary made no answer; she only continued studying the dark figure pacing below.

"I hope you two have not quarreled," prompted Elizabeth, to no avail. "Have I mentioned how very much we both like your Mr. Farnsworth, Mr. Darcy and I? We could not be more delighted that you have found someone so perfectly suited to you."

"He is far from perfect, as it turns out."

"I did not mean to say that he was. We all have our faults. We all make mistakes, I believe... perhaps even *you*, Mary dear."

Elizabeth was right, of course. What was there of moral high ground left to her, after all? Portions of her behavior over the past year were mortifying enough to remember, but when she recollected her *thoughts*... Pride and folly abounded, but there was far worse. Had she not distinguished something akin to murder in her heart when Kitty betrayed and Tristan deserted her? And what of her feelings for Mr. Farnsworth? If she looked more closely, might she discover that her first symptoms of desire for him had germinated when he was still another woman's husband?

If God could forgive her such things – and she knew that He could – what right had she to hold past offenses, already confessed and cleansed, against Harrison Farnsworth?

Mary abruptly abandoned her window and snatched up a handy shawl. "Thank you, Lizzy," she said brightly as she threw it about her shoulders.

"For what?"

Mary was already halfway out the door.

With a light heart, she sailed through the passageway and down the stairs. She had always been so severe on people who were not perfect and so unwilling to show any sign of frailty herself. Now, however, she rejoiced in her own weaknesses, so flagrantly displayed over the last year, because it made accepting Mr. Farnsworth's past failings not only possible but compulsory.

She crossed the hall and flung wide the front door.

Twenty feet away, Farnsworth heard the sound and stopped in his place. He turned and lifted his face to her – a face dripping with rain and laden with the weight of an unanswered question.

Mary paused on the threshold a moment, her breath catching in her throat as she regarded her beloved in all his tarnished splendor. What a kind convenience, she thought, that she had been taught to properly know herself just in time – in time to accept this marred yet magnificent man who had offered her his heart.

Down the steps she ran, and into the crush of Mr. Farnsworth's eager embrace. "All is well," she told him, as water from his sodden coat soaked through to her skin. "All is well."

"Then you have forgiven me?"

"There is nothing for me to forgive, dear Harrison. The past is past. Let us leave it there and make a new start... together."

~~*~~

That evening, with calm and comfort restored, Mary and Harrison Farnsworth attempted to reconvene their discussion in the saloon near the fire. Most the others of the household instinctively understood their need for private conversation, and they kept their distance. Mrs. Bennet proved the exception, however. But for Mr. Darcy's heroic intervention, she would have remained seated alongside Mary the entire evening, for the purpose of flattering her future son-in-law and frequently saying how very pleased Mr. Bennet would have been with the match.

"Come with me, Madam," said Darcy in a commanding tone as he crossed the room to offer Mrs. Bennet his arm. "Do be good enough to accompany me to the drawing room. I wish to hear more of what you were saying earlier about your opinion for how the room should be freshly furnished." For this gallant sacrifice, he received the couple's silent gratitude and a very promising look of admiration from his wife.

Their isolation thus happily restored, Farnsworth said, "Your brother-in-law is a prince among men."

"Truly, he is," agreed Mary. "And Mama will not always be so intrusive, I trust. It is only that our engagement is new, and she is caught up in the excitement of the thing."

"I cannot fault her for that; I am rather caught up in the excitement as well."

Mary blushed with pleasure.

After a thoughtful pause, Farnsworth continued. "Dear Mary, I could not be more gratified that we have laid the past to rest and come to a right understanding between ourselves. One thing I still wish clarified, however."

"Yes? What is it?"

"Your reason – or reasons – for leaving Netherfield so abruptly. I know you blamed yourself for Michael's accident and evidently believed everybody else would too, including myself. And yet your parting note hinted at something else. I have my theory, but will you not now tell me the rest?"

Mary dropped her eyes and for a long minute studied her hands, clasped tightly in her lap. "It is to do with Clinton," she finally said in little more than a whisper.

"Just as I thought," said Farnsworth with controlled intensity. He got to his feet, strode to the hearth, and then returned. "I was told that he virtually attacked you in the servants' quarters. How long had this been going on, these unwanted attentions?"

"There had been a few, more minor incidents in the months prior."

"And why did you not report his misconduct?"

"I did. When I woke one day to find him in my bedchamber, watching me, I went to your sister. She said she would have Haines speak to the man. It apparently did no good, however."

"Hmm. I wish you had come to me instead."

"As I recall, you were out of charity with me at that time. And when the last, violent event occurred... Well, you had more important matters on your mind."

"I am sorry I was not available to you when you needed me most, Mary. It shall not occur again. You may be somewhat comforted to know that Clinton is gone and will never set foot on the grounds of Netherfield again."

"How did you know? Who was it that informed on his behavior?"

"Haines. It was he who saw what happened in the servants' quarters and later told me of it. I immediately sent Clinton packing, but by then you had already gone. Haines said nothing of any past offenses, however."

"Perhaps your sister forgot to tell him."

"Yes, perhaps," he muttered, "although I am not at all certain it was forgetfulness. Deliberate neglect, more like."

"But, why? I have asked myself a hundred times why she first befriended and then later turned against me. I was inclined to lay it to *your* charge, thinking you might disapprove of your darling sister keeping company with a governess."

"Not I, no! Truth be told, I think you would find that Monsieur Hubert was the cause of my sister's change in sentiments."

"Monsieur Hubert! What can he have to do with the business?"

"I gather his copious praise of you, samples of which I heard for myself on more than one occasion, became a cruel thorn in Lavinia's side. *'Miss Bennet has such an ear for music, such a talent. Why cannot you play more like her, Miss Farnsworth, instead of in this clumsy manner? You must practice day and night if you ever hope to measure up to Miss Bennet.'* You can imagine that such comparisons, made by her beloved music master, would hardly have endeared you to the lady. If she had suspected that the man was in love with you as well, you might have been murdered in your bed."

"If that was truly the source of the trouble, our relations are sure to improve hereafter. I doubt that dear Monsieur Hubert will be singing my praises any longer." Then Mary laughed.

"What is it, my love?"

"I was just thinking that perhaps Miss Lavinia will prove to be his new favorite. How would you feel about having Monsieur Hubert for a brother-in-law?"

"He is welcome to my sister, so long as he leaves my wife alone."

51

Epilogue

Happy for all her maternal feelings was the day on which Mrs. Bennet got rid of her last daughter. Mary, in a fine gown, standing up in church next to a comfortably rich man in his prime – it was a sight that good lady had never expected to see. And yet now it seemed to her perfectly right and reasonable that one of her offspring should again preside at Netherfield.

Mrs. Bennet's enjoyment had not ceased since her return from Derbyshire. First, she had the satisfaction of announcing to all her friends that her daughter Kitty was now Mrs. Tristan Collins and would be remaining at Longbourn as its mistress. Then, when the furor had died down, the upcoming nuptials between Mary and Mr. Farnsworth had been publicized, prompting another gratifying round of felicitations.

In all this merriment, there was one occasion for sadness, however. At the church, the empty place in the pew beside Mrs. Bennet was a poignant reminder of the absent head of the family. Had Mr. Bennet known what revolutionary changes would occur that year, he surely would have found it worth his while to remain on earth a little longer. As it was, he was consigned to observe these events from afar, from his seat amongst the angels.

Although Mr. Bennet was not present in body on the day Mary and Harrison Farnsworth exchanged their vows, a cloud of witnesses were there to represent him: his widow, his five daughters, their respective husbands, and a growing throng of grandchildren. With all these to bear testimony to the mark he had left on the world, there would be no doubt of his memory living on into the foreseeable future.

To the sum of his natural grandchildren, Mr. Bennet could that day add those he was acquiring by Mary's marriage – a healthy-looking boy of nine and a pair of fine girls, twelve and fourteen years of age, all of whom were in their best clothes and behaving tolerably well. These were much regarded and much talked over by those interested persons who had never before set eyes on them. During the wedding breakfast at Netherfield, following the ceremony, Kitty observed that the three appeared very happy about their father's marriage. Jane viewed the trio with sympathy and said how pleased she was to know that the children would now have a mother again.

Lydia's thoughts on the topic were less charitable. "I do not envy Mary," said she. "Three to care for, and not one of them her own! I daresay the only saving grace is that they are already half grown, and she may hope to be soon rid of them."

Elizabeth, who saw signs of mischief in the boy especially, was of the opinion that Mary would have her work cut out for her there.

"Your sister will manage very well, with her new husband's help," Darcy told her. "He is not the sort to tolerate tomfoolery for long, and I would wager nothing much gets the better of him – certainly not one small boy."

With an arch look, Elizabeth told him, "Ah, but I have seen with my own eyes the power of one small boy to bring a proud man to his knees. And where there are three children, the poor man does not stand a chance against them."

Darcy answered dryly, "How lucky, then, if he has a sensible wife to stand in the breach, lest the man be completely undone. No one wants that."

"I feel certain it is no longer Mary and Mr. Farnsworth of whom we are speaking, Mr. Darcy, but of ourselves." She then continued in a whisper. "That being the case, sir, I must disagree with you and say that I think I should rather *like* seeing you completely undone."

Whilst Mr. Darcy joined his wife in the indulgence of these private musings, the rest of the company continued unawares. They ate and they drank. They toasted the happy couple, wishing them health, wealth, and length of days. Then finally they waved as the newlyweds departed on their wedding journey to Spain.

For an idyllic month, Harrison and Mary Farnsworth escaped the English winter to bask in the temperate heat of the Mediterranean sun and of each other's company. They often strolled along the beach and dined on the sumptuous local cuisine before once again retreating to the privacy of their rented villa overlooking the sea. If sufficient warmth were ever lacking, which it hardly ever was, either he or she was sure to find some inconsequential point of differing opinion that admitted spirited debate. Were the wines of Spain superior or inferior to those made in France? Which was the more beautiful – the sunset they were currently enjoying or the one of the previous night? The friction of the ensuing argument never failed to kindle a fire of a kind best enjoyed behind closed doors. In this form, the bride and groom were able to carry home a share of the romantic Spanish atmosphere to enjoy ever after.

Mr. Farnsworth had arranged that certain changes be made at Netherfield whilst he was away, in order to make his bride's homecoming more agreeable. For one, all of her belongings were to be properly installed in the house, with special care taken over her books, which henceforth would occupy a section of their own in the main library. Secondly, a new suite of rooms was to be fitted up for their mutual use, so that the second Mrs. Farnsworth would not be obliged to sleep in the very shadow of the first. Most importantly, however, the more recent mistress of Netherfield was to be completely exorcised from the house. Miss Lavinia Farnsworth had been instructed by her brother to pack her things and go, not to return even as a visitor until she was prepared to make a full apology to Mary for her many acts of grievous ill-usage.

These things accomplished, Netherfield stood ready and in eager anticipation of the return of its master and new mistress. When Mr. Farnsworth handed his wife out of the carriage at the front door, she was hardly recognizable to the household's servants, who had assembled in welcome. Gone were the weeds of a daughter in mourning. Gone were the severe dress and coiffeur of the governess, replaced by a softer, more stylish and elegant picture. No one was likely to mistake the lady for a servant again.

"Welcome home, Mrs. Farnsworth," said Mrs. Brand at the front of the receiving line.

Mary smiled and nodded her head to her housekeeper friend, and then acknowledged the succession of other familiar faces in a similar fashion. Lastly, she and her husband came to the children, who were waiting on the porch, and here all formality gave way. Nothing less than a fervent embrace would do for each of them, and then everybody seemed to be talking at once. Questions flew back and forth with no time for the answers.

"Are you well, Michael?"

"Did you see any bull fights in Spain, Papa?"

"How are your studies progressing, Gwendolyn? Have you had any letters from your Bancroft cousins?"

"What did you bring us from your trip?"

"Dear Grace, how are you?"

All these ran together before one question stood out from the rest.

"Oh, what shall I call you now?" Grace asked Mary.

Mary was taken aback and silenced.

"I cannot continue calling you Miss Bennet any longer, can I?" the girl added.

"No, I suppose not," Mary answered, looking to her husband for assistance.

Mr. Farnsworth crouched down to make himself equal to his young daughter's height. "Would you like to call her 'Mama,' Gracie?" he asked. "It would be perfectly acceptable if you would."

Grace vigorously nodded her head, and so it was settled for the two younger children. Gwendolyn, who retained a stronger impression of her natural mother, received permission to call Mary by her given name for the time being.

Mary had been in training for the children's mother over all her years as their governess. And four weeks in Spain with Harrison had taught her the first important lessons in the art of being his wife. Now another month was required to make her equally confident as mistress of Netherfield. After that period had elapsed, the Farnsworths gave a ball to celebrate their marriage with all their friends and neighbors.

The Bingleys and the Darcys came from the north, but Mary's other two sisters were too far advanced with child to appear. There was a delegation of select friends from London invited, as well as the usual families from that corner of Hertfordshire where the Netherfield family resided.

Gwendolyn and Grace came in to watch Mary dress that evening. "Please, Mary," said Gwendolyn, "may I not come to the ball tonight? I am nearly fifteen."

"Oh, Gwen," Mary answered, stroking her new daughter's cheek with her gloved hand, "you must not be in such a hurry. You will have balls and parties enough in another year or two, and we shall be sure to include your Bancroft cousins," she added with a wink. "For tonight, however, you must be content to watch the dancing from the doorway."

The girl's eyes twinkled with fun. "Like when we crept down and spied on the ball last summer?"

"Exactly, only this time you need not be so secretive because you and Grace have my permission, and your father's."

So Grace and Gwendolyn were there to observe the general splendor of the scene in the ballroom that night. Mary looked every inch the lady as her distinguished husband led her out onto the floor to begin the first dance.

"The moment is here at last, my love," he told her.

"I am not certain I understand you, Harrison."

"Nine months ago, I made you – I made myself – a promise. You would not dance with me that night in the library, but I vowed then and there that another time you would. Now, here we are. I have kept my word by bringing it to pass," he said, ending in a tone of triumph.

"Ah, yes," said Mary wryly. "How well I remember your words on that occasion. You cannot take full credit for their accomplishment, however."

"And why not?" he asked indignantly. "I should like to know who else claims a share in it."

"Have you forgotten the part Elizabeth played? And *I* must demand a portion of the credit as well, if wishful thinking counts for anything." Mary looked straight into the cool, blue fire of her husband's eyes. "For I assure you that not a day has passed between that night and this when I have not pictured myself being swept away in your arms."

Harrison Farnsworth returned her penetrating gaze, and one side of his mouth curled decidedly upward. He tugged his wife a bit closer; the music of the opening dance began; and with its heady strains, they moved off together as one.

The End

About the Author

Author Shannon Winslow specializes in writing fiction for fans of Jane Austen. *The Darcys of Pemberley*, her popular sequel to *Pride and Prejudice*, was her debut novel in 2011. *For Myself Alone* – a stand-alone Austen-inspired story – followed in 2012. Now comes *Return to Longbourn*, the next chapter in the continuing *Pride and Prejudice* saga. She has something entirely different waiting in the wings, though – a contemporary "what if" novel entitled *First of Second Chances* (date of publication yet to be announced). After that, she has in mind a *Persuasion* tie-in, which is currently in the planning stage.

Her two sons grown, Ms. Winslow lives with her husband in the log home they built in the countryside south of Seattle, where she writes and paints in her studio facing Mt. Rainier.

For more information, visit www.shannonwinslow.com.
Follow Shannon on Twitter (as JaneAustenSays) and on Facebook.

Appendix

Author's Note: Below you will find all the direct Jane Austen quotes used in this novel. In some cases, slight changes were made from the original text to allow the excerpted passages to fit more seamlessly into the manuscript. The reader may recognize other familiar phrases, too short and numerous to cite here, which also point to Miss Austen's work.

Key: References are followed by their **source** – book title and chapter, in abbreviated form. Abbreviations are as follows: P – Persuasion, NA – Northanger Abbey, S&S – Sense and Sensibility, P&P – Pride and Prejudice, E – Emma, MP – Mansfield Park.

Chapter 1: It is a truth universally acknowledged...P&P, opening line. Mrs. Bennet was really in a most pitiable state. P&P-23. "You look pale. How much you must have gone through. P&P-47. I was going to look for you...She followed him thither [; and] her curiosity to know what he had to tell her [was] heightened by the supposition of its being in some manner connected with the [letter] he held. P&P-57.

Chapter 2: [Elizabeth] lifted up her eyes in amazement, but was too much oppressed to make any reply. P&P-47. It sometimes happens that a woman is handsomer at twenty-nine than she was ten years before. P-1.

Chapter 3: It did come, and exactly when it might be reasonably looked for. NA-26 "What is there of good to be expected?" P&P-49. Three thousand pounds [! He] could spare so considerable a sum with little inconvenience. S&S-1.

Chapter 4: Bless me, how troublesome they are sometimes! P-6. ...not at all afraid of being long unemployed. There [are] places in town, offices where inquiry would soon produce something. E-35.

Chapter 5: ...must be in want of a wife...the rightful property of [some] one or other of [their] daughters. P&P-1. They proceeded in silence along the gravel walk that led to the copse. [Elizabeth] was determined to make no effort for conversation... P&P-56. I feel myself called upon by our relationship... to condole with you on the grievous affliction you are now suffering under, of which [we were] yesterday informed by a letter from [Hertfordshire]. P&P-48.

Chapter 6: "And what am I to do on the occasion?" P&P-20. "I will make no promise of the kind." P&P-56.

Chapter 7: "I do assure you, Sir, that I have no pretensions whatever to that kind of elegance which consists in tormenting a respectable man." P&P-19.

Chapter 8: "For heaven's sake, madam, speak lower. What advantage can it be to you to offend Mr. [Darcy]? You will never recommend yourself [to his friend] by so doing." P&P-18. The [Frank Churchill] so long talked of, so high in interest, was actually before her. E-23

Chapter 9: "I wish I were too. I read it a little as a duty, but it tells me nothing that does not vex and weary me." NA-14.

Chapter 10: "I have not the pleasure of understanding you." P&P 20

Chapter 11: ...he bore with the ill-judged officiousness of the mother, and heard all her silly remarks with [a] forbearance and command of countenance...P&P-55. ...when suddenly the clouds united over their heads, and a driving rain set full in their face... to which the exigence of the moment gave more than usual propriety; it was that of running with all possible speed...S&S-9

Chapter 12: [we] are so very, very different in all [our] inclinations and ways, that I consider it as quite impossible [we] should ever be tolerably happy together... MP-35

Chapter 13: "I have the greatest dislike to the idea of being over-trimmed." E-17

Chapter 14: He took her hand, pressed it, and [certainly] was on the point of carrying it to his lips when, from some fancy or other, he suddenly let it go. Why he should feel such a scruple, why he should change his mind when it was all but done, she could not perceive... The intention, however, was indubitable. E-45

Chapter 15: "There is a stubbornness about me that never can bear to be frightened at the will of others." P&P-31

Chapter 17: [They] must be a great loss to your family. P&P-45 I know he has the highest opinion in the world of [all your family,] and looks upon you[rself]...quite as his own sister[s]. S&S-22

Chapter 20: What praise is more valuable than the praise of an intelligent servant? P&P-43, They descended the hill, crossed the bridge, and drove to the door... P&P-43

Chapter 21: "It is not time or opportunity that is to determine intimacy; it is disposition alone. Seven years would be insufficient to make some people acquainted with each other, and seven days are more than enough for others." S&S-12

Chapter 22: ...she felt it to be her duty, to try to overcome all that was excessive, all that bordered on selfishness, in her affection for [Edmund]. To call or to fancy it a loss, a disappointment, would be a presumption for which she had not words strong enough to satisfy her own humility. To think of him as [Miss Crawford] might be justified in thinking, would [in her] be insanity. To her he could be nothing under any circumstances; nothing dearer than a [friend]. MP-27.

Chapter 24: Under these unpromising auspices, the parting took place and the journey began. NA-2

Chapter 28: "[Mr.] Bennet, have you no more lanes hereabouts in which [Lizzy] may lose her way [again today]?" "...walk to Oakham Mount [this morning.] It is a nice long walk, and [Mr. Darcy has] never seen the view." Etc. P&P-59

Chapter 29: "You must be satisfied with such admiration as I can honestly give. I call it a very fine country – the hills are steep, the woods seem full of fine timber, and the valley looks comfortable and snug – with rich meadows and several neat farm houses scattered here and there. It exactly answers my idea of a fine country, because it unites beauty and utility. And I daresay it is a picturesque one too, because you admire it." S&S-18. "I will hear whatever you like. I will tell you exactly what I think." E-49

Chapter 33: "let me intreat you to say and look everything that may set his heart at ease, and incline him to be satisfied with the match." E-46

Chapter 34: Her heart sunk within her... exertion was indispensably necessary, and she struggled so resolutely against the oppression of her feelings, that her success was speedy, and for the time complete. S&S-22

Chapter 36: "Is there no one to help me?"...as if all his own strength were gone. P-12

Chapter 37: "Say nothing of that... It has been my own doing, and I ought to feel it." P&P-48

Chapter 39: "I am determined to go directly. I have said nothing about it to any body. It would only be giving trouble and distress." E-42

Chapter 41: A speedy cure must not be hoped, but everything was going on as well as the nature of the case admitted. P-13

Chapter 42: "You may ask questions which I shall not choose to answer." P&P-56. "Do anything rather than marry without affection." P&P-59

Chapter 43: "A most suitable connection every body must consider it – but I think it might be a very happy one." P-17. "A little sea-bathing would set me up forever." P&P-41. "The only wonder was, what they could be waiting for, till the business [at Lyme came]; then, indeed, it was clear enough that they must wait till [her brain was set to right.]" P-18.

Chapter 48: ...made the important communication. The effect was most extraordinary; for on first hearing it, Mrs. Bennet sat quite still and unable to utter a syllable. Nor was it under many, [many] minutes that she could comprehend what she heard... She began at length to recover, to fidget about in her chair, get up, sit down again, wonder, and bless herself. "Good gracious! Lord bless me!" P&P-59

Chapter 49: "I must go farther back." S&S-31, "You may imagine what I felt and how I acted." P&P-35

5353748R00150

Printed in Great Britain
by Amazon.co.uk, Ltd.,
Marston Gate.